Property

ALSO BY LIONEL SHRIVER

The Mandibles: A Family, 2029–2047

Big Brother

The New Republic

So Much for That

The Post-Birthday World

We Need to Talk about Kevin

Double Fault

A Perfectly Good Family

Game Control

Ordinary Decent Criminals

Checker and the Derailleurs

The Female of the Species

PROPERTY

STORIES BETWEEN

TWO NOVELLAS

LIONEL SHRIVER

HARPER

An Imprint of HarperCollins*Publishers*

PROPERTY. Copyright © 2018 by Lionel Shriver. All rights reserved. Printed in the United States of America. No part of this book may be used or reproduced in any manner whatsoever without written permission except in the case of brief quotations embodied in critical articles and reviews. For information, address HarperCollins Publishers, 195 Broadway, New York, NY 10007.

HarperCollins books may be purchased for educational, business, or sales promotional use. For information, please email the Special Markets Department at SPsales@harpercollins.com.

FIRST EDITION

Designed by Fritz Metsch

"The Self-Seeding Sycamore" was originally written for the short story collection *Reader, I Married Him*, edited by Tracy Chevalier and published by William Morrow Paperbacks. "The Royal Male" was first published in the *Telegraph* (London), "Exchange Rates" and "Negative Equity" in the *Times* (London), "Kilifi Creek" in the *New Yorker*, "Repossession" in the *Guardian*, "Vermin" on *Stylist*, and "Paradise to Perdition" in *Raffles Hotels & Resorts Magazine*.

Library of Congress Cataloging-in-Publication Data has been applied for.

ISBN 978-0-06-269793-6

18 19 20 21 22   LSC   10 9 8 7 6 5 4 3 2 1

I bought a wood [. . .]. It is not a large wood—it contains scarcely any trees, and it is intersected, blast it, by a public footpath. Still, it is the first property that I have owned, so it is right that other people should participate in my shame, and should ask themselves, in accents that will vary in horror, this very important question: What is the effect of property upon the character? [. . .]

If you own things, what's their effect on you? What's the effect on me of my wood?

In the first place, it makes me feel heavy. [. . .]

In the second place, it makes me feel it ought to be larger.

—E. M. FORSTER, "My Wood"

Contents

Property

The Standing Chandelier

A NOVELLA

In bottomless gratitude, to Jeff and Sue.
This is not about you.

JILLIAN FRISK FOUND the experience of being disliked bewildering. Or not bewildering enough, come to think of it, since the temptation was always to see her detractor's point of view. Newly aware of a woman's aversion—it was always another woman, and perhaps that meant something, something in itself not very nice—she would feel awkward, at a loss, mystified, even a little frightened. Paralyzed. In a traducer's presence, she'd yearn to refute whatever about herself was purportedly so detestable. Yet no matter what she said, or what she did, she would involuntarily verify the very qualities that the faultfinder couldn't bear. Vanity? Flakiness? Staginess?

For an intrinsic facet of being disliked was racking your brain for whatever it was that rubbed other people so radically the wrong way. They rarely told you to your face, so you were left with a burgeoning list of obnoxious characteristics that *you compiled for them.* So Jillian would demote her garb from *festive* to *garish* or even *vulgar,* and suddenly see how her offbeat thrift shop ensembles, replete with velvet vests, broad belts, tiered skirts, and enough scarves to kill Isadora Duncan three times over, could seem to demonstrate *attention-seeking behavior.* A clear, forceful voice was to the leery merely *loud,* and whenever she suppressed the volume the better to give no offense, she simply became inaudible, which was maddening, too. Besides, she didn't seem capable of maintaining a mousy, head-down demeanor for more than half an hour, during which the sensation was tantamount to a Chinese foot binding of the soul. Wide gesticulation when she grew exuberant was doubtless *histrionic*. Smitten by another smoldering black look from across a table, she would sometimes trap her hands in her lap, where they would flap like captured birds. But in a moment of inattention, the dratted extremities always escaped, flinging her napkin to the floor. Her full-throated guffaw would echo in her own ears as *an annoying laugh*. (Whatever did you do about an annoying laugh? Stop finding anything funny?) Then on top of all the ghastly attributes she embodied, merely being in the presence of someone who she knew couldn't stand her slathered on an additionally off-putting surface of nervousness, contrition, and can't-beat-them-join-them self-suspicion.

But then, Jillian should have known better by now, having enough times withstood the gamut from distaste to loathing (yet rarely indifference). When people didn't like you, if this doesn't seem too obvious, they didn't like *you*. That is, the problem wasn't an identifiable set of habits, beliefs, and traits—say, a propensity for leaning against a counter with a jauntily jutted hip as if you thought you were hot stuff, overusage of the word *fabulous*, a misguided conviction that refusing to vote is making a political statement, a tendency to mug the more premeditative with a sudden impulse to go camping this very afternoon and to make them feel like spoilsports when they didn't want to go. No, it was the sum total that rankled, the whole package, the essence from which all of these evidences sprang. Jillian could remain perfectly still with her mouth zipped, and Estelle Pettiford—a fellow crafts counselor at the Maryland summer camp where Jillian worked for a couple of seasons, whose idea of compelling recreation for fifteen-year-olds was making Christmas trees out of phone books in July—would still have hated her, and the girl would have kept hating her even if this object of odium didn't move a muscle or utter a syllable through to the end of time. That was what slew Jillian about being disliked: There was no remedy, no chance of tempering an antipathy into, say, forbearance or healthy apathy. It was simply your being in the world that drove these people insane, and even if you killed yourself, your suicide would annoy them, too. More *attention seeking*.

Glib, standard advice would be not to care. Right. Except that shrugging off the fact that someone despised you was impossible. The expectation was inhuman, so that, on top of having someone hate you, you cared that someone hated you and apparently you shouldn't. Caring made you even more hateable. Your inability to dismiss another's animus was one more thing that was wrong with you. Because that was the thing: these sneering, disgusted perceptions always seemed to have more clout than the affections of all the other people who thought you were delightful. Your friends had been duped. The naysayers had your number.

There was Linda Warburton, her coworker during a stint leading tours at the Stonewall Jackson House, who grew insensibly enraged every time Jillian brewed strong coffee in the staff kitchen—Jillian made strong everything—as the girl preferred her java weak. After Jillian began going to the extra trouble of boiling a kettle so that Linda could dilute her own mug to her heart's content, the accommodation to everyone's tastes seemed only to drive the lumpy, prematurely middle-aged twenty-five-year-old to more ferocious abhorrence: Linda actually submitted a formal complaint to the Virginia Tourist Board that Jillian Frisk wore the bonnet of her costume at "an historically inaccurate cocky slant." There was Tatum O'Hagan, the clingy, misbegotten roommate of 1998, who'd seemed to want to become bosom buddies when Jillian first moved in—in fact, the brownie-baking sharing of confidences became a bit much—but who, once Jillian inserted a merciful crack of daylight between the two, came to find her presence so unendurable that she posted a roster of which evenings one or the other could occupy the living room and which hours—different hours—they could cook. There was the officious Olivia Auerbach only two years ago, another unpaid organizer of the annual Maury River Fiddlers Convention, who accused her of "distracting the musicians from their practice" and "overstepping the necessarily humble role of a volunteer." (And how. Jillian had a sizzling affair with a participant from Tennessee, who knew how to fiddle with more than his bow.)

Tall and slender, with a thick thatch of kinked henna hair that tumbled to her elbows, Jillian had trouble being inconspicuous, and that wasn't her fault. She supposed she was pretty, though that adjective seemed to have a statute of limitations attached. At forty-three, she'd probably been downgraded to *attractive*—in preparation, since postmenopausal flattery went unisex, for *handsome*; gosh, she could hardly wait for *well preserved*. So she might plausibly dismiss this bafflingly consistent incidence of female animosity as bitchy takedown in a catwalk competition. But when she glanced around Lexington, which flushed every fall with an influx of fetching freshmen from Washington and Lee—whose appearance of getting younger each year helped track her own decay—Jillian was often awed by the profusion of beautiful women in the world, not all of whom could have been unrelenting targets of antagonism. To the contrary, in her high school days in Pittsburgh, when Jillian was gawky and still uncomfortable with her height, students flocked to sunny blond bombshells, who often benefited from a reputation for kindness and generosity purely for bestowing the occasional smile. Her problem wasn't looks, or looks alone, even if the hair in particular seemed to make a declaration that she didn't intend. Jillian had hair that you had to live up to.

So looking back, it had been naive in the extreme to have innocently posted photographs of various homespun creations in the early days of social media, in anticipation of a few anodyne responses like, "Cute!" or "Super!"—or in anticipation of no response, which would have been fine, too. When instead her set of handmade dishware attracted, "You're a talentless, amateur hack" and "Suggest trampling these misshapen atrocities into landfill," Jillian drew back as if having put a hand on a hot stove. By the time that comments on such applications escalated to routine rape threats, she had long since canceled her accounts.

It did seem to irk some sorts that Jillian was a self-confessed dabbler.

She taught herself a sprinkling of Italian, for example, but in a spirit of frivolity, and not because she planned to visit Rome but because she liked the sound—the expressive *mamma mia* up and down of it, the popping carbonation it imparted even to *little pencil*: "piccola matita." Yet the phase was to no purpose, and that was the point. Jillian pursued purposelessness as a purpose in itself. It had taken her some years to understand that she'd had such trouble settling on a career because she didn't want one. She was surrounded by go-getters, and they could have their goals, their trajectories, their aspirations—their feverish toiling toward some distant destination that was bound to disappoint in the unlikely instance they ever got there. Some folks had to savor the world where they were, as opposed to glancing out the driver's window while tearing off somewhere else. This was less a prescriptive ideology than a simple inclination to languor or even laziness; Jillian cheerfully accepted that. She wasn't so much out to convert anyone else as to simply stop apologizing.

It was curious how furious it made some people that you didn't want to "make something of yourself" when you were something already and had no particular desire to change, or that you could declare beamingly that you were "altogether aimless" in a tone of voice that implied this was nothing to be ashamed of. Jillian had recently been informed at the bar of Bistro on Main that, for an expensively educated woman with a better-than-middle-class background who enjoyed ample "opportunities," having no especial objective aside from enjoying herself was "un-American."

Jillian had the kind of charm that wore off. Or after enough romantic diminuendos, that's what she theorized. Even for guys, whose gender seemed to preclude the full-fledged anaphylactic shock of an allergic reaction, the profusion of her playful little projects, which were never intended to make a name, or get a gallery, or attract a review in the *Roanoke Times*, might appear diverting and even a measure entrancing at first, but eventually she'd seem childish, or bats, or embarrassing, and men moved on.

With one crucial exception.

* * *

SHE'D MET WESTON Babansky while taking a poorly taught English course when they were both undergraduates at Washington and Lee. Their instructor was disorganized, with a tendency to mutter, so that you couldn't tell when he was addressing the seminar or talking to himself. She'd been impressed by the fact that after class Weston—or "Baba," as she christened him after they'd grown to know each other better—was reluctant to bandwagon about Steve Reardon's execrable lectures with the other students, who railed about paying tuition through the nose for this rambling, incoherent mishmash with a relish that alone explained why they didn't transfer out. Instead Baba was sympathetic. The first time they had coffee, he told Jillian that actually, if you listened closely, a lot of what Reardon said was pretty interesting. The trouble was that qualifying as an academic didn't mean you were a performer, and teaching was theater. He said he himself didn't imagine he'd be any better up there, and on that score he was probably right. Weston Babansky was inward, reflective, avoidant of the spotlight.

Already subjected to multiple aversions, Jillian appreciated his sensitivity—although there was nothing soft or effeminate about the man, who was three or four years older than most of their classmates. No sooner did he express an opinion than he immediately experienced what it was like on its receiving end, as if firing a Wile E. Coyote rifle whose barrel was U-shaped. It was one of the many topics the two had teased out since: how careless people were with their antipathy, how they threw it around for fun; how these days people indiscriminately sprayed vituperation every which way as if launching a mass acid attack in a crowded public square. Sheer meanness had become a customary form of entertainment. Since the disapprobation she'd drawn that she knew about was doubtless dwarfed by the mountain of behind-the-back ridicule that she didn't, Jillian herself had grown ever more reluctant to contrive a dislike even for celebrities who would never know the difference—pop stars, politicians, actors, or news anchors, whose high public profile presumably made them fair game. She'd catch herself saying, "Oh, I can't stand him," then immediately hear the denunciation with the victim's ears, and wince.

It turned out that Baba was also a northerner, and in respect to his future, equally at sea. Best of all, they were each on the lookout for a tennis partner—ideally one who wouldn't scornfully write you off the moment a wild forehand flew over the fence.

Lo, from their first hit they were perfectly suited. They both took a long time to warm up, and appreciated wit as well as power. They both preferred rallying for hours on end to formal games; they still played proper points, which would be won or lost, but no one kept score—more of Jillian's purposive purposelessness. It didn't hurt that Baba was handsome, though in that bashful way that most people overlooked, with the stringy, loose-jointed limbs of a natural tennis player. He was ferocious, hard hitting, and nefarious on court, but the killer instinct evaporated the moment he exited the chain-link gate. His tendency to grow enraged with himself over unforced errors was Jillian's secret weapon. After three or four of his backhands in a row smacked the tape, he did all the hard work for her: he would defeat himself. He was complicated, more so than others seemed to recognize, with a dragging propensity for depression to which he admitted as a generality, but never actively inflicted on present company.

She also found his understated social unease more endearing than the facility of raconteurs and bons vivant who greased the skids at parties by never running out of things to say. Baba often ran out of things to say, in which case he said nothing. She learned from him that silence needn't be mortifying, and some of their most luxuriant time together was quiet.

Baba was something of a recluse, who kept odd hours and did his best work at four a.m.; Jillian had joked that if the courts had lights, she'd never get a point off him. She was the more gregarious of the two, so after they'd exhausted themselves bashing balls back and forth it was Jillian who delivered the bulk of the stories for their ritual debrief on a courtside bench. For a man, he was unusually fascinated with teasing out fine filaments of feeling. Thus they used each other as sounding boards about the friends and lovers who came and went. Baba was neither perturbed nor surprised when one of the seniors in Jillian's dormitory suite came to so revile her company that the moment Jillian entered the suite's common area the girl flounced back to her room. "You have a strong flavor," he said. "Some people just don't like anchovies."

"Liver," Jillian corrected with a laugh. "When I walk in, she acts more like someone slid her an enormous slab of offal—overcooked, grainy, and reeking."

In fact, which badinage proved the more engaging was a toss-up: the assertion and reply on court, or the tête-à-tête when they were through. One conversation seemed a continuation of the other by different means. As a walloping approach shot could be followed by a dink, Baba would no sooner have questioned on the bench whether it was really worth his while to complete his degree at Washington and Lee (the interest he was rounding on was computer networks, a field transforming so quickly that most of what he was studying was out of date) than Jillian would mention having discovered a great five-minute recipe for parmesan chicken. The conversational ball skittered across all four corners of their lives, from lofty speculative lobs about how, if energy was neither created nor destroyed, could that mean there was necessarily life after death—or even life before life?—to single put-aways about how *Jerry Springer* had a campy appeal at first, but ultimately was unendurable. It was with Baba that Jillian first began to haltingly explore that maybe she didn't want to "be" something she wasn't already, and with whom she initially considered the possibility of making things outside the confines of the pompous, overwhelmingly bogus art world. Together they agreed on the importance of owning their own lives, and their own time; they viewed the nine-to-five slog of a wage earner with a mutual shudder.

After graduation—Jillian finally settled on a suitably diffuse degree on cross-fertilization in the arts (which got her adulthood off to a thematically pertinent start by serving no earthly purpose), while Baba's major had more of a science bent (she could no longer remember what it was)—she loitered in Lexington, tutoring lagging local high schoolers in grammar, vocabulary, and math, often for SAT prep. That was the mid-1990s, when the internet was taking off, and as a freelance website designer Baba easily snagged as much work as he cared to handle. So from the start, they both did jobs you could do from anywhere.

But if you could be anywhere, you could also stay put. Lexington was a pleasant college town, with distinguished colonial architecture and energizing infusions of tourists and Civil War buffs. Virginia weather was clement, spring through fall. And what mattered, other than Jillian's pointless, peculiar projects—the hand-sewn drapes with hokey tassels, the collage of quirky headlines ("Woman Sues for Being Born")—was being able to play tennis with your ideal partner three times a week.

Tired of having to defer to the teams, the two retired from the college courts where they might have continued to play as alumnae, preferring the three funky, more concealed public courts at Rockbridge County High School, which were sheltered by a bank of tall trees and blighted with just enough cracks to add an element of chance (or better, something to blame). Especially summers, they'd retire to the bench and muse for an hour or two, while the humid southern air packed around them like pillows. Jillian would ruffle the crystallized sweat on her arms and sometimes lick it, having become, as she said, "a human Dorito." They still shared recipes and disparaged television programs, but their mainstay was the mysteries of other people.

"Okay, I know I said I wouldn't, but you predicted it, and you were right," Jillian once introduced. "I slept with Sullivan on Friday. Now, it wasn't terrible or anything, but get this: in the throes of, ah, the thing itself, he starts announcing, full voice, 'I'm so aroused!' Over and over, 'I'm so *aroused*.' Now, who says that?"

"People say all kinds of things during sex," Baba allowed. "You ought to be able to say whatever you want. Maybe you should be a little easier on the guy."

"I'm not criticizing exactly. But still, it's so abstracted. Removed. Like he was watching himself, or . . . I mean, most people get off on stuff that goes back to puberty or even earlier, and 'I'm so aroused' sounds so hyperadult. Stiff and formal and almost third person. *I'm so aroused?* Tell me that's normal."

"There is no normal."

"But you can't imagine how *unarousing* it is to be officially informed that your partner is 'aroused.' Though at least Sullivan's swooning beat Andrew Carver's. That guy kept crooning, 'Oooh, baby! Oooh, baby, baby, baby!' Made my skin crawl."

"That's it," Baba announced. "I'm not sleeping with you, Frisk, if you have to have script approval."

That was a vow he would break. Perhaps tragically at different junctures, each fell in love with the other—abruptly, hard, all in. The first go-round, Baba had a steady girlfriend, and they conducted a torrid affair on the side until, feeling guilty over the disloyalty to his main squeeze, he reluctantly called it off. During their reprise—two, three, four years later? The chronology had grown hazy now—Jillian misinterpreted their reinvolvement as the idle entertainment of what were then called *fuck buddies* and later *friends with benefits*. So when she had a weekend fling with a dashing bartender, she naturally told Baba all about it after tennis. He was literally struck dumb—collapsing so inertly onto their regular bench that it was a wonder he was not still slumped there to this day.

In this one-two punch, which of the two had suffered more grievously was a matter of some dispute, and after both sexual terminations there ensued an agonizing interregnum during which they didn't talk or, worse, play tennis. Jillian would never forget migrating on her lonesome to their regular after-hit bench, kneeling on the ground, and resting her forehead on the rough, paint-peeling front slat in a position that could only have been called prayerful. And then she wailed, that was the word for it, and the cries emitted from the very center of her diaphragm, the part of the body from which one is taught to sing in opera. The theater would have been melodramatic had anyone been watching, but at least to begin with she was by herself. Until a teacher rushed to the parking lot and shouted, "Are you all right?" He must have thought she was being attacked—which in a way she was. Intriguingly, she could no longer recollect whether she made that pilgrimage in the aftermath of being rejected or doing the rejecting, for it was a hard call which role had been the more awful.

Weston Babansky and Jillian Frisk were best friends—a relationship cheapened by an expression like *BFF*, which notoriously referenced a companion to whom you wouldn't be speaking by next week. They had known each other for twenty-four years, and never in all that time had an interloper laid claim to the superlative. That exercise in mutual devastation was inoculating, and raised the relationship to what at least felt like a higher spiritual plane. Post-romance, post-sex, neither was tortured with curiosity about the twining of each other's limbs. Baba wasn't circumcised; Jillian refused to shave her bikini line: their secrets were out. It was a certain bet that, having survived the worst, they really would be *best friends forever*, thereby proving to the rest of the world that there was such a thing.

THE MILLENNIUM ONWARD, Jillian had lived in a sweet, self-sufficient outbuilding of an antebellum estate, which she kept an eye on when the owners were abroad. She lived rent-free, and received a modest stipend in addition for receiving packages, retrieving the mail, taking trash cans to the curb and back, watering the potted plants in the main house, holding the gate open for the gardener, and agreeing not to take overnight trips if the Chevaliers were away. It was a cushy situation that all those aspirants desperate to be film directors might have seen as a trap. But the four-room cottage was just big enough to accommodate flurries of industry—the melees of crepe paper, plywood, rubber cement, and carpet tacks when Jillian plunged into another purposeless *project*. She'd been given free rein to redecorate, so refinishing the oak flooring, stitching tablecloths, tiling the bathroom, stripping tables, and repairing rickety rocking chairs kept her agreeably occupied when more elaborate creations weren't commanding her attention. A few years back, Baba had finally bought a house, like a good grown-up—an unconventional A-frame whose rough-hewn, homemade quality always reminded her of a tree house—but Jillian enjoyed all the advantages of a homeowner, as far as she could see, without the grief.

Patching together the stipend and a variety of odd jobs, Jillian approached earning her keep like quilting. She continued to tutor, in addition to subbing at Rockbridge County High School, so long as the gig didn't involve supervising any after-school activities on Mondays, Wednesdays, or Fridays, her regular tennis days. She got on well with children; if nothing else, they seemed always to love her hair. Having youngsters in her orbit took the sting out of the fact that it was looking as if she'd never have a family of her own. Having had plenty of exposure, she wasn't sentimental about kids, and often suspected their parents were a little envious that when her lessons were done she got to go home alone.

About the absence of a lover who stuck around, she was more wistful. Yet the urgency of finding a lifelong soul mate that had infused her twenties and thirties had given way to a state far more agreeable than some sullen resignation. She was still open. She had not given up. But she would rather be on her own than go through yet another roller-coaster ride of mounting intoxication and plummeting heartache. She had a rich life, with a smattering of interesting friends. She had tennis, and she had Baba.

Who had himself run through a surprisingly large population of women. Contrary to type—the subtle misfit, the mild sociophobe, the loner who might be expected to fall hopelessly head over heels once his defenses dropped—Baba had ended nearly all these relationships himself. The very ear for individual notes in an emotional chord that Jillian found so captivating meant that one or more of those notes, for Baba, was always a touch off-key. We are all audiences of our own lives, and in listening to the symphony of his feelings, Baba was like one of those musical prodigies who could detect one missing accidental—B flat, not B natural—in the fifth chair of the viola section, ruining the whole piece for him, while less attentive concertgoers would find the performance tuneful.

Yet for the last couple of years, a duration unheard of, he'd been seeing a somewhat younger woman who worked in admissions at Washington and Lee, and a year ago—another first—Paige Myer had moved into his house.

Jillian wasn't precisely jealous; on second thought, not at all jealous. When he started seeing Paige, Weston Babansky was already forty-five, and a lasting attachment was overdue. Jillian loved Baba in a round, encompassing, roomy way, and if she still found him technically attractive, the sensation was purely aesthetic. She enjoyed being in his physical company the way she enjoyed sitting in a smartly decorated restaurant. This pleasing feeling didn't induce any need to do something about it, any more than she ever experienced the urge to fuck a dining room.

So far, only once had Paige Myer's entry into Baba's life caused Jillian genuine alarm. It was a fall afternoon, on their usual bench at Rockbridge, a few months into this new relationship.

"By the way," he introduced. "I've been teaching Paige to play tennis."

Jillian narrowed her eyes and glared. "You're trying to replace me."

He laughed. "You're such a baby!"

"On this point, yes."

"You and I aren't exclusive, you know. We both sometimes play with other people. Sport is promiscuous."

"There's having a bit on the side, there's being a whore, and there's also throwing over an old, predictable partner for sexier fresh meat. *And* there are only so many days in the week. Why wouldn't my three afternoons seem imperiled?"

He was enjoying this. It was the kind of jealousy in which one could bask, and he brought it to a close with obvious regret. "Well, you can relax. The tennis lessons have been a disaster."

Jillian leaped up and did a little dance. "Yay!"

"It isn't becoming to take that much joy in another woman's suffering," he admonished.

"I don't care whether it's *becoming*. I care about nailing down my Monday, Wednesday, and Friday slots." She sat back down with zest. "Tell me all about it."

"I made her cry."

"You didn't."

"It's just—it would take years to narrow the skills gap. She's a complete newbie, and she wasn't doing it because she especially wanted to play tennis. She just wanted to do something with me—and in that case, we're better off going to the movies. I'm not sure she has much aptitude, and I definitely don't have the patience. The boredom was claustrophobic. I don't know how the pros can stand it. I had to call a halt to the lessons, because if we kept torturing ourselves we were going to split up. She made me feel like a tyrant, and I made her feel inadequate."

"Did you two come here?" Jillian asked warily.

"No, I took her to the university courts."

"Good. Rockbridge would have been traitorous."

"The guys next to us, the last time we went on this fool's errand— Paige sent so many balls into their court that they started smashing them back two courts over. You'd have loved it, you ill-wishing bitch," he said fondly.

"I'd have loved it," she concurred. "Except I'm *not* ill wishing. At least so long as she stays off my fucking tennis court."

ADMITTEDLY, THE FIRST time they all met could have gone better. Inviting Jillian to dinner sometime that January, Baba had been unusually anxious about the introduction, her first intimation that this relationship was hitting a harmonious major chord. Getting ready that night, Jillian considered that it might have been politic to bunch back the hair into a less in-your-face look, but she hadn't timed her shower well, and the tresses were still damp. Going back and forth over what to wear, she worried that plain jeans would seem disrespectful of the occasion, so she went the opposite direction. In retrospect, the fawn-colored boa was a mistake, even if the finishing flourish had presented itself as irresistible in her bedroom mirror. But it wasn't the boa that got her into trouble.

When she first burst into Baba's kitchen, she realized she must have been anxious, too, since in the flurry of delivering the wine and divesting herself of the tiny present wrapped in birch bark, she forgot to really take in the new girlfriend—what she looked like, how she seemed. Although nearly as at home in Baba's A-frame as she was in her own cottage, Jillian was officially the guest. Thus she naturally got confused at first about whose job it was to put whom at ease. "I've been doing a little beadwork, see," she babbled with her coat still on, nodding at the package. "You can find all kinds of wild costume jewelry from yard sales, thrift shops, whole boxes of the stuff on eBay . . . Anyway, you get a lot more interesting effects when you break up the strings and mix the elements in different combinations . . ."

One didn't exactly unwrap birch bark, and the gratuity simply fell out of the fragile assemblage into Paige's palm. In her hand, suddenly the necklace looked a little cockamamie. "Oh," she said. "How nice."

"I'm still experimenting," Jillian carried on, "throwing in other found materials, like pinecone, gum-wrapper origami, pieces of eraser, even dead batteries . . ."

Paige's gaze scanned slowly back up. "Don't you think," she said, "that after all the progress we've finally made on animal rights, it might not be wise to be seen in public wearing a fur?"

Jillian gestured dismissively at her wrap. "This old thing? I picked it up secondhand years ago for five bucks. I've no idea what it's made of—muskrat, beaver? I don't much care, because even in this polar vortex what-all, it's incredibly warm."

"And it's incredibly uncool," Paige said.

"I guess *warm* and *uncool* mean kind of the same thing," Baba inserted gamely, and the girlfriend glowered.

It took Jillian a moment to register that she and Paige had managed a disagreement, a serious disagreement, with Jillian not two minutes in the door. "I bet the animals that gave up their lives for this coat were dead before I was born," she submitted. "Even if we leave aside the question of whether they'd have been bred and raised in the first place without a fur trade, my refusing to wear this coat doesn't bring the critters back to life, does it? I mean, why not redeem their sacrifice?"

"Because walking around in a barbaric garment like that is like voting," Paige countered. "It's advertising the killing of animals for the use of their body parts."

"Isn't that what we always do when we eat meat?" Jillian asked tentatively.

"I don't eat meat," Paige said stonily.

"Well, then, you're admirably consistent. Fortunately it's nice and warm in here," Jillian said, slipping off the *barbaric garment*, "so we can dispatch with the conversation piece." She braved a despairing glance at Baba, and she probably shouldn't have.

Once the threesome was settled in the living room—it might have been more graceful if Jillian had a date, too, but she hadn't been about to rent one—she was able to take the measure of Baba's new heartthrob. Late thirties; shorter than Jillian, but then most women were. After they did the whole where-are-you-from bit, it was clear that the girlfriend's Maryland accent had been thoroughly compromised by a northern education and academic colleagues from all over the map, leaving her vowels appealingly softened yet any suggestion of the hayseed picked clean. Paige had a compact figure and a somber, muted style: neat, close-cut hair, sweater, wool slacks, and now rather out-of-fashion Ugg boots. She was nice looking, though an incremental disproportion about her features made her face more interesting than plain old pretty. In any case, her expression was etched with an alertness, or with whatever elusive quality it was that wordlessly conveyed intelligence, which made mere prettiness seem beside the point. If her bearing was a shade wary and withholding, that could have been the result of circumstance. After all, a forgivable shyness and social discomfort could easily be mistaken for their more aggressive counterparts: aloofness and hostility. Jillian made a big effort thereafter to seem affable, expressing if anything excessive appreciation of the lentil salad and quinoa—but the whole rest of the evening was one long recovery from the fur coat.

In any event, that mild debacle was long behind them. By the time Paige graduated to Baba's Longest-Lasting Girlfriend Ever, Jillian made getting along with her a priority. There may have been an indefinable disconnect between the two women, but Jillian was sure they could bridge the void with the force of their good intentions. She wanted to have amicable relations with her best friend's girlfriend, and obviously Paige would want to have amicable relations with her boyfriend's best friend. Some inexorable transitive principle must have applied. If A likes B, and B likes C, then A likes C, right? And vice versa. Jillian wasn't a moron, either, and recognized the importance of taking a step back from Baba when Paige was present. Having known the woman's boyfriend for twenty-some years conferred an unfair advantage. Paige doubtless knew, too, that Jillian and Baba had slept together, and that was awkward.

Accordingly, Jillian came to pride herself on inserting an artificial distance between herself and her best friend during the numerous instances that she popped around for a drink or had the two of them over for dinner, sometimes further diluting the undiplomatic intensity between the two tennis partners by inviting another couple as well. In Paige's presence, she would ask Baba formal questions about the websites he was working on, when she was acquainted with them already, and had been discussing their particular annoyances après tennis for weeks. She was equally solicitous of Paige's travails in admissions, entering into the difficulty of balancing academic excellence with racial and economic diversity, or asking how you kept applicants from private schools from always having the edge—though this was the kind of stiff, topical discussion that Jillian didn't especially enjoy.

All told, she assessed her friend's transition to coupledom as a success for everyone concerned. Paige was on the serious side for Jillian's tastes, but as Baba pointed out, she had admirably strong convictions, of which Jillian had learned to be respectful (well—had learned to sidestep). Once Paige relaxed (which took at least a year), a sly, cutting sense of humor emerged—for example, in regard to college applicants who in their essays cast skiing holidays as "making a contribution to local communities." Jillian had come to appreciate Paige Myer, and she was grateful that finding a kindred spirit had so contented her best friend that he was considering coming off Zoloft. Jillian didn't quite understand what drew them together, but she didn't have to. She assumed that in private Paige shared her boyfriend's passion for parsing emotions and divining the fine points of complex relationships.

For that matter, Jillian largely failed to understand what drew anyone to anyone. It was one of those mysteries of the universe that the vast majority of people were able to convince someone else to singularly adore them, when any given suitor was free to choose from billions of alternatives—and these successful bondings encompassed portly shop assistants with prominent nose hair, severe-looking Seventh-Day Adventists with a penchant for hoarding felt-tip pens, and timid Filipina housemaids with wide, bland faces and one leg shorter than the other. It was astonishing that so many far-fetched candidates for undying devotion managed to marry, or something like it. Were it up to Jillian to fathom why her peers might logically invite lifelong ardor in order for them to pair off, the species would dwindle, until our worldwide population could snug into a boutique hotel. So what the hell, she'd long ago given up on second-guessing romantic attraction.

Meanwhile, Jillian had embarked on her most ambitiously futile project yet. Forty-three seemed just old enough to afford a retrospective. Were she a writer, she might have accrued sufficient experience to start a memoir. She was not a writer, but still being something of a curator of her own life, and having remained in the same cottage for fourteen years, she'd accumulated all manner of flotsam—the residue of multifarious adventures that she might convert from clutter to precious construction materials. At first she titled the assemblage "The Memory Palace," but the expression was derivative. At length, she settled on a fresher designation: "The Standing Chandelier."

AMBLING INTO THE living room in his bathrobe, Weston seemed to have walked into a conversation that, one-hand-clapping, was already under way.

"You know, this pretense Jillian has," Paige said, apropos of nothing, "that she's not really an artist—"

"Frisk likes to make stuff," he objected, rubbing his eyes. "That's all. It's posing as an Artist that's pretentious."

Paige was dusting. While any given day of the week was as good as any other to him, weekends meant something to her, and this swabbing, scouring, and polishing on a Saturday seemed a waste. The A-frame did have a more focused feel to it once she finished, even if he couldn't consciously detect how anything had changed. Yet the swish-swish of the cloth today conveyed an impatience. It may have been three in the afternoon, but he'd just gotten out of bed (having had to set his alarm to do so), and this was far too much vigor in his surround before coffee.

"But not really doing anything, and all her dumb little jobs. There's something a little spoiled about it."

"I don't follow," Weston said.

"It has to do with . . . class, really. Like, if she came from humble roots, having no ambition, and not participating in the art world proper, would seem like having low self-esteem. But because her father's a surgeon, being a big nobody is supposedly brave or something. Admirable and daring and original. Whereas the truth is that Jillian won't play the game because she doesn't want to lose." *Swish-swish,* went the cloth. "She's just afraid of judgment."

"Who wouldn't want to avoid *judgment?*"

"People who can make the grade, that's who. There's nothing upsetting about being judged if it turns out that everyone thinks you're wonderful."

"Uh-huh. And these days, when does that happen? Look at the internet. It's nothing but a lynch mob, braying about how shit everything is. I don't blame Frisk for not wanting to stick her neck out. Perfect formula for getting your head chopped off."

"She doesn't call herself an artist, because then she'd have to be a bad artist. Most of the junk she cobbles together is just—kooky. God, I wish you could find a way of telling her to stop bringing by those necklaces, made of feathers and, like, bat guano. You'd think she'd notice I never wear them."

This interchange required some serious caffeine, so Weston passed on the caffetiere and went straight for the espresso machine. He was reminded that one thing he liked about Paige was pushback. When he and Frisk conferred, they tended to agree on everything, which was restful, but it wasn't sharpening. "*You* tell her to stop with the necklaces, then," he said.

"No, if I start telling Jillian what I really think, there's no telling where it will lead. Like, I can't bear the way she calls you 'Baba.' It's such a dumb name. Like rum baba, or baba ghanoush. Or like Bill Clinton's white trash nickname—*Bubba*."

"So is your problem that it's culinary, or that it's redneck?"

"My problem is it's not your name. And it's presumptuous. This little claiming, like, 'You're my special friend with a special name that I gave you that only I get to use.' You'd think she'd have the good grace to at least call you *Weston* when I'm around."

"It would sound artificial," he said wearily. "After well over twenty years? Like coming here and suddenly calling me 'Mister Babansky.'"

"I could live with 'Mister Babansky,'" Paige muttered. "A little regard for *boundaries* would be more than welcome."

Weston always woke slowly, emerging from bed in a bumbling, bearlike state that Paige commonly found beguiling; on more promising Saturday afternoons, she'd have tackled him back to the sheets. One of the perks of keeping such different schedules was that sex was a daytime activity, which had nothing to do with sleep. Paige was an inventive lover, with an appetite her low-key apparel and cropped, easy-maintenance haircut might seem to belie. He was well aware that Frisk found his relationship a measure perplexing—she was never good at keeping such thoughts to herself, even if she imagined she was being tactful; Frisk's version of discreet was everyone else's foot-in-mouth disease—and the often psychotropic frenzies with Paige, whose exquisitely subtle breasts drove him wild, were a big piece of the puzzle. A piece he tended to underplay with Frisk. Guys had been thin on the ground for her recently, and he didn't want to rub her nose in his good fortune.

"The truth is," Paige continued, having moved on to Windexing the wineglass rings on the coffee table, "it kind of grates when you call her 'Frisk,' too. Like you're football buddies in a locker room. That last-name thing, it's a gruff, shoulder-clapping palliness you usually get over after high school."

Weston wondered whether he could train himself to refer to Frisk as *Jillian* at home. The rechristening would take vigilance, but if it made a difference to Paige, the effort might pay off. On the other hand, such constant mental editing was a drain. He didn't think of his tennis partner as *Jillian*, and he was well aware that a first-name basis in this instance would amount to a demotion. He would be humoring Paige, too, and that wasn't a direction he wanted to go. A matter for private debate later. In the interim, he would try to stick to pronouns.

Taking a slug of espresso, he shot an anxious glance at the clock. "What's biting your butt today?"

"Oh, we'd talked about asking Gareth, Helen, and Bob over in a couple of weeks—our usual History Department crowd—and then I thought, right, great, you're no doubt expecting we'll ask Jillian, too."

"We don't always ask her." Jesus, this was exhausting.

"No, but the last time we didn't, you just *had* to tell her all about the evening with Vivian and Leo—"

"I couldn't resist telling her about that nightmare 'free-form berry tart.' How the cream cheese pastry kept springing leaks and we had to put it in the freezer—"

"You said you thought she felt hurt."

"That may have been my imagination. She doesn't expect to come over every time we *entertain*." He didn't think of himself as someone who *entertains*.

"But whenever we knock her off the guest list, you feel guilty."

"A little guilty," he said, having considered the question for a moment. "And a little relieved. I don't enjoy being caught in the middle."

"Then don't put yourself in the middle."

"*Finding* yourself in a position isn't the same as *putting* yourself there."

"Oh, no? Anyone with volition in a position he doesn't like can move somewhere else."

He didn't have time for this. He pulled the chilled thermos from the fridge, collected his cell, wallet, and keys, and put them by the door. "At least if we did ask her," Weston tossed off on the way to the bedroom to dress, "with Gareth-and-Helen, and Bob, it would be balanced."

"Bob doesn't balance anything, because Bob is gay," she called after him. "I wish Jillian would at least get another boyfriend."

"You couldn't bear the last one!" Weston called, pulling on his shorts.

"He was an idiot. Jillian has terrible taste in men."

Tennis shoes in hand, Weston came back out pushing his head through his T-shirt. "Thanks."

Paige looked up sharply, taking in the garb. "But you're not 'a man.' To her. Supposedly." Her demeanor had suddenly frozen over.

"I'm running late. This'll have to wait." Weston yanked his laces, and headed to the carton of balls in the corner to withdraw a new can.

"But it's Saturday."

"Frisk . . . she . . . got inexplicably caught up in something she's working on yesterday, and lost track of the time. Not like her, but anyway, we rescheduled. May not get our two hours on a weekend, but one's better than nothing. See you around six or so. Seven at the latest." With a wisp of a kiss, Weston snatched his racket and fled. If they did play two hours, he would not be home till eight.

He hadn't wanted it to be true, and Weston was as capable of self-deceit as the next person, whatever his pretensions to self-knowledge. So it had taken him too long to pick up the pattern. On Mondays, Wednesdays, and Fridays, Paige got in a bad mood.

WESTON KNEW THIS much about himself: he was prone to confuse thinking about something with doing something about it. So as far as he was concerned, in often turning his mind to Paige's exasperating and no-little-inconvenient antagonism toward Frisk, he was doing his job.

That Saturday afternoon they were freakishly able to play not two hours but three. Afterward, as Weston kept glancing at his watch in the dimming dusk, Frisk urged him to attend a private unveiling of her latest project, about which she'd been oddly secretive for months. But despite all Weston's industrious cogitating, it was more challenging than it once had been to arrange to stop by Frisk's cottage on his own. He introduced the idea to Paige the following week with an ingratiating cynicism that made him dislike himself.

"I have no idea what it is," he said, paving the way for what he didn't wish to regard as "permission" to visit his best friend after hours. "I only know she's made a big deal out of it, and she's been working on it for a bizarrely long time. You can be sure it's a little crazy, per usual."

"Can't she just bring it along this weekend, now that she's virtually invited herself to dinner with the history crowd? She could wrap it up in *birch bark*."

"I got the impression it doesn't transport easily. And whatever it is, I'd think you'd be glad to get out of pretending to admire it."

Weston himself had tried to maintain a studious neutrality in relation to Frisk's creations. He took at face value her reluctance to participate in the professional art world, and one upside to her having carved out the right to "make stuff" outside the aegis of galleries—she did give things away, but she never sold anything—should have been release from assessment. Yet it was infernally difficult to suspend your critical faculties. In cosmopolitan culture—and the better educated in isolated college towns like Lexington held on to every signature of sophistication for dear life—the impulse to appraise was deeply ingrained: this knee-jerk need to no sooner see, hear, taste, or read a thing than to determine how "good" it was. The fashioning of an opinion was almost synonymous with apprehension of the item in question, so that you hardly had a chance to take something in before you got busy deciding what you thought of it—as if failure to come up with an instantaneous verdict made you remiss, or slackwitted. So Frisk's often whimsical contrivances had given him practice at detachment. Surely there was something to be said for simply looking, without immediately going to work on an estimation, as if you were expected to value the article at hand for insurance purposes.

He did appreciate Frisk's refusal to acknowledge the artificial boundary between fine art and craft, a line she crossed merrily back and forth all the time. And in one respect he didn't resist discernment: whatever she made, she made well. If his casual attendance at various galleries in Lexington and even DC was anything to go by, that made her the exception among most would-be artists, whose technical proficiency was often woeful.

Frisk was a better-than-competent carpenter and a skillful welder. The phantasmagoric tiling affixed to her claw-foot bathtub was neatly grouted. Her coffee table slatted together from logoed yardsticks, which hardware stores gave away to customers for free advertising in the 1970s, wasn't only ingenious, and nicely variegated with accents of red and yellow, but flat. Composing her pointillistic self-portrait made entirely of buttons, she had meticulously picked the residual threads from the holes of the secondhand ones, and had sacrificed several of her own shirts when the color of their fasteners helped fill out the demanding proportion of the surface taken up by the mass of hair—even if the resultant facial expression was unnervingly dazed. However wonky and unwearable Paige might find those strings of beads and found objects, the necklaces would never fall apart—much to his girlfriend's despair.

Moreover, whatever withering appraisals others might level at what she never even dignified as "her work," Frisk wasn't hurting anybody. Every time he entered the house of horrors of a major newspaper, Weston elevated sheer harmlessness to the pinnacle of achievement.

She wasn't asking for much, either: a smile, a handclap, or a good long stare. Such modest acknowledgment was the least he could supply her, and having showered after tennis on a Wednesday in May, he braved Paige's tight-lipped silence and promised to be back for dinner.

Frisk met him at the door in one of her floor-length getups. Once black and dotted with tiny red chrysanthemums, the dress had grayed and relaxed from multiple washings. The fabric looked soft—not that he was about to touch it. The near rag had doubtless been cadged from a church basement jumble sale, but especially with the hair it cast her as a Pre-Raphaelite Ophelia. She'd arranged the living room lighting so low it was almost dark. In the middle, resting on her hand-hooked shag rug, loomed an obscure object over six feet tall, poking here and there against the drape of its bedsheet.

"Don't look now, but your house is haunted," he said, kissing her cheek hello.

"And how," she said, insisting on uncorking a Sauvignon blanc before the viewing. She wasn't usually this dramatic about unveilings, which had never been so literal. Ordinarily, whatever she'd made would be propped in a corner, and she'd point.

"I call it 'The Standing Chandelier,' and if I'm honest with myself, this time I really want you to like it." She clinked her glass against his. "Ready? Close your eyes."

Weston played along. There was a rustle, then a click.

"Now."

If a "chandelier," it was upside down. The object was more of a standing candelabra, with multiple branches welded onto a central trunk in an irregular, botanical pattern. It glittered with dozens if not hundreds of tiny lights, most of them white, with a few incidental accents of yellow and blue. On examination, the lights illuminated a host of miniature assemblages, like individual installations on a minute scale. He knew her life in sufficient detail to infer the provenance of their constituent parts. Her wisdom teeth—pulled in her midtwenties. An admission ticket to the Stonewall Jackson House, where she used to work. The ebony trident-shaped mute would be a memento from that hot fling with a violinist during the fiddlers' convention. The lavender roll tied with a bow he recognized as the last grip she replaced on her trusty Dunlop 7Hundred, and there were other tennis references, too. One of the arms of the candelabra was neatly wound with a busted string; another enclosure included a rubber vibration dampener and a puff of chartreuse that could only have been shaved from their usual Wilsons (extra-duty felt for hard courts). She'd discovered that delicate curlew skull on a walk along the Maury River, the long tweezer of a beak still perfectly intact; it was one of her prize possessions. He spotted some keys, perhaps to old apartments, like the share with that O'Hagan shrew; a diminutive pewter cowbell, a souvenir from the solo Alpine hike through Switzerland on which she got lost for three days; a ribbon-wrapped coil of hair, a distinctive henna with the odd blond highlight, which could only have been snipped from her own head.

There were signatures of childhood: a small windup helicopter (which still worked); an inch-high troll doll trailing pink hair, meant to fit on the end of a pencil; a red-and-gold kazoo and a plastic whistle. The pair of red salt and pepper shakers hailed from her very first airplane journey—museum pieces, from a domestic in-flight meal. One round, green cloth cameo was embroidered with a spool of thread, another with a tent—though the merit badges were few, because Frisk hadn't lasted long in the Girl Scouts. The 1981 Susan B. Anthony silver dollar was a present from her father on her graduation from sixth grade, the shining feminist symbolism dulled somewhat when the coin was pulled from circulation.

She'd even fabricated exquisitely reduced versions of earlier handiwork. The self-portrait was duplicated with minuscule beads instead of buttons (and at two inches square, the facial expression was more focused). She alluded to the yardstick coffee table by gluing together a dollhouse edition made of painted flat toothpicks, their enamel repeating the red and yellow accents of the life-size version. The claw-foot bathtub was now shrunken to a hollow half acorn, its tiling painstakingly approximated by individual squares of glitter. A woven rug, about the size of a commemorative stamp, echoed the colors of the very carpet on which the chandelier stood.

But this contraption wasn't a tree of junk; it wasn't like opening a jumbled drawer in a study whose owner never cleaned out her desk. Each collection of objects was a composition, often enclosed in inventive containers: a bright Colman's mustard tin with windows cut out; a classy Movado watch box with its dimpled satin pillow, from Frisk's one splurge on jewelry that wasn't from Goodwill; a wide-mouthed, strikingly faceted jar that he recognized as having once held artichoke-heart paste, because he'd given it to her on her last birthday. Some of the boxes were made of tinted transparent plastic, while the cardboard ones were wallpapered inside, with velvet carpeting or miniaturized hardwood floors. Each still life was lit, and she'd been scrupulous about hiding the wires in the tubular branches. As ever, the workmanship was sound, and when he gave the trunk a gentle shake, nothing rattled or fell off. What's more, the lamp spoke to him. It conveyed a tenderness toward its creator's life that would invariably foster in the viewer a tenderness toward his own.

"Well?" Frisk prodded. "You haven't said anything."

For once Weston didn't have to concentrate on withholding judgment. As Paige had observed, there was nothing to be feared from judgment when everyone would say that what you'd made was wonderful. So that's what he did. He said, "It's wonderful."

"You like it!"

"I love it. It reminds me a lot of Joseph Cornell."

Her face clouded. "Who's that?"

"Well, so much for Washington and Lee's art education. Paige and I saw an exhibit of his work at the National Gallery. He put all these bits and pieces in little boxes, and hung them on the wall."

"So you're saying it's imitative?"

"You can't copy someone you've never heard of. And the comparison is a compliment. That retrospective was one of the only exhibits Paige has dragged me to that wasn't a waste of time. Cornell strikes a great balance between serious art and a childlike, kind of sandbox fucking around. And to my knowledge, he never made any 'standing chandelier,' either. You know, what's especially amazing," Weston noted, taking a couple of steps back, "is that it works on every level. Each little arrangement is perfect. But it also works as a whole. It's like a Christmas tree you can keep lit year-round."

She was so excited that it broke his heart to turn down her spontaneous invitation to stay for dinner. Nonetheless, they finished the Sauvignon blanc.

WESTON HAD BEEN contemplating the matter for a while, and it was a rare rumination that he hadn't chosen to bounce off Frisk. Paige came across at first as a little unadorned and sexless, which is why it had taken him a while to notice her when he was working with the admissions office on the William and Lee website. But that was before you took her clothes off. She had a perfectly proportioned body that made so many other women seem like mere packaging. To his surprise, too, the heat between them hadn't cooled once the novelty wore off. To the contrary, the more familiar they became with each other, the more they relaxed and let fly. Maybe it was advantageous that she didn't advertise herself as a honeypot—disguise would keep other men's hands off her—and he liked the sensation between them of having a secret. He recognized something in her, too—a difficulty in figuring out just how to be with people. When he saw this awkwardness in someone else, he could see how attractive it was when you didn't like artifice, and would rather be genuinely uncomfortable than insincerely at ease. He'd come to treasure her faux pas, like that fracas over Frisk's fur coat. Blurting about the "barbaric garment" had hardly oiled the wheels that night, but she couldn't help but say what she was thinking. Which made it so much easier to trust her.

Paige was the more determined to overcome this inbuilt ungainliness, and her being more sociable than he was—the sociability was a discipline; her doses of company were almost medicinal—had so far been beneficial. Since they'd been together, he'd increased his circle of acquaintances by a factor of three, and now, haltingly, counted one or two as friends. She took an interest in the arts, especially visual art. While many of the exhibitions they'd traveled to see had left him cold, there were memorable exceptions. After years of Frisk's jaundiced views of the museum and gallery establishment, he was grateful to be introduced to a few painters and sculptors who weren't phony. Paige conceived fierce opinions, while he was more wont to see multiple sides to an issue, so she pushed him profitably to stop waffling: yes, on balance, it did seem that the bulk of climate change was probably manmade. Few women would have been so tolerant of his late hours, too. (Some internal clock in him was six to seven hours out of sync with other people's. Try as he might, he could never hit the sack at midnight. Aiming for a more civilized schedule, he'd set an alarm for nine a.m., not arise until eleven, and still feel so cheated of sleep that the following day he'd snooze through the afternoon.) What's more, Paige accepted his mood swings. When he stopped talking and sank in front of late-night TV for days on end, she recognized the funk for what it was and didn't take it personally.

He'd worried at first about the vegetarianism, but they'd worked it out. At home, he'd eat legumes and eggplant, and the new dishes she brought to their table richly expanded his gastronomic range. He was "allowed," if that was the word, to order meat when eating out, so long as he brushed his teeth as soon as he got back.

He was forty-eight. He was pulling in a good living at last, and was surprised that making money made him feel more emotionally grounded; perhaps financial precariousness induced instabilities of other sorts. In the last thirty years, he had sampled enough women to have lost interest in variety. An isolate, he'd always thought of himself as a man who treasured his solitude above all else. Yet the last year and a half of cohabitation had been effortless, which wasn't so much a tribute to Lonely Guy Gets a Life as it was to Paige Myer in particular. He suffered under no illusion that he'd grown into a more accommodating character. The women he could put up with who could also put up with him were very few, if indeed there was more than one.

Leery of restaurant theatricality, Weston didn't feel the need to conspire with a chef to plant a ring in the molten middle of a flourless chocolate cake. Yet the day after the viewing of the chandelier, he did offer to make dinner (a zucchini lasagna with pecorino and béchamel), and he opened a red whose cost exceeded his usual $12 limit. It wasn't ideal to have chosen a weeknight, but he was eager to erase Paige's irritation that he'd stayed too long at Frisk's the previous evening, for which a motherfucking marriage proposal was sure to compensate. Eagerness outweighed anxiety. He was optimistic.

"But from your description," Paige said, digging into her lasagna, "it sounds goofy. Busy and trashy and kitchen sink."

The confounded thing was that Paige bent over backward to see the goodness in just about anybody else. She had a weakness for social strays, dragging home office assistants with bottle-bottom glasses and bad dandruff the way other women adopted mangy, big-eyed kitty cats with no collar. The only person in the world about whom he'd heard her be overtly unkind was Jillian Frisk.

"Then you'll have to take my word for it." He didn't want to get short tempered, this of all nights. "I thought it was beautiful."

"Still." She wouldn't let it go. "You have to admit that the whole concept is on the egotistical side—"

"It's a celebration," he cut her off. "Of a life, and it could be anyone's life. Warmth toward your own past, and a sense of humor about your idiosyncrasies, doesn't make you self-obsessed."

He was overdoing the defense, but Weston was tired of being enticed into criticizing his best friend, which made him feel weak and two-faced. Yet somehow he had to imbue this meal with a more convivial vibe or put off his proposal for another time. For that matter, maybe what was making him testy was having an agenda and not addressing it. He and Paige were now sufficiently attuned that whenever one of them suppressed a thought, the atmosphere queered. So, with a deep breath, he refilled their glasses to announce, "Look, I was going to wait until after dinner, but if I don't get this out I'm going to bust."

She immediately looked frightened—withdrawing from her food with a stricken wince, as if he'd just destroyed her appetite. If he weren't so determined to plow ahead, he might have considered that terrified reaction. He trusted her, but maybe the trust didn't run both ways.

He moved the plates out of the way, leaned in, and slid his glass forward until it kissed hers. "I shouldn't really be taking this hand," Weston extemporized, holding her fingers between his, "when I want to ask for it."

Either the construction was too clever, or fear had clouded her wit. She looked uncomprehending.

"I'm asking you," he spelled out, "to marry me."

"Oh!" Breaking the clasp, she sprang back, and her eyes filled with tears.

Now it was his turn not to get it. "Is that a yes?"

"I don't know."

This wasn't going the way he expected. The lasagna was starting to congeal.

"It's too soon? Too sudden? Too . . . what?"

Paige stared at her lap, worrying her napkin. "I want to be able to say yes. But I talked about this for a long time with my sister, more than once. I made her a promise, which was really a promise to myself. I can't tell you how hard it is for me to be disciplined about this. I'd love to throw my arms around you and say, 'What took you so long?' But I can't accept unconditionally."

"What's the condition?" A lump was already wadding in Weston's gut. He didn't bother to formulate to himself the nature of her stipulation, since she would spit it out soon enough. But he could have anticipated the ultimatum without much strain.

"Jillian," she said.

Lord, how lovely it would be, once in a while in this life, to be surprised.

"You know how you meet some people and think they're really great right away?" Paige continued. "But then they don't wear well, and what was superficially appealing is disappointing or even annoying in the long run. And then there are the other people, who you don't take a shine to at the start—who seem like creeps, or drive you nuts. But you stick with it, and get to know them better, and little by little they grow on you after all. So it can turn out that it's the very people who put you off at the beginning who you end up liking better than anybody."

Despite himself, Weston's expression must have looked hopeful.

"Well, this thing with me and Jillian isn't like either of those," Paige said, meeting his eyes at last, and that was that for feeling hopeful. "I couldn't stand her when I met her, and I can't stand her now that I've gotten to know her better. She acts as if her not doing anything professionally makes her so special, when most people don't do anything. She absolutely has to be the central focus in any given group of people, and whenever conversation strays from *her* latest goofball project, or *her* latest goofball outfit, she stops paying attention. She's basically undersocialized. She only pretends to be interested in anyone else—though I guess the pretending means she's socialized to a point—and whenever she asks about my life, it's obvious she's only going through the motions and doesn't care. I'm not even convinced she's that interested in you. You're just a great audience for her, and that's the main thing she needs from anybody. She has no sense of tact—which is just another form of being inconsiderate, of not bothering to pay attention to anyone else. So it never occurs to her to maybe keep her mouth shut about how great *fracking* is, because other people present might find her idiotic opinions offensive. For that matter, her opinions about anything important are all over the map. Since she doesn't read newspapers or even watch TV news, I've come to the conclusion that she doesn't *have* opinions—she just tries on a position like another outfit. She's not a serious person, West! She lives her life in, like—a playroom! And there's something so *crafted* about her. All presentation, no substance. With these big stagey entrances she makes. With all the feathers and jumped-up enthusiasm. It's fake. I have no idea what's behind the prima donna song and dance, aside from a woman who's hopelessly self-centered, and maybe a little lost. Like a lot of people who come across as egotistical, all that high-octane vivacity *could* be just overcompensating for underconfidence—since she's clearly too frightened to go out into the world and make her mark. That's me bending over backwards to be understanding, but I'm not a gymnast. I can't maintain that position for very long."

This—whatever you call the perfect opposite of *ode*—came out in such a rush that Paige was breathing hard. Weston asked dryly, "Is that all?"

"No, come to think of it. She also drinks too much. Way too much, making her a bad influence. Every time you go over there without me, you come back soused."

"Are you trying to convince me to despise my own best friend?"

"No, this is obviously my problem—but it's getting worse. Like those private coinages of hers that she repeats all the time whenever we go over for dinner, and she *always* serves popcorn as an appetizer? Which is cheap, by the way, in every sense. Practically free, and déclassé. So a substandard bowlful always has 'low loft.' Having only a few dead kernels at the bottom indicates a 'high pop ratio.' A batch lifting the lid on the pot is 'achieving lidosity.' You think it's enchanting, and I'm glad for you about that, I guess. But I couldn't find it enchanting on pain of death. I think it's dorky. Every time she says this stuff it's fingernail-on-a-blackboard for me. Her very *voice* grates. You'd think she'd learn to speak at a volume that isn't pitched for the hard of hearing! The stress of pretending to get along with her is wearing me out."

"If you want to keep the socializing to a minimum—"

"If it were just a matter of your friend getting on my nerves, maybe I could simply avoid her, and we could keep making excuses for why I'm busy and can't come with—though if we're really talking about getting married, a there's-somewhere-I-gotta-be routine could be hard to keep up over a lifetime. She'd figure it out. And then it would be an issue, and she'd get all touchy and wounded the way she does. Still, maybe that would be manageable. If that were the only problem, we could choreograph some sort of elaborate dance and never end up in the same room.

"But it's worse than that. She acts as if she owns you. I'm never sure what you two are talking about all that time after tennis—because you're always gone for way longer than the couple of hours you play. I can't help but worry that you're talking about me. And I worry the discussion isn't always nice, since nice things are usually a little boring, and for some reason they never take very long to say. I can't bear this paranoia. It's worse than when you go see your shrink. At least a shrink is supposed to keep his mouth shut, and be a little objective. If you also need to confide in a regular person, a civilian, and I'm going to be your wife, then you should be confiding in me."

"I can confide in more than one person, can't I?"

"You can confide in more than one person who's a *man*. You're going to claim I'm 'insecure.' Maybe I am, but maybe I have a right to be. If you two always had a platonic relationship, that would be one thing. But you've been involved with each other, you said, not once, but twice. You've played it down, but I've gotten the impression that both times it was kind of a big deal."

"We've both been involved with multiple people since. That's ancient history."

"It doesn't come across as ancient history. I still pick up a feeling between you two. It's not—well, it's not wholesome. There's an electricity, an energy, and it leaves me out. When she's around, you hardly touch me, have you noticed? Structurally, this situation is lopsided, too. I've had boyfriends, but then I've broken up with them or they with me, and we've gone our separate ways. I don't have anyone in my life who remotely duplicates Jillian's role in yours. I don't see anybody else socially three or four times a week, not even a girlfriend. I'd appreciate your trying to picture how you might feel if I saw one of my exes that often. And we hung out on a park bench for hours at a time and shared each other's secrets. Wouldn't that make you anxious? Wouldn't you worry what we talked about?"

"Half the time, it's about how many minutes you should sous vide salmon."

"Right—*half* the time. Wouldn't you worry about the other half? And imagine if this male pal of mine went through long periods of being unattached, and gave every sign of being emotionally dependent on me, to say the least. I think you'd get the jitters. Especially if this hypothetical guy was—I'll give Jillian this much, and I might feel a little different if she weren't—fucking good-looking." Paige didn't often curse.

Maybe this was where he was supposed to say, *Only up to a point*, or *But she's not aging very well*, or *I've never noticed one way or another*, or *Fair enough, but not my type*, further gilding the lily with the white lie, *I may not have mentioned it, but truth is we were a lousy match in the sack.* Maybe out of loyalty he was even supposed to claim, *Give me a break! Between the two of you, you're the knockout in my book.* There was no way any man in this position could remain in the realm of credibility and win.

"It's hardly her fault that most people would consider her reasonably attractive." Judicious. But even his insertion of *reasonably* was pure suck up, and probably backfired. The qualifier made him sound evasive and condescending.

"The issue isn't 'most people.'"

"I don't think of her that way."

"So you've told me repeatedly. Whatever folks say over and over starts sounding shifty. As if they're trying to talk themselves into something."

"I don't know what else I can say to make you feel safe."

"There's nothing you can say. That's the point. There's something you'd have to do."

Weston wished that real life had a pause button. When watching a smart TV, you could always freeze the frame before an exciting scene, and leave to take a leak or grab a snack. Meantime on-screen, no one pushed the protagonist off a ledge to fall twenty stories to the pavement. As if to activate his personal remote control, he found himself sitting perfectly still. If no one spoke, and no one moved, he and Paige could remain in this instant and not the next one. As soon as the program advanced, they would be living in a different world where his life was bound to be worse. For when you said things, there was no taking them back. That was the other button real life lacked: a rewind.

Paige said, "You have to stop seeing her."

"That's out of the question." The answer was reflex.

She started to cry. Weston realized they'd been talking several feet apart, and any man who did not rise and comfort his lover when she was weeping was a monster. He was not a monster.

"That was what I told my sister you would say." She snuffled on his shoulder and got a string of watery snot on his shirt. "And it's okay. It's all my fault, in a way. This isn't the first time I've fallen in love with the wrong man. I just didn't—read the situation right. I took you at your word that you were free, but you're not free. Because all this time I think you've been in love with Jillian. With *Frisk*. She probably loves you, too, and I don't know why you two aren't together already. It seems like a bad-timing problem, but I wish you'd figure it out, or you'll just put your next girlfriend through the same thing. I wish I'd understood what was going on sooner, because for me it's too late. Now I'm going to feel horrible. I'd have loved to marry you. I thought that after so many dead ends I'd finally found someone. But it's like Princess Diana said: 'There have always been three people in this relationship.' I can't marry you if it means constantly having to look over my shoulder. Wondering where you are and what you're saying about me and why it's taking you so long to come back from the tennis court."

* * *

THEY HAD SEX that night, but in a spirit of Paige's sacrificing herself on the altar of him. She was too wide open, defenseless, almost splayed. The feel was a little warped. As they coupled, too, he couldn't help but notice the odd tear drizzle down her temple and pool in her ear. He was so afraid that she was thinking this was the last time that he couldn't ask. When her alarm went off, though neither was rested, he got up with her, as if now she were the one who shouldn't be trusted, and had to be watched.

Before she left for work—where she would be useless, and coworkers would ask if something was the matter; her face was puffy and bruised looking, her eyes squeezed and red—he sat her down. Listen, he said. What she was asking was monumental. He and Frisk had been fast friends for—Yes, yes, Paige interrupted wearily. *Twenty-five years.* He wasn't refusing to comply with her wishes outright, he said. But he wasn't an impulsive man, and it took him longer than most people to know his own mind. So she had to let him consider this. In the meantime, he said, he had to know what he was considering. The details. She wasn't saying that he had to see Frisk less often, or with a chaperone, but that he had to cut off the friendship altogether? Paige nodded. And that included tennis? When he asked for that last clarification, it was hard to get the words out. In some ways, she said, especially tennis. Okay, he said, so what was the time frame? (He worried he was sounding too businesslike, but there was clearly an element here of drawing up a contract.) For the first time since she imploded the night before, Paige looked a measure less crestfallen—no, a measure less *destroyed.* She had never looked *crestfallen,* but *destroyed.* The time frame? she repeated. In the instance that he'd really do as she asked? So that they were getting married after all? Well, she had obviously put up with this situation as his girlfriend, she said, and for longer than she should have. But she wasn't putting up with it as his wife. Assuming they weren't talking about some old-fashioned long engagement, he would have until their wedding day to sort it out. To say good-bye, and give Jillian his good wishes, or whatever it was that people did when they'd never speak to each other again.

"This is a small town," he reminded her. "We'll run into each other regardless."

"Okay, I'm not being ridiculous," Paige said, rolling her eyes. "You can still say hi. But you might find in the end you'd be doing her a favor. I mean, why *is* a woman that good-looking still single in her midforties? She may not realize it, but she could be holding out for you. In any case, she certainly uses you as a crutch. If you let her go, she might find someone. As things stand, she doesn't feel the need to do online dating or anything. She always has her *Baba*, like a stuffed bear."

There was a final condition. About the wedding, if there was one— here and only here did Paige sound a note of vengefulness—"*She's not invited.*"

WHEN HE RERAN that conversation with Paige after she left for the university, Weston was alarmed by how rapidly their tenses had changed, from the conditional/subjunctive to the simple future to the present. "You *would* have until the wedding" had slid to "We *will* run into each other," until Paige was allowing, "You *can* still say hi." Although officially no decision had been taken, the very grammar of this dilemma was moving too fast and getting away from him.

It would have to be a tennis day. Having clocked the day of the week, Paige had charged at the door, "You're going to tell her, aren't you? About the whole conversation, and my awful ultimatum, and then you'll decide what to do about it *together.*"

The nasty twist of that parting shot, which he left unanswered, alone illustrated how impossible this situation had grown overnight. Preserving his nonaligned status by being so stoically methodical with Paige before she left, he had tried to carve out extra time for himself, in which to examine all the angles. Yet absent resolution, staying in the same house with Paige even one more day could prove untenable. The longer he delayed giving his girlfriend an answer, too, the more he'd express being torn—the more he'd indicate that marriage to Paige wasn't important enough for him to pay a price for it, and the more he'd indicate that his friendship with Frisk was *too* important. Weston's mind was forever chewing mental cud, and he wasn't accustomed to having to do something rather than merely mull it over. Starkly, either he announced this very evening that a detonator was ticking on his friendship with Frisk, or Paige moved out.

Over a sodden bowl of muesli, fragments of that excoriation of Frisk kept hitting his brain like shrapnel. He supposed that, looked at a certain way, some of his girlfriend's accusations were sort of true. Frisk was a little self-. . . self-centered, self-involved, self-absorbed? But who wasn't self-something? It might not have been obvious from the outside, but he himself was wholly and unapologetically self-absorbed. His own nature may have been the source of endless frustration, but of tireless fascination also, to the point where he regarded the study of Weston Babansky as his real career.

Besides, he wondered if you couldn't describe just about anyone in terms that were both accurate and lacerating. You could probably savage the personality of everyone on the planet if you wanted to, though there remained the question of why you would want to. And some folks were destined to stand more in the firing line than others. Frisk had a flamboyance that thrust her head above the parapet. She was something of an acquired taste, but Weston had acquired it, and he worried that Paige's aspersions might make him more critical, more susceptible to perceiving what had so recently seemed his best friend's strengths as her flaws. After all, any virtue could be cast as a defect. Optimism might look like credulity; self-assurance could come across as conceit. So while he clearly shouldn't repeat any of Paige's broadside to Frisk, he'd also have to be mindful about not rehearsing the diatribe in his own head. The recollection made him shudder. It was called "character assassination" for good reason. He felt as if he'd witnessed a murder.

Exhausted, he'd be sluggish on the court. How extraordinary, that he wasn't looking forward to a hit.

Mobilizing his gear that afternoon as if sloshing through floodwater, Weston acknowledged that the one thing he did owe his girlfriend was some serious soul searching. Maybe there was something wrong with his relationship with Frisk, something unsavory. Maybe they crossed a line. Truly, Paige didn't demand the same broad-mindedness from him. He had difficulty conjuring a mirror image in which Paige ran off to spend hour upon hour with another man, of whose intentions he was suspicious. The imaginary rival remained a paper doll. Yet she had to be right. He wouldn't like it.

PRESUMABLY WHEN MEETING as veritable strangers on the street they would learn to say hi, but they didn't bother with formal greetings yet. Leaning against her bike, helmet off and headband on, Frisk simply raised her eyebrows and laid a censorious finger on her watch. He was fifteen minutes late.

Silent chiding sufficed, and she let the annoyance go. "You know, I've been flying on such a high ever since you came to see the chande-lier," she jabbered en route to the net post. "I'm so excited you like it!"

He wanted to ask, *Do you worry that my reaction to your lamp thing, or anything else really, matters too much to you?* But he didn't.

"You're quiet," she noted, unsheathing the Dunlop 7Hundred.

"I didn't get much sleep."

"You're not getting down in the dumps again, are you?"

"You could say that," he conceded.

Frisk's magenta shorts were on the skimpy side, and as he watched her sashay to her baseline Weston concluded that she wasn't wearing underwear. She should be wearing underwear, shouldn't she? Some-thing sporty with wide elastic—a little baggy, cotton, and plain.

Was he still attracted to her? Well, what did that mean? That he wanted to jump her? That he actively thought about fucking her? No, he didn't. He didn't think he did. He had, after all, fucked her already, which strangely enough, though he was not a linguistic prude, he didn't like the sound of. He could naturally recall those two periods when they got down to it—perhaps the affairs were only a few months apiece, though in his head they took up the space of a few years. The memories were stored more as a jagged sequence of stills than as video. In the rare instance that these images strobed his mind, he tended to flinch. He no sooner summoned what she looked like naked than made the picture go away.

"Baba, I know you're tired," she shouted across the net. "But I don't usually start a point and you just stand there!"

"Sorry," he called from his baseline. "Distracted."

She was a comely woman and he was a hale heterosexual whose testosterone levels had not yet dropped to zero. She had good legs—long and sinewy, with well-developed calf muscles, though in her forties the skin above her knees was starting to crinkle, from years of too much sun. She had a taut figure, and hilarious hair. He loved her face, though he didn't know what that meant, either, except that it was true: he loved her face. Blue eyes with shocks of green, thin lips and a mouth slightly too wide, and he liked it wide. Yet this breakdown was unhelpful. He treasured her *presence*. He was accustomed to her *presence*, at ease in her *presence*, and her appearance was utterly inseparable from the whole of her: the whooping laugh, the zany ideas, the unreliable crosscourt backhand. So the answer to his point of inquiry was a worthless *I don't know*.

Weston did at last bear down on the ball, focus on which reprieved him from still more mental cud chewing that resolved nothing. They were well matched in a broad sense, but who was beating whom swung drastically back and forth from session to session and hour to hour, and by the end he was getting the better of her. In fact, during the final thirty minutes he marshaled a degree of sheer power from which he may often have sheltered her, perhaps subconsciously. She could hit a heavy ball for a woman, but he still had the gender advantage if he chose to employ it.

"You know, you seemed almost angry," she said on the bench. "I'm used to your getting mad at yourself, but toward the end there you seemed mad at me."

The distance between their thighs was about an inch. Which wasn't enough if she didn't have any panties on, and Weston discreetly rearranged himself farther away.

"I'm not angry at you. I was just trying to really connect for once."

He was dismayed that she accepted the denial so readily—"You sure wore me out, anyway!"—before segueing to her current fixation without dropping a beat: "By the way, you were right about that Christmas tree quality. I've started leaving the chandelier on at night while turning all the other lights off, and it's magical. Every December when I was little, I used to get up at six a.m. even when school was out—so I could listen to 'Pavane for a Dead Princess' turned down low and bask in the glow of the tree. I was always crushed whenever my parents finally decided it was too dried out and a fire hazard. Now I don't ever have to take down the tree."

She was irritating him, and it was a terrible feeling. Maybe Paige was right, that this chandelier contraption was egomaniacal. And he'd never noticed before how often his tennis partner touched his arm while she talked.

Frisk went on to explain about how she'd started making her own kimchi and the smell was taking over the whole cottage. He shared a recipe he'd tried recently, a new twist on crab cakes, but his heart was so little in the telling that he forgot to mention the mango chutney—and that was the twist.

Weston's subsequent non sequitur was not premeditated. Nevertheless, he needed to investigate the question pressing in on him: *Is there something wrong here, have we all along been doing something wrong?* So after she related how last week during a tutorial her student kept emitting such evil farts ("there must be an intermediate state in physics that's halfway between a gas and a solid") that she had to keep excusing herself for a bathroom break or drink of water just to get out of the room, he said, "Oh, right. I asked Paige to marry me last night."

Dropping that bombshell was an observational experiment. He watched her face. The face that he loved—that he either loved innocuously or loved dishonestly. Whatever was happening in that face, it was complicated. Which meant something in itself. And her pause implied a reckoning. Did one *reckon* with good news?

"Wow," she said after the elongated beat. "You've sat here all this time, telling me a slightly lame recipe for crab cakes, and then it's like, also, I'm getting married, and don't forget the cilantro?"

"We've never been hung up on telling stories in hierarchical order."

"If an extraterrestrial spaceship had landed on the Chevaliers' lawn this morning, I think I might have let you know before telling the anecdote about Fart Boy."

Equates Paige with invader from outer space.

". . . was this proposal something you've been planning for a long time?"

From the very outset, solely concerned with whether Baba has been concealing his intentions from her.

"Awhile."

"I'm surprised you've never mentioned the idea. Mister Mysterious!"

Inference corroborated. Subject cares more about enjoying privileged communication with ostensible "best friend" than about life-changing content of revelation. Indicative of narcissism and/or unhealthy obsession with Baba–Frisk relationship.

"I don't tell you everything," he said.

"Oh, you do, too!" she exclaimed, prodding his arm again.

"I don't even tell myself everything."

"You tell me what you haven't told yourself. That's one of the main things I'm for."

"I do occasionally talk to my own girlfriend," he reminded her.

"All lovers require editing. That's why I can tell you that 'I'm so aroused!' is a turnoff, but I wouldn't have told Sullivan that in a million years."

Implicitly relegates Baba–Paige relationship to subsidiary status. Marriage proposal = emotional trump, palpable evidence that Baba–Paige relationship is primary. Subject in denial.

"You know, you still haven't asked if Paige said yes," he said.

"Well, of course she did. She's smitten with you. It's amazing you didn't call to cancel tennis, because she'd already dragged you off to the registrar at town hall."

Instinctively associates Baba getting married with not playing tennis. Good guess, by coincidence, but for Frisk, not playing tennis = end of world [see ET mention above; Paige = calamity/Armageddon]. Once again, Paige/marriage = threat.

On reflection, since he had plenty of experience with therapy, Weston added a second note: *Describes Baba–Paige relationship in terms suggesting unequal emotional involvement. More comfortable with Paige being "smitten'" w/Baba than w/Baba being smitten with Paige. Assumes Paige must be driving force behind marriage ("dragged" to town hall), imputing passivity or unwillingness to Baba.*

"You don't seem all that happy about my news," he submitted carefully, as if dropping a catalyst into a test tube with a pipette.

"I might be happier if you seemed happier. But you're acting so morose. I asked before we played if you felt down, and you said yes. That's not the way I'd expect you to feel after popping the question. Hey"—another touch, on the shoulder—"maybe not leaping and frolicking, but at least a smile?"

Actively looks for signs that Baba does not really want to marry Paige.

His obligatory smile was pained.

"Are you sure this is a good idea?" she pressed on.

Actively dissuades Baba from marrying Paige.

"When am I ever sure of anything?" he said. "Except that obviously, if I did propose, then on balance I decided that yes, it's a 'good idea.'"

"Then why are you so disturbed?"

Deliberately exaggerates what Baba believes is carefully controlled affect. But Weston could no longer sustain a clinician's arch distance, and put down his mental pen.

Why am I disturbed? he considered. *Let me count the ways. Because*

I am starting to see things from my lover's point of view, and I don't want to. Because from that perspective, I am either a cruel two-timer or conveniently delusional. It seems that I have been trying to have it both ways at a good woman's expense. I put my would-be fiancée through unnecessary suffering out of selfishness. I have heard my whole life that men and women can never be friends. I have nursed the vain notion that you and I are exceptions to that rule, not because this is necessarily true, but because being a supposed exception suits my purposes: I can have my cake and play tennis with it, too. But I am also disturbed because I love you, and whether that love is corrupt, or covertly flirtatious, or interfering with my ability to fully embrace another woman without holding something back, it is still love, in all its near-indestructible dreadfulness, and I am about to take a sledgehammer to my own heart.

"Oh," Weston said lightly. "You know me, I'm moody."

JILLIAN INEVITABLY CONTEMPLATED the matter, and would have liked to have been happier, which wasn't the same as being happy. But then, while many people are overjoyed when they decide to get married themselves, it's hardly normal practice to hoot and sing hallelujah when someone else does. Understandably, too, Baba's new circumstances underscored her own—she hadn't even dated for over a year—and thus his announcement moved her to feel a tad pensive, a degree more concerned that she for one was destined to remain single. Worse things could happen, of course. Having proved in Jillian's experience more durable than romance, friendship often provided a form of companionship as good as marriage, if not better.

When she scrutinized herself—which made her feel like Baba—she didn't appear to feel doleful or pissed off or excluded, because she was already integrated into Paige and Baba's social life. Paige was already acclimated to her boyfriend's amity with an old college classmate, which had lasted his adulthood through. So there was no reason that anything would change after a wedding. Apart from a possible honeymoon, it would be back to tennis and a musing debrief thrice a week, punctuated by twosome, threesome, and several-some dinners, liberally lubricated with libation.

Any self-interested consternation that Baba was taking himself off the market would be irrational. Back in the day, they had each had opportunity to pursue the other as marriageable material, and they had each walked away. The two of them as an item were not meant to be. What was meant to be was exactly what they were. In fact, in the more recent go-round, Jillian had been the one who'd cut it off, and she could never bear women who got huffy when other women picked up their discards. You either wanted a guy or you didn't. If you didn't, it made no more sense to get retroactively possessive than it did to become incensed that a neighbor was walking around in a shirt that you'd donated to the Salvation Army.

Yet the following several weeks felt indefinably out of kilter. If this summer were a bed, it would be rumpled and unmade. Baba canceled tennis dates more often than he once did (that is, he canceled at all). Shit happens, and she'd overlooked his being late that afternoon in May when he delivered the perplexingly leaden report of his proposal. But the tardiness grew chronic. She'd wait around for twenty minutes, fidgeting in anxiety that they'd lose no. 3—their favorite, if only for being customary—because a lone player couldn't hold a court. By the time Baba finally showed up, Jillian would have grown cross, which meant playing in a humor at odds with the buoyant spirit of the whole endeavor.

This was the summer, too, that she developed an odd glitch in her forehand follow-through—a destructive crook of the wrist as the ball left the strings that hooked the shot to the net. One of the commonalities that suited them to each other on court was a tendency to exasperation with the shortcomings of their own games and an inexhaustible patience in relation to the other's frustrations. So Jillian would have expected to grow provoked by the spastic innovation herself, but not for Baba to find it just as infuriating.

"You should really consider taking a few lessons," he announced testily on a water break. "Iron it out."

She was nonplussed. "Since when do we take lessons?"

"A little humility goes a long way in this sport, and a few sessions with a professional can be invaluable. I'm sure you could find a coach at Washington and Lee who moonlights. And it's not that expensive. If you don't think you can afford it, you can always go back to leading those tourist walkabouts around Lexington landmarks."

He knew full well she'd given up that part-time job because they weren't accommodating about releasing her on Monday, Wednesday, and Friday afternoons.

"But I know what I'm doing wrong," she said. "I just can't seem to stop."

"When I know I'm doing something wrong," he said tightly, "I stop."

Most disconcerting was Baba's new reluctance to linger after a session. There was always an appointment, or he'd promised to have an early dinner with Paige. Was he trying to establish some new protocol now that he was getting hitched? Meanwhile, Jillian had issued a routine dinner invitation to the couple—she reminded Baba that his fiancée had still not seen the Standing Chandelier, about which so far other friends had been spectacularly enthusiastic—but those two could never arrive at a date. She knew he'd come to cast a wider social net with Paige—all to the good, since in times past, tennis aside, unless Jillian hauled him through the door, he was capable of spending weeks on end holed up with a computer—but she hadn't thought he'd become one of those gadflies out and about every night. Hard to arrange anyway, in a town of eight thousand people.

She'd have understood his being busy and distracted if he and Paige were in the process of planning a massive wedding. But the event on August twenty-sixth was meant to be modest. The invitations apparently went out by email to a guest list of under fifty (Jillian was surprised they could even marshal these dozens of well-wishers when Baba had long been such a hermit, but then everyone had cousins). They were eschewing the catered cakes, goodie bags, and hired

DJs of the marriage-industrial complex for a simple ceremony followed by a potluck picnic. That night, to make the day more of an occasion for out-of-towners, they'd have a party with drinks and snacks back at the A-frame, with music streamed from Baba's Mac. About all that would have been taking up her tennis partner's time was putting together the playlist.

Jillian had offered to ask the Chevaliers if they'd be open to letting the picnic take place on their grounds. In August, the estate's owners would be down in Byron Bay, Australia, and she was sure that they'd happily grant permission so long as everyone cleaned up after. The hills were rolling, the lawn luscious. It would be so much more private than the Boxerwood Nature Center, and not as impersonal as the Golf and Country Club, which would charge an arm and a leg—

"Jordan's Point Park," he cut her off. "It's pretty, it's public, and it doesn't involve easily offended rich people. But thanks anyway."

He didn't sound very thankful. "Okay, never mind, then."

BY THE FOURTH week of July, Jillian's follow-through glitch was worse than ever, losing her every third point or so. Constant apologizing made her meek, and meekness weakened her strokes, when one of the aspects of her game that Baba had always relished was that she gave as good as she got. She was playing like a girl. She was playing like a girl who sucked. Tennis was a hard enough sport without the additional burden of worrying that your partner was bored or otherwise not having a good time. And he was not having a good time—or at least that's what it looked like from the other side of the net that Friday, when he started losing numerous points from his own unforced errors, his motions phlegmatic, as if he couldn't be bothered to chase her dreary little shots. Careful not to seem pouty or petulant or weepy and instead making a matter-of-fact and indisputable observation that this wasn't working, Jillian suggested as they gathered balls at the net that they call it quits prematurely. It was the first time in twenty-five years that they'd curtailed their play in the absence of rain, dark, injury, or hail.

With the half hour's early retirement, for once Baba couldn't claim that he had to rush off elsewhere.

"Sorry," she said again on the bench. Though it must have been ninety degrees, so frequently had she futzed up that she'd barely worked up a sweat. "Maybe I should take those lessons."

"Yeah, maybe," he said, staring glassily straight ahead. He didn't seem very attached to the advice anymore.

When neither said anything for a couple of minutes, there was none of the serenity that usually characterized their silence. It was awkward. Awkward the way it would have been with just anyone.

"Baba." She took a breath. "Is there some reason that you and Paige can never find a single free evening to come to the cottage for dinner?"

"We have been pretty busy. But," he added, "it's possible I feel protective."

"How's that?"

Kneading his knees, he seemed to struggle with and overcome some impulse, and then to proceed in a spirit of grim resolution. "Well, face it, Frisk. As for the whole getting-married thing, you haven't exactly been on board."

"How can you say that? I think it's great! I think Paige is great! I think you make a great couple! One of those—unpredictable couples. Who might not be spit out as checking all the boxes on Match dot com, but who make a more interesting combination as a consequence of being unlikely."

"Is that a tortured way of telling me that you think Paige and I are a bad fit?"

"No, that's not what I meant, and not what I said, either. What's with you? I swear, all summer you've been so out of sorts! Constantly taking things the wrong way. Being grumpy and distant. Ever since—"

"That's right, *ever since*. Is this another plea to get me to call off the wedding?"

"When have I ever—"

"When have you not? It was obvious when I first told you we were getting married that you opposed the idea, and were hoping to talk me out of it. I don't know what your problem is with Paige—"

"I don't have a problem with Paige." He wouldn't look at her, so she leaned into his lap until he met her gaze. "I don't. I like her. We have a few negligible differences of opinion. I don't mind wearing a beat-up, used fur coat to keep warm. I could never give up veal chops. I'm of two minds about fracking because Virginia needs the money and I like the idea of energy independence, but that argument was stupid because I don't actually care that much one way or the other. What's important is she's honest, and sincere, and genuine, and forthright. She's nice-looking, she's obviously loyal, and she must be pretty smart if she went to Middlebury, though I like the fact she doesn't show off how much she knows. She's got a way bigger social conscience than I do."

Somehow the more Jillian piled on the compliments, the hollower they sounded, which drove her to pile on still more. "There's something disarming about her—something vulnerable and unguarded, so I guess I understand your impulse to 'protect' her, but she doesn't need protection from me. Why should she, when she's been nothing but nice to me, to a point where I've almost been embarrassed—giving me that fringed shawl she found in Lynchburg, or the fig preserves from the Wine and Music Festival? Never mind if a present isn't all that expensive, it's the gesture. Thinking of me, even when I'm not there, and making a good guess as to what I might like. She's never seemed wary or territorial, despite the fact that you and I are so close. Which is pretty amazing, actually."

Throughout this panegyric touting the many fine qualities of his wife-to-be, Baba looked only the more miserable.

"Or we used to be close," Jillian added, sitting back.

"See?" Baba pounced. "That's what I mean. That kind of cutting aside, which says it all."

"Oh, all *what*? I'm very, very glad you've found someone. I don't know how to spell it out more plainly. Because what I appreciate most about Paige is that she loves you. It's obvious every time she looks at you. In fact, there are times she can't even bear to look at you, because it's too much, it makes her feel too much. Why wouldn't I want that for you?"

"That's what I ask myself," Baba said.

"I'm sorry if I didn't burst into tears of joy, or whatever you hoped for when you told me. You seemed in a terrible frame of mind, like someone had died or something, and I was trying to understand why, not 'talk you out of' getting married."

Yet the further she extolled his fiancée's merits, the more Jillian was reminded of that feeling in the presence of a woman who detested her: that no matter what she said, she was digging her own grave.

ONCE BACK HOME, Jillian showered and put her feet up with a glass of wine in the glow of the chandelier. She considered whether the problem wasn't talk itself, with its deserved reputation as cheap. She could blah-blah herself blue in the face, and Baba would never be sure that she wasn't merely mouthing what he wanted to hear. That very afternoon, hadn't Jillian sung the praises of the gesture, which spoke so much more forcefully than words? Perhaps in this case a gesture of larger proportions than a jar of fig preserves.

When the ideal course of action presented itself, she felt a twinge, like a stitch in the side—which is how she could tell it was right. A grand gesture should cost you. The agonizing back and forth on a second glass of Chablis was self-theater. She had already made up her mind, and by the third glass had moved from fraudulent indecision to the early stages of mourning. Baba would believe that she was thrilled he was marrying Paige Myer only when he saw how much she was willing to surrender to make the point.

PACKAGING UP THAT weekend was anxiety provoking, and required half a roll of six-foot Bubble Wrap and a full roll of packing tape. When tennis was rained out that Monday, Jillian was relieved; neither her game nor her friendship with Baba was going to settle until her alleged antagonism toward his impending nuptials was conclusively demonstrated to be all in his head. Though she didn't want him to feel ashamed of himself. She wanted him to be touched. Cancel that; she wanted them both to be touched.

On Tuesday, the weather cleared. After the Chevaliers' gardener, Lance, had finished for the day, he generously agreed to provide the services of his van. So extravagantly had Jillian wrapped her offering that, even with both of them manipulating the monster wad of pillowy plastic, it barely fit through the back doors. Lance drove, while she stayed in back to ensure their cargo didn't rock, and he was equally sweet about helping her unload. "I didn't go to this much trouble for me and my wife's twenty-fifth!" he said, pulling on the bundle's back end. "That sixty-inch Sony flat screen was a box of safety matches in comparison. Whoever these folks are, sweetie, you sure must like 'em."

"Yeah, that's the message, all right," Jillian said. It wasn't all that heavy with the two of them, but it was unwieldy, and got stuck again as she shoved it from behind. "Careful!" she cried. "Don't put any pressure on it. Let's just *ease* it back and forth."

She hadn't given Baba a heads-up about her visit, lest he be driven to "protect" his fiancée from her fearsome disapproval. Besides which, you didn't give fair warning about a surprise; that was what made it a surprise. It was barely seven thirty p.m., still light, and Baba's Escort was in the drive.

"Where you wanna carry this, missy?" Lance asked, once the bundle had cleared the van's doors.

Dismally, Jillian appraised the A-frame's entrance. If her delivery jammed between the roof and floor of the van, it wasn't going to fit through the front door. "I'm afraid that to get it inside, I'll have to unwind the outside layers. If you keep it steady upright, I'll start slicing tape. Fortunately, I brought an X-Acto knife."

This was poor dramatics. She had hoped to make the present look less like a lifetime supply of plastic wrap by belting it with the red ribbon tucked in her shorts pocket. But it was too late for the flourish, because their commotion had already drawn Baba to the door.

In the middle of his front lawn, she was in the midst of walking another layer off the wad, which with all the packaging stood eight feet tall. To keep from having to feed the accumulating Bubble Wrap between Lance and the bale, she'd sliced off a couple of sections, now fluffing in the breeze and trashing up the yard. As Baba emerged onto the porch, she had to chase after one of the rectangles to keep it from blowing away.

"What's this about?" he asked, with an expression she couldn't read. If he knew what the object was, he gave no indication, but he might readily have guessed had he applied himself.

She smiled shyly, arms full of plastic. "It's your wedding present. I think I can get it through the door now. Want to help?"

The two men helped negotiate the slimmer but more fragile bundle, while Jillian, who was familiar with which bumps were the most delicate, directed its orientation. Once in the living room, she had them rest it on one side so that she could go at the bottom with the X-Acto knife, cutting away the packaging until she revealed the metal base. She'd been so busy with the logistics that it was only then that she looked up to meet Baba's gaze, though he had to have surmised some time before what they were unwrapping. His smile was warm enough, but also colored by a wan quality.

"Are you sure you want to give this away?" he asked quietly.

"To just anybody, no. To you—to you and Paige—sure as shootin'."

"But that thing took you six months."

"Longer. But if it didn't mean anything to me, it wouldn't be a good present."

They raised the new addition to Weston Babansky's already eclectic decor to its upright position, and with the base unpacked it was stable. Jillian assured Lance that she could take it from here, thanked him effusively, and wished him good-night. Yet it was several more minutes before Paige finally emerged from downstairs, carrying a basket of clean laundry. Had Jillian heard visitors muffling overhead, while the scraping of an obscure object penetrated the ceiling of her utility room, curiosity would have gotten the better of her sooner. Some women had a vigilant relationship to a load in the dryer.

"Jillian!" Paige's face quivered briefly, as if she were about to sneeze. "What on earth? Is this that—chandelier thing?"

"I was thinking"—Jillian had unwound the big sheet now, and was down to snipping the smaller squares cushioning each individual assemblage—"that during the party on the night of the wedding, it would be nice to have a centerpiece. Which also provides romantic, indirect lighting."

"So this is a loaner?" Most people were a little graceless or flustered when on the receiving end of extreme generosity, and she wouldn't have meant to sound so hopeful.

"No, no," Jillian corrected. "That would make for a pretty feeble wedding present. It's yours, and the welds are solid. As your grandchildren will discover, should you choose to go that direction."

Insofar as Jillian had envisioned this presentation, she'd imagined a bit more hubbub, especially since Paige had never seen the "chandelier thing" before. But the betrothed couple was unnervingly muted, so that when Paige offered a cup of tea, Jillian said maybe a glass of wine instead, if a bottle was open. A steadier. The trouble was, the unveiling was too fiddly and protracted, what with unwinding the individual strips of Bubble Wrap first from the miniature toy box and then from the helicopter inside, unpacking the cotton balls from around the curlew skull, checking that the wisdom teeth were still securely glued in place, and peeling off every little scrap of residual tape from the structure. On reflection, the theater would have been flashier had she delivered the gift while Baba was home during the day. Then Paige could have walked in, and voilà! Jillian could have switched on the power. As it was, unpacking was so time-consuming that Paige drifted off to work on dinner, and Baba started reading "Talk of the Town" in last week's *New Yorker*. With no outlet in reach, she had to ask for an extension cord, and lacking spares on hand Baba had to resort to a power strip whose disconnection would disable his stereo speakers.

At last, after Jillian had whisked around the floor filling three enormous black trash bags with Bubble Wrap, she tied her ribbon (alas, crumpled) around the trunk, and the moment was upon them. Baba called Paige away from her cutting board, and she returned to the living room, wiping her hands on a dish towel. Baba had helped Jillian position the lamp at its most becoming angle—though some rearrangement of furniture might be required in order to show off her creation to its best advantage and make it look at home here. She hit the switch.

"Well," Paige said. "That's really something, isn't it."

Baba seemed to take in the chandelier anew. When he said, "It's wonderful," he hit a note of wistfulness as well as awe, and the assertion didn't flush Jillian with quite the same heat as the first time he said that. But then, these infusions of perfect satisfaction don't necessarily come around more than once.

"Thank you," Paige said formally. "I'm sure no one else will give us a wedding present anything like yours. And it's always going to remind us of you, isn't it?"

As Jillian explained the derivation of a few elements, Paige's expression remained more polite than fascinated, and she cut the museum tour short. No one sat down. She was mildly surprised not to be asked to stay for a bite, though she'd arrived without warning, and maybe they had only two stuffed peppers or something. While that shouldn't have precluded a refresher of the wine, that glass must have been the end of a bottle. And sure, it wasn't a long walk back to the cottage; the summer evening was soft. Still, even if she'd have declined, it might have been nice to have at least been offered a ride home.

"YOU HATE IT." They had waited to speak until hearing Frisk crunch safely to the end of the gravel drive.

"I hate the fact of it," said Paige. "Though I'll grant it's not *quite* as ugly as I'd pictured."

"I don't know what we're going to do with it if you find it a torture."

"For now, we're not going to do anything," she said, U-turning briskly to the kitchen to resume chopping onions. "One upside of the long-term prospects for that friendship—meaning, it *has* no long-term prospects—is that after the wedding, we can do whatever we want with it, and she'll never know. In the meantime, on the off chance she comes back here again—unannounced, with the standard presumption—I guess we haven't any choice but to let that hulking contraption take up a third of our living room to keep from hurting her feelings."

It hit Weston then, the absurdity of protecting Frisk's feelings for four more weeks, only to summarily crush them. The illogic recalled capital cases in which condemned men fell ill, and the state devoted all manner of expensive medical care to reviving convicts it planned to kill.

"I know you think she means well," Paige recommenced at dinner. "But it's so inappropriate! For a wedding present? For one thing, it's physically intrusive. It's huge. And I'd never seen it. She had no idea whether I'd like it."

"Most people like it," Weston mumbled.

"But anything that occupies that much space is an imposition."

"I realize how hard it is for you to take it this way, but that chandelier is important to her, and I'm sure it was hard for her to part with it. That was a lavish gift. Emotionally lavish."

"In which case, it's even more inappropriate. It's excessive, as usual. She has no business giving you an 'emotionally lavish' gift. What's wrong with a set of coasters?"

"That chandelier was a labor of love."

"A labor of love for herself! Those knickknacks glued every which way are all about *her*. A wedding present should be about us. Honestly, I no sooner begin to see the horizon beyond which we can stop fighting over that woman than she moves into our house. As a leering, beady-eyed monstrosity, peering at us while we eat. It's not any different than if Tracey Emin gave us her filthy bed. With used condoms, cigarette butts, and smears of menstrual blood on the sheets."

"Now it's not only Frisk who's going overboard. You can't equate a used condom with a toy whistle."

"I'm just having fun." Paige leaned over to kiss him, and the discussion was over—for tonight.

IN RETROSPECT, THE expectation had been crazy. For three solid months, Weston would bop around the court with Frisk, interspersing chatty, musing dinners, in the full knowledge that at the knell of August twenty-sixth a curtain would drop on the whole relationship. In this loopy version of events, the friendship would still perk along as if nothing were the matter. Frisk would keep bearing down on that erratic but occasionally devastating crosscourt backhand. Weston would share his recipe for quick-pickling fresh vegetables in miso paste. And then one day—August twenty-*fifth*, say—it would be, Oh, by the way, we're never going to meet again, so long, it's been real.

In contrast to this fantasy, his treatment of Frisk all summer had been perfectly wretched. Unconsciously or otherwise, he'd been trying to gradually widen a distance between the two—just as you work a baby tooth loose with your tongue until it clings by a thread, making the extraction itself almost painless. Well, so much for the application of dentistry to human relations. He'd been subjecting Frisk to flat-out torture. Were his accelerating remoteness meant to make the imminent severance any less agonizing for himself, even there the technique had backfired. Acting like a prick had made him feel only worse, and for weeks, he'd done nothing but suffer.

An alternative to the working-the-baby-tooth model glared. What's less excruciating, inching into a cold swimming pool, or diving in? Peeling a Band-Aid slo-mo, or ripping it off? So why not get it over with?

Because he didn't want to. He didn't want to, he didn't have to yet, so he wouldn't.

Weston Babansky was a coward. He hadn't taken a bold, difficult decision in May; he'd taken half a decision. The easy half. Ever since the announcement to Paige that he would comply with her terms—ever since his sorrowful, downcast concession that he could see why no wife should be asked to tolerate another woman waiting in the wings, another confidante, an ex-lover of all things, and a rather intemperate one at that, who wasn't always artful about negotiating the spiky geometry of the triangle—day-to-day domestic life had certainly been more tranquil. The late-night scenes over his best friend had subsided. Paige was patient with his continuing to see Frisk on court, albeit with a tinge of triumphalism. He hated to think that she would take enjoyment in another woman's impending pain, though Weston had a bad habit of holding others to standards he wouldn't meet himself. Anyone would feel the frisson of victory on summarily trouncing a perceived rival.

A lifelong procrastinator, he'd been cashing in on the benefits of ditching Frisk while not paying the price. The hard part was the other half of the decision, which, being the hard part, was obviously the whole decision: telling Frisk. Because he had just enough wit to realize that, when you announce a relationship is going to be over, it is over right then.

The sole argument in his defense was that if he was trying to eat and have cake, it had not so long before been very good cake. Overoptimistic and idiotic, obviously, the aspiration was also tender: he'd hoped to safeguard one last summer with his favorite tennis partner.

Yet predictably, his fiancée's having articulated all that was wrong with the woman had made Weston more irritable with Frisk—which is to say, at all irritable—and more inclined to nitpick. That paean to Paige, for example, had been so strained, so conspicuously trying-too-hard, that he'd wanted to hit her. The unremitting corruption of her forehand (why ever would a player with a perfectly serviceable stroke suddenly install a fatal flip of the wrist—for *variety*?) actually moved him to rage, and expressing the fury as mere frustration required ungodly self-control. However curtailed their courtside debriefs, he found himself listening with a different ear: there she was, talking about herself again. When he told her about revisiting the National Gallery with Paige, her questions were flat, few, and generic. It must have been true, after all, that Frisk didn't really care for him, that she used him only as an audience.

It goaded him, too, how insensitive Frisk remained to the fact that Paige disliked her. Was his best friend dense? She'd had enough experience with detractors by now, so how could she still be so poorly attuned to positively semaphoric social cues? What did it take for Frisk to get the message? Did Paige have to march into the room wearing a T-shirt printed I HATE YOU? Physically attack her with a coal shovel?

In times past he'd have been endeared, yet even the billowy overkill of Bubble Wrap around the chandelier had been vexatious. Showing up at the A-frame out of the blue, staging a trashy striptease on the lawn, taking over the living room for an hour and a half, appealing to Paige for a bowled-over gratitude that would never be forthcoming . . . The whole production demonstrated Frisk's weird obliviousness to other people, her blindness to the fact that what they wanted might be contrary to what Frisk wanted. For Christ's sake, if she'd simply *asked* him whether he thought the lamp would make a suitable wedding present, he might have figured out a diplomatic way of fending the present off.

But here was the super weird thing: he was delighted to have it. Though Weston was not about to emphasize as much to Paige, he adored the Standing Chandelier, which melted him, and induced an emotional falling sensation, every time he laid eyes on it. Since the lamp had arrived in their possession, he had routinely basked in its glimmer for the long hours after Paige went to bed. Maybe Frisk did have a problem with alcohol, because something about the light it gave off went irresistibly with whisky.

Obviously with a D-day looming, Weston was always going to find it a challenge to have a wonderful time while steeped in dread. Yet if his intention was to conduct a final halcyon season as a monument to all the bucolic seasons that went before it—to which he might later refer as a keepsake, raising his hands to the memory of the summer sun as he warmed himself at the woodstove, once an uncommonly lonely wintertime advanced—it made absolutely no sense, did it, to be mean to Frisk. Ironically, Frisk alone would have been able to understand that being mean to Frisk was one surefire method of being mean to himself. For it seemed that Weston had become the bad guy coming and going. He was a terrible person because he was unfaithful to his fiancée, and he was a terrible person because he was unfaithful to his best friend. Mooning over Talisker, Weston would suppose morosely that if he simply disappeared himself from this equation, both women would be fine. To retreat into self-pity was cowardly, but recall: he *was* a coward.

The better course for the month of August wasn't to stop feeling sorry for himself, but to start feeling sorry for the other parties, too. He had already to battle resentment in relation to the woman he was pledged to marry, which was no fit state in which to embark on a life together. But any expectation that Weston would accede to her wishes gladly was absurd. Cutting off the friendship with Frisk was bound to feel like cutting off his arm. Then again, the more sizable a sacrifice his fiancée appeared to be demanding, the more amply it was demonstrated that she was right to demand it.

AS THE RECKONING neared, feeling sorry for Frisk came naturally. The way this scenario was playing out, Weston and Paige would walk off into the sunset hand in hand. Frisk would be left with nothing— not even her most cherished possession, relinquishment of which Paige only held against her. (That said, several guests from William and Lee had been entranced by the lamp, as a consequence of which she had grown somewhat less hostile toward the object itself.) So partly as a reward for the chandelier, since it was the only reward that Frisk would reap, from the wedding present onward Weston was kind to her.

Too kind? He worried that his compassion was oppressive. Perhaps he was afflicting her with the same good intentions that must suffocate the terminally ill, whose friends and relatives continuously testify to the upstanding character of the dead-to-be. After the stink of all those flowers, the relentless puff of praise and pillow plumping, he wouldn't be surprised if cancer patients come to beg for the restorative of a harsh word.

For he would catch himself announcing, apropos of not much, that the hours spent with Frisk were "some of the most enjoyable of his life," or over-reassuring that despite the inexplicable disintegration of her forehand he "still loved playing with her more than anyone." She'd eye him suspiciously, wondering what his problem was. Theirs was a knockabout friendship, and they were supposed to be taking each other for granted.

"Do you ever wonder what it would have been like if you and I had made a go of it?" Frisk asked idly on the bench, a few days into the Month of Nauseating Niceness.

"Not really," Weston said quickly. She was making him anxious. "Dwelling on the counterfactual is a waste of energy."

"The *counterfactual*! Well, la-di-da. Maybe we'd have bombed because you have a rod up your ass."

"It doesn't bear thinking about," he reiterated firmly.

"Well, that's weird. And fancy-pants, too. *It doesn't bear thinking about.* As if you're afraid to think about it. And since when are you afraid to think about anything? I was only speculating. It's not as if I'm about to rip your clothes off or something."

He tucked the exchange away, as evidence that he had made the correct decision. There wasn't a great deal of evidence accumulating along these lines, so the encounter became strangely precious.

IT WAS AUGUST fifteenth, a Wednesday. Considering that memories of their summer assignations tended to blur into one long, searing session, the fact that Weston would later recall the exact date would alone prove depressing. Frisk's demeanor was bubbly, as it had been ever since delivering her wedding present, which she appeared to believe had magically pressed a reset button. In Frisk's view, his warmer disposition was an effort to make up for having been churlish, crabby, and detached for months. She'd no doubt dismissed the dyspeptic humor as one more funk of the sort they'd survived for decades: arising from no cause, subsiding from no cure.

"I thought the Wrist Epilepsy wasn't so bad today," she announced.

"Yes, your forehand's been much more solid the last three or four times we've played," he said. This was true. That deadly flopping forward during her follow-through seemed to be a barometer of something, and he'd established this much: when he was mean to her, it got worse.

"Hey, I've been meaning to ask," she said. "This wedding-and-picnic thing. What's the dress code? Are we still supposed to ritz it up, with heels and flounces? Or is the idea more checkered tablecloth, and even jeans are fine?"

Weston focused on the rookies flailing on court no. 2, as if strokes better suited to badminton were terribly fascinating. "The concept is casual, but it is a wedding, so some women are likely to dress up."

"Well, what's Paige wearing? I gather you're not supposed to show up in anything that outshines the bride."

"You know her tastes." Squinting, he followed the incompetents' ball as it sailed over the fence, regretting that they hadn't hit it in this direction, so that he could fetch it for them. Anything to interrupt this line of inquiry. "Simple, no lace."

"I'm picturing a sleeveless sheaf, matte finish, all clean lines no trim, but with killer shoes."

The description was so astonishingly on target that for a moment he had to question whether Frisk really paid no attention to other people. "Something like that," he said vaguely.

"See, I was considering red, and I was worried about being too loud."

He turned to her. "Since when do you worry about being loud?"

She laughed. She didn't take the rejoinder the wrong way, and she should have.

"Also, I wanted to ask you about the food," she continued. "I assume your family coming from Wilmington, and Paige's from Baltimore, means they'll probably show up empty-handed, or at best bring, like, commercial pie. So I'd be happy to bring more than one thing. Either that, or I could make a serious quantity of something, because the problem with potluck is all these tiny dishes, and then everyone takes a timid tablespoon, and you end up with a plate that's incoherent—"

"We're having a barbecue," he cut her off.

"Oh!" she said, as if taken aback by his tone. About time, too. "I'm surprised you haven't mentioned that before. If you need someone to mind the coals, you know you can trust me not to burn the chicken."

"Paige's friends from the History Department are manning the grill."

Weston had moved on to looking riveted by a nondescript brown bird foraging in the crabgrass, thus keeping his gaze trained a good hundred degrees from his tennis partner's face. But he could tell she was peering at him.

"What about setup? I could help to put up tables, and lug cases of champagne—"

"All the bases are covered."

The fact that she hadn't pulled up short by now suggested experimental intent, as if she were delivering an escalating electrical shock to a lab rat and recording its response. "Still . . . It might be good to have, say, a carb—enough that everyone could have some? I told you about that Lebanese *freekeh* with roasted vegetables, which came out smashing. The recipe would be easy to multiply—"

"Frisk!" For this lab rat, the fibrillation had crossed a critical threshold. "You're not invited to the wedding! Why *else* do you think you never got the email?"

He'd been afraid he would explode, and he had exploded. That announcement had not been on the agenda for the afternoon.

Skipping even the clichéd incredulity of "*What?*" she dropped the boppy deportment cold. She was still and grave. "Why. Not."

"Paige doesn't like you." He hadn't intended to say that, either. He hadn't intended to say that, ever.

"Ah." She sat back on the bench. Her expression reminded Weston of doing a find-and-replace in a large Word file. There was a lag, and then a window popped up, 247 REPLACEMENTS MADE. "I've been having dinner with you guys for coming up on three years. You'd think I would have noticed."

"Yes, well. I've been surprised you haven't."

"Here I was thinking your girlfriend and I got on pretty well."

"I think it's a chemistry thing," he said, unsure whether the irremediable nature of chemistry made it better or worse.

"Is it?" He might have expected her to cry, but instead she was cool and clear. Unsettlingly composed, in fact. "Something inexpressible, then. Nothing she could put her finger on."

"Sort of," he said glumly.

"So she wouldn't have cited any of her problems with me in particular."

"Oh . . . She has mentioned your being, well, a little showy, a little self-involved. You know, her whole style is lower profile and more self-effacing. But I don't see what's to be gained from going into any detail. It would just hurt your feelings."

"No, we wouldn't want to do *that*."

They sat.

"I can only infer," she resumed, "that this 'dislike' goes back a ways?"

"She's felt uncomfortable around you for a while, yeah."

"So you and I have been chatting after tennis for years, and you've never said a word about Paige being 'uncomfortable.'"

"It's not nice, is it? I don't even think I should have told you just now."

"Because you and I only tell each other nice things."

"We tell each other what's helpful, or try to."

"We used to tell each other the truth. And now we've gone this whole summer, you sitting there knowing I'm not welcome at your wedding, and letting me prattle on about what to wear."

"I'm sorry. I was putting off telling you, obviously. This isn't easy for me, either."

"This *discomfort*, which I hadn't realized before is a synonym for *loathing*—it's not only because I'm too colorful for quiet, unassuming Paige, is it? I mean, it wouldn't have anything to do with *jealousy*, would it?"

"You could call it that."

"Good. Let's call it that."

He'd never have expected her to be so icy. "She finds you a little possessive. Of me."

"I do possess you. In my way. Or I used to."

"Then you can see why that might be difficult for her."

"No, I can't. She possesses you, too, in a different way. I don't see why there's a conflict."

"You usually have a more nuanced sense of how people work."

"Here's my nuance: if she trusts you—and if she doesn't, she has no business marrying you—then she should be cool with inviting your best friend to your wedding, even if I'm not her favorite person in the world. Since I assume everyone else on the guest list hasn't been vetted for being too 'showy' or 'self-involved.'"

When Paige had laid out her case, the just course seemed so clear. Weston had to stop himself from clapping his hands over his ears. "That's the way it seems to you."

"Of course it 'seems that way to me'; that's why I'm the one who's saying it. But it also *seems to me* that this situation is a great deal more complicated than my now being free to make other plans for August twenty-sixth. It's not just that I've been absolved of any requirement to make a big vat of *freekeh* beforehand. Because if I'm not invited to your wedding"—she leaned forward—"*what else am I not invited to?*"

Weston pressed the pads of his fingers to his forehead, now granular with salt. *My life*, he thought. *You are no longer invited to my whole life.* She'd been his best friend cum beloved tennis partner for a quarter century, and she was right. He owed her the truth.

It might have been tasteless or insensitive, but pure force of habit moved him to say when they parted, "See you on Friday." Yet he'd actually been planning to play with her, too, as he would also have shown up at Rockbridge County High School with his racket, water, sweatband, and a new can of Wilsons on the twentieth, twenty-second, and twenty-fourth the following week. All summer, he had clung to Paige's permission that he could run out the season with Frisk until August twenty-sixth, and it was merely the fifteenth. Only when Frisk stared and said, "Have you lost your mind?" was the new order real to him, as it would be even more so on Friday—sleeping feverishly into the late afternoon because there was no four p.m. tennis date for which to wake.

BY THE FOLLOWING summer, Jillian had found three other people to hit with in a rotation every week, and the variety was probably better for her game. But she was surprised to discover that she didn't care about her game. She kept up the sport to get relatively painless exercise, but tennis as she had once conceived it—the soul of the present tense, the one activity that from moment to moment was exactly what she wanted to be doing and nothing else, a pure kinetic joy—had long been synonymous with her friendship with Baba, and playing with anyone else wasn't the same.

At least seeing the three poor substitutes put her in contact with a handful of other adults besides the parents of her students. For a long time after the breakup—she didn't think you were supposed to "break up" with friends, but she didn't know what else to call it—she avoided people.

She could no longer trust her own judgment. Competent animals could sniff out threat. They instinctively distinguished their own kind, and anodyne adjacent wildlife, from predators. So it was in the spirit of biological imperative that she reviewed her many intersections with Paige Myer. Their first meeting: That hadn't been a slightly inept young woman with a tendency to blurt her fiercely held convictions. It was an outburst of immediate, uncontrollable aversion of a kind Jillian should have recognized. Because Paige would already have heard as much about Jillian as Jillian had heard about her, chances were high that Paige had *prehated* her, much as one preorders a book, or a burial plot. Some characters might be so beguiling on introduction that they are able to penetrate a shield of prepared enmity with the sword of their fearsome charm, but examples of prevailing against prehatred are probably few.

Thereafter: Paige wasn't bashful, and she wasn't quiet. She was subdued around Jillian because that's what people were like when the whole night through they were shoving a fist in their mouths and waiting for a guest to leave.

The presents (the shawl, the fig preserves): camouflage.

Various admirations (of the necklaces, the button self-portrait, even the high-loft popcorn): fake. Jillian made a note to self: she was as big a pushover for flattery as every other bozo.

Jillian's respectful efforts to act more formal with Weston Babansky in Paige's presence: wasted. Read as patronizing. Though it wouldn't have helped had she acted in another manner instead, as any alternative approach would have backfired, too.

The point was, if Jillian Frisk couldn't tell the difference between a shy, diffident, openhanded new acquaintance and a nemesis gunning for her most precious asset from the get-go, she shouldn't be allowed out in public.

The near agoraphobia following that awful August was aggravated by a still more pernicious mistrust. Launching into the outside world requires feeling faintly palatable. At the least, in social settings you have to adopt the default assumption that others' initial reaction to you will be neutral, and healthy characters walk into a room expecting to be actively liked. But for months, Jillian felt hateable. Lest she appear "showy," she dressed in small colors, wearing slack T-shirts and tired jeans that disguised her figure. She kept her hair bunched, and often skipped showers so that its tendrils wilted. Lest she seem "self-involved," she conducted all phone calls with such a paucity of autobiographical content that her mother in Philadelphia accused her of being secretive. When she met the disappointing tennis partners, she volunteered little enough about her off-court life that they stopped asking, and consigned the relationship to the sports friendship, a perfectly agreeable but utilitarian arrangement whereby you never saw one another other than to play. In general, Jillian tried to say and do as little as possible, because whatever she expressed and however she behaved was bound to inspire disgust.

Mind, one of the primary reasons most people dislike someone is that the other party doesn't like *them*; thus so many antagonisms come down to a chicken-and-egg issue of who started it. Yet Jillian found Paige Myer strangely difficult to despise in return. There simply wasn't that much prospectively odious material to work with. Baba's renunciation naturally feeling like a betrayal, Jillian might have taken refuge in righteous indignation—alas, a deflective, huffy emotion, in this case hopelessly subsumed by sheer woundedness. She couldn't hate him, either, which would only pile betrayal upon betrayal. You were supposed to love a wife more than a pal, right? So it made sense that Baba had thrown their friendship under a bus, the way earlier generations of gallants threw capes over puddles.

Consuming the better part of a year, her bereavement was so deep and enduring that she might have wondered whether, as Baba had insinuated that dreadful Wednesday, the undercurrents of the friendship were indeed improper. Except that no romance had wrecked her this thoroughly for this long, regardless of how besotted she'd been to begin with. In the end, the unique severity of the loss seemed to exonerate their amity as innocent after all.

Inevitably, she would catch sight of him. He did give their old courts wide berth; it was tacitly understood that she'd been awarded Rockbridge, as if having been bequeathed no. 3 in a divorce settlement. But downtown Lexington was tiny, its eateries few. The first time she spotted Baba coming out of Macado's on Main Street, she ran away, cowering around the corner on West Henry. Not an adult response. She got better at fielding these intersections, nodding from down the block if she caught his eye, sometimes cracking a despondent half smile. He was always the one who broke the gaze first to look down at the side-walk. Then he'd glance back up and flutter a lifeless wave, having trouble raising his hand, as if the once keen sportsman had contracted some terrible muscle-wasting disease. On each sighting, he looked thinner—unattractively so. All that vegetarianism.

By late spring, however, Jillian started to feel hardier, and reconsidered the plan she'd conceived over the winter to pick up stakes. She had a sweet arrangement with the Chevaliers that she was unlikely to duplicate elsewhere. She loved her cottage, its floors refinished with darker lines patterning the edges of the rooms like tribal tattoos. Her reputation as a lively, infectiously enthusiastic tutor had spread widely enough—to nearby Kerrs Creek, Mechanicsville, and Buena Vista—that she didn't want for work, even if her secret with the boys was that most of them developed crushes. It was a comely, close-knit municipality that she had made her home, and on the face of it, the rejection of a tennis partner was a lunatic reason to leave town.

As the weather warmed and her skin turned golden, she began to feel braver, donning more revealing skirts and the flouncy thrift shop tops she had shunned for months. She went back to wearing hats—wide brimmed, straw, with ribbons. She let her hair down in every sense, and kept it washed. She rediscovered that a broad grin in Sweet Things Ice Cream Shoppe was all it took to win an extra-generous scoop and free sprinkles. A widowed client raising two sons, who by the by was rather dishy, had started asking her to stick around after lessons for a glass of wine. The only individual in her orbit who appeared to find her "hateable" was Jillian herself. So she tried the Ice Cream Shoppe smile in her bedroom mirror, and the reflection smiled right back.

Whether she precisely forgave Baba—whom she was starting to think of as *Weston*—was a moot point. The purpose of forgiveness was to lay planks over a gorge in the interest of forging ahead, and instead her erstwhile soul mate had raised one of those stark black-and-yellow END signs meant to alert motorists to the termination of a cul-de-sac.

How she felt about Paige, likewise never again actively germane to Jillian's affairs, was equally irrelevant. Although forevermore a particular place in her mind was destined to ache when she brushed against it, she was apparently capable of moving on.

But as the loss of her best friend gradually healed over, another hole in her life continued to gape.

The back right quarter of her living room was empty. She had never chosen to rebalance the room by returning the armchair there. What was done was done: *Weston* had forsaken their friendship to appease his wife. But one injustice could be righted.

On the exact date at the end of July marking the one-year anniversary of a big mistake, Jillian wrote the following email:

Dear Weston,

I hope you don't mind my contacting you this way. While I do miss you sometimes, I am well, and I am not trying to stir up trouble. I trust that you and Paige are very happy.

A year ago, I gave you and your fiancée a wedding present that cost me a great deal of time, energy, and love. The materials I used to construct it, like my own wisdom teeth, are irreplaceable. So it was very difficult for me to give away my handiwork—which was literally imbued with my own DNA. Had things gone differently between the three of us, however, rest assured that I would still be delighted to have given my creation a new home, where I could be certain it would be cherished.

As it happens, you accepted the gift under false pretenses. The evening I bestowed it, you were already planning to bring our friendship to a permanent close. You were also keenly aware that your wife-to-be disliked me, a fact that you concealed from me, allowing me to make a fool of myself by proceeding as if she and I had warm, harmonious relations. Had I benefited from access to both these pieces of information at the time, I would never have given you the Standing Chandelier—of which I am now not only dispossessed, but which I can't even visit.

I would like it back. I don't mean to be an Indian giver. (Paige wouldn't approve; I think that expression is no longer PC, though I don't know of another expression that has replaced it.) We could arrange an exchange, just as many newlyweds take their ugly ceramic cheese boards back to Pottery Barn and trade them for store credit. I'll replace the chandelier with a set of nice wineglasses or something, and then you can break them.

In any case, I can't imagine Paige treasures a reminder of someone she detests. I would even think that an intimate memento of our long but cruelly truncated friendship would be painful for you also. I would be glad to come by to pick it up when neither of you are home. Perhaps you could leave a key and instructions with a neighbor. I would even bring the bubble wrap.

Yours sincerely,
Jillian Frisk

"That is so completely lacking in class," Paige announced over Weston's computer in the A-frame's second-floor alcove. It was before dinner in early August. "Okay, sure, once in a while a wedding is called off. Then, yes, a couple with any integrity returns the presents—voluntarily, I might add. But I've never in my life heard of anyone giving a wedding present and then demanding it *back*."

"It's a little more complicated than that, isn't it?" Weston said tentatively.

"It is not. You always want to make everything out as complicated. This is straightforward. It's crass."

"While she obviously tried to write that email politely, I agree that the request itself is a little spiteful. So what do you want to do?

Knowing she begrudges our having it—I don't know how I'd feel about keeping that thing."

Paige gave him an affectionate poke. "You never know how you feel. Maybe we could consult a year from now and take a barometric reading of the Babansky soul."

She was right. He functioned on emotional hold, operating a more protracted version of the seven-second delay on radio broadcasts to check for Federal Communications Commission obscenity no-nos. He had put off showing Paige the email for the last three days, because his own reaction to it was so undiscernibly mixed—a sludge of dread, sorrow, and irritation.

"One thing I don't understand," Paige added. "If she was going to be so gauche, what took her so long? It's been a year."

"Maybe it took her a while to figure out what she felt, too."

"That's generous. As usual, given the subject matter. I would have hoped she's just been getting on with her life, but clearly she's been stewing this whole time. Writing that same email over and over in her mind. And even so, she can't control herself! That line about how she could give us some glasses instead, 'and then we could break them.' The bitterness, it's like having a double espresso thrown in your face, no sugar."

The bitterness was two-way. Paige herself was sounding a note he hadn't heard since the previous summer. She was not in the main given to recrimination or viciousness. The only topic that drew these qualities from Paige was Jillian Frisk. Best let his wife get the vitriol out of her system, then. Maybe he should be positively grateful for having obtained such a home remedy. The subject of his old friend could extract the residual traces of rancor from his wife's character like a poultice.

"And you said she was polite. But the cordiality is fraudulent," she carried on, having bent again over his computer. "'*I trust that you and Paige are very happy*,'" she read in a mincing tone. "Notice she can't resist getting in a dig at me with that crack about not being 'PC,' when what she really means is that she's a cultural troglodyte. Because she's right, you're not supposed to say 'Indian giver' anymore, as if anyone should ever have said it in the first place. And when you realize that, you don't *write* 'Indian giver,' you write something else. Oh, and I like her saying she doesn't 'mean to be' an Indian giver, when that's exactly what she's being."

Now was not the time to observe that Paige had just used the very expression that she claimed to deplore. He found it mysterious that she still got so worked up over Frisk, whom she had vanquished in every way. He'd have thought she would feel a touch of pity, or nothing.

"Oh, and notice how it's *your* fault that she 'made a fool of herself,'" Paige went on. "Just because she's socially oblivious and never picked up that she got on my nerves. The melodrama, too! Your 'cruelly truncated friendship.' And I have to 'detest' her. It's not just that Jillian isn't my cup of tea."

This email forensic was curiously heavy on beverages. "Well," Weston allowed. "You did say you 'couldn't stand her when you met her' and you 'couldn't stand her when you got to know her better' either. I'm not sure what you call that but detesting someone."

"I can't believe you can quote word for word something I said that long ago."

"It was memorable."

"Detestation—if that's the noun—is a feeling that eats you up. So it's hardly pertinent to someone I never think about."

Uh-huh, Weston stifled. "I know I said I wouldn't communicate with her. But even if you find the email overwritten, or inaccurate about your feelings, I think it deserves a reply. That's why I showed it to you. So we could decide what to say."

"Of course you showed it to me. I'd be alarmed if you didn't. You haven't been corresponding with her all along, have you? And are only showing me this one because it involves us both?"

"We haven't been corresponding," Weston said flatly. He might have gone on at greater length, either in umbrage or with fervid reassurance, but amid the range of emotions he battled whenever Frisk arose in their discussions the most dominant was exhaustion, and he kept the denial short. "The point is, she wants the lamp back. So I guess we should let her have it."

"You must be kidding! It was a *wedding present*!"

"I thought you didn't like the chandelier anyway."

"I don't like calling it a 'chandelier'—that part is true. It's not a 'chandelier,' which is a pompous, totally inane thing to call a *lamp*. Still, even if it's not entirely to my taste, it's grown on me. Or at least I've gotten used to it. And we rearranged the whole living room to accommodate that thing."

In truth, Frisk's addition to their household cornerstoned the decor of the whole ground floor. It was a great conversation starter with new dinner guests, who often exceeded exuberant enthusiasm to confess to outright envy. Bill from the History Department had gleefully rechristened it "The Memory Palace," a branding he seemed to believe was sparklingly original; having contrived a new name also encouraged the guy to act weirdly proprietary, as if he were a museum director and this artwork was only resting in their living room on loan. The light the lamp cast was uniquely soft, enclosing, and warm, and Weston couldn't imagine ever finding a proxy that would duplicate these qualities in a world of glaring compact fluorescents. He still routinely worked beside it during the wee smalls in his regular rocking chair, the radiance emitting from the windows of the Colman's mustard tin mingling with the glow of his computer. In all honesty, the object reminded him less and less of Frisk; he was now capable of spending whole hours in its presence without her crossing his mind even once.

Catching himself in this admission moved him to remind Paige, "But this isn't about a thing. It's about what it means. Frisk really put her heart into that—" He was about to say *chandelier*, and thought better of it. "So for her, it's symbolic of, well, giving her heart. Which we sort of stepped on, or that's how she would see it."

"Is that the way you see it?"

"It's just, I'm getting the impression you definitely don't want to give it back."

"Better believe it."

"Which would seem, to Frisk, like stepping on her heart twice."

"The symbolism? That present is symbolic of Jillian for once in her life doing the traditional, decent thing and giving an acquaintance of long standing a wedding present—even if the present itself was a little weird. For us to acquiesce and let her snatch it back would be to say, yet again, that the rules governing everyone else don't apply to her, and she can behave as badly as she likes and get whatever she wants, other people be damned."

Weston let *acquaintance* slide. "You didn't say at the time it was 'a little weird.' You called it 'inappropriate' and 'an imposition' and 'a beady-eyed monstrosity.' You compared it to Tracey Emin's bed."

"You're doing that again. Quoting me verbatim from last summer. What, did you run off and take notes, so you could hang me with them later?"

"If that lamp is symbolic of anything, it's symbolic of my friendship with Frisk. Because she's right on one point: it's always going to remind you of her. So why on earth would you want to hang on to it?"

"Because it distresses me that all this time later, with one lousy go-fetch email, you'll still do her bidding. Which makes me wonder."

"Don't *wonder*," he said with annoyance. He was no longer wondering himself. *That lamp doesn't only remind my wife of her adversary. It reminds her of winning.* "But what on earth can I write back?"

"I could draft that email in a heartbeat. 'Dear Jillian: What you're asking goes so beyond the limits of decorum that it's off the charts. A wedding present is forever, just like my marriage. Have a nice life.'"

"I guess I'll have to think about it."

Her laughter had an unpleasant color. "What a shock."

WESTON HAD NOT replaced Frisk—or, to the degree that he had, he had replaced her with Paige. The confidences, the day-to-day anecdotes, the many ambivalences with which he wrestled, even the recipes, successful and disappointing alike, he shared with his wife. That was as it should be, he supposed. As a consequence of this substitution—this wife swap, if you will—it was possible that some small slice of himself was stifled. But that's what solitude was for: exploring the unsayable. He was becoming one of those commonplace men whose sole intimacy was with a spouse, while friendship, exclusively with other men, was reserved for talk about movies and football. Except that Weston wasn't interested in football.

He was still interested in tennis, and had finally joined the local club, which he could now afford. His partners there were male, and they always played formal matches. He was rising on the ladder. No longer merely rallying with Frisk three times a week, he'd improved his serve.

It had not been optimal to begin his marriage in a spirit of sacrifice. But he had instructed himself on the necessity of the Frisk forfeiture enough times to begin to believe it. On reflection, Paige's request had been so justified, its reasoning so solid, that it was astonishing earlier girlfriends hadn't laid down the same law. (Some of his wife's romantic predecessors had also found the Frisk situation fishy, but they'd kept the grumbling to a minimum. Either they hadn't loved him enough to put up a stink, or they knew he didn't love them enough to capitulate.) Weston being Weston, he had naturally examined the question of whether he should feel guilty about Frisk from every angle. The answer was no. Human relations had a calculus, and sometimes you had to add up columns of gains and losses with the coldness of accountancy. He was a happier man married. Although he would eternally suffer from funks, they were fewer and shorter now. He was glad to have put to rest a quest that would otherwise fester— biology ensured that—and to have escaped the fate of men forever single into their fifties, who reliably earned reputations as strange, gay, emotionally dislocated, or all three. Settledness suited him. Only women were meant to care about safety, but safety was a universally appealing state, and men could snug into it, too. He enjoyed the regular rhythms of his days with Paige, like the rise and fall of swells on a coastal vacation. During his boyhood in Wilmington, an hour's drive from the Jersey shore, Weston had spent many tireless hours lulled up and down beyond the breakers. If the cost of installing this sensation in his inland adulthood was doing without an alternative rhythm three times a week, so be it.

After they'd rehashed the *Indian giving* yet again after dinner and Paige had gone to bed, he poured himself a double Talisker and switched on the chandelier. He was frankly surprised that Frisk had brought herself to rescind the gift, because Paige was right: it wasn't classy. You'd think Frisk would have restrained herself, if only out of pride.

Yet after a few sips of whisky, the explanation fell into place. Pride was predominantly a social construct, having to do with witness. And why would Frisk fear his contempt for making an appeal that was beneath her? Aside from those few torturous bumpings into each other downtown—more like hauntings, or disquietingly vivid memories, than proper encounters—Weston played so little a part in her life now that he might have been dead. As for her own witness of this mean-spiritedness, which might invite regret: however inevitable their parting of ways, even Weston couldn't persuade himself that Frisk deserved his desertion. Whether or not the friendship was unacceptably tinged by mutual attraction, she'd never actually tried to kiss him again, had she? She hadn't tried to lure him back to bed. Not once convicted of a moving violation, she hadn't, strictly speaking, done anything wrong. Yet she had been roundly punished. So for Frisk, any passing private chagrin over *Indian giving* was bound to be swallowed by a far greater sense of grievance. Or grief? Idly, he checked the etymologies online. Both *grievance* and *grief* derived from the Old French *grever*, "to burden." That was about the sum of it. He had burdened her.

To resume: you obeyed conventions because you cared what other people thought of you. If Frisk and Weston were no longer friends, then Frisk had no cause to care what he thought of her. She'd have been well aware that the revocation of a wedding present was crass. So? His repudiation of their friendship had freed her from the bonds of seemliness. She had no reason to avoid asking something embarrassing, or even reason to feel embarrassed. For embarrassment as well was a social construct. Without relationship, there is no society. The ties between the two parties had been severed. All that remained was stuff. Thus she had nothing to lose by savaging his good opinion of her, and one thing to gain: her chandelier.

Here in this living room, the same paradigm repeated. Neither he nor Paige retained an investment in what Jillian Frisk thought of them. Plausibly, the only faux pas more crass than demanding the return of a wedding present was having a nuptial gift rudely retracted and refusing to give it back. So? They had nothing to gain by remaining theoretically in Frisk's good graces, and one thing to lose: the chandelier.

Structurally, then, a single disparity distinguished the two squared-off factions: he and Paige had custody of the item at issue, and Frisk didn't.

Were he to return the gift, he would do so over his wife's dead body. What was in it for him, taking all that flack, when at best he'd receive a single thank-you in his inbox as compensation? And Weston liked the chandelier, even liked calling it that, if it might take Paige a few more years to warm to the tag. The grand, eccentric centerpiece had already grown into the very being of the A-frame, as if the trunk of the lamp had extended roots through the oak flooring that were penetrating the ceiling of the utility room and gnarling around the pipes. Secreting its many objets d'art, miniature dioramas, and natural wonders like the curlew skull, the arboreal assemblage gave off enough hint of Yuletide to evoke the ringing refrain *And a partri-idge in a pear tree.* Squirm as she might to avoid admitting as much, Paige liked the chandelier, too—liked it very much, in fact, and she would come to like it more and more as the years advanced.

The lamp wasn't a symbol. All the meaning had been sucked out of it the afternoon he sank back onto their regular bench at Rockbridge to deliver the bad news, its limp elucidation taking so much less time than the rambling rationalizations of his rehearsals. They would all three continue to pretend that the chandelier was a symbol, when really it had become a thing. Frisk wanted the thing. Weston wanted the thing. Improbably, even Paige wanted the thing. A thing of which possession was ten-tenths, like most of one's belongings.

The Talisker was finished. At last Weston composed the shortest email he could muster:

> Have discussed. Paige finds request violates social custom. Will continue to enjoy chandelier.

He'd signed it "B." to begin with, then changed that to "W.," couldn't bear the W, and didn't sign it at all.

Though he sent it at past three a.m., the response was immediate:

> She just wants to keep her *scalp*.

He'd promised, and this was bordering on *correspondence*. After deleting not only Frisk's reply but also its ghost in TRASH, he swiftly closed the computer like the lid of Pandora's box.

The Self-Seeding Sycamore

JEANNETTE HAD NO idea that plants could inspire so much hatred.

For years, she'd left the garden to Wyndham. Weekends outdoors provided an antidote to the windowless stasis of his lab. Though their plot was sizable only by London standards, she'd humored him. (Whatever was there to do? A little watering during dry spells, a ten-minute run of the hand mower round the lawn.) Having begrudged the dear man neither his solitude nor his superfluous pottering, she treasured snapshots of her husband in muddied khaki trousers, bent over a bed, doing heaven-knew-what with a characteristically intent expression. Now, of course, she knew exactly what he'd been doing. How much he'd spared her.

While still cosseted by mutual spousal existence, she'd scanned with indifference bitter first-person articles about how fiercely people avoid the bereaved—a revelation her own friends had amply illustrated for a year or more. She didn't blame them. Unintentionally, she and Wyndham had fallen into the heedlessly hermetic unit of two that's so off-putting from the outside. If she didn't need friends then, she'd no right to demand their attentions now. Besides, she'd grown less compelling to herself. A widow of fifty-seven had both too much story left, and not enough. It was narratively awkward: an ellipsis of perhaps thirty years, during which nothing big would happen. Only little things, most of them crap.

The big story that was over wasn't interesting, either. Pancreatic: swift and dreadful. Yet the pro forma tale did include one poignant detail. Two years ago, she and Wyndham took early retirement, he from private biochemical research, she from her job as a buyer for Debenhams. Some colleagues had quietly disapproved, and soon no one would be allowed to stop working at fifty-five, but to Jeannette and Wyndham that argued for a leap through the closing window. They'd not found each other until their forties, and had made extravagant travel plans for while they were still in rude health. The reasoning was sound; the arithmetic, not. The diagnosis arrived a mere ten weeks after Wyndham's farewell party.

She hadn't kept track of whether fifty-seven was the new forty-seven, or thirty-five, or sixty-four—but in any event, whatever age she'd reached was not the age she was. Not long ago, she and Wyndham had mourned his every strand that clogged the plughole, each new crease in her neck when she glanced down. Now? She could not get older fast enough.

Convinced that a garden took care of itself—it grew, bloomed, browned, and without prodding renewed the cycle—other than hiring a boy to mow, for the year following Wyndham's death she left the back to its devices. In truth, she missed the sharpness of those first few months, whose high drama would have been impossible to maintain without its sliding into a humiliating fakery, a performance for herself. While still free flowing and unforced, the grief had been so immersive, so rich and pure and concentrated, with the opacity of Cabernet, that it verged on pleasure. Yet from the start the anguish had been spiked with an awful foreknowledge that the keenness of her loss would blunt, leading to a second loss: a loss of loss. Some soft, muffled bufferedness was bound to take over, as if she were buttressed by excess packaging. Unlike the searing period, with its skipped meals and feverish lie-ins, a bufferedness could last forever, and probably would.

Sure enough, the stab ebbed to ache; a torturous residual presence gave way to absence. Jeannette took refuge in self-sufficiency. She would take nothing, and expect nothing. There must have been millions of such Britons: perfectly neutral social quantities, mutely shopping and tidying up. She would take care of herself, as the garden did.

So late this April, she was surprised to note on an aimless stroll beyond the slug-trailed patio, simply to escape the house—which had never felt suffocating when she shared it—that flowering shrubs past their prime were pooping mounds of rotting pink blossoms, under which matted grass skulked, dying or dead, a urinary yellow. Ineffectually, she raked the piles of petals with her fingers off the moribund lawn, in idle amazement that flowers could kill. The silky mulch had a nice heavy wetness, reminiscent of her cheeks after an inadvisable third glass of wine. Its original perfume mixed with an aroma deader and flatter, like sweet but fading memories intermingling with her present *self-sufficiency*.

She surveyed the beds on both sides. Pooping flowers were the least of it. Unafflicted by Wyndham's "superfluous" attentions, the ceanothus had bushed out in scraggly extrusions like an unbarbered afro, blocking the stone path to the toolshed and poking her in the eye. Ivy choked the herbs; the ferns drooped with snails. The lawn had dead patches from peeing foxes, vermin she'd been too apathetic to shoo. She couldn't speak for the human sphere, but apparently in the botanical world, without the constant intercession of a benevolent higher power, evil triumphed.

At first anxious about uprooting her husband's beloved something-or-others, Jeannette soon mastered the gardener's rubric: anything that grows fast and well is malevolent. Weeding, she was tortured by a cliché that circled her head like a successful advertisement jingle: *Nature abhors a vacuum.* She came to match each invader with a uniquely flavored dislike. Burrowing into the mortar of the property line's brick wall, a pretend-attractive plant with small, devious leaves inspired an impatient disgust; its roots remaining behind, the crafty, low-lying wallflower would be back in a week. Allowed in the passivity of her grieving to rise six feet high, a gangling daisylike species with disproportionately small, stupid yellow flowers had spread thick white ropes of lateral roots so quickly and so thickly that in another month's time the towering, insipid plants would have taken over the world. That aversion was laced with fear; she pursued their extermination with the grim, stoical thoroughness of genocide. In this merciless laying of waste, the institution of her private scorched-earth policy, she came closer than she had in seventeen months to joy.

Yet Jeannette reserved her most extravagant loathing for clusters of innocent-looking seedlings that seemed to erupt in concert on a single day, as if obeying a battle plan. Oh, on its own, a single sample of this anonymous item seemed innocuous and easily vanquished. A mere three inches high, two never-mind-me leaves splayed on a spindly stem. But when snatched from the ground, lo, the tiny flagpole had sunk into her property a good four inches below—and virtually overnight.

Besides which, any organism in sufficient quantity is gross. Bulging clusters of these seedlings, pushing against one another in their blind, ignorant bunching, sprouted en masse through the bark cover around the toolshed. The impertinent would-be trees cropped up in the lightless murk below the shrubs. They perforated the lawn every two inches. They penetrated the ivy that had killed the chives, and threatened the ivy, too.

Thus by May, her every hour in the garden was devoted to massacring seedlings by the *thousand*, creating whole burial mounds of the shriveled fallen, and still they came. The slaughter recalled a certain kind of asymmetrical warfare, whereby a better supplied, more technologically sophisticated army is overrun by forces in rags with sticks, the adversary's greatest weapon its leadership's utter obliviousness to casualties on a staggering scale.

Any child soldier she failed to slay right away would stake a territorial claim. Within days an overlooked seedling jagged out in aggressive, multipronged foliage with the rough nap and variegation of *real tree leaves*. The fragile stem woodened to sturdy stalk; the taproot plummeted and grew clinging hairs. Her attempts at jerking these interlopers from the ground were no more effective than the Home Office's feeble efforts to deport asylum seekers.

No mystery, the source of the assault. On the opposite side of the party wall, a monster of a tree rose over three stories high, its trunk inches from the brick, ensuring that nearly half its branches extended over her own garden. It was a charmless thing, blocking light from the herb bed, and already grown pregnant with *more seedpods*, its branches sagging from the weight of their great ghastly clumps. So eclipsing did her antipathy for this verdant vandal grow that she failed to note: this was more than she had felt towards any living thing, one way or another, since Wyndham's flatline.

A vastly more beguiling tree, the flaming Japanese maple was growing inexplicably lifeless, so Jeannette booked an appointment with a tree surgeon. He wasn't much comfort—"The poor tree's time has come, missus"—but so long as he was at hand, she pointed to the ogre overhead. "Speaking of trees whose time ought to have come," she said, "what's *that*?"

The surgeon grinned. "A self-seeding sycamore."

The name rang a bell. Wyndham must have mumbled it once or twice. It pained her that her patient husband had eradicated half a million seedlings every spring with so little complaint. What other suffering had he disguised, especially in those last months?

"A volunteer," he went on. "*Nobody* plants a self-seeding sycamore on purpose. It's a pest tree." He looked it up and down, as if measuring it for a coffin. "Three fifty, and I'll cut it down for you."

THE HOUSE ON her eastern side was owned by a man she gathered from a misdelivered credit card solicitation was called Burt Cuss. It was an ugly name, like a one-two punch. Perhaps also in his fifties, he had a hulking, furious bearing, and either he seldom left the house or for extended periods he wasn't there. Sightings were rare. In all seasons, she'd spotted him always in a black crew-neck T, black jeans, neo-Nazi boots, and a buzz cut. She'd never spoken to him, which should have been unusual, but in London wasn't. She and Wyndham had speculated about their neighbor—as one does. Given the biceps and hard stomach, her husband assessed the man as ex-army. Jeannette surmised he was divorced. Soon after Burt moved in, he'd burnt a pile of papers out back, in which she'd spied photographs. Irrationally, she was a little afraid of him. If only because they *hadn't* spoken, she rushed inside in the uncommon instance that he ventured into his own garden—if you could call it that.

Burt's garden was subject to near-total neglect. It hadn't been landscaped in the slightest. Other than the manically propagating sycamore, its only plant life was scrub grass, which grew a foot high before Burt, no more than twice a year, thwacked it to jaundiced nubs with a scythe. Nearer the house, bits of furniture slumped in the rain. Plastic bags that blew onto the long, narrow plot would flap there for weeks.

Most Londoners would have sold their firstborns into slavery for fertile terra firma a fraction of that size, a blank canvas begging to be painted with azaleas, and in times past the dismal waste ground had aroused her dismay. From the master bedroom on her first floor, she had a panoramic view of this unsightly patch, which might even have dropped the adjoining property values a tad. Yet now that she'd seized on the tree surgeon's offer—to be spared that malignancy of seedlings every spring, £350 was a bargain—suddenly her neighbor's obliviousness to horticulture seemed a stroke of good fortune.

Sometimes going for days without saying a word, Jeannette had to steel herself to interact with anyone. Even the encounter with the tree surgeon had been draining. She'd lost the knack for small talk. But a firm purpose was fortifying.

It felt odd to knock formally on the front door when she gawked daily at her neighbor's unkempt inner sanctum. The peephole cover swung. Multiple locks.

"Right?" he said gruffly, in the usual uniform. Up close, his eyes were green.

"I'm sorry, we've never been—"

"You're in ninety-two," he cut her off, jerking his head towards her house.

But of course: While you're supposing about neighbors, they're supposing about you. "Jeannette Dickson." He nodded curtly, keeping his own name to himself. "I was hoping we might talk about your tree."

"What about it?" It was astounding that Burt was even aware of having a tree.

"I hate it." No self-respecting Brit would confess to such ferocious feelings about a plant. She'd just cast herself as a kook.

"What'd that tree ever do to you?"

"More than you'd expect," she said, trying to sound sane. "Its seedlings. They erupt by the thousands. I spend hours and hours pulling them up."

"Sounds terrible," he said, and the deadpan grated.

"I now have some appreciation for the experience of being taken over by aliens," she said. "The point is, I'd be willing to pay to have it cut down."

"Sounds a bother. What's in it for me?"

"Well—you must have at least as bad a problem with seedlings yourself."

"Problem I ain't even noticed can't be much of a problem."

"We'd both have more light, and your own, ah, *garden* would feel larger and more open." It was the best she could do, on the spot.

"No sale. Rather have my privacy."

She was getting flustered. He stood before her too squarely, blocking the door in an unfriendly fashion, arms folded, forearms rippling. The T-shirt was tight, his pectorals formidable. She wondered how a man who seemed rarely to go outdoors had got that tan. He was a brute, monosyllabic and sullen, nothing like Wyndham, who was tall and lanky, with a sly humor he saved for her; not big on exercise, beyond the pottering, but sinewy, with no waste on him, which made the end come faster, with so few reserves on which to draw. If also not a big talker, he was brilliant, they all said so at the lab, unlike this animal, and when Wyndham did say something, he'd made it count.

"My tree surgeon says no one would deliberately plant such a 'pest tree'—"

"*Your* tree surgeon?"

"Why's that funny?"

"I don't even have a GP."

"What I meant is, that's the opinion of an expert."

"Darling," Burt said. "I been through this rigmarole before, and you lot got your answer. Ask your husband."

So: Wyndham had tried to negotiate this very solution, to no avail.

"I'm afraid my husband passed away, nineteen months ago." Ergo, *Here I am, still grieving, and I'm spending all my time ripping up your filthy seedlings.*

But Burt didn't easily embarrass. "Tough luck," he said dispassionately.

"Could you consider my proposal? I'd make all the arrangements. Please? As a favor. It would mean so much to me."

"Lady, I spent seventeen years doing *favors* for a bird not so different from yourself, and in the end it didn't mean nothing to her at all."

He shut the door in her face. Confirmation: divorced.

THE FOLLOWING FEW days, Jeannette spent more than one tiresome afternoon in a state of suppressed rage, grumbling about that tosser next door while pulling single sycamore seedlings from a busy cover of woodbine, something like plucking individual gray hairs from a heavy beard with tweezers. Meantime, incredibly, seedlings she'd already ripped out and left to wither were still struggling their wounded roots back into the bark cover. Good God, it was like watching privates who'd had their limbs blown off shimmy bloody torsos across the battlefield and pick up guns with their teeth.

Yet infeasibly, when Jeannette peered over the party wall, she could not discern, in Burt's foot-high scrub grass, *any seedlings at all.*

Armed with a sheaf of printout, she knocked on Burt's door for round two.

"Don't tell me," he said. "I'm meant to dismantle my upper floor, so's you get more sun in your sitting room."

"It's all over the internet." Jeannette brandished the sheaf. "On blogs, social media, on botanical websites. Everyone detests those trees—"

"Speaking of trees," he interrupted, giving her a once-over. "You've *spruced up*."

She blushed. True, ever since Wyndham died she'd been rather careless in the sartorial department, and this afternoon she had taken advantage of a snappy wardrobe from years as a Debenhams buyer who was encouraged to bring home samples. The hasty makeover was merely more strategy—to look presentable, like a neighbor anyone would want to please. So, fine: she'd washed her hair.

"They're not even native to Britain," Jeannette carried on. "It's an invasive species from the Continent. Sycamores have only been here a few hundred years."

"The toffs in *Downton Abbey* only been in Britain 'a few hundred years.'"

Jeannette frowned. "You don't seem like the costume drama type."

"So what do I seem like?"

Awkwardness made her honest. "Someone who does loads of press-ups."

That won her a half smile, a first, perhaps a prelude to a full smile, which she precluded by pressing her case. "If you'd simply take a look at these . . ." She held out the sheets of A4. "There's a uniform consensus . . . We'd be doing a community service."

"You're a terrier, you are. Know the type. Just wear you down. Don't work no more, not on me."

Before he had a chance to shut the door again, she burst out, "Nearly half of that tree is on my side of the property line. I've checked with the council. I'm within my legal rights to cut off any of that sycamore that's sticking over the wall!"

He shrugged and said, "Be my guest," perhaps missing her parting shot: "It'll look ridiculous!" As if he cared.

UNFORTUNATELY, WHEN SHE contacted the tree surgeon again, allowing that the actual owner of the sycamore was uncooperative, he turned the radical pruning job down by text, though he needed the work if he was still using a mobile without autocomplete: Dodgy in evry wy. Physicly difficlt. + any idea hw ugly disputes ovr evn wee shrbs in ths cntry gt, btw neibrs? Rd th papr? Ppl gt killd ovr less! Stying out of it.

Very well. But she was not simply rolling over. The alternative was year upon numbing year, toiling away as an ever more elderly pensioner in the gardening equivalent of the salt mines, to strip away yet another crop of seedlings, budding with idiot hopefulness, perking and poking and flopping about with garish green naïveté. Unless she took a stand, each year her futile Sisyphean extermination would be undertaken in a spirit of submission and impotence.

First off, she would demonstrate the extent of what Burt refused to label a problem. Thus after another mass murder of seedlings by the log store—an empty structure that made her feel wistful and remiss, for she hadn't reordered fuel for the wood burner, around which she and Wyndham had lingered through many a toasty winter evening—Jeannette gathered the hairy pile of crushed blades and dangling taproots, marched to Burt's front door, and deposited the gratuity on his step with a note: "Sorry, I believe these belong to you." Within minutes—he could have heard her scuttle away, and she was braced for a blast of effing and blinding—a belly laugh carried to her patio, round, resonant, and loose.

Jeannette rifled through the toolshed the next morning. Even if Wyndham had kept a chain saw, which it seems he hadn't, she'd have been too afraid of the monstrosity to use it. But she did dig out a trusty handsaw, whose rudimentary technology she understood, and which in a moment of inattention was unlikely to amputate her arm. Yet the identifying "rip-cut teeth cross-cut" on its cardboard sleeve sounded suitably violent.

The sky-blue shorts with decorative pockets she wore for the project that afternoon were sensible for a warm spell in June, though they were nearly new, and showed off legs little veined and rather shapely for a woman her age. The crisp yellow crop top was also airy and cool; at Debenhams, she'd always maintained that good styling needn't be impractical. Drawing the sword of vengeance from its scabbard, she climbed from bench to wall, then scrambled onto the roof of the log store (already shaggy with helicopter seedpods, lying in wait for next year). From here she enjoyed ready access to a fat lower branch of the sycamore, right where it thrust presumptuously across the property line. Gripping the branch with her other hand for balance, she traced a starter cut with the tips of the teeth. The blade juddered.

By the time she'd established a notch, she was sweating; the yellow crop top would soon be a write-off. The green wood continually grabbed the saw's teeth and brought each wobbly stroke to a standstill. After half an hour of rasping, and stopping to catch her breath, she'd got not an inch through a branch whose diameter ran to half a foot. At this rate, she'd be sawing sycamore branches in all seasons for the next year. Already, her upper arm ached, and her right forefinger had blistered.

What she needed was the smallest symbolic satisfaction. That meant removing one full branch to start with—much more doable if she climbed farther up into the tree itself to attack a higher, thinner limb. Aiming for a vulnerable-looking bough ten feet overhead, Jeannette dusted off her climbing skills from a tomboy childhood.

Goodness, she must have been a brave little girl. When ascending many a tree to nearly its summit on family holidays in the Lake District, she didn't remember feeling this terrified. Struggling both to pull herself up and to keep hold of the saw, Jeannette remembered from painting the loo ceiling during the first footloose fortnight of retirement: fear destroys balance. Only once she'd hoisted to within striking distance of the target branch did she get her confidence—or at least she stopped shaking.

Braced against the trunk, she got purchase on the bough. Her elbow kept running into a branch behind her, preventing a full stroke. The project grew so consumingly tedious that she lost all trace of vertigo. At long last, the cut opened up from the weight of the bough, which splintered off with a crack. What a pity that she'd been keeping steady by gripping the severed side of the branch.

HE KEPT THE sitting room dark, with curtains drawn, though on a long summer's day it was still bright at nine p.m.

"I should really go home," she said weakly from the sofa.

"Rubbish, you can't walk," Burt said, bringing whisky. "Keep that leg elevated."

There was the broken ankle, a cracked rib, a sprained right wrist, and naturally she was pretty scratched up. *Mortified* didn't begin to cover it.

He wasn't ex-army, but a medic for the Red Cross, who flew out at a moment's notice to Haiti or Sierra Leone. A medic certainly made for a more providential neighbor than a retired women's clothing buyer who was a fool. The moment she fell, he had streaked out, then crudely splinted her ankle with duct tape and the *Independent* (not, as she'd have expected, the *Sun*). At a lope, he carried her several streets to their local clinic. Those expert administrations as she woozed in his overgrown grass were hazy, but she did remember the black T-shirt bunched under her head, its distinctive must, and the vivid, bumpy journey to the clinic. Jeannette hadn't felt the clasp of a man's arms for nineteen months. Pain or no, the sensation was thrilling.

Burt interrupted her anxious internal reverie about the many daily activities that a woman avowed to "take nothing, and expect nothing" would now have trouble doing for herself. "You'll need help. Got kids?"

"No," Jeannette said. "Wyndham and I did not *self-seed*." The shorts were soiled, silly and too exposing, and she was grateful for the sheet he'd brought her, even in the heat.

"I feel part responsible," he said, nipping at his drink. "Should have stopped you when I first spotted you climbing that wall. With

a *handsaw*, for fuck's sake. Figured I'd let you learn your lesson.
Thought it was funny."

"I suppose it *was* funny."

"So what was the plan? You'd never have lopped more than a branch
or two."

"Over time, I was hoping to cut off enough to kill it."

"But what's so bloody important about a few little plants? You're
bigger than them."

"*Few?*" She turned away, groping, unsure of the why of it herself. "I told you, I hate them. So mindlessly cheerful and impossible
to discourage. Just starting out in life. Willing to give it a go, even in
bark chips. Then the mess of them. They're rioting, insane. Running
roughshod over all my husband's tending and discipline. Invading, uninvited, *out of control*. And I feel an obligation, to honor Wyndham's
creation, in memoriam, to not let the garden go to hell in a handbasket
on my watch. I only found out recently how much effort a garden is,
how much work he must have done, which I was blithely unaware of, or
even scoffed at. Besides. Also. There's something horrible. The repli-
cation. The burgeoning is grotesque. I can kill them in the thousands,
but still I can't win over them as a mass. I know they're so much smaller
than I, but together, as a profusion, they're bigger, and they make me
feel helpless and defeated all over again." It was the fatigue, and shock,
and the blurring of the painkillers, but the plethora of personification
must have verified the verdict: without question, a kook.

"And you?" she added. "What's so important about that tree? I haven't
sensed any love lost."

"Had my fill of female willfulness, I reckon," he said. "Willfulness
begets willfulness. Spirals, and never ends well."

"Doesn't it?" she asked with a smile, as he freshened a drink they
both knew conflicted with the advisory on her prescription.

AFTER SHARING HIS takeaway, he insisted she settle for the night
on his sofa. She slept hard and long, stirring only from a loud, high-

pitched buzz outside. The council, ironically, must have been finally pruning the London plane trees along the pavement.

Rising midday with chagrin, Jeannette hobbled with her NHS crutch under her good arm out the back double doors. She knew her way around. The houses on this stretch were identical.

Right at the back, Burt was splitting the last of the big logs, using the stump of the self-seeding sycamore as a chopping block. In wonderment, she could see through the slats: Rising on her side of the party wall, the log store was nearly full, its contents neatly stacked. An offering—or was it a proposal? As she approached, he remembered to put on his chain saw's safety catch. Off to the right, fat, fluffy twigs of felled pod clusters piled bonfire high.

After landing a decisive blow on the wedge with his sledgehammer, Burt announced gruffly, "Sycamore seasons fast, and burns hot."

"If Wyndham is to be believed," she returned, "so do I."

WHEN HE WAS not away treating cholera patients, they would recline in the glow of incinerating sycamore in her wood burner, watching the concluding Christmas special of *Downton Abby*, and later the repeats—though Burt drew the line at *Poldark*, which he ridiculed as a sappy bodice ripper, and she accused him of being jealous of the lead. They would stay in separate houses; the arrangement maintained a courtliness, an asking, that they came to cherish. Every spring, the seedlings returned. According to the Royal Horticultural Society website, the sycamore lays a seedbed that will recrudesce for years. But it had laid her own bed also. *Nature abhors a vacuum.*

Domestic Terrorism

"BY ABOUT SEVENTEEN," Harriet despaired, "*I* couldn't wait to fly the coop. Emory appealed if only because it was about the farthest school from Bellingham that I could find. My parents lobbied for the University of Washington, so I could commute from home. They were clingy. While I was dying to get up to no good, and do everything for myself. I was frantic for my adult life to begin. Which Liam's hasn't."

"Liam's never seemed to find adult life especially compelling," Court granted.

As ever, the couple was holed up in the master bedroom of their split-level in Atlanta, voices held to stage whispers. Liam had a room and bath below, which should have afforded them the run of upstairs, and a modicum of privacy. But no, their son preferred to prowl the upper floor, closer to the refrigerator. The switcheroo had not gone unremarked upon: the parents had become the teenagers, bulwarked in their antisocial lair.

Harriet plumped her pillow and raised the volume of the eleven o'clock news for better cover. The stream of unaccompanied children pouring over the Mexican border from Honduras was unabated. "He has no motivation to leave. How's a community college dropout going to afford a whole house in leafy, middle-class Morningside, a twenty-minute bus ride from downtown? With a juicer and espresso machine?

At least in our day, parents were dark on sex and drugs, with rules against cursing and drinking. They marched into your room and turned the music way down without asking, and then ordered you to take out the trash. We let him do what he wants."

"We could join some obscure cult," Court proposed, "and turn into hard-ass killjoys overnight. No Godless whore music by Beyoncé, only revivalist hymns, like 'Shall We Gather at the River.' Jocanda's sauntering downstairs would be against our religion—or sauntering, *period*. We'd have to defend our pure minds from the rays of the devil, so we could ban the internet! I'd buy you a bonnet. We could disavow motorized transportation and modern medical care. Get a horse and buggy and sell the car."

"I wish you wouldn't always address this situation with *whimsy*." On another evening, she might have spun the fantasy forward, conjuring the draconian laying down of God's law on Wildwood Place, the pouring of liquor down the drain. But they'd spent too many nights fabricating fanciful solutions, and they just weren't that funny anymore.

She couldn't fathom her own impotence. It was their house. But unlike many of their friends' children, who'd returned home in their twenties, Liam had never left, which eliminated the juncture at which he might at least have had to *ask* for his old room back.

Harriet might have blamed indulgent parenting, in which case being saddled with a lifelong adolescent was just deserts for failing to raise a functional human being. But Liam's younger sister, Alicia, had evolved into a competent striver, living with two other young women in Peoplestown while working as the sous chef at Tap. Despite being the firstborn, typically the more intrepid, Liam had never exhibited an appetite for independence as a child. Whereas Alicia grew furious if, in a hurry, you tied her shoes for her—"I want to do it *my-sehwf*!" became her ringing prime directive by age three—Liam wouldn't even fold over his sneakers' Velcro. He threw screaming fits at four when Harriet insisted he learn to wield utensils; he preferred spoon-feeding. Once when he got separated from Harriet at Six Flags, she'd raced the grounds for half an hour before spotting a lone, immobile figure beside the Great American Scream Machine. It hadn't occurred to the nine-year-old to take some initiative—to locate the Meeting Place, to approach a security guard, or even to attract adult attention by bursting into tears. To the contrary: head swiveling languidly as if taking in the sights, he didn't race to embrace Mommy in relief, but acknowledged her approach with a nonchalant wave. He'd always possessed an unshakable faith that, come what may, someone else would take care of him.

Obviously, a boy who felt safe and secure was all to the good. Yet the complacency grew less than heartening. Throughout his school years, he let his bicycle rust, content to be ferried to Kmart for supplies. When he was a teenager, she actually wished that he seemed at least a *little* embarrassed to be seen with his parents. They'd had to veritably foist a first cell phone on the boy in high school, and he never learned how to text or retrieve voicemail; he didn't keep it charged or do the updates, so that it rapidly transformed into fallen space junk. When his other classmates enrolled in driver's ed, Liam preferred a nondescript elective called Civic Responsibility, a selection his mother found bleakly comic in retrospect. He still didn't have a license. Indeed, so little command of an automobile did he enjoy that in the midst of some theoretical metropolitan emergency, of which, say, his poor parents were early victims, while long lines of cars on I-85 fled a viral plague or hordes of flesh-eating zombies, she pictured him sitting inertly in the passenger's seat in their driveway and poking at the radio.

He couldn't cook. He couldn't sew on a button or work the washing machine. Not that she hadn't taught him these things, or tried. Is a lesson taught if it doesn't take? No matter how many times she demonstrated which point on the dial corresponded with a load of whites—for heaven's sake, it said WHITES—and which button started the cycle, he would amble upstairs the next time and ask to be instructed again. Or he'd select the wrong setting for colors and ruin the load. Ineptitude of this magnitude required a genius. But calling incompetence a gambit didn't change the fact that it worked.

"I feel a little had, frankly," she confessed to Court, finishing her mint tea. Meanwhile, on the news idealistic young lawyers were streaking to detention centers on the Texas border, eager to provide unaccompanied Central American minors help with negotiating the immigration system or locating distant relatives in Wichita. "When he was a kid-kid, I was more than glad to bake peach crumbles, buy his spiral notebooks, and get him vaccinated. But just because we're technically still his parents— well, I feel taken advantage of. He never lends a hand. He never vacuums or unloads the dishwasher or shops."

"Have you asked him?"

Harriet guffawed.

"I know you find his still living at home a little trying. But have you wondered why you want him out of here? He's an extra expense, but he doesn't cost us that much."

"We're on the cusp of entering a whole new chapter of our lives. Once we retire, it might be nice to, I don't know, travel."

"Nothing stops us from traveling. He's thirty-one. Leave him alone, and we're not going to be arrested by social services for neglect."

"Given his vast incapacities, we probably should be." She didn't want to travel.

"Do you not . . ." Court hazarded in a discomfited whisper, "like him?"

"No, it's not dislike . . . All that idleness is *oppressive*. It lowers the barometric pressure of the whole house. And there's not that much to like or dislike either way, is there?" She worried this formulation of awful neutrality definitely tilted toward dislike. She'd never wanted to be one of those tiresome embodiments of "maternal ambivalence."

"So what do you really want to change?" Court was a musing, mischievous man, and the sobriety was refreshing.

"I want to feel able to get him out of here," she determined. "I'd like a choice in the matter. Then, who knows? I might even be okay with his staying."

The soft, rasping paw on the door was a triumph of patient

coaching—Liam's lifelong impulse was to barge into his parents' bedroom unannounced—but he didn't wait to be invited before popping his head in. His face was broad and bland, like a parking lot. "That raspberry crumb coffee cake is gone. And we're out of paper towels. I thought you'd want to know."

"But there were two extra-large rolls—" Harriet began.

"I spilled a soda."

"I've asked you, please don't use yards and yards of that pricey reinforced double-ply on the floor. There's that big sponge under the sink." Liam wasn't an idiot. Imagining that her son would comply with this request if she issued it twenty-five times after he'd ignored it for twenty-four made Harriet the idiot.

In his usual summer uniform of T-shirt and boxers, his flat feet bare and spreading like melting ice cream on the wooden parquet, Liam continued to stand in the doorway, being. It was his habit. One of the many responsibilities he shirked was keeping up his end of conversation. He seemed to regard the sheer fact of himself as both comment and reply. While never having been talkative, he was possessed of a weighty presence, and this sense of mass was literal only in part. Sure, he got no exercise and was on the heavy side, but becoming outright obese would have required ambition on a scale beyond him. He forever exuded the baffled, slightly dazed, not unpleasantly surprised quality of having just been transported to another universe, and of still being unsure of how things in the seventh dimension were done. *Try this*, Harriet thought: *In the seventh dimension, we use a sponge.*

"Well," Harriet said, after an amount of time in which normal people could have done twenty sit-ups or made a cup of instant coffee. "Good night."

Liam was socially awkward in a way that he didn't appear to experience as awkwardness. Liam felt fine. He made other people feel awkward. "Right," he said at last, floating back down the hall, and failing to close the door behind him.

Harriet heaved from the bed and closed the door. "We've got to talk to him."

Court reminded his wife, "We have talked to him."

THERE HAD INDEED been much earnest discussion about Liam's occupational future. Environmental campaigning? Maybe Liam could get experience by volunteering for a lobbying organization at the state legislature. Or the hospitality trade, did that appeal? Because Atlanta's tourism industry did nothing but expand, and entry-level hotel jobs required minimal qualifications, maybe . . . But his parents did most of the talking, and they might as well have been speculating about the fate of a television character in a series slated to be canceled. "He's just not an aspiring kind of guy," his father had recently reasoned out of their firstborn's earshot. "You can't change his nature."

"He could *become* the kind of young man who aspires to something, if he wanted to," Harriet insisted.

"I think that's called *assuming the conclusion*," Court said. "The whole problem is not wanting to want to."

Liam had been diagnosed in the days before everyone routinely put an *H* between the *AD* and *D*, but Ritalin, then Adderall, had only ensured that he did the bare minimum in class a little faster. Because over half of his schoolmates were on the same prescriptions, in a relativistic sense the medications simply maintained what often seemed a carefully calibrated position in the academic pack: not at the very back, but behind the middle—a location that, naturally, attracted the least attention. For if Liam was guilty of nursing a single objective, it was to be left alone. When as a young mother Harriet had dutifully grubbed onto the floor to play with her son, her participation proved an intrusion. He preferred solitary pursuits, of a maximally purposeless variety—filling a cup with pebbles, emptying it out, and filling it up again. She sometimes wondered, when this proclivity for a veritably Buddhist circularity persisted into adolescence, whether he lived on an elevated metaphysical plane, having an inborn sense that this earthly life is chaff, that seeking is only for its own sake, that all grasping after satisfaction is fated to end only in more fruitless, gnawing desire. His affect into adulthood grew only airier. His smooth, pleasant face could entertain such a lofty, pityingly scornful smile that she worried it might someday earn him a sock in the jaw.

Yet when he did venture from the house, he somehow provoked something else entirely. Harriet couldn't imagine his being perceived as a catch—his body was soft from inactivity, his features engendering the same behind-the-middle position in the comeliness stakes that his schoolwork had achieved in the educational one—so it must have been that very aura of knowingness, of finding everything faintly amusing though in what way he wasn't about to say, of having mastered a mystery whose solution had been withheld from the multitudes, that explained why Liam had more than once pulled in a stunning girlfriend who would appear to be out of his league. He had something they wanted, or he seemed to have something they wanted, which being indistinguishable from genuine enlightenment was equally enticing—for what they wanted, what all young women most wanted whether or not they knew so consciously, was not to want. To be spared the ceaseless tyranny of yearning, to escape their own desire to please. To stop giving blow jobs because they didn't like the taste and to be able to say so. To be replete. For that was what Liam Friel-Garson gave off in spades: repleteness.

Other words for *replete* were less complimentary: smug, self-satisfied, and static.

In her own youth, Harriet wasn't precisely driven. A better word was *directed*. Neither she nor Court could quite claim to be a child of the sixties, which in her teenage years had made her feel cheated, but which she understood by college to have been a narrow miss in her favor. Beyond the few issues of consequence like civil rights and the war, the whole *Laugh-In* la-di-da had been a commercial contrivance to sell beads and flares. She'd also been spared so much retroactive mortification, like the photos of her older sister Eileen in body paint shooting peace signs. Young people in that era thought they were so original and special, and it never occurred to Eileen and her friends that in that case *why did they all look identical?* The cohort that came of age in the late 1970s was more practical, spurning the overobvious attractions of the creative professions for achievable career choices that were solid second bests. So Harriet had majored in arts *administration*. The trouble with this strategy was that aiming for second best often meant attaining third best—at best. Harriet's having finally worked her way *up* to booking talent for the Woodruff Arts Center was a miracle.

Though she'd never blame him outright, her husband's underactive sense of agency might have borne some genetic responsibility for their son's full-blown inertia. For privately she regarded Court as a specimen: the type who just out of college takes an acceptable job with acceptable pay, because it's there, because it will do, and because it seems a respectable placeholder for surveying an array of beckoning better options. As time lolls infinitely up ahead, promotion ensues. The pay improves. Until suddenly our hero is old enough to have looked up his pending Social Security payments online, and he's still managing the bookstore in Ansley Mall. Lo, though he has a degree in journalism from Georgia State, apparently he "decided" to be a bookstore manager when he grew up. This process of expedience sliding to what, for mortals, passes for permanence recalled that weary aphorism about life and other plans, and the pattern was far more standard than fixing on a goal and getting there. Court was cheerfully resigned, though his work put only a thin intellectual gloss on removing cuboids from boxes. The Local Bookie was now sponsoring events to counter online sales, and congenial jawing with visiting writers helped compensate for the fact that only five people showed up. Independent bookstores had achieved the same edgy, right-on quality of Eileen's peace rallies, which made running in the red feel a cut above ordinary bankruptcy.

Court was a boyish, toss-a-baseball-in-the-street type of guy, sexy in his day, still sexy in his way. Maybe it was the cowlick, or an innocuous touch of the prankster that one associates with about age ten, but others always mistook him for younger. Of the two, he was the laissez-faire parent, and while she was reluctant to label him passive, he was too amenable. Were it up to her husband, Court would have granted their son the rather exalted-sounding status that her expatriated college roommate had finally won in Britain: *indefinite leave to remain.*

But turning fifty-nine in March had hit Harriet with an unexpected starkness. She'd always been a rounder-up in relation to birthdays, and no sooner turned one age than readied herself for the next. Effectively, she was as good as sixty. Much media verbiage serviced the notion that sixty was the new middle age, but Harriet rejected this view on arithmetic grounds; she wouldn't live to 120.

She accepted that her job had its funky side, but of all the work in the world she wouldn't have dreamed as a girl of casting about Peachtree Center for a black silk robe for a prima donna hip-hop star's dressing room. She didn't mind having ended up in Atlanta, a vigorous, mixed city with terrible traffic that sometimes didn't even seem part of the South—but she wasn't confident that she had chosen it rather than come by it, as Court had come by Ansley Mall. Much like her husband's, the course of her own life exhibited a deficit of intention, and she was running out of time to intend. Granted, in physics "what happens when a stoppable force meets an immovable object?" didn't pose much of a paradox. She still refused to simply submit to the fact that Liam would be lumped downstairs till the day she died.

BEFORE MAKING A frontal assault, Harriet slipped behind enemy lines to lure a defector.

A force of nature in her latter twenties, buxom and bright in every sense, for going on two years Jocanda had made free with the house on Wildwood Place, to Harriet's delight. She had a swooshing physical presence and a booming, anarchic laugh. The girl gleaned the funniest cat videos from YouTube and the wisest home remedies from her mother, whose advice to treat discolorations on beech wood with lemon juice had recently rescued Harriet's blotched butcher-block kitchen island. As for her being African American, Harriet was very proud of her son's racial open-mindedness, but had never figured out a way of telling him so, since to commend his choice of girlfriend on this basis sounded closed-minded.

Yet the young woman's CV was disconcerting. She had qualified as a veterinary technician—something short of the full medical whack, the very sort of *achievable, solid second-best career choice* that Harriet could only applaud. Jocanda was a sophisticate in so many respects. She wore flowing, monochromatic garb made of draping, upscale synthetics, in that orchard of subtle colors in-between the primaries, like *tangerine* and *plum*. She preferred *Django Unchained* to *Twelve Years a Slave*, and could elucidate with great eloquence why the swashbuckling revenge fantasy was actually more empowering to her community than another sobering epic of abuse. Enthusiasm for Obama didn't blind her to the dubiety of his extrajudicial drone killings in Pakistan. Still, this intelligent woman conceded cheerfully that she'd never researched the availability of employment in the veterinary field before applying to Gwinnett Tech. Jocanda was part-timing at Staples.

Yet Liam's girlfriend did have mighty powers. Although she was forever snitching incremental wedges of Harriet's freshly baked rhubarb cream pie until she consumed two or three slices in the guise of a taste, ferrying away Harriet's dinner leftovers and never returning the snaplock containers, and availing herself of Harriet's washing machine, often running a whole load to launder one wraparound and a pair of leggings, Harriet lived in terror of escaping the girl's good graces, and fell all over herself to be ingratiating. Still officially living with her divorced mother in South DeKalb, Jocanda stayed over only about four nights a week; on the nights she was gone, the feeling upstairs went dumpy and stale, and Harriet would old-lady the evening away mending, watching improving documentaries, and filing clipped recipes. Atmospherically, that girl pumped up the Friel-Garsons' home to a near-bursting beach ball, and sucked the air out with her when she left.

Alas, the who-curried-whose-favor dynamic put Harriet at a manipulative disadvantage. One evening when earphones safely tethered

Liam to his computer in the den, she dangled a timorous question to Jocanda in the living room: "Don't you and Liam ever wish it was just you two, you know, in your own place?"

"Not really," Jocanda said, stretching her shapely bare feet onto the coffee table. The single cornrow spiraling from around her crown to below her ears was mesmerizing, and reminded Harriet of *The Twilight Zone*. "Raised with three brothers, you get used to bumping into folks in the hall. And you and Court make me feel real welcome, don't you worry about that."

"But you must sometimes want to be able to have a screaming match, and not worry about being overheard?"

Jocanda tilted her head. "Liam and me don't have screaming matches. You and Court at odds over something? Sounds like projection to me!" Languidly, Jocanda scratched the family tabby, Fluffernutter, who acted every bit as smitten with Liam's girlfriend as Harriet was. "As for whatever else you might *overhear* from upstairs," she said, eyes aglitter. "It's kind of a turn-on, if you want to know the truth."

Having long before owned sex with the same possessive sense of discovery that every generation did, Harriet refused to be embarrassed. "I realize there are only so many openings at veterinary practices, and you have to be patient. But Liam—I mean, he has so many gifts—it does seem as if maybe it's about time that he, well, *did something* with his life. And I was thinking—he's not going to listen to his mother—but I'm sure he'd listen to you."

Dismissing the cat in a gesture of getting down to serious human business, Jocanda reared back, while eyeing her hostess through the roseate glow of her Negroni—a cocktail whose name made Harriet anxious. "This whole idea of 'doing something' with your life, it's wrong-headed. Ask Liam—you maybe don't realize, but your son, he's into some profound shit. You *are* your life. It's not outside you. You can't 'do something with it' like a toaster on a table. Liam already *is*, know what I'm saying? He don't need to *become* nothing. This whole *goal* thing, keeping your head in the future, it's where most folks get all, like, subdivided. Like, some big part of them's off in a time and place that don't even exist and may never exist, 'stead of right here and right now." Harriet was reluctant to call the downtown touches in Jocanda's speech an affectation. Still, the girl had been raised in an affluent suburban black neighborhood in Sandy Springs that Harriet and Court could never afford.

"Ah, don't you think, maybe Liam could still be present in the way that I think you mean and still get a job?"

But Jocanda was on a roll. "Whole country always waiting, and planning, and striving, and educating, trying to 'get somewhere' or 'get ahead' so they don't notice where they already at. That's what don't wash about the 'American dream'—that it's a *dream*. Like all them wiggly screens in old movies. Liam and me, we *awake*. Liam and me, we happy as clambakes, right here and right now. We're not itching to *head* or *get* or *become*, and that's the whole secret, the whole ball of wax, know what I'm saying?"

"Well, I'm awfully glad to hear you're so contented with each other!" Harriet declared.

"*Contented?* Honey, we blast-into-the-stratosphere, off our butts with bliss!" She rattled her ice. "Now, what say we go for a refill? Double up that bliss." Jocanda's teeth shone, while Harriet grinned with her mouth closed, self-conscious about how yellowed her smile had grown, here on the threshold of sixty.

IF THE MOUNTAIN'S girlfriend wouldn't come to Mohammed, then Mohammed would go to the mountain—although any proverb with *Mohammed* in it made Harriet anxious, too.

Hands flat on the kitchen table later the same week, she announced, "We really think it's time for you to find a job and move out."

Liam's head bobbed. "I can see how you might think so. But I'm not trying to hear that."

"What's 'I'm not trying to hear that' supposed to mean?" Jocanda had a late shift at Staples, and Harriet was feeling forceful.

"Hon, don't ride him too hard," Court said. "We're just exploring possibilities."

"In allowing you to stay here for the foreseeable future, we're being lousy parents. It's child abuse."

"That's nice of you to worry," Liam said politely. "But I'll be all right. Kids sticking around—it's a thing."

"He's right about that," Court contributed unhelpfully. "It is a thing."

"Well, I'm hugely sympathetic with the likes of the Sawyers," Harriet allowed. "You know their daughter Julia—she got a master's from Duke, and now she's back home trying to pay off a quarter of a million bucks in student loan debt. Lucy says they're having to get her treated for depression. But your loans are a fraction of that, and we've *almost* paid them off." Harriet was privately convinced that Liam's brief infatuation with a degree in court reporting hailed directly from his watching too much *Law & Order*.

"I do wish you'd let that go," Liam said pleasantly. "It was the stenography. They decided I must be dyslexic."

"Voice recognition software will eliminate those positions anyway," Court said. "Liam dodged a bullet, in my view."

"But don't you want to have a career, raise a family? Make the world a better place?"

"That whole, you know—it's not my bag." Liam continued to sound affable. From childhood, he'd lacked the shame gene. If a parent went nuclear with, "I'm so disappointed in you" regarding his substandard grades—and by the time Liam was in school, to get anything less than a B you really had to go out of your way—he took in the assertion congenially as a point of information. Corporal punishment was out; using food as reward or chastisement was said to foster eating disorders; "grounding" was meaningless when there was nowhere their son especially wanted to go. So Liam's immunity to their displeasure had reduced disciplinary options to zero.

"Well, what is your *bag*?" Harriet charged.

"Manhole covers," Liam said promptly.

Not that this was news. Liam spent hours per day on ManHole .com—an address that initially moved his mother to assure him that they'd have no problem with his being gay. But no, it was a website for enthusiasts of manhole covers. They traded photographs of different designs, scans of pencil rubbings, anecdotes about sewer-gas explosions, and stories of car-axle breakages when metal thieves stealing the big iron discs left the cavity agape. Obsessed with a cramped urban version of *Journey to the Center of the Earth*, hole spotters with more catholic interests explored a sideline in municipal drains, debating parallel versus perpendicular gutter grates, while one pull-down menu listed big digs, roadworks, and water pipe replacements. The very arbitrariness of the absorption was clearly its attraction: more filling a cup with pebbles and dumping them out again. Harriet would have liked to infer from her son's fascination with substructure a metaphorical determination to eschew surface for deeper substance, to get to the bottom of things, to master underlying patterns and derive the gist, but she couldn't help but associate holes in the ground with pet burials and sandboxes.

"I'm not sure we're going to be able to exploit that. But what if we told you," Harriet veered, "that we're thinking of offering your room to a Central American refugee?"

Court looked alarmed. They hadn't discussed this.

"Why take in one refugee," Liam said smoothly, "only to create another?"

"You'd hardly be on a par with someone fleeing violence and hardship. You've had all the advantages. A nice home, clothes, plenty to eat—"

"So as punishment for these *advantages*," Liam said, "I have to give them up. Though I'd at least be fleeing persecution, if this discussion is anything to go by."

"Buddy boy," Court said, "we sure don't mean to twist any screws—"

Liam stood up; they were dismissed. "It seems crazy to pay for a whole other pad when there's a bedroom downstairs. You always go on about carbon footprints. Well, I use fewer resources this way, too. Unless you don't *like* having me here?"

"Of course we do!" Court said. "We love having you here! Don't we, pumpkin?"

SO MUCH FOR the talking to.

Applying the new political fashion for the "nudge," phase two involved an unnerving outlay of cash. But Harriet argued that presenting Liam with a fait accompli would introduce him to the thrills of autonomy—to which he would become sufficiently accustomed that the prospect of living with parents in one's thirties might reachieve the stigma it had apparently lost. So the couple sought out a one-bedroom apartment that listed for $1,250/month in the rapidly revitalizing Intown neighborhood of Old Fourth Ward. They put down the deposit and prepaid two months' rent.

They presented the plan to Liam with a giddy gaiety that may have bordered on hysteria: The two months' free ride should give Liam time to find work, so that by the third he could pay the rent himself. They promised him a stipend for the transitional period, and help in locating job openings. MARTA having crabbed in all directions from the center of town, lack of a driver's license shouldn't pose a problem, so long as he avoided delivery work. They would admire his determination, Harriet emphasized, even if he started at a rudimentary job like minding a cash register—although historically Liam had proven as indifferent to parental approval as he had to their disappointment. Throughout this presentation, he continued to forge his way through a carton of fudge nut ripple, pausing only to dig out and lick clean the almonds, which he preferred to eat plain.

"It's a cute place!" Harriet enthused. "With a balcony. You're not far from the Carter Library, and the trail through Freedom Park. O4W is becoming really hip, you know, and super integrated."

"You mean I'd be displacing an African American," Liam said, scraping the last of the ice cream.

Harriet blushed. There was truth to the charge. "Blacks and whites living side by side immeasurably improves the social health of this city."

That smile again, the one that could get him decked someday, and pretty soon Harriet could be volunteering to do the honors herself. "You should consider becoming a flack for one of those big developers. You've got the knack."

His parents spent the following weekend scouring thrift shops and yard sales for secondhand furniture. Liam went amicably along for the ride, but claimed to have hurt his back doing a manhole cover rubbing on North Rock Springs Road, and let them load the serviceable single bed frame, fold-up table, and upright caned chairs into their VW wagon with the same vicarious engagement with which Norwegian television viewers were said to have watched the stoking of a woodstove on camera for hours on end. The apartment was a one-floor walk-up, and as his aging progenitors struggled to lift a sofa over the banister, Liam provided helpful pointers from below.

Harriet set up the new router that came with the Comcast one-year contract—though the password she picked, *Liberty4ME!*, did raise the question of liberty for whom exactly—folded clean clothes into his dresser, and packed the refrigerator with a generous Kroger shop that included more fudge nut ripple. She made up the bed with worn sheets from home, though the pillows were new, while Court registered for a free two-week trial subscription to Netflix on Liam's laptop. She unpackaged a new toothbrush, popping it in one of the *Family Guy* glasses from the yard sale on Windemere Drive, and stacked the cabinets with the set of floral stoneware—on the ugly side, but with one plate chipped and a dessert plate missing, the as-is dinnerware had been a steal for six bucks.

Struggling to equalize the bedroom blind, Harriet remembered kitting out her own first digs. When you got older and more financially capable of devising domestic space in keeping with your tastes, your very agency gave rise to dissatisfaction—leading couples their age to continually make over kitchens, build new extensions, and tear down walls. Because the real inadequacy was one of imagination, the wealthier you became, the more utterly you erected a monument to your own limitations.

Yet in her youth the simplest making do had been exhilarating. Back then, chance acquisitions worked accidental magic, coming together in a way that never would have fallen into place by design. Odds and ends of crockery had complemented one another with slant juxtaposition, like the parts of a Schoenberg quartet. A fake-Victorian blue-and-white dinner plate would strike chords with a parti-colored polka-dotted soup bowl and hit serendipitous harmonics.

After Harriet graduated from Emory and was outfitting her first apartment in Little Five Points ("Little Five" if you were with it), her parents had driven out from Bellingham to help, making a vacation of the project and stopping to see Eileen in Kansas City en route. Harriet had felt both comforted and crowded. True, the gifts of small furniture and used housewares were a welcome economy, and her father had used a tape measure to hang the Cars and Steely Dan posters at the same height. She'd scrounged through her mother's boxes of family castoffs for the red-fringed tablecloth she'd grown up with, printed with tiny dustpans, brooms, and 1950s fridges. Yet she'd been desperate to be left to her own devices, and didn't really want to be taken out to eat in the Old Spaghetti Factory in Underground Atlanta, but ached to prepare her own meals in her own kitchen, whatever and whenever she liked. When her parents finally cleared off, she cranked up *Can't Buy a Thrill* to dance in celebration at two a.m., until the resident of the apartment below furiously pounded his ceiling.

For all that glorious self-sufficiency there would be a price to pay, of course, one steeper than the ire of a neighbor who felt excluded from all the fun: nights when the bottom fell out for no reason, and freedom converted to ordinary loneliness, hollow and dragging; on certain Gethsemanes, the loneliness descended to desolation. But you only realized later that it was supposed to be that way—that the very precariousness of young adulthood was what made it so heady—that balancing on the edge of a sheer drop conveyed heroism to mere standing up. To this day, the pop tunes of that era, like "Baker Street," filled her with a soaring sense of possibility that none of the highbrow symphonies at Woodruff could stir.

Thus in Liam's place, she'd have been twirling with delight that the teal sofa from Goodwill fit perfectly beneath the bay window—the while chafing for her parents to go. Liam, however, stood in the middle of the main room, equidistant from every object as if to express a perfect lack of attachment to each foreign appointment. As he had when lost at Six Flags at nine, their son didn't look frightened or unsettled, but he did seem to be waiting, less for his parents to leave, which they were preparing to momentarily, than for his parents to come back.

"But what will I do for dinner?" he asked.

"There's the makings for ham sandwiches, or a burger," Harriet said. "I left you some chicken, sweet peppers. You could try a stir-fry . . ." She could as well have told him that he could also order Chinese from a takeout place on the moon.

In the end, they stayed and christened his new apartment with a meal she whipped up herself, a useful exercise. He also needed a serving spoon, a vegetable peeler, and a mixing bowl.

ON THE PRETEXT of getting help choosing job openings on Craigslist, Liam returned the next day for lunch. Once back from Ansley Mall, Court helped him go at it until after seven, at which point it was easy enough to put out a third plate for the bolognese. By the following week, Harriet was stricken with Provender Pity. The sliced ham in Liam's fridge would be acquiring a fetid slick, the chicken would be toxic, the ground beef oxidized. Oh, their son returned to his apartment to sleep, but Court often broke down and gave him a ride. They were paying $1,250/month to outsource a mattress. Thus far having eliminated the perk but not the problem, she missed Jocanda.

The job search was more pebbles and cups, and Harriet grew alarmed when Liam started to enjoy it. Given his appetite for numbing circularity, that meant the process never threatened to end anywhere other than where it began. It seemed the interviewer at the Four Seasons had commented that his applicant "didn't really seem to *want* the job" of receptionist at the plush downtown hotel, and their son had then credited the man with being "keenly observant." What was she supposed to do, come with him?

The third month, they piled Liam's furniture at the back of the carport, after which the VW wagon would no longer quite fit under its roof. Once the war of independence was battled in reverse, the fact that Liam had lent a hand in packing up the floral stoneware, the worn sheets, the charming print tablecloth from Harriet's childhood, and his brand-new mixing bowl was purely discouraging. It was at least gracious of the landlord to let them break the lease without penalty. He was sympathetic, he said. His brother in Saint Louis had four grown kids, and in short order after college every single one of them had come back home.

It was winter now, and their firstborn had turned thirty-two.

BY SPRING, HARRIET was crazed. Fundamentally, the predicament was zoological. Like the time a badger had gotten into the toolshed and simply skulked farther back by the rakes the more they shouted at it. A large animal had invaded her territory, and it would not scare out. But you couldn't put an apple in a cage in the backyard and wait for your son to trip the latch.

Alicia stopped by in May. It pained Harriet that her daughter seemed to pay these biannual visits—too evenly spaced, the way one schedules dental check-ups—in the same spirit of fatalistic obligation in which Harriet had visited her own parents. So she knew the drill. Having shown up on the early side, Alicia would pick at her dinner, though she'd always been a night owl with a creditable appetite; her *real* evening would commence once she fled. Yet they'd tried to be companionable parents—broad-minded, unrestrictive, and nonjudgmental to such a degree that, in relation to Liam anyway, admonition had built up in Harriet's system like mercury poisoning. Did nothing ever change? Didn't anyone *like* their parents and look forward to seeing them? Or did all grown children shoot surreptitious glances at their father's watch, gauging whether they'd served enough of their sentence that they might get time off for good behavior?

At twenty-six, Alicia possessed a knowing sourness that Harriet recognized. It was a weak disguise of knowing absolutely nothing and having unrealistically high expectations of everything and everybody. Harriet had imagined herself a cynic at that age as well, until she chanced across snapshots of her own postgraduate years in the 1980s: big-eyed, soft-lipped, the facial expressions perfectly undefended—a beautiful idiot. In oversize black jeans and a boxy, mannish sports jacket, Alicia did her damnedest to disguise how pretty she was. Harriet had lost track of whether her daughter was currently "gender queer" or "gender nonconforming"; having looked up both terms online, she still couldn't have told you the difference with a gun to her head. When Harriet was growing up, women were trying to immolate gender stereotypes. These days, you preserved the stereotype, the better not to correspond to it. She wasn't sure what the difference was there, either, but with Alicia she wasn't looking for a fight.

Mother and daughter had a brief window on their own, since Court had been making an effort to share Liam's fascination with manhole covers, and the two men had launched into Druid Hills to track down a retro design.

"Any progress on finding Little Liam another tree house?" Alicia asked, sipping rosé on the back patio.

"Your brother doesn't seem very interested in making his own way in the world," Harriet said.

"Why should he be? He's got everything he needs here. I've half a mind to move back home myself. Jack, you remember her—she's back with the folks, saving to buy her own place. She'll have enough for a down payment, too, by the time she's fifty-five."

"I realize that property prices for your generation—"

"Oh, screw it. I don't want a house. But these *parasaito shinguru* who waitress at Tap—"

Harriet frowned.

Alicia translated, "'Parasite singles.' Common parlance around here now, but the Japanese coined it, so they've obviously got the same thing-that-wouldn't-leave problem in Tokyo. The waitstaff who live with their parents—you have to be super nice to them, because if you so much as say *boo* they'll quit in the middle of their shift. No rent to pay—nothing to lose. Their tips and wages are just especially generous forms of an allowance. So they go out all the time, and wear shit-hot gear, and always have the latest iPhone. I still have a *five*."

"You have what money can't buy: self-respect. And that's why you don't really want your old room back."

Alicia chuckled. "I made you nervous. Admit it."

"It's our home gym now, as you know very well. I'd have nowhere else to put the StairMaster."

"You could put it in the utility room."

"I can't stand that thing without TV!"

"See? You are. You're nervous."

"What am I supposed to do about your brother?" Harriet lamented.

Alicia shrugged. "Kick him out. Get all Darwinian on his ass."

"We can't throw our own son on the street. You know, home is where they'll always take you in and all."

"I never knew you were such a sucker for poetry."

"He's not able to take care of himself, and you know it, sweetie."

"He was useless in school because he could get away with being useless, and he's useless here for the same reason. He's not mentally challenged, he's fucking smart, and he knows exactly what he's doing. Meanwhile, you've disabled his survival instinct. It's like, unplugged. Or at least rerouted. He can survive here; he's got that sorted. But force him to survive somewhere else, and my money says he won't end up in the morgue."

"Alicia!"

"All I know is it's not fair. You cover all his expenses, and I cover all of mine. You're paying off his student loans, and I'm paying off my own loans. He gets meat and two veg every night, and I'm living on pot noodles. Useless pays. He makes me feel like a sucker."

"But honey, standing on your own two feet—it's so much more admirable!"

"I don't need your admiration. I need more *money*."

"What I don't understand is—what does Liam expect to happen, in due course? We're getting older. Life doesn't stand still."

"You and Dad will get feeble and dotty and move into an assisted-living facility and eventually a nursing home. Beforehand, because Liam knows you're planners, way in advance of Medicaid's 'look-back period' you'll have steadily transferred any remaining assets, and finally this house, into Liam's name. Once you're down to two grand in cash, at least on paper, you'll qualify for Medicaid—though he tells me that you can still keep one car. This way the government will pick up the tab for your long-term care, so some larcenous geriatric outfit won't eat up your savings. Voilà. Liam stays in his room. If, over time, the assets dwindle, he can sell the house and downsize."

Harriet was stunned. "I can't imagine our Liam figuring all that out."

"Then you don't know him very well."

"I think that's the sort of thing that as a loyal sister you're not supposed to be telling me." Alicia had been a terrible tattletale as a girl.

"*Loyal sister* was invited in on the deal. He said I could move in, too, once you're addled. Though I think he just likes the idea of keeping someone on hand who can drive."

Court and Liam returned, rubbing proudly in tow. While Harriet rustled up tacos, the other three lounged at the kitchen table, with CNN yammering behind them. This summer the Central Americans had been eclipsed by the European refugee crisis. To the left of Alicia's head, discarded orange life jackets littered a Greek beach. Many of the life jackets, Anderson Cooper explained, were defective.

"If you actually look at who's in those boats," Liam said, pointing at another rescue at sea, "tons of them aren't from Syria. They're from Africa. Like, it's kind of obvious, if you get my drift. You don't exactly have to check their passports."

"So?" Alicia said.

"So they're not running away from a war. They just want the good life." For Liam, this was unusual engagement with the news. Ever since Harriet's mumble about perhaps replacing him with a waif from Honduras, he'd felt competitive with the wretched refuse of anyone's teeming shore.

"You of all people," Alicia said, "are incensed by *economic opportunism?*"

Even his sister had trouble ruffling her brother's feathers. "All of Africa and the Middle East can't move to Germany," he said mildly. "It'll get crowded, and the Germans will get sick of them. They should stay home."

"You'd know about that," Alicia clipped.

Chopping green peppers, Harriet wondered whether recipients of charity were naturally suspicious of other recipients of charity; for Liam, that had been an impassioned speech. Clearly, he resented the genuinely desperate and dispossessed for making him seem capable and prosperous in comparison.

Weakness was a weapon, and a fiendishly effective one. Harriet increasingly experienced their son's poor education, domestic ineptitude, off-kilter social skills, and broad unemployability as a form of blackmail. Yet this brand of extortion—*I have thrown myself on your mercy; if you don't take care of me, I will make you look like a monster*—depended on physical presence. The moment those poor migrants set one foot on Greek sand they ceased to be an African or Syrian problem and transformed into a European one. The temptation to pole those populous dinghies from the shore must have been stupendous, although with the cameras rolling no one on Lesbos wanted to look that callous—or, to give the good Greek people more credit still, they didn't want to *be* that callous. Yet surely you were a bit of a patsy to allow your own finest qualities to be used against you: your sympathy with the *vulnerable*, as anyone who drew a short stick of any description was now labeled incessantly; your self-consciousness about your own privilege; your sense of responsibility for the defenseless; your decency, your kindness, your generosity. Okay, but if weakness conferred power, Harriet realized joyously, so did being an asshole.

IT HAD TAKEN days of cajoling to get Liam to join an expedition in sewer spelunking sponsored by his buddies on ManHole.com, the better for their son to be out of the house a whole Saturday. Harriet sneak-thiefed downstairs, come to ransack her own home. In big plastic containers allegedly purchased as protection for sweaters, she folded her son's shirts in neat stacks, filling empty crevices with rolled boxers and bunches of socks. The exercise might have recalled packing Liam's bags for summer camp, except that Liam had never cared to go to camp. The books were few; he wasn't a big reader.

Helping lug the containers up to the foyer, Court plunked the first on the floor in befuddlement. "But what are we going to do with this stuff?"

"Once it's on the other side of that front door," she said, dragging the box labeled JEANS/SLACKS over the threshold, "the only question is what Liam's going to do with it."

Court was queasy about the scheme, which his wife had sold as "a sociological experiment." The locksmith arrived at noon.

By the time a fellow hole spotter dropped Liam back home at six p.m., the front yard was stacked with their son's belongings, the containers secured with a tarp in case of thunderstorms. Huddled at the kitchen table clutching glasses of the wine they'd largely forgone for years—if they kept it in the house, Liam drank it all—Harriet and Court heard the key crunch into the side-door lock and then *snick-snick* when it wouldn't turn. "Mom?" Typically, the call was indolent, untroubled. Then the same soft mauling that often afflicted their bedroom door, a soughing sound that brought to mind "The Monkey's Paw." "Something's wrong with the lock."

"There's nothing wrong with the lock." Harriet's voice had gone squeaky. "This motel has no vacancies. No room at the inn. I'm afraid you're on your own."

He might have inferred the futility of the circuit, but Liam still went through the theater of shuffling to the front door, to the patio sliding door, and to the separate back entrance to his own former warren downstairs, the better to underscore how much bother his own parents had gone to in order to batten down the hatches against their only son. Listening to the old house keys jam each time made Harriet feel trapped, as if she hadn't locked her boy out but herself inside. In a horror movie, they'd be goners.

"This is awful," Court mumbled. "I'm not going to be able to hold out."

"You will hold out, and so will I. This is the hard part. We just have to keep our nerve, and not go soft and gooey."

"You know what a customer at the Bookie called stay-at-home adults? *Failed fledglings*. But what happens when you push a little bird from the nest, and it still can't fly? It's not a pretty picture."

"Liam's not a little bird. We've come this far. And I'm scientifically curious what he's going to do."

For the time being, what Liam did was return to the side door and stand there. He didn't keep pawing, and he didn't beg. But the silhouette of his blunt, impassive form lurked behind the thin curtains, like a paper target at a shooting range. The reproachful shadow would be able to discern them more clearly in the light of the overhead, merrily preparing a meal that their son wasn't invited to join, toasting the abandonment of their firstborn with a feisty Pinot Gris. At length, Harriet grew so uncomfortable that she corked the bottle and took their plates down the hall, barricading themselves in the bedroom on the queen-size mattress just as they'd hidden out when Liam was still home.

Jocanda had apologized that her mother didn't exactly welcome a white boyfriend, which was why she and Liam always spent the night together over here. So Harriet had rather assumed that her ousted son would end up bunking with Alicia. It was more unfairness, dumping the girl's brother in her lap, but Harriet was sure that Alicia's hardworking roommates would refuse to carry a slacker for more than a few days. Then Darwin would work his magic.

Yet the next morning, their neighbor from across the street, Judy Leavenson, phoned as early as acceptable on a Sunday. "I knew it was getting bad downtown," she said. "But I'm a little surprised that it's spread to Morningside. Don't get me wrong, my heart goes out to the urban poor, but are y'all aware that there's a homeless person sleeping smack outside your front door?"

Harriet peeked through the den's venetian blinds. Sure enough, the plastic containers were stacked in a fort formation, inside of which the tarp was laid over the grass. She recognized the disordered swaddling around the motionless lump in the center as the light-blue sheets and thin-weave yellow blanket they'd provided Liam for his truncated stint in O4W, which he'd topped with the cherry-red, housewares-dotted tablecloth, whose vibrancy called attention to his dilemma. That Liam had ventured no farther than the front yard was dispiriting, but locating the box of linens still stashed beneath the carport displayed more resourcefulness than she'd seen him manifest in thirty-two years.

"That's a homeless person, all right," Harriet said. "It's Liam. We decided it was time he found alternative accommodation."

"Mercy me, Harriet, that's simply extraordinary!" The proclamation was studiously impartial. "You mean you've chucked that boy out?"

"We've suggested that our *young man* take responsibility for himself, yes."

"My dear," Court said in her ear. "Sorry to interrupt, but he's going to get hungry."

"Isn't that the *point*?" Harriet exclaimed, covering the receiver. She was flustered, if only because she'd been thinking the same thing.

"Isn't getting hungry the very essence of your survival instinct kicking in?"

Yet by the time she finished trying to explain to Judy their tough-love philosophy in terms that didn't make them seem like animals, a second peek through the blinds revealed a plate beside their stirring petitioner, with a freshly toasted bagel and cream cheese, drizzled with strawberry jam—just the way Liam liked it. Court wasn't cut out for this stuff.

Word of Liam's plight spread rapidly down the lane, and neighbors cleaved down the middle. To a portion of their peers, the pitiless Friel-Garsons lacked any normal nurturing impulse and had no appreciation for the daunting financial obstacles confronting young people today. To others, they were brave crusaders finally laying down the law to a coddled, work-shy generation that adults were obliged to put aside childish things, and that included their old bedrooms.

Harriet and Court's supporters were given to high fives and shoulder claps, but Liam's sympathizers were more proactive. Thus a large purple domed tent with nicely sealed seams, zippered half-moon entrance, and net windows for cross-ventilation was now pitched in their front yard. Other well-wishers obliged with a light sleeping bag and air bed—doubles, the better to allow for conjugal visits. Locally resident backers provided access to convenient bathrooms, so that Liam actually took more showers as a refugee than he had as an overstaying houseguest. Cases of soda and iced coolers of beer appeared, along with a coterie of his fellow spongers, who would linger into the summer evenings as the heat subsided, perching on Liam's plastic containers while playing catch-and-release with fireflies.

It took little more than a week for the banner to unfurl. Painted in purple letters to match the tent, PARENTHOOD HAS NO STATUTE OF LIMITATIONS stretched from a dowel driven beside the driveway to the trunk of the far magnolia. Chagrined, and anxious that their son might take advantage of an open door to push back inside, both parents took to coming and going by the back entrance, which meant scuttling through the hollow scold of Liam's old haunt. They skulked shiftily in and out of the car, like squatters keeping their heads down and uneasy about the arrival of police.

The supplicant on their lawn was unlikely to starve. To the contrary, the Friel-Garsons' trash cans began to fill up with discarded wax paper from deli sandwiches and Styrofoam containers sticky with barbecue sauce. Liam left emptied Pyrex casserole dishes by the mailbox for retrieval. There he also deposited bags of dirty laundry that vanished and rematerialized fresh and neatly folded, just as his clothes had miraculously rejuvenated themselves his whole life.

In attracting a flock of other *failed fledglings*, Liam had at last located his social milieu, as well as a sizable enough national constituency—highly motivated by fellow feeling and bald self-interest, eternally online, and chronically underoccupied—to keep their young man in short ribs and sides of coleslaw for some time to come. Harriet had never seen him so chatty and at ease around other people, many of whom appeared to revere him as a celebrity icon, though her son had never before evidenced what she'd call leadership qualities. One of his comrades in the cause—a core quintet had labeled itself proudly "The Freeloading Five"—produced a device for a Wi-Fi hotspot, the better to rally support farther afield. Donations from other bedroom barnacles poured into their website from as far away as Oregon and Maine. And who was the inspirational organizer of this fund-raising, as well as the primary publicist, the logistics mastermind, indeed, the chief strategist of the whole campaign? *Jocanda.*

Its environs increasingly trashed, like the site of a recently vacated flea market, the split-level on Wildwood Place also became subject to pickets, during which a contingent of millennials shuffled the sidewalk prodding smart phones while shouldering placards: SAFE SPACE IS A HUMAN RIGHT and PETER PAN RULES! Gawkers from other neighborhoods, along with some motorists with out-of-state plates, began rubbernecking slowly past their address in sufficient numbers that neighbors complained. The whole reason they'd moved to a cul-de-sac was to avoid this kind of traffic.

"I think we're losing the hearts and minds war," Court worried at dinner after they'd endured the notoriety for three weeks. It had hit them both as a particularly low blow that Fluffernutter had defected to the purple tent just that morning. "I wonder if we should install one of those Central Americans after all. Better for our rep than advertising that getting Liam's room back has made it possible to store bulk purchases from Costco."

"Central Americans are old hat this summer," Harriet said. "It would have to be a Syrian refugee."

"Not sure you can get one on Amazon. Maybe I could ask my cousin George to move in. He's got dark hair, and this time of year he'd have a tan."

Whimsy wasn't much help when the inevitable occurred: news teams descended from WSB-TV and Fox 5. As his parents peered around the carport, Liam held forth for the cameras with more lucidity than he'd ever employed at the dinner table, suggesting that perhaps his eviction would be the making of the man after all. Harriet couldn't discern the whole interview, but did catch snippets—about "the well-off's indifference to the plight of the less fortunate" and "the disenfranchised simply seeking a better life," phrases he had clearly lifted wholesale from the coverage of the European migration crisis, as well as despair of "intergenerational inequality" and "the sacrifice of affordable housing to the scourge of luxury condominiums."

Neither parent hungered for the limelight, but Harriet thought it vital that someone put the case for their side. So once a journalist again stalked toward the couple returning from work, she emerged onto the driveway. Having been conferring passionately with their supporters for the last month, she imagined that her arguments about young people only thriving from shouldering responsibility for themselves were in good order. But she hadn't counted on the pounding terror that hit the moment the furry mic lunged at her face like a rabid stuffed animal. "But I *liked* living . . . When I was that age . . ." she blithered. "Little Five. Plates. They didn't match, but they still went together."

The journalist had that thank-God-this-isn't-going-out-live look, and turned to Court. "What do you say to the charge some of your neighbors have made that throwing your own child out on the street is brutal and unfeeling?"

"I wouldn't call a springy zoysia lawn the same as the street," Court said defensively. "Besides, our son is always welcome in his own home."

The man appeared put out. Obviously, if what Court just said was true, this was a nonstory. "So you're officially inviting Mr. Friel-Garson to move back into the house? And this whole tent in the yard display is a stunt."

"My wife wanted to make a point. It wasn't my idea—all this commotion. Liam's a good boy. And he's wise beyond his years. Some young people—they're too sensitive for this world. Forcing the likes of Liam to work reception at some downtown hotel—well, it would be a terrible waste of human capital."

"*Our son is always welcome in his own home?*" Harriet quoted him back furiously once the news crews had packed up. "I sure don't call that having my back!"

"I'm sorry," Court said. "But I need to show you something." He pulled out the family tablet and brought up supportthefreeloadingfive .com (whose fund-raising counter now read $21,347.50), albeit only to locate a link. "See? There was this guy Brian Haw in London, who camped out on Parliament Square to protest British foreign policy or something. Iraq and stuff. Everybody brought him food. Know how long he lived in that tent, which was covered in artwork and buttons, banners and placards—a massive eyesore in the center of London, for thousands of Chinese tourists to trip over? The whole time, constantly shouting down a megaphone at members of Parliament trying to work across the street and driving them nuts? *Ten years.*"

"I can't imagine Liam having that kind of stamina."

"I think stamina is exactly what he's got," Court said, with a rare contrariness. "And if their site is linking to Brian Haw, we may not have awakened his survival instinct so much as his competitive one. I bet he'd like to set a record."

Harriet slumped at the kitchen table. She considered the indefinite plunking in their bedroom doorway, the inert keeping watch through the curtains when they first changed the locks, that improbable patience with cups filled, emptied, and filled again that went back to Liam's toddlerhood. Inadvertently, in ejecting the boy from downstairs, they had converted their son from deadbeat to dissenter. They'd allowed him to find his calling. "So you want us to cave."

"This Haw guy. They made documentaries about him. He ran for municipal office. He didn't win, but he did win in the big picture. He won every day he stayed camped on that square. Meanwhile, Parliament tried passing all kinds of laws to get rid of him, and they didn't work."

"What did work, then? Finally, after ten years?"

"He died of cancer."

"If we're going head-to-head on mortality," Harriet conceded, "I guess Liam's got the edge."

"Meanwhile, as far as most of the public is concerned, we look like jerks. We have a two-salary income and a full fridge and a four-bedroom empty nest that we don't want him to keep living in on principle. But what's the principle? That it's better for him, and the country at large, for young people to bootstrap themselves the way we did. But when we came of age, housing and education were cheaper. Adjusted for inflation, wages were higher. So the 'principle' really comes down to *we don't want him here.* Because it's our house, and we've done our bit, and our hospitality has been exhausted. Because, you know, *enough is enough already.* We can make that case all right, but it sounds mean spirited."

"Like, we don't have to take care of him, so we won't," Harriet recapitulated. "But does it matter, what other people think?"

"Theoretically, maybe not. Realistically—yeah, it probably does. And this is an impasse. Even if we stand firm and take the flak, what's the endgame? We don't have one."

* * *

THE BUNDLES OF paper towels and cases of tuna fish from Costco got stacked in the corner of the master bedroom. To reclaim the space, Harriet stopped abjuring her son not to waste whole rolls of Bounty on swabbing kitchen spills. Alicia found the O4W furniture under the carport a godsend when she established her own apartment. The round of dead grass from the tent never did grow back, and marked the front lawn forever after like a giant manhole cover. Jocanda got pregnant. If softened on the cracker boyfriend, her mother still had much less room in a luxury condo, so Jocanda moved into Wildwood Place once the little girl, Pebbles, was born; Germany had absorbed over a million migrants the previous year, in comparison with which taking in one mother and child couldn't even count as bighearted. It made sense for Harriet and Court to shift downstairs, allowing Liam and Jocanda to assume the master bedroom—right across from the erstwhile home gym, now redecorated as a nursery. They lugged the StairMaster to the utility room. In the fullness of time, naturally the couple retired, and into their seventies displayed early-warning forgetfulness. According to their lawyer, the protocol was standard. Medicaid's "look-back period" in Georgia was five years, so in order to keep from being penalized for transferring assets at under fair market value, advance planning was of the essence.

The Royal Male

THE FIRST TIME was occasioned by his bad knee. After onerously following the rise and fall of the coast, Gordon Bosky's postal route in Newquay veered inland and passed right by his own semidetached. The ache had been sharpish, so he pulled the trolley into his vestibule, fixed a cup of tea, and fell asleep. When he awoke it was too late to finish the delivery without drawing a torrent of complaints, and the following morning there would be yet more mail—too much to fit in the trolley without removing the undelivered tranche. So he loaded the orphaned post into a bin liner, which remained at the foot of the stairs for some time. Nobody noticed; the sun still rose in the sky.

Of course, his neighbors might have objected had their post ceased to arrive altogether. Thus with impressive psychological acuity and mathematical cunning, Gordon learned to calculate just how often a trolley full of envelopes and packets could go missing with no one the wiser. As for why? He was overworked and underpaid. The Royal Mail demanded that routes be completed far too double-quick for a man with a dodgy knee. From his own discerning perusals, the post these days was chock-full of such rubbish that his customers were well spared: a catalog flogging motorized salt cellars, or rebukes from the Revenue in brown envelopes so cheap and grim that you'd think it was still World War II.

But perhaps most of all because nary a soul ever posted an envelope to Gordon Bosky himself. It was hardly fair for the means by which a man earned his crust to rub it in on a daily basis that he was alone in this world. He'd originally shifted to Cornwall on the assumption that a holiday destination would be teeming with sex-starved widows and rich American divorcées. Instead, Newquay was overrun with lean, cliquish surfers who looked right through a fifty-five-year-old postman as if he were a jellyfish.

Thus as the bin liners burgeoned, Gordon came to look on his stash as his own sort of tax, or more kindly, a *tithe*. Since no more did beholden customers hand their postman a discreetly folded tenner or even a sodding fruitcake at Christmas, he was therefore obliged to extract an additional gratuity around the holidays, when the pickings were more choice. Or they once were. Enragingly, indolent shoppers were now purchasing the tastier gear through Amazon, which shunned the Royal for couriers. Really. As if postmen weren't to be trusted.

Combing through his booty was hard work, and the council might have commended his diligent recycling—the blue boxes out front forever bulging with circulars, bank statements, blood-test reports, and Tesco coupons that regrettably he couldn't use because their bar codes didn't match his Club Card. Accordingly, Gordon felt he'd earned the few usable bits of kit he salvaged, like fleece-lined slippers only a size too small. Alas, rare personal correspondence merely confirmed that his neighbors were a tedious lot: cranky complaints about a tube of toothpaste full of air, or handwritten hate mail for some poor journalist on Jubilee Street—scrawled in green ink, dripping exclamation marks, all in capital letters, every other word underscored three times.

But one elegant envelope caught his attention in September. The handwriting of the address was fluid but firm, and what's more it was *legible* (for the bane of a postman's life of late was tosspots raised on computers whose cursive rendition of *Newquay* was indistinguishable from *Moscow*). Inside, on quality stationery:

Dear Erskine,

Forgive my impertinence, but my daughter located you for me on Facebook (an enigma quite beyond my ken, I'm afraid). You may not remember me, but we attended school together at Bergen Grammar in Peterborough. After thirty-nine years, I can finally admit that I fancied you then. I admired not only the confidence with which you managed your difficulties, but also the shrewdness with which you used hardship to your advantage.

My daughter claims that you're single, and describes your photograph as "roughly handsome". My husband died some years ago. Would you care to meet up? I'm attending a film festival in Newquay the first week in November.

If I don't hear from you, perhaps your life is too full to accommodate a virtual stranger, and no offence taken.

Best regards,

Deirdre St James (the girl in the little red hat)

Poncey name. Still, Gordon and Deirdre must have been about the same age, and after four decades you could have turned into anybody. He surely qualified as "roughly handsome," if with a tad too much emphasis on the adverb. A shut-in who'd never so much as peered through his letter box, the real Erskine Espadrille (*very* poncey name) had recently vacated his dwelling without taking the judicious precaution of purchasing redirection services. A skinflint whom Deirdre (about whom he already felt proprietary) was better off without. Gordon wrote back.

Pleasantly, his letter did not land in the hands of a postman like himself, and achieved its mission. When she rang the number "Erskine" had enclosed, Deirdre's voice engendered the same clarity and firmness of her handwriting. A mischief in her laugh was consonant with a little girl who had sported a quirky red hat. They arranged to meet at a café not far from the Lighthouse Cinema, between screenings she was keen to catch; a proper film buff, was Deirdre.

A well-kept, stylish woman with neat, short gray hair entered the café right on time, per their agreed signal wrapped in a bright red scarf, a token of her girlhood trademark.

"Deirdre!" Gordon tried to imbue his clasp with the *confidence* she'd admired in her schoolmate. "Figured you might not recognize me after all these years."

"*Erskine*," she stressed, gaze aglitter. "I might not have recognized you at that."

They ordered tea. Formerly a functionary in Swindon's Building Control and Planning, Deirdre had taken early retirement, the better to pursue a range of outside interests. After Gordon shared his anxiety about rumors that the Royal might be privatized, the two commiserated. Scandalously, these days the whole nation seemed to resent its public workforce. "As if we're parasites," Deirdre said. "There's no appreciation. Would people in the vaunted 'private sector' want these jobs? I don't think so. The term is civil *servant*. So I got out while I could still get a proper pension. Having sacrificed so much, a body has to take advantage of the *few* perquisites."

"Right you are," Gordon—or Erskine—agreed heartily. "The punters take us for granted. You wouldn't credit the rudeness—mums with strollers going head-to-head with my trolley on the pavement, expecting an agent of the state to give way! Deliver one letter to the wrong address, and it's heaps of abuse. Are they glad for the hundreds of items delivered to the *right* address? Never."

Deirdre invited him along to the cinema, where Gordon was in such fine humor that he overcame his aversion to subtitles. Indeed, for the rest of the week, Gordon joined her for afternoon screenings, his attendance facilitated by stashing the majority of his morning's postal delivery unceremoniously in his vestibule. They took walks on the coastal path (his knee having uncannily improved), caught sunsets on Fistral Beach, and dined with views of the sea. He wooed her with thoughtful little presents from his postal trove: a packet of exotic dried mushrooms, a restaurant guide to Cornwall, and, by a stroke of fabulous good fortune thanks to some biddy with time on her hands in York-shire, a hand-knit woolen watch cap in red.

Of course, there was awkwardness. Gordon would forget to look round when his date called him *Erskine*. Settling bills, he rushed the credit card into his wallet, lest she glimpse the account holder. A Google search on "Bergen Grammar Peterborough" may have enabled wistful remembrance of an ivy-covered amphitheater, but when Deirdre reminisced about particular teachers and fellow students, Gordon could only nod. He'd had to scramble, too, when one of his few customers who actually knew it hailed him by name—a nickname, he explained afterwards, from his fondness for gin. Gordon was subsequently obliged to order G&Ts, though he preferred lager.

Yet when she hinted that for her last evening it would be nice to eat at his house, the whole charade was in danger of collapse. Dining in was a reasonable request, but he'd be hard-pressed to justify the GORDON BOSKY on his bell or the disparity between his address and the one to which she'd sent her query. His home was riddled with tiny details that would betray him, like the name on the prescription pain medication for his knee. Most of all, how could he rationalize the mountains of bin bags? In truth, he had come to fancy her madly, but sooner or later with this "Erskine Espadrille" palaver some slip would do him in. They had no future.

So he acceded to her wishes, and welcomed her that evening with a funereally hung head. If she noticed any anomalies, Deirdre politely refrained from observing them aloud. Stepping over a bin bag, she did ask decorously if he had a penchant for hoarding.

"Of a sort," he said miserably. The merest glimpse in one bag would give the game away, and there's some who would take a less than charitable view of his customers' involuntary *tithe*. It was over—a week hitherto the finest of his life.

At dinner—candlelight minimizing bin-liner glare—Gordon had little appetite, and finally came clean. "Deirdre, love. I'm not Erskine Espadrille."

"Of course not," she said readily.

"You knew?"

"Erskine was born without a right hand. Prosthetics have advanced, but they're not *that* lifelike. I've been captivated by your enterprising spirit. Though I'm curious. However did you gain possession of my letter?"

With nothing to lose, Gordon confessed.

As Deirdre laughed, that chime of mischief pealed into full-tilt naughtiness. "What good fun! I'm a dreadful snoop, and can't think of anything more delightful than poking through other people's post. But from the looks of this place, you're not up to the job alone. What say we take on that bag by the door after pudding?"

Thereafter, deploying the same efficiency with which Deirdre St. James had denied planning permission for sheds in back gardens, the operation became more professional, and they cleared the backlog. Gordon would tackle the recycling as his wife-to-be read out belligerent passages in correspondence. Both tenderly reserved premium discoveries for what would prove a cracking Christmas. Sensibly, they unearthed the occasional object so improbably ugly or useless that the easiest means of its disposal was to deliver the packet, albeit belatedly, to the hapless addressee. Gordon Bosky's efforts having schooled his customers in the art of appreciation, they never groused over the delay, but acted suitably grateful to have got any post at all.

Exchange Rates

KEEN TO SELECT a profoundly British venue, Elliot had arranged to meet his visiting father at a funky gastropub on the Cut, a London street name that itself embodied his adoptive country's quirky nomenclatural charm. (Elliot collected oddball street names. A recent business trip to Beverley had netted the beguiling byways *Old Waste* and *North Bar Within*. The penchant was an economy. A collection of Victorian teapots, say, would have run to thousands of quid; street names were free.) The Anchor & Hope was within walking distance of his Bermondsey flat, but the slog was just long enough to discourage his father from strolling back for coffee to discover that his son, at the humiliating age of forty-three, was living with roommates like some scraping grad student. His father wouldn't understand that single adults with full-time jobs teaming up to share a flat was commonplace in this city, where in Elliot's conversation the adjectives *exorbitant*, *larcenous*, and *extortionate* had grown impotent from overuse.

Still, while straining to read the specials on the chalkboard, Elliot's father, Harold Ivy, though a retired history professor whose specialty was seventeenth-century England, didn't wax eloquent on how the Thames once froze so solid that merchants sold their wares in "frost fares" on its surface. No, he couldn't stop talking about what everything cost. Like every American who'd visited Elliot in London the last few years, Harold remarked in indignation on the fact that, while the exchange rate was two-to-one, a pound and a dollar bought roughly the same thing. "This 'baby beet-leaf salad' with duck 'shreds,'" Harold said, pointing. "Eight pounds—that's sixteen dollars! In a bar! For an appetizer!"

"They'd call it a *starter.*" Elliot felt at once responsible for the prices, and proud of himself for surviving them. In his head, he now routinely doubled the cost of British goods into dollars, to heighten the outraged sticker-shock; on visits back home, he halved $18.99 into pounds to make the most recent Coldplay CD, *X&Y*, seem cheerfully cheap.

"It's not just restaurants, it's everything," Harold fumed. "When I was in Oxford making some last-minute notes on my guest lecture, my roller-ball went dry. I pick up a little packet of three at a stationery store—six pounds! That's four bucks apiece!"

"Welcome to my world," Elliot said. "There are only two bargains in the UK: marmalade, and breakfast cereal. Meanwhile, everyone here is taking buying-binge trips to New York. They think everything is half price."

"Never mind a few shopping sprees, I don't know why the whole population of Britain doesn't pick up and move to the United States. We may have an idiot president, who keeps sending the US army on walkabout in Middle Eastern quicksand. But at least you don't have to take out a second mortgage to buy a sandwich."

Harold opined about how relieved he was that Oxford was covering his London overnight, especially once he got a look at the hotel's rates. "Still," he added, puffing up a bit, "they put your old dad in some pretty fancy digs! Lavender-whatnot shampoo, heated towel racks. And carte blanche on the minibar! Feels good to be on expenses again."

There was a note in his father's voice that Elliot would retrieve only weeks later, but at the time he was distracted by the image of Harold stuffing all the chic hotel toiletries into his luggage, and washing his hands with plain water so he didn't have to unwrap the soap, the better to spirit the booty back home. Maybe he'd even remember to haul back a swag bag of Rose's thin-cut lemon-lime and Weetabix.

Naturally Elliot joined his cheapskate father in declining to order a starter, and a full bottle of wine was out of the question. It went without saying as well that they'd skip dessert. This had always been the form when eating out with his parents: one main course, tap water, *maybe* a glass of wine if they were feeling extravagant, and then the bill, ensuring that at least these oppressively scrimping occasions were short.

It wasn't that Elliot didn't like his father, a vigorous seventy-three with a full head of knurling white hair that gave Elliot hope for his own unruly mop in old age. Granted, the guy's having put on some serious weight in the last few years was concerning; the elderly—a word that Elliot applied to his father with something between disquiet and consternation—were prone to becoming bizarrely obsessed with food. Nevertheless, among the student body his father's passion for "the *real* Civil War" had been famously infectious, and he still pronounced commandingly on issues of the day as if the whole world were perched on the edge of its collective chair, waiting to hear the final verdict from Professor Ivy. Teaching conferred the arbitrary yet absolute authority of tin-pot dictatorships, and was bound to go to anyone's head eventually. Besides, Elliot was glad that his father hadn't slid into the passive apathy of so many seniors, who take refuge in bewilderment, or who revel in a grim satisfaction that the likes of climate change and desertification would wreak their worst destruction on someone else. Harold Ivy had retired from Amherst; he had not retired from planet Earth.

No, the trouble was Elliot's sense of filial inadequacy, made doubly shameful for being trite. Harold didn't condescend to his younger son exactly, and Elliot hated to think that he might still be yearning for his father's approval (though he probably was). It was more that Elliot's life didn't *interest* his father much. Whereas his father had been bent on becoming a scholar by his freshman year at Princeton, Elliot had never enjoyed a strong sense of occupational calling. After an aimless major in history at Brandeis that in retrospect was sycophantic, he'd cofounded a catering company that went bankrupt after a client sued over an *alleged* food-poisoning incident. He'd taught English to unsalvageables in South Boston; when one of his own students held him up at knifepoint, he'd rebelled against thankless do-gooding for next to nothing, and spent three years in middle management with AT&T—which was as boring as it sounds. Making the mistake of many of his fellow seekers in the same department at Boston U, he began a master's in clinical psychology under the illusion that the aim was to sort out his own confusions, rather than to become an assured, well-adjusted graduate capable of sorting out the confusions of *other* people. Little matter, since he aborted his second year, having fallen hard and helplessly for a sly, sarky British tourist he'd met at the Plough in Cambridge—the copycat Cambridge—who was heading home to London the following month.

Personally, Elliot could see a pattern: a pendulum swing between finding meaning and making money. But that structure had to be imposed on a narrative that to his father was simply incoherent. In Harold Ivy's terms, about the only half-intriguing thing that Elliot had ever done was move to the UK, although the initial motivation—to marry Caitlin, who was from Barnes—didn't seem quite respectable for a guy. Elliot did feel that he'd found his professional footing at last; everyone at the engineering society for which he worked said he was a natural at events planning. But his father could never come up with anything to ask about his job. Harold's idea of proper "events planning" was preparation for the Battle of Marston Moor.

Fortunately, their single course of wild boar and salsify stew (not altogether distinguishable from pork roast and parsnips) was readily occupied with family news—his mother's successful hip replacement, his brother's latest coup (a big commission to install solar panels on a public library; it was irksome how Robert managed to conceal with a cloak of virtue that he was really just a salesman), and an awkward inquiry about Caitlin, to which Elliot was obliged to reply that he had no idea. Harold pored over the bill before paying in cash. Elliot didn't need to see the printout to be sure that the tip was puny.

"By the way," Harold appended, pulling several twenty-pound notes from his wallet. "You know, I'm flying back to Logan tomorrow morning. But just to keep the bureaucracy down, Oxford paid my honorarium and per diem out of petty cash. No use to me in Massachusetts, and I've got most of it left. I stopped in a bank, and they charge a five-pound commission. Ten bucks! Seemed like throwing money away. I thought, since you spend sterling all the time . . ."

Cheered, Elliot mentally retracted his unkind exasperation with his father's parsimonious approach to dining out. The sheaf looked like well over £100—not enough to have an improving effect on his thus-far apocryphal property deposit, but a little extra pocket money never went amiss. He'd just arranged a surprised-but-grateful expression when his father kept talking.

"And you still have an American bank account, right? So I thought you could change the money for me, and I could skip that scandalous fee."

Elliot's face twitched from surprised-but-grateful to plain surprised. "Well, I don't have any dollars on me . . ."

"That's okay, just slip a check in the mail." Harold counted the bills. "I make that one-sixty. Don't worry, I trust you. No receipt required!"

"Yes, but do you trust me not to charge you a five-pound fee?"

The humor felt strained. When they parted outside, Elliot's elaborate instructions for how to get to the tube stop at Waterloo right around the corner were meant to cover for an abrupt irritability. The evening felt spoiled, and when he hugged his burly father good-bye his heart wasn't in it. He'd remember the embrace later: its inattention, its merely gesturing back pat, the tense, lopsided twist of his own insincere smile.

HUNCHING HOME, HANDS jammed in his pockets, braced against a chill far too sharp for spring, Elliot considered why, exactly, his father using his son as a *bureau de change* was quite so irksome. Since exchange rates were always rigged in the bank's favor, he himself maintained a hard-and-fast policy of never changing currencies. Modest birthday and Christmas checks from his parents (they wouldn't spring for international postage on presents) and commercial rebates from his own spending sprees Stateside (only a moron bought a computer in the UK) he always deposited in his Boston Citibank account, which also held his savings from that lucrative stint with AT&T. Especially since the value of American currency had plummeted—Britons now regarded a dollar as a small green rectangle for wiping one's bum—he wasn't about to effectively halve its buying power by transferring his precious $37K and change to NatWest. Instead, he was hoarding his few spare pounds for a deposit on a flat. And now he was expected to do on his father's account what he never, ever did on his own: trade dollars for pounds.

Moreover, his father doubtless expected Elliot to pony up the exchange rate quoted on the evening news—recently, about $1.97 to the pound, give or take. But peons didn't get anywhere near $1.97 at banks, whose exchange rates' relation to the currency market was capricious to nonexistent. At NatWest, his father would have been lucky to get $1.85. Instead, Elliot would be expected to write his father a check for $320—rounding up the rate to a tidy 2:1.

All right, it wasn't that much money. Yet there was a principle at stake. On however miniature a scale, his own father was taking advantage of him, all in the interest of saving five miserable quid. Elliot wasn't too clear on the details, but Harold Ivy's financial circumstances had to be healthy. If nothing else, his parents owned their own home, free and clear, which they had bought in that sane era when a house was still a normal acquisition purchased by normally salaried people that they paid off in a normal time frame of perhaps twenty years. These days even a poky two-bedroom walk-up in a dubious "transitional neighborhood" had become an unimaginable luxury that lowly wage earners like himself would own outright only by moonlighting until age 159. As for a proper *house*, well, that was a pipe dream, like a private trip to the moon, within the means only of lottery winners, Arab sheiks, and City of London shysters.

Hunkering down Webber Street, Elliot glared at the smug yellow-bricked terraces with their prissy white curtains and self-congratulatory flowerpots. Before he moved to Britain, his reigning ambition had never been to own property. Nevertheless, he'd lived for the last ten years amid an unprecedented real estate frenzy, and he felt left out. All around him people were making fortunes by flipping one hovel after another, and meantime he was numbly forking out £800 a month for a single room (okay, the largest room) of a shared three-bedroom, and he felt like a sucker. For all its postclass pretentions, modern Britain was just as feudally cleaved into serfs and landowning gentry as it had been in the Middle Ages, and entering his own middle age Elliot was still a serf. Gleaming brass escutcheons seemed to be locking Elliot Ivy personally out, while gloating facades on either side of the road rose implacably against this poor asshole American who hadn't the brains to have swung onto the much-vaunted "housing ladder" when he'd had the chance. Now the end of that ladder was dangling a hundred feet in the air, and all the slaphappy homeowners carousing on the bottom rung were pointing down at him and cackling.

It was all his parents' fault.

Throughout his upbringing they'd pinched their pennies—buying single-ply toilet rolls, with its notorious "poke-through" problem, clothing Elliot in Robert's hand-me-downs, and foreswearing air conditioning, which meant that his friends would boycott his house all summer. Made from quick-sale vegetables with their ignominious yellow stickers, stir-fry suppers had exuded the ammoniated whiff of mushrooms gone slippery. Less from necessity than catechism, his mother never bought herself a dress at Filene's Basement that wasn't on sale. As much as he resisted such joyless thrift in theory, like it or not the tightwad gene was buried deep in his own DNA. Elliot bought single-ply, too.

The year he'd moved to London turned out to be a watershed, and not because Labour came to power. In hindsight (though of course making decisions "in hindsight" would make everyone rich), he should have urged Caitlin to sell her flat, that they might embark on married life in a new home that they purchased together. Back then, he might easily have transferred his Citibank savings (during a now-nostalgic era of exchange rates sometimes as low as $1.40) to go fifty-fifty on a deposit. Instead, with the accommodating deference of a stranger in a strange land, he'd contributed his half of her mortgage payments for four years, during which Caitlin's flat nearly doubled in value. It was news to him when they split that all along he hadn't been building a share in the escalating equity, but, the initial pittance of a deposit being Caitlin's, paying "rent." Bitterness was never an attractive quality, but on this point—the monies at issue running to about £55K, more than enough to have set him up in his own place—Elliot was well and truly bitter. The real test of lovers wasn't how they dealt with illness, whether they were "supportive" or sexually faithful; you discovered what people were made of only once on the pointy end of how they handled money.

In hindsight, too, as soon as he gave up on the marriage (Caitlin was under the deluded impression that she had kicked him out), he should again have availed himself of his American savings to buy the first crappy dive he could snag. But by that point, British property already appeared wildly overvalued. Fatally, then, he had rented the flat in Bermondsey with two workmates and resolved to sit tight. Since, property had appreciated another staggering sixty percent. Would his mother be dismayed, or gratified? Elliot had been waiting in vain for houses to go on sale.

As he trooped up Pilgrimage and rounded on Manciple (both street names long ago added to his collection), even the blocks of ex–council flats seemed to be sneering with schoolyard contempt, "We were bought before 1997, *nyah*-nyah-*nyah*-nyah-*nyah-nyah!*" Because one couldn't walk any distance in this city without passing residential dwellings, even brief scuttles home like this one wore him out with resentment.

Unlocking the front door of his shared loft conversion on Long Lane, Elliot supposed morosely that he could always go back to the States. When asked by uncomprehending Brits why he stayed in this bleak, godforsaken country, he would often promote some twaddle about "culture," but an honest answer was closer to "furniture." In an ostentatious display of largesse that helped cover for some tiny trace of embarrassment over screwing him on the flat, Caitlin had made a great show of dividing the appointments they'd bought together strictly down the middle. Thus he was possessed of a handsome two-hundred-year-old dining table whose rugged, manly cut he quite fancied. Currently the social center of the loft, it was a heavy walnut affair that expanded to seat eight—too massive to ship, too cherished to abandon. He could see himself living in this city for the rest of his life, manacled to the legs of that table.

Besides, taunted by those fatuous facades of self-satisfied brick, buffeted by the hostile forces of $4 roller-balls, Elliot did not want to admit defeat.

TYPICALLY, HIS FATHER'S £160 quickly frittered from Elliot's wallet on dull rubbish. He may have treated himself to a couple of proper lunches instead of meagerly filled M&S chicken fajita wraps, but otherwise lost the packet to new batteries for the Long Lane radio-controlled thermostat, Sainsbury's thievingly priced non-bio laundry detergent because he couldn't be bothered to go all the way to Lidl, a scandalous dry-cleaning bill . . . In all, the kind of expenditures that provide nothing that you didn't have before.

Now that the money was spent and he still had to write his father a check, Elliot experienced a fresh burst of exasperation. Wouldn't it have been more *gracious* for Harold simply to have given his son the cash? Did the guy really need $320—a *rounded-up* $320? The folderol now required was hardly worth five quid: writing the check, addressing the envelope, and queuing the usual forty-five minutes for an airmail stamp at one of London's few remaining post offices, now that Britain considered the post office as outlandish a luxury as a place to live.

More important, didn't this amount of bother to save a fiver epitomize all that was wrong with his parents? His father's pettiness at the

Anchor & Hope mirrored the killjoy stinting that had tyrannized El-liot's boyhood. Store-brand white bread bought in two-pound loaves, a fraction cheaper per weight than the one-pound size, had guaranteed that the sandwiches in his second week's bag lunches would be stale, with spots of mold pinched off the crusts. The kitchen drawers of his childhood were cluttered with the tat of Green Stamps and ten-cent-off coupons for Tang. On phone calls with his grandparents, he and Robert had been distracted by pointed reminders to "keep it short" be-cause the call was—always iterated in hushed, reverential tones—"long distance!" Now all his grandparents were dead. How was that for *long distance*?

As it happened, while Elliot foot-dragged on returning Harold's honorarium in dollars, the pound slumped to its lowest rate in years, and was now trading in the markets at $1.78. Determined to teach his father a lesson, although he may have been a little hazy about what les-son, he popped into NatWest on his way to work. The bank was selling dollars at the predictably less generous rate of $1.69. Back home at his desk that night, Elliot punched the numbers into his calculator. That £160 wasn't worth anywhere near $320, but $270.40. In a fit of exacti-tude, before writing a check for the amount to the penny, he subtracted another $1.27—the 75P for an airmail stamp.

THUS A WEEK later an email arrived in Elliot's personal Gmail account from prof.harold.ivy@aol.com whose subject line read, "Miscalcula-tion?" Its text was terse and lacked a greeting: "got the check. seems a bit short. 160 pounds = $269.13????????"

This response was strangely satisfying. It wasn't like his father, a stickler for grammatical correctness even in this conventionally slap-dash medium, to fail to capitalize or to omit the subjects of his sen-tences. The juvenile profusion of question marks was hardly in keeping with Harold Ivy's commonly restrained style, and indicated that the message—whatever it was—had struck home.

Lingering over his reply with a glass of Rioja that evening, Elliot assumed the same tutorial tone to which he himself had been subjected during countless edifying dinners as a boy. He patiently explained about the currency market, and how the rates in the *Boston Globe*'s financial pages were not remotely representative of exchange rates on the High Street here in London. He noted that the pound had recently dipped, alas in this instance to Harold's disadvantage. He rued with lighthearted despair that UK postage was "far more dear"—a pleasingly British way of putting it—than that of US mail; hence the deduction of $1.27. Signing off with an allusive flourish, Elliot typed, "Welcome to my world," and hit Send.

Yet when he received no reply over the following several days, Elliot's sense of triumph rapidly ebbed to a tormenting hollowness. And then the phone rang.

ELLIOT KNEW SOMETHING was wrong as soon as he heard his mother's voice. Though industry deregulation had radically cheapened the international phone call, Bea Ivy was still averse to "long distance," and was wont to communicate with emails that were long, chatty, and free. Unless she'd gotten so scatty as to forget the five-hour time difference, she must have realized that in London it was four a.m.

Impressively practical and matter-of-fact, his mother delivered the end of the world as she knew it. "I'm so sorry to have to tell you this, and I know it will come as a shock. His last checkup gave him the all clear. But shortly after dinner tonight, your father had a heart attack. I just came back from the hospital. As far as I could tell, the doctors did everything they could. But Elliot . . ." The line rustled for a second or two with static. "Your father didn't make it."

NATURALLY, SHE SUFFERED bouts of weeping. But Bea also inhabited moments of repose, one of which descended during the memorial gathering back at the house in Amherst after the funeral.

"I'm so relieved that you saw your father in London last month," she told Elliot, politely accepting a skewer of chicken satay proffered by the catering staff, then disposing of it discreetly on the mantel. "In a way, you got to say good-bye."

"In a way," Elliot said.

"And I'm especially grateful that Harold got that opportunity to speak at Oxford. I can't tell you how much that invitation meant to him. I suppose I tried to shelter you from his moodiness. You have your own life, in such a big, exciting city, where you're out on the town all the time—I *hope* looking for a young woman with better taste than that Caitlin." To his mother, his ex was always *that Caitlin*, a syntax she may have picked up from Bill Clinton.

"Well, my life in London is hardly one big party." Ever since he'd heard the news, Elliot's demeanor had been hangdog.

"Anyway, these last five years have been—were pretty hard for your father. He was used to being so busy, flying off to academic conferences all over the world. Always working on a paper after dinner, or drafting a new curriculum. Unlike most of the faculty, Harold didn't give the same set lectures over and over. He was always refining, doing new research and polishing his ideas. Then, retirement—it just didn't sit well with him. He'd never been a potterer. He had no interest in the garden, or in doing frivolous, time-filling things like taking a class in Indian cooking. He'd read, but even reading wasn't the same. He was used to reading for a reason."

"You mean he was depressed."

"I suppose that's what you'd call it. The phone rarely rang, and some days he got no emails at all. At Amherst, he used to complain so about being inundated, about how email had become a plague! But, you know, be careful what you wish for."

"He still got a few emails," Elliot said heavily.

"I was thrilled when they asked him to speak in Oxford—the cradle of his sacred dictionary! It was such a compliment, since obviously the British have plenty of historians who specialize in seventeenth-century England in their own country. When the invitation came in, it changed his whole . . . Well, he was back to his old self."

"Yeah, he did seem pretty energized when we had dinner." For the first time, Elliot realized that he'd never even asked his father what his lecture had been about.

"It wasn't only the invitation. Being flown across the Atlantic again, at someone else's expense. A hotel, being wined and dined. Even getting an honorarium, when he used to be paid to speak all the time. Oh, I think the college paid him a pittance, you know, as a gesture. Oxford doesn't have as much money to throw around as the likes of Harvard, I don't need to tell you that! Still, to finally earn something again, instead of just drawing down his retirement accounts . . ."

Feeling a little sick, Elliot deposited his smoked-salmon canapé next to the satay skewer on the mantel.

"I think too little is made of the satisfaction of earning money," his mother said philosophically. "I discovered it myself when I started doing that freelance editing, and then I kicked myself for not having brought in a bit of my own income a long time before. Oh, it was only part-time, and we didn't especially need the extra money. But I loved the way those checks in the mail made me *feel*. I was worth something, literally worth something, in terms that other people take seriously. We make such a fuss over the joy of spending. But I think *earning* money is a much richer experience than buying some new trinket. Your father certainly felt the same. When I finally started working myself, I was even a little piqued, as if Harold should have let me in on the secret. As if all along instead of generously supporting our family he'd been selfishly indulging a private pleasure."

Though under the circumstances remarkably self-possessed, Bea couldn't have been so coolly collected that she was feigning innocence; clearly, his father had kept his irritation over the light Citibank check to himself. But successfully burying the episode made Elliot feel only worse.

Glumly accepting a third glass of wine and already planning on a fourth, Elliot rehearsed the evening at the Anchor & Hope. Why, he'd simply taken it for granted that his father would pay the bill. That's what parents did. But he was forty-three, with a full-time job, not some teenager saving for a motorbike by flipping burgers. Would it have killed him to treat his father to a meal in Elliot's own city? Astonishingly, he could not recall even once eating out with his parents and picking up the tab. He had never taken his father out to dinner, and now he never would.

Making a mental subtraction whose difficulty suggested that a fourth glass of wine was a bad idea, Elliot calculated that in giving his father the "real" exchange rate instead of rounding up to two-to-one, he had saved himself the princely sum of $50.87.

Maybe the problem really was genetic.

AFTER THE FUNERAL, his mother had evinced a peculiar resolution, a firm sense of direction that seemed to Elliot premature at the time. His parents' marriage of forty-eight years had been close, and he wouldn't have expected her to achieve this forward-looking determination half so quickly. But he had misinterpreted her sense of purpose. It wasn't that unusual, when the marriage was sound. Within a handful of weeks, she died.

Thus after the wheels of probate finished turning, he and Robert were settled with an inheritance far more sizable than Elliot would ever have anticipated.

Once the money landed in Citibank, he didn't visualize it as rows of zeros, stacks of banded bills, or bars of gold bullion. Rather, he pictured a tat of Green Stamps and ten-cent-off coupons for Tang; mounds of mildewing discount dresses, mountains of molding store-brand white bread, and teetering towers of toilet roll—single-ply. Rotting somewhere in a vault in Boston were hundreds, perhaps thousands of unordered appetizers, forgone desserts, and undrunk cups of restaurant coffee. And it was freezing in there—icy with forty-eight summers' worth of air conditioning that his parents had lived without.

At however poor an exchange rate, Elliot could now readily purchase a respectable home in London—where during a precipitous economic downturn property prices had finally started to slide, and it might indeed be possible, he thought wanly, to find a house *on sale*. Toward this end, he could apply not only his inheritance, the nest egg in pounds at NatWest, and his original American savings of $37K and change, but an outstanding check for $269.13, which had never been cashed.

Kilifi Creek

IT WAS A brand of imposition of which young people like Liana thought nothing: showing up on an older couple's doorstep, the home of friends of friends of friends, playing on a tentative-enough connection that she'd have had difficulty constructing the sequence of referrals. If there was anything to that six-degrees-of-separation folderol, she must have been equally related to the entire population of the continent.

Typically, she'd given short notice, first announcing her intention to visit in a voicemail only a few days before bumming a ride with another party she hardly knew. (Well, the group had spent a long, hard-drinking night in Nairobi at a sprawling house with mangy dead animals on the walls that the guy with the ponytail was caretaking. In this footloose crowd of journalists and foreign-aid workers between famines, trust-fund layabouts, and tourists who didn't think of themselves as tourists if only because they never did anything, the evening qualified them all as fast friends.) Ponytail Guy was driving to Malindi, on the Kenyan coast, for an expat bash that sounded a little druggie for Liana's midwestern tastes. But the last available seat in his Land Rover would take her a stone's throw from this purportedly more-the-merrier couple and their gorgeously situated crash pad. It was nice of the guy to divert to Kilifi to drop her off, but then Liana was attractive, and knew it.

Mature adulthood—and the experience of being imposed upon

herself—might have encouraged her to consider what showing up as an uninvited, impecunious houseguest would require of her hosts. Though Liana imagined herself undemanding, even the easy to please required fresh sheets, which would have to be laundered after her departure, then dried and folded. She would require a towel for swimming, a second for her shower. She would expect dinner, replete with discreet refreshments of her wineglass, strong filtered coffee every morning, and—what cost older people more than a sponger in her early twenties realized—steady conversational energy channeled in her direction for the duration of her stay.

For her part, Liana always repaid such hospitality with brightness and enthusiasm. On arrival at the Henleys' airy, weathered wooden house nestled in the coastal woods, she made a point of admiring soapstone knickknacks, cooing over framed black-and-whites of Maasai initiation ceremonies, and telling comical tales about the European riff-raff she'd met in Nairobi. Her effervescence came naturally. She would never have characterized it as an effort, until—and unless—she grew older herself.

While she'd have been reluctant to form the vain conceit outright, she might plausibly have been tempted to regard the sheer insertion of her physical presence as a gift, one akin to showing up at the door with roses. Supposedly a world-famous photographer, Regent Henley carried herself as if she used to be a looker, but she'd let her long, dry hair go gray. Her crusty husband, Beano (the handle may have worked when he was a boy, but now that he was over sixty it sounded absurd), could probably use a little eye candy twitching onto their screened-in porch for sundowners: some narrow hips wrapped tightly in a fresh kikoi; long, wet hair slicked back from a tanned, exertion-flushed face after a shower. Had Liana needed further rationalization of her amiable freeloading, she might also have reasoned that in Kenya every white household was overrun with underemployed servants. Not Regent and Beano but their African help would knot the mosquito netting over the guest bed. So Liana's impromptu visit would provide the domestics with something to do, helping justify the fact that bwana paid their children's school fees.

But Liana thought none of these things. She thought only that this was another opportunity for adventure on the cheap, and at that time economy trumped all other considerations. Not because she was rude, or prone to take advantage by nature. She was merely young. A perfectly pleasant girl on her first big excursion abroad, she would doubtless grow into a better-socialized woman who would make exorbitant hotel reservations rather than dream of dumping herself on total strangers.

Yet midway through this casual mooching off the teeny-tiny-bit-pretentious photographer and her retired safari-guide husband (who likewise seemed rather self-impressed, considering that Liana had already run into a dozen masters of the savanna just like him), Liana entered one eerily elongated window during which her eventual capacity to make sterner judgments of her youthful impositions from the perspective of a more worldly adulthood became imperiled. A window after which there might be no woman. There might only, ever, have been a girl—remembered, guiltily, uneasily, resentfully, by her aging, unwilling hosts more often than they would have preferred.

DAY FOUR. SHE was staying only six nights—an eyeblink for a twenty-three-year-old, a "bloody long time" for the Brit who had groused to his wife under-breath about putting up "another dewy-eyed Yank who confuses a flight to Africa with a trip to the zoo." Innocent of Beano's less-than-charmed characterizations, Liana had already established a routine. Mornings were consumed with texting friends back in Milwaukee about her exotic situation, with regular refills of passion fruit juice. After lunch, she'd pile into the jeep with Regent to head to town for supplies, having tolerated the photographer's ritual admonishment that Kilifi was heavily Muslim and it would be prudent to "cover up." (Afternoons were hot. Even her muscle T clung uncomfortably, and Liana considered it a concession not to strip down to her running bra. She wasn't about to drag on long pants to pander to a bunch of uptight foreigners she'd never see again; career expats like Regent were forever showing off how they were hip to local customs and you weren't.) She never proffered a few hundred shillings to contribute to the grocery bill, not because she was cheap—though she was; at her age, that went without saying—but because the gesture never occurred to her. Back "home," she would mobilize for a long, vigorous swim in Kilifi Creek, where she would work up an appetite for dinner.

As she sidled around the house in her bikini—gulping more passion fruit juice at the counter, grabbing a fresh towel—her exhibitionism was unconscious; call it instinctive, suggesting an inborn feel for barter. She lingered with Beano, inquiring about the biggest animal he'd ever shot, then commiserating about ivory poaching (always a crowd-pleaser) as she bound back her long blond hair, now bleached almost white. Raised arms made her stomach look flatter. Turning with a "cheerio!" that she'd picked up in Nairobi, Liana sashayed out the back porch and down the splintered wooden steps before cursing herself, because she should have worn flip-flops. Returning for shoes would ruin her exit, so she picked her way carefully down the overgrown dirt track to the beach in bare feet.

In Wisconsin, a "creek" was a shallow, burbling dribble with tad-poles that purled over rocks. Where Liana was from, you wouldn't go for a serious swim in a "creek." You'd splash up to your ankles while cupping your arches over mossy stones, arms extended for balance, though you almost always fell in. But everything in Africa was bigger. Emptying into the Indian Ocean, Kilifi Creek was a river—an impres-sively wide river at that, which opened into a giant lake sort of thing when she swam to the left and under the bridge. This time, in the inter-est of variety, she would strike out to the right.

The water was cold. Yipping at every advance, Liana struggled out to the depth of her upper thighs, gingerly avoiding sharp rocks. Regent and Beano may have referred to the shoreline as a "beach," but there wasn't a grain of sand in sight, and with all the green gunk along the bank, obstacles were hard to spot. Chiding herself not to be a wimp, she plunged forward. This was a familiar ritual of her childhood trips to Lake Winnebago: the shriek of inhalation, the hyperventilation, the panicked splashing to get the blood running, the soft surprise of how quickly the water feels warm.

Liana considered herself a strong swimmer, of a kind. That is, she'd never been comfortable with the gasping and thrashing of the crawl, which felt frenetic. But she was a virtuoso of the sidestroke, with a powerful scissor kick whose thrust carried her faster than many swimmers with inefficient crawls (much to their annoyance, as she'd verified in her college pool). The sidestroke was contemplative. Its rhythm was ideally calibrated for a breath on every other kick, and resting only one cheek in the water allowed her to look around. It was less rigorous than the butterfly but not as geriatric as the breaststroke, and after long enough you still got tired—marvelously so.

Pulling sufficiently far from the riverbank that she shouldn't have to worry about hitting rocks with that scissor kick, Liana rounded to the right and rapidly hit her stride. The late-afternoon light had just begun to mellow. The shores were forested, with richly shaded inlets and copses. She didn't know the names of the trees, but now that she was alone, with no one trying to make her feel ignorant about a continent of which white people tended to be curiously possessive, she didn't care if those were acacias or junipers. They were green: good enough. Though Kilifi was renowned as a resort area for high-end tourists, and secreted any number of capacious houses like her hosts', the canopy hid them well. It looked like wilderness: good enough. Gloriously, Liana didn't have to watch out for the powerboats and Jet Skis that terrorized Lake Winnebago, and she was the only swimmer in sight. Africans, she'd been told (lord, how much she'd been *told*; every backpacker three days out of Jomo Kenyatta Airport was an expert), didn't swim. Not only was the affluent safari set too lazy to get in the water; by this late in the afternoon they were already drunk.

This was the best part of the day. No more enthusiastic chatter about Regent's latest work. For heaven's sake, you'd think she might have finally discovered color photography at this late date. Blazing with yellow flora, red earth, and, at least outside Nairobi, unsullied azure sky, Africa was wasted on the woman. All she photographed was dust and poor people. It was a relief, too, not to have to seem fascinated as Beano lamented the unsustainable growth of the human population and the demise of Kenyan game, all the while having to pretend that she hadn't heard variations on this same dirge dozens of times in a mere three weeks. Though she did hope that, before she hopped a ride back to Nairobi with Ponytail Guy, the couple would opt for a repeat of that antelope steak from the first night. The meat had been lean; rare in both senses of the word, it gave good text the next morning. There wasn't much point in going all the way to Africa and then sitting around eating another hamburger.

Liana paused her reverie to check her position, and sure enough she'd drifted farther from the shore than was probably wise. She knew from the lake swims of childhood vacations that distance over water was hard to judge. If anything, the shore was farther away than it looked. So she pulled heavily to the right, and was struck by how long it took to make the trees appear appreciably larger. Just when she'd determined that land was within safe reach, she gave one more stiff kick, and her right foot struck rock.

The pain was sharp. Liana hated interrupting a swim, and she didn't have much time before the equatorial sun set, as if someone had flicked a light switch. Nevertheless, she dropped her feet and discovered that this section of the creek was barely a foot and a half deep. No wonder she'd hit a rock. Sloshing to a sun-warmed outcrop, she examined the top of her foot, which began to gush blood as soon as she lifted it from the water. There was a flap. Something of a mess.

Even if she headed straight back to the Henleys', all she could see was thicket—no path, much less a road. The only way to return and put some kind of dressing on this stupid thing was to swim. As she stumbled through the shallows, her foot smarted. Yet, bathed in the cool water, it quickly grew numb. Once she had slogged in deep enough to resume her sidestroke, Liana reasoned, *Big deal, I cut my foot.* The water would keep the laceration clean; the chill would stanch the bleeding. It didn't really hurt much now, and the only decision was whether to cut the swim short. The silence pierced by tropical birdcalls was a relief, and Liana didn't feel like showing up back at the house with too much time to kill with enraptured blah-blah before dinner. She'd promised herself that she'd swim at least a mile, and she couldn't have done more than a quarter.

So Liana continued to the right, making damned sure to swim out far enough so that she was in no danger of hitting another rock. Still, the cut left her rattled. Her idyll had been violated. No longer gentle and welcoming, the shoreline shadows undulated with a hint of menace. The creek had bitten her. Now fitful, the sidestroke had transformed from luxury to chore. Possibly she'd tightened up from a queer encroaching fearfulness, or perhaps she was suffering from a trace of shock—unless, that is, the water had genuinely gotten colder. Once in a while she felt a flitter against her foot, like a fish, but it wasn't a fish. It was the flap. Kind of creepy.

Liana resigned herself: this expedition was no longer fun. The light had taken a turn from golden to vermilion—a modulation she'd have found transfixing if only she were on dry land—and she still had to swim all the way back. Churning a short length farther to satisfy pride, she turned around.

And got nowhere. Stroking at full power, Liana could swear she was going backward. As long as she'd been swimming roughly in the same direction, the current hadn't been noticeable. This was a *creek*, right? But an African creek. As for her having failed to detect the violent surge running at a forty-five-degree angle to the shoreline, an aphorism must have applied—something about never being aware of forces that are on your side until you defy them.

Liana made another assessment of her position. Her best guess was that the shore had drifted farther away again. Very much farther. The current had been pulling her out while she'd been dithering about the fish-flutter flap of her foot. Which was now the least of her problems. Because the shore was not only distant. It stopped.

Beyond the end of the land was nothing but water. Indian Ocean water. If she did not get out of the grip of the current, it would sweep her past that last little nub of the continent and out to sea. Suddenly the dearth of boats, Jet Skis, fellow swimmers, and visible residents or tourists, drunken or not, seemed far less glorious.

The sensation that descended was calm, determined, and quiet, though it was underwritten by a suppressed hysteria that it was not in her interest to indulge. Had she concentration to spare, she might have worked out that this whole emotional package was one of her first true tastes of adulthood: what happens when you realize that a great deal or even everything is at stake and that no one is going to help you. It was a feeling that some children probably did experience but shouldn't. At least solitude discouraged theatrics. She had no audience to panic for. No one to exclaim to, no one to whom she might bemoan her quandary. It was all do, no say.

Swimming directly against the current had proved fruitless. Instead, Liana angled sharply toward the shore, so that she was cutting across the current. Though she was still pointed backward, in the direction of Regent and Beano's place, this riptide would keep dragging her body to the left. Had she known her exact speed, and the exact rate at which the current was carrying her in the direction of the Indian Ocean, she would have been able to answer the question of whether she was about to die by solving a simple geometry problem. A point travels at a set speed at a set angle toward a plane of a set width while moving at a set speed to the left. Either it will intersect the plane or it will miss the plane and keep traveling into wide-open space. Liquid space, in this case.

Of course, she wasn't in possession of these variables. So she swam as hard and as steadily as she knew how. There was little likelihood that suddenly adopting the crawl, at which she'd never been any good, would improve her chances, so the sidestroke it would remain. She trained her eyes on a distinctive rock formation as a navigational guide. Thinking about her foot wouldn't help, so she did not. Thinking about how exhausted she was wouldn't help, so she did not. Thinking about never having been all that proficient at geometry was hardly an assist, either, so she proceeded in a state of dumb animal optimism.

The last of the sun glinted through the trees and winked out. Technically, the residual threads of pink and gray in the early-evening sky were very pretty.

"WHERE IS THAT blooming girl?" Beano said, and threw one of the leopard-print cushions onto the sofa. "She should have been back two hours ago. It's dark. It's Africa, she's a baby, she knows absolutely nothing, and it's dark."

"Maybe she met someone, went for a drink," Regent said.

"Our fetching little interloper's *meeting someone* is exactly what I'm afraid of. And how's she to go to town with some local rapist in only a bikini?"

"You would remember the bikini," Regent said dryly.

"Damned if I understand why all these people rock up and suddenly they're our problem."

"I don't like it any more than you do, but if she floats off into the night air never to be seen again, she is our problem. Maybe someone picked her up in a boat. Carried her round the southern bend to one of the resorts."

"She'll not have her phone on a swim, so she's no means of giving us a shout if she's in trouble. She'll not have her wallet, either—if she even has one. Never so much as volunteers a bottle of wine, while hoovering up my best claret like there's no tomorrow."

"If anything has happened, you'll regret having said that sort of thing."

"Might as well gripe while I still can, then. You know, I don't even know the girl's surname? Much less whom to ring if she's vanished. I can see it: having to comb through her kit, search out her passport. Bringing in the sodding police, who'll expect chai just for answering the phone. No good ever comes from involving those thieving idiots in your life, and then there'll be a manhunt. Thrashing the bush, prodding the shallows. And you know how the locals thrive on a mystery, especially when it involves a young lady—"

"They're bored. We're all bored. Which is why you're letting your imagination run away with you. It's not that late yet. I'm sure there's a simple explanation."

"I'm not bored, I'm hungry. Aziza probably started dinner at four—since she *is* bored—and you can bet it's muck by now."

Regent fetched a bowl of fried chickpea snacks, but despite Beano's claim to an appetite he left them untouched. "Christ, I can see the whole thing," he said, pacing. "It'll turn into one of those cases. With the parents flying out and grilling all the servants and having meetings with the police. Expecting to stay here, of course, tearing hair and getting emotional while we urge them to please do eat some lunch. Going on tirades about how the local law enforcement is ineffectual and corrupt, and bringing in the FBI. Telling childhood anecdotes about their darling and expecting us to get tearful with them over the disappearance of some, I concede, quite agreeable twentysomething, but still a girl we'd barely met."

"You like her," Regent said. "You're just ranting because you're anxious."

"She has a certain intrepid quality, which may be deadly, but which until it's frightened out of her I rather admire," he begrudged, then resumed the rant. "Oh, and there'll be media. CNN and that. You know the Americans—they love innocent-abroad stories. But you'd think they'd learn their lesson. It beats me why their families keep letting kids holiday in Africa as if the whole world is a happy-clappy theme park. With all those carjackings on the coast road—"

"Ordinarily I'd agree with you, but there's nothing especially *African* about going for a swim in a creek. She's done it every other afternoon, so I've assumed she's a passable swimmer. Do you think—would it help if we got a torch and went down to the dock? We could flash it about, shout her name out. She might just be lost."

"My throat hurts just thinking about it." Still, Beano was heading to the entryway for his jacket when the back porch screen door creaked.

"Hi," Liana said shyly. With luck, streaks of mud and a strong tan disguised what her weak, light-headed sensation suggested was a shocking pallor. She steadied herself by holding on to the sofa and got mud on the upholstery. "Sorry, I—swam a little farther than I'd planned. I hope you didn't worry."

"We *did* worry," Regent said sternly. Her face flickered between anger and relief, an expression that reminded Liana of her mother. "It's after dark."

"I guess with the stars, the moon . . ." Liana covered. "It was so . . . peaceful."

The moon, in fact, had been obscured by cloud for the bulk of her wet grope back. Most of which had been conducted on her hands and knees in shallow water along the shore—land she was not about to let out of her clutches for one minute. The muck had been treacherous with more biting rocks. For long periods, the vista had been so inky that she'd found the Henleys' rickety rowboat dock only because she had bumped into it.

"What happened to your *foot*?" Regent cried.

"Oh, that. Oh, nuts. I'm getting blood on your floor."

"Looks like a proper war wound, that," Beano said boisterously.

"We're going to get that cleaned right up." Examining the wound, Regent exclaimed, "My dear girl, you're shaking!"

"Yes, I may have gotten—a little chill." Perhaps it was never too late to master the famously British knack for understatement.

"Let's get you into a nice hot shower first, and then we'll bandage your foot. That cut looks deep, Liana. You really shouldn't be so casual about it."

Liana weaved to the other side of the house, leaving red footprints down the hall. In previous showers here, she'd had trouble with scalding, but this time she couldn't get the water hot enough. She huddled under the dribble until finally the water grew tepid, and then, with a shudder, wrapped herself in one of their big white bath sheets, trying to keep from getting blood on the towel.

Emerging in jeans and an unseasonably warm sweater she'd found in the guest room's dresser, Liana was grateful for the cut on her foot, which gave Regent something to fuss over and distracted her hostess from the fact that she was still trembling. Regent trickled the oozing inch-long gash with antiseptic and bound it with gauze and adhesive tape, whose excessive swaddling didn't make up for its being several years old; the tape was discolored, and barely stuck. Meanwhile, Liana threw the couple a bone. She told them how she had injured her foot, embellishing just enough to make it a serviceable story.

The foot story was a decoy. It obviated telling the other one. At twenty-three, Liana hadn't accumulated many stories; until now, she had hungered for more. Vastly superior to carvings of hippos, stories were the very souvenirs that this bold stint in Africa had been designed to provide. Whenever she'd scored a proper experience in the past, like the time she'd dated a man who confided that he'd always felt like a woman, or even when she'd had her email hacked, she'd traded on the tale at every opportunity. Perhaps if she'd returned to her parents after this latest ordeal, she'd have burst into tears and delivered the blow-by-blow. But she was abruptly aware that these people were virtual strangers. She'd only make them even more nervous about whether she was irresponsible or lead them to believe that she was an attention seeker with a tendency to exaggerate. It was funny how when some little nothing went down you played it for all it was worth, but when a truly momentous occurrence shifted the tectonic plates in your mind you kept your mouth shut. Because instinct dictated that this one was private. Now she knew: there was such a thing as private.

Having aged far more than a few hours that evening, Liana was disheartened to discover that maturity could involve getting smaller. She had been reduced. She was a weaker, more fragile girl than the one who'd piled into Regent's jeep that afternoon, and in some manner that she couldn't put her finger on she also felt less real—less here—since in a highly credible alternative universe she was not here.

The couple made a to-do over the importance of getting hot food inside her, but before the dinner had warmed Liana curled around the leopard-print pillow on the sofa and dropped into a comatose slumber. Intuiting something—Beano himself had survived any number of close calls, the worst of which he had kept from Regent, lest she lay down the law that he had to stop hunting in Botswana even sooner than she did—he discouraged his wife from rousing the girl to go to bed, draping her gently in a mohair blanket and carefully tucking the fringe around her pretty wet head.

PREDICTABLY, LIANA GREW into a civilized woman with a regard for the impositions of laundry. She pursued a practical career in marketing in New York, and, after three years, ended an impetuous marriage to an Afghan. Meantime, starting with Kilifi Creek, she assembled an off-beat collection. It was a class of moments that most adults stockpile: the times they almost died. Rarely was there a good reason, or any warning. No majestic life lessons presented themselves in compensation for having been given a fright. In contrast to, say, the rescue of a child from a fire, most of these incidents were in no way heroic. They were more a matter of stepping distractedly off a curb, only to feel the draft of the M4 bus flattening your hair.

Not living close to a public pool, Liana took up running in her late twenties. One evening, along her usual route, a minivan shot out of a parking garage without checking for pedestrians and missed her by a whisker. Had she not stopped to double-knot her left running shoe before leaving her apartment, she would be dead. Later: she was taking a scuba-diving course on Cape Cod when a surge about a hundred feet deep dislodged her mask and knocked her regulator from her mouth. The Atlantic was unnervingly murky, and her panic was absolute.

Sure, they taught you to make regular decompression stops, and to exhale evenly as you ascended, but it was early in her training. If her instructor hadn't managed to grab her before she bolted for the surface while holding her breath, her lungs would have exploded and she would be dead. Still later: had she not unaccountably thought better of lunging forward on her Citi Bike on Seventh Avenue when the light turned green, the garbage truck would still have taken a sharp left onto Sixteenth Street without signaling, and she would be dead. There was nothing else to learn, though that was something to learn, something inchoate and large.

The scar on her right foot, wormy and white (the flap should have been stitched), became a totem of this not-really-a-lesson. Oh, she'd considered the episode, and felt free to conclude that she had overestimated her swimming ability, or underestimated the insidious, bigger-than-you powers of water. Or she could sensibly have decided that swimming alone anywhere was tempting fate. She might have concocted a loftier version, wherein she had been rescued by an almighty presence who had grand plans for her—grander than marketing. But that wasn't it. Any of those interpretations would have been plastered on top, like the poorly adhering bandage on that gash. The message was bigger and dumber and blunter than that, and she was a bright woman, with no desire to disguise it.

After Liana was promoted to director of marketing at BraceYourself—a rapidly expanding firm that made the neoprene joint supports popular with aging boomers still pounding the pavement—she moved from Brooklyn to Manhattan, where she could now afford a stylish one-bedroom on the twenty-sixth floor, facing Broadway. The awful Afghan behind her, she'd started dating again. The age of thirty-seven marked a good time in her life. She was well paid and roundly liked in the office; she relished New York; though she'd regained an interest in men, she didn't feel desperate. Many an evening without plans she would pour a glass of wine, take the elevator to the top floor, and slip up a last flight of stairs; roof access was one of the reasons she'd chosen the apartment. Especially in summertime, the regal overlook made her feel rich beyond measure. Lounging against the railing sipping Chenin Blanc, Liana would bask in the lights and echoing taxi horns of the city, sometimes sneaking a cigarette. The air would be fat and soft in her hair—which was shorter now, with a becoming cut. So when she finally met a man whom she actually liked, she invited him to her building's traditional Fourth of July potluck picnic on the roof to show it off.

"Are you sure you're safe, sitting there?" David said solicitously. They had sifted away from the tables of wheat berry salad and smoked tofu patties to talk.

His concern was touching; perhaps he liked her, too. But she was perfectly stable—lodged against the perpendicular railing on a northern corner, feet braced on a bolted-down bench, weight firmly forward—and her consort had nothing to fear. Liana may have grown warier of water, but heights had never induced the vertigo from which others suffered. Besides, David was awfully tall, and the small boost in altitude was equalizing.

"You're just worried that I'll have a better view of the fireworks. Refill?" She leaned down for the Merlot on the bench for a generous pour into their plastic glasses. Resorting to a standard fallback for a first date, they had been exchanging travel stories, and impulsively—there was something about this guy that she trusted—she told him about Kilifi Creek. Having never shared the tale, she was startled by how little time it took to tell. But that was the nature of these stories. They were about what could have happened, or should have happened, but didn't. They were very nearly not stories at all.

"That must have been pretty scary," he said dutifully. He sounded let down, as if she'd told a joke without a punch line.

"I wasn't scared," she reflected. "I couldn't afford to be. Only later, and then there was no longer anything to be afraid of. That's part of what was interesting: having been cheated of feeling afraid. Usually, when you have a near miss, it's an instant. A little flash, like, *Wow. That was weird.* This one went on forever, or seemed to. I was going to die, floating off on the Indian Ocean until I lost consciousness, or I wasn't. It was a long time to be in this . . . in-between state." She laughed. "I don't know, don't make me embarrassed. I've no idea what I'm trying to say."

Attempting to seem captivated by the waning sunset, Liana no more than shifted her hips, by way of expressing her discomfort that her story had landed flat. Nothing foolhardy. For the oddest moment, she thought that David had pushed her, and was therefore not a nice man at all but a lunatic. Because what happened next was both enormously subtle and plain enormous—the way the difference between knocking over a glass and not knocking over a glass could be a matter of upsetting its angle by a single greater or lesser degree. Greater, this time. Throw any body of mass that one extra increment off its axis, and rather than barely brush against it you might as well have hurled it at a wall.

With the same quiet clarity with which she had registered in Kilifi, *I am being swept out to sea*, she grasped simply, *Oh. I lost my balance.* For she was now executing the perfect backflip that she'd never been able to pull off on a high dive. The air rushed in her ears like water. This time the feeling was different—that is, the starkness was there, the calmness was there also, but these clean, serene sensations were spiked with a sharp surprise, which quickly morphed to perplexity, and then to sorrow. She fit in a wisp of disappointment before the fall was through. Her eyes tearing, the lights of high-rises blurred. Above, the evening sky rippled into the infinite ocean that had waited to greet her for fourteen years: largely good years, really—gravy, a long and lucky reprieve. Then, of course, what had mattered was her body striking the plane, and now what mattered was not striking it—and what were the chances of that? By the time she reached the sidewalk, Liana had taken back her surprise. At some point there was no *almost*. That had always been the message. There were bystanders, and they would get the message, too.

Repossession

ON FIRST VIEWING the two-story semidetached on Lansing Terrace, Helen Rutledge dismissed outright the absurd impression that she was not welcome here. She was a sensible young woman—all right, no longer *that* young—who routinely privileged the *should* over the *was*. This *should* be the perfect house for her; ergo, it *was*. Three bedrooms, for herself, a study (perhaps in time a nursery?), and guests: *tick*. Not one of those decrepit Georgian headaches whose renovations were hog-tied by preservation orders, the structure was at least postwar: *tick*. Granted, the nondescript semi of yellow brick was located in deep South London, but any property whose purchase someone in Helen's income bracket could swing was bound to involve a hefty commute to a job in NW1. Indeed, that was the clincher: the house was a steal. *Tick, tick, tick!*

As for whether she harbored any reservations about 21 Lansing Terrace having been repossessed, the answer was certainly not. A tax accountant, Helen held rules in high esteem. She had no sympathy for people who didn't exert control over their circumstances—who allowed their lives to go higgledy-piggledy and so created messes for responsible citizenry to clean up. For Helen, the prospect of being unable to pay any bill slipped through her letter box was mortifying. If the previous owner had purchased a property beyond his or her means, such culpable foolhardiness ought rightly to be punished, and that's all there was to it.

Given the paltry asking price—or paltry in London terms—she was surprised to face no competition, and the estate agent acting for the bank accepted her offer with a hastiness that more seasoned house hunters might have found alarming. But as a first-time buyer, Helen wasn't about to look a gift house in the mouth. She would continue to rent her flat in Dulwich for a month after the closing in order to do a spot of spiffing up. The persistent unpleasantness that imbued the interior—nothing whose source you could quite identify, and therefore nothing—could surely be ameliorated with a few licks of paint.

Handy for her gender and generation, Helen spent her first Saturday as a homeowner covering the sitting room walls in a vibrant, nervy color that she'd found in the *Guardian Weekend*'s interior design pages: a dazzling aqua popular for plastic toys. By late afternoon, a beaming second coat had obliterated the somber underlying shade, a light gray with a queasy purple undertone, as if the room had been bruised. Even if the new paint job hadn't, somehow, settled—the panels of blue-green seemed to float slightly forward of the plasterboard—she'd introduced a splash of vivacity to the ground floor.

She returned the following morning to have a go at the skirting boards. Yet her key simply would not turn the upper lock, though she jiggled it this way and that for a solid ten minutes. *Whoosh*, up the homeowner's learning curve: when it was your property, you couldn't ring the landlord to come and fix it, and Helen fought an urge to cry. The house didn't like her and didn't want her inside.

The sensation of personal rejection being flagrantly ridiculous, she got a grip and located a locksmith on her mobile, then sat on the step to wait. It was autumn, and she noticed too late that a scraggly tree growing at a deranged angle overhead had dropped stinky violet berries onto the step. So now her jeans looked bruised as well, their seat stained with purple blotches that would never wash out. Worse, once the locksmith rocked up, he tried the key once and the door swung wide, open sesame. He still charged a call-out fee, quite a packet to part with for the privilege of feeling like a dunce.

In the entryway, the quality of the light glooming from the sitting room doorway was inexplicably dingy and sulking, although the south-facing front windows still had no curtains and the sky was clear. Helen ventured in to admire yesterday's daring makeover, only to find the walls a color that would never be employed for a toy. The shade was still blue, of a sort, but sullen. Rather than refract the sunshine shafting through the windows, this hue consumed the light, sucking every photon from the rays like a child slurping the last of a soda. When she came closer, it was clear the paint hadn't dried, either, or just enough to have grown mucky and thick. The surface was bubbling, making creepy little pipping sounds, and in long vertical streaks the old purplish gray glowered through. Since obviously the whole job would have to be done again, she touched the paint that had looked so jaunty and dashingly modern when she locked up on Saturday, and it stuck to her finger, stringing like bubblegum when she pulled away. It was as if the outrageously defective product that she'd slathered on her sitting room was dissolving earlier layers of paint beneath.

Which was the only explanation for what rapidly emerged on the far wall. At first she thought it was a trick of the queer light, or an accidental arrangement of streaks and blisters. But no, those were letters—in black, crudely formed and dripping, as if slashed with a wide, over-laden brush, and underscored for good measure:

MY HOUSE!

So spiteful were some delinquent homeowners, it was said, that they vandalized their own homes before being evicted. The bank would have arranged for any damage to be tidied before putting the house on the market. And now her warped poor luck with a bad batch of paint— she might as well have covered the room in battery acid—had exposed some ghastly deadbeat's defiant parting graffiti.

"It's not your house anymore!" Helen announced aloud—though the walls ate the sound as voraciously as the light, and her voice sounded terribly tiny.

She returned the remains of the paint in a state of righteous indignation, but the salesman at B&Q was skeptical—even more so once she'd described the burbling horror show in gory detail. "Never heard of *that*, love. Sure you didn't just apply the second coat before the first was dry?"

"If I can execute the directions in 11,520 pages of Her Majesty's tax code," she huffed, "I can follow the back of a tin." But he clearly delivered her refund only to get this crackpot out of his hair.

By the time she stopped back by Lansing Terrace midweek it was evident that the paint would never cure. The sticky mess couldn't be called "Island Breeze" now, for it had now churned into a vomitty miasma of a hue more like "Caribbean Twister." So Helen was obliged to hire a contractor to replace the plasterboard. When it came time to choose a color for the sitting room again, she found she'd lost her nerve, and opted for an innocuous shade the contractor recommended as popular called "Moonlit Sky"—which turned out to be light gray with a queasy purple undertone.

For her next home improvement project in the master bedroom, Helen fancied ripping up the lumpy, nubbled beige carpet and refinishing the floorboards. All the magazines indicated that carpet was naff. Chic Londoners now opted for burnished wood accented with arty throw rugs.

But even tearing up the old wall-to-wall was exhausting. The carpet had been fanatically tacked, and the nails pierced her work gloves until her hands were sore and swollen. Slicing the carpet into the short widths that the council required for pickup entailed more than one slip with the box cutter. The painful nicks so slowed her typing of spreadsheets at work that a colleague in the next cubicle needled her for regression to hunt-and-peck.

Once she rented the sander, the real frustration began. She *knew* you had to remove any nails from the flooring, and numerous tacks had pulled through the carpet padding and remained behind in the wood. So she had fanatically smoothed her puffy bare hands over the boards to search out even the smallest bit of metal, countersinking stray spikes with a hammer and using pliers to tug out the tacks with heads. Yet whenever she started the machine—a deafening, unwieldy monster that was honestly rather frightening—it shrieked immediately on a raised nail, which shredded the sandpaper. The belts were pricey as well as bothersome to replace, and by the day's end she must have gone through a dozen—even after repeatedly caressing the whole floor on her hands and knees, checking every square inch for extrusions.

That night, at her wit's end and having ruined yet another sandpaper belt within sixty seconds, Helen Rutledge drew the kind of conclusion that the more self-possessed rendition of her character would have found preposterous. The floor was obviously growing nails. It was growing nails as surely as her fingers did. As a demented experiment, she meticulously traced a little patch at one corner, then turned her back. By now, she wasn't even surprised. When she returned to the patch, it sported six or seven raised, snag-headed tacks, which had popped up like toadstools.

"Have it your way, then," she told the floor. Sanded fitfully in disconnected sections, the surface had a mangy quality, like a diseased urban fox. So she was at a loss to comprehend how it still managed to look smug.

When choosing a replacement carpet, she erred on the side of caution, selecting a sample of nubbled beige. The whole tedious operation dispatched, the bedroom looked exactly the same. So far, after much expense and effort, Helen the new homeowner had made no impact on this property whatsoever.

"SAY, AREN'T *you* brave!"

Helen was on the pavement keeping an eye on the removal men, making sure they didn't scratch her mother-of-pearl inlaid antique sideboard. An older woman had leaned over the picket fence between their adjoining properties. She had the stout build and burst-capillary complexion of this "up and coming" area's pregentrification residents. Before she could stop herself, Helen thought reflexively, *On benefits.*

"I don't know how 'brave' I am when they're doing all the work," Helen said, trying to sound friendly to cover for her uncharitable assumptions.

"I mean taking that place on," she said. "Has quite the reputation round here, that house."

"Oh?" Helen's tone cooled. She'd nursed an aggressive lack of interest in her property's history, especially in whatever loser had lived there who was feckless enough to have faced foreclosure.

"Your last owner, Judith. Determined to go down with the ship, she was!"

"Except the ship"—Helen nodded at her front door—"is still afloat."

The woman mistakenly imagined that the new owner was desperate to hear the story. "There's not many what realize it, but Judith weren't all that far from paying off the mortgage free and clear. But her husband had died a ways back—something with the kidneys—and Ron'd brung in the bacon. Bus driver, if I recall rightly. Your bereavement payment is a one-off, your bereavement allowance lasts only a year, and Judith weren't old enough to draw a pension. So money got well tight. Kids were wasters. Which didn't keep her from slipping them two boys the odd tenner when she had it to spare. Only reason they ever called round, if you ask me. Judith was a generous soul. Just had her limits. She'd a long fuse on her, but she did have one fearsome temper once she was riled. All that dosh pitched to the bank for donkey's, she weren't about to let 'em take that house off her."

"But apparently they did." With every new scrap of superfluous information, Helen's heart had steadily sunk. The last thing you wanted was a motormouth for a next-door neighbor. This woman could make simply getting out the door for the smallest trip to the shops take forty minutes. But Helen was under the misimpression that keeping her own comments to a minimum would discourage chat, when in truth her terseness simply left her neighbor all the more conversational leeway to let fly.

"Not without a fight! Soon as Judith get that summons, she start hammering. A proper racket for me, you can imagine, and I come out to see she's banging up big plywood sheets over the windows, like you do for rough weather—but these boards is on the *inside*. They say she padlock the doors from the inside as well, top and bottom, front and back. She'd a great towering stack of food and drink in the cellar, the way them religious nutters ready for the end of the world. Might not be much to look at to some—no offense intended—but to Judith it were her house, where she spend most of her marriage, where she raise her boys."

"Sounds a pity, then," Helen said, powerfully disapproving of any such illegal sit-in. If you owed a payment, you raised the money from somewhere or accepted the consequences. Irked that her curiosity about how the story ended had been piqued despite herself, she apologized that she had to mind the removal men and fled inside.

THAT NIGHT, SURROUNDED by cartons, Helen flopped into bed without having flossed. Nothing was more exhausting than moving house, and before dropping off she made the commonplace vow (as commonly broken) that she'd never pull up stakes again.

Her slumber might have been deep and dreamless, were it not for the persistent strains of "Jerusalem" chorusing over and over from the direction of the party wall. She'd once found the tune rousing, until a workmate at Manson & Ross had started using the first three bars as a ringtone, after which she'd found its pompous strains unbearable. She didn't want to make enemies of this woman when their properties were attached at the hip, but some laying down of ground rules was in order.

The following Sunday morning, Helen relished the Christmas sensation of unwrapping treasured keepsakes from their newsprint swaddling. Unpacking was like being given everything you owned all over again. When she arranged her trove of CowParade figurines and smaller

"mini-moos" atop the antique sideboard, the familiar bovine art repro-
ductions made a declaration of sorts: MY HOUSE! (Helen wasn't a natural
collector, but a single gift of a brightly striped resin cow had triggered
a cascade of presents from the same series. It seems one's personality
wasn't always of one's own making, but could be a joint effort.) Maybe
the previous owner had been on to something, too, and defacement was
the ultimate form of possession, since pounding picture hooks into the
plasterboard was strangely exhilarating; Helen would never have dared
to drive holes into the walls of her rental flat in Dulwich. The framed
photo of the whitewashed cottage where her family had always holi-
dayed in the Cotswolds pleasingly linked where she had been to where
she was now. Even if she hadn't exactly *read* them, her embossed classics from the Folio Society marked her new digs as a household of taste,
education, and refinement.

Contented by festooning her first proper home with the dozens of
touches that turned mere quadrants into rooms—rooms with character,
rooms that had been mastered—she managed for most of the morning
to ignore the insistent smell. A piercing odor of ammonia suggested
that whoever had tarted up the house for sale had gone overboard with
violent cleaning products, although the ammonia was contaminated
with an undersmell of diesel, and laced with a burnt singe. Residual
wafts of detergent should have begun to dissipate; this pong was growing stronger.

If only to escape the mysterious reek, Helen took a break and headed
out to her local Sainsbury's; switched on for a full day, the fridge should
be cold by now. But of course she didn't make it to her front gate before
the busybody next door popped out to ask how she was getting on, and
to finally introduce herself as Gertrude.

"So you're a fan of 'Jerusalem,' I gather." Helen had to force herself
to bring it up.

Gertrude reared back. "Quite the opposite! Had to hear it again, I
might top myself."

Helen frowned. "But I heard quite distinctly—"

"Judith, now. Couldn't tell if she specially fancied it or specially despised it, but either way that carry-on made for a fiendish weapon. Once the authorities get heavy—no surprise the bank bring in the council, and the council the police—Judith blast that recording on her stereo nonstop, all hours. Never sure what she mean by it, but for me, by the end, you could shove your *'green and pleasant land'* right up England's arse."

It wasn't clear what Gertrude's game was, but at least the woman had been put on notice about her sound system.

Helen returned from the supermarket with an enormous shop, from which she immediately extracted the honeysuckle air freshener and sprayed the kitchen until the aerosol was half exhausted. But poorly masking the stench with artificial scent just made the room smell like a petrol station toilet. After hastily stocking the fridge-freezer, she retreated to the sitting room with chamomile tea to settle her stomach.

The photo of the Cotswolds: it was turned to the wall. The Folio Society hardbacks as well were now facing backwards, presenting a bank of blank deckle-edged pages. The cows on the sideboard had vanished. On a hunch—British burglars weren't known for eccentric reshelvings of *Moby-Dick*—she opened the sideboard's top drawer, and there were her kaleidoscope cows—seemingly unharmed, but on their sides, shoved out of sight.

Sheer mischief! Might that Judith woman have provided Gertrude a spare key for emergencies? Yet if so, why would her neighbor sneak inside when Helen was out shopping and mess with her things? Nothing seemed to have been taken, so the lady might simply have been nosey parkering, but didn't most snoops make a point of leaving everything as they found it?

Still, the ploy, whatever it was for, was oddly effective. As Helen righted the photo, reversed the Folio books, and restored the resin cows to their rightful place on the sideboard, she felt more unnerved than she had been by the hostile front lock, the boiling paint job, the nail-sprouting floorboards, the bombasts of William Blake, or even that awful smell—although as she recited it, she realized that there was a list, and that it kept getting longer.

Running late for work that Monday morning, still underslept from more penetrating strains of "Jerusalem," Helen whitened the coffee that would have to suffice for breakfast, only to watch the milk resurface in bobbing curds. That semiskim wasn't a day old! But when she checked, the fridge was warm; the frozen food was melting. Surely she'd heard the comforting hum of the appliance as she unpacked dishware the day before. But now the socket was switched to the off position, and everything she'd bought at Sainsbury's was ruined.

There was nothing for it but to switch the socket back to On and deal with the disaster after work. Perhaps she'd imagined the hum, and neither she nor the removal man who'd connected the white goods had remembered to activate the outlet.

Yet when she returned from work that evening, the outlet switch was back in the off position. Chicken juice from the freezer pooled on the floor. Furiously, Helen pitched the breast fillets, venison burgers, sausage rolls, lamb chops, smoked salmon, and packets of prewashed baby lettuce into a bin liner. After dumping the bag of costly foodstuffs into her wheelie bin, she marched round the picket fence and pounded on Gertrude's door.

Alas, her neighbor's expression of affable innocence looked so genuine that Helen's consternation crumbled to embarrassment. If she accused this near stranger of barging into her property solely in order to turn off the refrigerator, she would sound unhinged. For that matter, confronted with the problem of a malicious intruder who must have a spare key, why hadn't a capable homeowner like herself simply changed the locks right away?

The answer was clear cut. When an inanimate CowParade collection freakishly transports itself from surface to drawer, safeguarding a rational explanation was tantamount to safeguarding one's sanity. So long as she didn't change the locks, she could always blame Gertrude.

In the event that any further goings-on might require a logical attribution, she didn't want to change the locks.

"Sorry, I—forgot to switch on the outlet for the fridge, and now all my food's spoilt. I wondered if you might have a bit of bread and cheese, to tide me over." It was all she could think to say, though half a dozen takeaway menus had already been shoved through her letter box.

"We can do better than that, treasure. You come right in."

Gertrude's house was cluttered, laid with clashing patterned carpets and lined with cutesy ceramic pigs, whose old-lady ambience might in time worrisomely confer itself on Helen's avant-garde cows. Still, the gas fire was lit, and it was a relief to feel welcome somewhere.

"Sure that outlet's being switched off was your fault?" Gertrude fished, slipping a ready-meal lasagna into the microwave.

"Who else's fault could it be? I'm on my own."

"And why would that be? Such a fine-looking girl. Don't fancy a body to keep you warm at night?"

"Oh, I've had my share of boyfriends," Helen exaggerated. "But right now I'm concentrating on my career. Enjoying my independence."

Gertrude glanced at her guest askance as she delivered a glass of lager (Helen would have preferred wine). "But what about a family? Getting late for you, I wager."

"Oh, I'm not sure children are in the cards. But they've never been a priority for me, really." The feisty assertion was undermined by a forlorn note.

As they sat down to their meal, Helen raised tentatively, "That face-off, with Judith. When she boarded up the windows, and padlocked the doors from the inside. How did it end?"

"Badly, of course," Gertrude said sorrowfully. "All manner of nasty notices pile up at the door. Officers pounding to be let in. Finally, didn't they drive up in a lorry with a battering ram, and bust through the entry. Don't know if you notice, but that front door of yours? It's spanking new. The old one was splintered to bits, like."

The old lock would have been done for as well. So much for the theory that Gertrude had a spare key. "So did they arrest her, or fine her? Say, for perverting the course of justice?"

Gertrude sighed. "Too late for that. They found Judith collapsed in the kitchen. Probably dead a day or two. She build one of them fertilizer bombs, if you can credit it. Researched the how-to on the internet; cops found the searches on a computer she'd used down at the library. Hadn't researched it too good, mind, since heaven be praised the contraption was duff. Poor wretch were overcome by the fumes when she try to set it off. Troubled me Judith didn't take into account how blowing up her house might of taken me own with it, but she couldn't of been in what you'd call a considerate state of mind."

"It was *her house*," Helen filled in. "If she couldn't keep it, then no one else was going to get it either."

"Figure that's about the sum of it."

NEVERTHELESS, SENSIBLE HELEN Rutledge couldn't countenance hocus-pocus, and throughout the following several years the *should* continued to take precedence over a great deal of *was*. A washer load of whites would come out a sickly pink, having been fouled by a pair of red socks, and Helen didn't own red socks. The dimmer switches in the breakfast room developed a constant tremble; the nervous sensation that the quavering halogen spots provided her evenings soon translated to her left eye, whose chronic twitch made clients at Manson & Ross worry that she was untrustworthy or hiding something. Electrical wiring began bulging from the plasterboard, branching in disquieting varicose veins, as if the whole house had high blood pressure.

Over time, mildew rose in a blighting speckle beside the shower stall, and to Helen the dusty pixels always formed a face—with beady, resentful eyes, frazzled hair, and pressed lips—much as visions of the Virgin Mary will appear to the devout on a piece of burnt toast. When Helen attempted to wipe off the spores, she simply smeared the expression from grimace to smirk. Disrobing under the moldy stare made her shy, and alone at home with the shades drawn Helen would bind a towel tightly under her arms to hide her breasts.

Trying to rejuvenate the disheveled back garden, Helen planted a row of forget-me-nots, in the hopes that the sheer helplessness and aching vulnerability of the tiny periwinkle blooms would protect the cover from harm. No such luck. The pretty little plants all withered and blackened within the week, while the garden suddenly reeked of ammonia and diesel, the smell to which she'd long before grown inured indoors.

Other misfortunes were more ruinous. During one workday, the bath spontaneously ran for hours and soaked the sitting room ceiling, which saved its collapse of soggy plaster for the moment of her return. Following some routine masonry repairs, both sinks backed up. When she swore herself blue that she would never pour wet concrete down her own kitchen drain, the plumber asked the obvious: "So who else did it?"

Even entertaining never went right. Guests spilled things, ate quickly, and left early. Perhaps the sense she'd had on first entering these quarters affected others as well. They didn't feel *welcome*.

When she finally invited a proper date round for a summer supper— Alan was a new hire, and rather dashing, for an accountant—he seemed ill at ease from the start, having been unsettled by the peculiar shelving of her Folio classics, which she'd given up standing spine-out. "She doesn't care for Jane Austen," Helen dismissed distractedly, basting the roast. While the two chatted awkwardly in the sitting room, the meat burnt to a cinder anyway, since *somehow* the oven dial got nudged up to gas-mark nine, and Alan had made a point of preferring his beef rare. But never mind the food, as once they sat down to a candlelit dinner on the little back porch the decking collapsed, breaking Alan's collarbone and ending their romantic evening in Accident and Emergency.

Sadly, Helen's resolve not to be defeated by mere bricks and mortar came at a cost. She developed an anxious, jumpy disposition, and workmates began to avoid her at lunch. Her appearance suffered; weight loss was aging, and due to a phobia about the shower, which got scalding with no warning as if suffering from menopausal hot flushes, her hair

was often greasy and flat. Proud independence slid without her noticing to reclusiveness. That forlorn note that had sounded at Gertrude's
about not giving "priority" to children became a dominant chord. Professionally, too, she felt increasingly perverse. Despite the smorgasbord
of careers from which she might have chosen when younger, she had
willingly plunged up to the eyeballs into the most odious aspect of modern life.

In the office, she'd once been a notorious stickler, insistent that expenses be entered in precise amounts to the penny. Yet now her decimal
points were wont to migrate willy-nilly two or three places. She would
forget to include buy-to-let profits, or neglect investment income. Consequently, one client in arrears with HMRC seemed to qualify for a
substantial refund. After the client had blown his windfall on a holiday
in Seville, he returned to face an audit and then criminal prosecution.
Helen was sacked.

She tried mightily to find another position, but she'd left the firm
without a reference. Months went by. Formerly substantial savings having been depleted by stamp duty, abortive DIY, and unanticipated bills
from tradesmen, she soon fell behind on her mortgage payments.

Helen imagined herself a reserved person, but 21 Lansing Terrace
had taken its toll. When the foreclosure notice from Barclays arrived,
she was incandescent. Was it her fault that the job market was so ane-
mic? Had she not arranged monthly direct debits for year upon year?
It was sheer larceny—the compulsory forfeiture of countless interest
payments, a fair whack of principal, and her deposit to boot! Was it
fair for slackers to get housing from the state for free, when responsible
taxpayers who fell on hard times were thrown on the street? True, she
hated this house, but mutual loathing had locked them into the embrace of lovers, and it was *her* house to hate. Indeed, no one would ever
revile this property with the ferocity of Helen Rutledge, who was not
about to abdicate its deed to anyone for whom her ultimate foe, her bête
noire, her personal nemesis, was merely an affordable bottom rung on
the UK's most worn-out metaphor.

Dear Gertrude having passed that autumn, and the council having yet to install another tenant in the adjacent semi, Helen searched the internet with a clean conscience. Moreover, she was still capable of calling up the exactitude and attention to detail that had once distinguished her performance at Manson & Ross. Only after exhaustive cross-reference and thorough perusal of shadily inquisitive threads on Ask.com and Yahoo did she settle on what appeared to be a foolproof recipe. So when Helen detonated her own toil and trouble, caldron bubble, accompanied by the rousing chorus of "Jerusalem," it worked.

The ChapStick

THE LOGIC WAS faulty: expressing his resentment of having to take this trip by leaving late for the airport. Dropping everything to fly to RDA was only worsened by traveling under stress. That foot-dragging in his Clinton Hill walk-up—clearing off coffee mugs that would have waited for his return—had merely ensured that Peter Dimmock would agitate in the taxi en route, shooting glances at the time blinking on the sedan's dashboard while glaring at the congestion on Atlantic. The jittering of his knee was probably driving the cabbie nuts. It would have been one thing to have announced firmly to his father's live-in home health aide—an illegal immigrant from Guatemala, paid in cash; this was America, after all, rich in its unique cultural *traditions*—that he had heard this death's-door business before, and this time he wasn't coming. To instead merely cut it close on catching the flight was like being passive-aggressive with yourself.

"When you fly?" asked the driver.

"Eight ten. JetBlue, terminal five." It was a stupid departure time, putting him smack in rush hour on the way to a stupid airport. But mid-evening from JFK was the only semiaffordable ticket he could scrounge at the last minute. "I'm running late, obviously. But with this traffic, there's no point in telling you to step on it." It was already nearing six o'clock, and they couldn't have gone more than half a mile.

"You go to . . . ?"

"Raleigh-Durham. Grew up there," he added gruffly, grateful that a Pakistani wouldn't have the ear or the interest, and so wouldn't comment on his passenger's lack of a Tarheel drawl. It was a boring conversation.

"This is warmer—than in New York?"

That was an even more boring conversation, earning only a grunt. "My father's dying. Supposedly. One more time." Having undercut the violin section, not wanting to be misread as bidding for sympathy, Peter added wistfully, "Although eventually it really is a wolf, isn't it?"

Silence seemed to indicate that the cabbie didn't get the allusion. For all Peter's skepticism, something told him that this time it was the wolf. If he hadn't left for the airport so late, he might have afforded a little reflection on how he felt.

"I am so sorry," the driver remembered to say at last—with a surprising passion.

IN HIS HEYDAY, Daniel Dimmock was the acknowledged Father of Modern Dialysis. Working circa 1960 at the embryonic form of what was now the vast and internationally acclaimed Research Triangle Park, he designed the revolutionary Dimmock Shunt—a mechanism that Peter still didn't understand, at fifty-eight. (Peter wasn't that dumb. He had failed to understand it on purpose.) Had the shunt been developed and patented through a commercial company rather than at a publicly funded nonprofit, Dr. Dimmock would have become a wealthy man—which the august medical researcher had noted himself a few hundred times. These many years after the man's retirement, Peter still couldn't assess with any confidence his father's importance in the wider world. In the small pond of renal research, his father had been a whale. Whether that made him a guppy in the ocean of human achievement or more like a grouper was anyone's guess.

In any event, Peter had been awed as a boy. He felt wistful about the adoration now, which he wouldn't have wanted to sustain through an unbecomingly fawning adulthood, but might have liked to revisit—like sampling one sumptuous bite of a cream bun otherwise sickly sweet for a mature palate. He'd boasted to third-grade classmates that his father wasn't a plain old doctor, but "more like a mad scientist." (Maybe it was the post-A-bomb paranoia, but in those days all scientists were "mad.") His father was lean, vigorous, and busy, and when you were a kid, or at least back then, nothing made grown-ups more impressive than the fact that they ignored you.

See, Dod hadn't been a cruel father. He was oblivious, which was worse. Cruelty at least entailed paying attention of a kind.

Funny, that *Dod*—the tag still cheered Peter up. All three kids had been schooled to call the guy "Father," a formal, old-fashioned term of address for the 1960s whose associations were too reverent, as in "Father of Modern Dialysis." "Father" was what bedraggled, brow-beaten children called their stern, religious-fundamentalist poppas in grim black-and-white art movies: "Yes, Father." "No, Father." "Of course you're right, Father, this dress is much too bright and whor-ish, what was I thinking." His older brother started it. Since Daniel Oliver Dimmock signed cryptic, bossy notes to their mother *DOD*, Luke appropriated the acronym, which outsiders often misheard as a snooty pronunciation of "Dad"; confronting paternal obstruction as a teenager, the eldest elongated the handle to "Department of Defense." An early discovery of childhood is the power of naming, one of the few weapons at the disposal of short people in the absence of capital, clout, or brawn. For Peter and his siblings, the rechristening of "Father" was a rare victory for their team, an impish pushback that Dod had never quite decided was insolent or affectionate, when it was both.

As a son, Peter had traveled an arc from awe to disenchantment that probably wasn't yet complete, with Dod on the cusp of oblivion at ninety-two. The filial disillusionment wasn't sourced in parental neglect, which was standard for family men married around 1950. It wasn't as if his father turned out to be a rather bad researcher, either, who did flawed work that killed people or something. There was no scandal, no embezzling of funds. No grievous private shortcoming like a gambling addiction or propensity for domestic violence fatally offset Daniel Dimmock's public accomplishment.

Be that as it may, the man often stayed late at the lab without bothering to pick up the phone, while his wife's lovingly prepared dinners would dry and char. He treated his children like annoyances, whom their mother hurriedly issued out of his way when he did come home. Conversation was dominated by which prestigious journal had accepted a paper, which colleague had cited his research, which medical conference had invited the great man to speak. He was competitive with his lab partners, and shamelessly voiced satisfaction when their experiments failed. If grant funding fell through, he didn't mourn the fact that a vital line of clinical inquiry would now not be pursued, but raged back and forth in the living room at the personal affront: "Would *I* have signed off on that application if it didn't have merit? Did those pinheads at the NIH ever notice whose name was on the title page?"

Thus by his latter teens, Peter began to register the real reason that his father wasn't a "plain old doctor." The revered MD might have had a taste for protégés, acolytes, and subordinates, but he'd little time for needy, smelly patients, much less for people as a broader class. The development of effective dialysis that could be repeated year after year was a technical challenge, likewise the refinement of a smaller, more portable machine that could be employed in domestic settings. What mattered to Dod was not the alleviation of suffering, but that if suffering was alleviated, Daniel Dimmock would get the credit. Renal research was of value only because he was good at it. In sum, the man was driven solely by self-aggrandizement. If by his own middle age Peter had tried to gentle the harshness of this assessment—most high achievers he'd encountered by then were powered primarily by narcissism, varying only in their capacity to conceal it—a boy's disappointment that his father was not, after all, a life-saving crusader but a self-serving egotist had never quite lost its bitter bite.

You'd think that at some point someone would have told a megalomaniac like Peter's father to stuff it. But no: the more egregious his behavior, the more the God's gift convinces the people he treats like dog shit that he must really be extraordinary, or long ago someone else would have told him to stuff it. Pricks get away with acting like pricks because they've always gotten away with acting like pricks, and no one wants to interfere with the natural order of the universe.

The same natural order was duplicated in the domestic sphere. Dod wasn't one of those pushy fathers who drove his children to succeed and so to manifest his hopes for them—a cliché that would surely have improved on a father who had no hopes for his children. For Daniel Dimmock had never displayed an appetite for passing on the generational baton. Though all three kids had the grades and test scores to make a bid for the Ivy League, he'd encouraged Luke, Esther, and Peter to take advantage of in-state tuition at local public colleges, when he himself had gone to Stanford. He didn't urge any of them to take on the big professions—law, the sciences—but promoted community service jobs like nursing or schoolteaching. Even these days, with so little to occupy his time, he never watched Luke's news packages online, checked out clients' enthusiastic reviews on Peter's webpage, or saved Esther's full-page profile in the business section of the *News and Observer* to boast about to friends. The good doctor had no intention of abdicating his position as the center of the familial universe, at however advanced an age. It couldn't have been coincidental that both boys were baptized with New Testament Christian names. They were raised to be apostles.

PETER HAD UNDERTAKEN the first of these missions of mercy to North Carolina after their father, then eighty-six, had fallen from a ladder while cleaning the gutters and broken his hip. This hackneyed beginning of the end presented an opportunity to make settling the estate after the inevitable occurred as graceful as possible. Once Luke had flown in from Portland and Esther from Beijing, the siblings conferred back at the house in Woodrow Park while their father was laid up in Rex

Hospital. Peter's brother and sister were in accord: in order to oversee their father's finances during a convalescence fated to end badly, Peter should get power of attorney. Esther was a poor candidate for the post, having moved to China. A television journalist who covered quirky, uplifting feel-good stories for local news in Oregon, Luke was often on the road, and was eager to avoid the aggravation of managing bills and investments. Besides, Peter had already been named the executor in their parents' will.

Like the decision to dub him executor, the fact that their father proved willing to give his youngest access to his accounts was a compliment, theoretically. A thriving consultant who helped American companies negotiate a foreign and no-little-devious business culture, Esther had further anchored herself to Beijing by marrying a native entrepreneur, thereby consigning herself to irrelevance in Raleigh. As the eldest, Luke might conventionally have stewarded their surviving parent's affairs, despite living farther away; in the online world, Portland and Brooklyn were right next door. Yet from childhood, Luke had exhibited a chameleon side, an unsettling capacity for being all things to all people—which is how he got away with presenting doggy, Pollyanna features about the finer side of human nature rising in the face of adversity when in private he was a cynic. He wasn't precisely a pleaser, which would have entailed actually pleasing people; he was a manipulator, which entailed seeming to please people. Given this lifelong slipperiness, neither their father nor their late mother entirely trusted Luke. Both parents regarded Peter as the moral anchor of their triad—the decent, dependable, faithful one, to whom it would never *occur* to take advantage of power of attorney by charging personal expenses to his father's credit card, or to discreetly siphon off a couple hundred grand in executor "fees," about which his siblings would never be the wiser.

Glowering at the haloed taillights of the sedulous traffic on South Conduit—it had started to sleet—Peter wondered whether being anointed as the trustworthy one might be a shade unpleasant. If he really wouldn't abuse his legal position to self-deal—and he hadn't—

the bovine rectitude suggested a lack of imagination. The expectation
that of course little Peter would unerringly toe the line imputed to the
youngest a cowed quality—if nothing else, a paralytic dread of being
caught. In pictures of Peter as a boy, his mouth dropped tremulously
open while his eyes widened, their pupils cast upward at an imploring
tilt. He'd been the weakest of the litter, the momma's boy, the crybaby
on the first day of school. The older two were always more rebellious,
more mischievous, less respectful (God love them)—and therefore, it
didn't take a psychological genius to decode: more independent, more
visionary, and less bludgeoned into submission to the Father of Modern Dialysis. So his parents had chosen their last-born to execute their
will because he was the tractable one, and would do their bidding. Too
timid to stray from the path of righteousness, Peter wouldn't have the
moxie to write himself checks on his father's account, lest lightning
strike him dead.

Being trusted was an insult.

Yet Peter Dimmock was fifty-eight years old, and that quivering
portrait from first grade, which had mocked him from the frame on
his parents' buffet for decades, was out of date. He was a larger, more
muscular man than his older brother, who didn't work out, and was
starting to look puffy on camera. In adulthood, Peter had developed a
temper that sometimes got him into trouble, though it was the return
of his primary-school timorousness, not wrath, that he blamed for the
recent demise of his second marriage. June had steadily lost respect
for her husband the longer he step 'n' fetched for her father-in-law.
Or maybe that wasn't the main reason she walked out, but it hadn't
helped.

When first awarded power of attorney, Peter felt a quiet sense of victory. In running his father's logistical life, he could turn the tables, take
control—all in preparation for receiving a baton that at last the man
couldn't withhold. At the time, Peter had estimated that his ailing father would last six months at the outside, just long enough to get the old
man's affairs in order—to consolidate his assets, locate the house deeds

and car registration, learn his passwords, and solicit a list of the music he preferred for the funeral in a spirit of discomfiture and sorrow.

It had now been six years. Apparently, the aged *usually* don't recover from broken hips, just as it's *usually* the daughters who squander their primes caring for elderly parents—and tell that to Esther the Wheeler-Dealer in Beijing. Dod was Peter's problem, and his siblings were ever so keen that he remain Peter's problem.

When first embarking on his fiduciary duties, Peter had been intent on demonstrating his competencies, in hopes that his father would be impressed. After his mother's death three years earlier, he'd lost his champion, who had long claimed that her second son's problem was having "too many talents." (Perhaps she was right, since you were far better off with only one talent.) His mother had encouraged her youngest to nurse all manner of arty, unrealistic ambitions, although he was also, of the three, the least likely to develop the resilient ego that pursuing arty ambitions with any success required. He tried acting at UNC Chapel Hill, where he was easily crushed by failed auditions; he'd hoped that his performances were *subtle*, but in retrospect a better word was *flat*. Doing wedding gigs after college with a killing barbershop quartet hardly paved the way to a career. When he turned to screenwriting, his dialogue was sharp, or what a hired editor called "clever," but he never registered that film was a visual medium in which something was supposed to happen that you could see.

Finally in his thirties he converted ignominy to enterprise. Having been cured of a childhood lisp by a sympathetic young man trained in the field, Peter qualified as a speech therapist. It was a humble occupation, which didn't transform renal medicine for all time, but did make a difference to individual stutterers and stroke patients. For a sense of importance, he leveraged his small usefulness by plying his trade in what, for a self-exiled North Carolinian, was still the greatest city in the world. Dod had never acted overtly disappointed by how Peter turned out, but he wasn't exactly wowed.

Furthermore, you don't readily impress as an underling. Power of attorney hadn't conferred conquest of any sort. It had designated Peter his father's errand boy. Daniel Dimmock had been accustomed to secretaries and lab assistants his whole professional life, so ordering around his son instead came naturally. Peter's position as paternal flunky brought out the timidity threaded through in his DNA that he most despised about himself. Overcompensating, he'd pick fights with June, shouting and breaking things. That didn't impress, either.

The near invalid didn't have much to fill his day, and thus spent much of it hectoring Peter from command central, a grand leather-inlaid desk in a study plastered with framed degrees and commendations. When Dod ran him ragged with demands—for a stair lift repair, a more adjustable shower chair—Peter swallowed his impatience and thanked God for online shopping. Many of Dod's requests were pretextual. Outliving multiple friends and colleagues, having avoided the "drooling imbeciles" of a nursing home, and tended by aides who barely spoke English, he had few people to talk to. By a good measure, then, Peter spent more time speaking to his father than keeping in touch with his own two kids. (One price when the calls were protracted: the pernicious return of the up-lilting southern accent that this proudly reconditioned New Yorker had shed. So contaminated, Peter had actually addressed the family of one Upper East Side client as *y'all.*) While not clinically demented, Dod did relentlessly repeat himself, and he would get exercised about the loss of small objects, blamed on sticky-fingered caretakers, that he'd merely mislaid. Why in this day and age would a semi-illiterate steal a fountain pen? When Dod alienated still another live-in aide by being accusatory, dictatorial, and unappreciative, Peter would numbly contact the Latino community center on New Hope Church Road, where another off-the-books unfortunate could be found. Meanwhile up in New York, each new medical crisis involved rescheduling a raft of appointments with clients whom a freelancer could not afford to lose, in order for Peter, who was also his father's health care proxy, to streak down south on flights like the one he was now in danger of missing.

He hadn't been running things; he'd been run. He did his father's taxes. He hired his father's gardener. If only to service his father's vanity, he kept the retired medical researcher's AMA membership paid up. He ordered his father a crate of ruby-red grapefruits from Florida every Christmas. He'd put his own personal life and career on hold, while his siblings got off with rare, distracted Skype chats. For all his manly biceps, Peter remained the little boy in that first-grade photo: meek.

ARRIVING AT TERMINAL five by 7:05 p.m. was little short of a miracle. He had twenty-five minutes before the flight would board, and he'd checked in online. Rolling only carry-on, Peter should squeak onto the flight, just. It all depended on security.

The line wasn't bad; February wasn't a month for heavy travel. He made a futile effort to repress his compulsive incredulity that every day millions of people were forced to go through this elaborate tedium of queuing, disrobing, and being X-rayed because of the freakishly high likelihood—any likelihood being freakishly high—that passengers will blow up their own planes. (*Don't say "blow up." Not even in a mumble.*) In other walks of life, the same assumptions about humanity's poor sense of self-preservation would dictate tall fences along every curb, lest pedestrians hurl themselves en masse into oncoming traffic. Or you wouldn't even allow such a thing as cars, lest drivers plow blindly into concrete stanchions the moment your back was turned.

Enough. For the rest of this journey, he should focus on its purpose. False alarms had inured him to this errand, but this time it was pneumonia—or "ammonia," as Dod had croaked on the phone, one of the several recent slips. If by now he might find in his father's passing an element of relief, ample time remained to admit as much in the years to come. Just now, he should prepare for grief.

In a line full of seasoned fliers, there's always one moron who waits until the last minute to pull all the crap from his luggage and holds everyone up.

Before he'd any firsthand experience of the parental fade to black,

Peter would have imagined a softening, a rounding of edges, on the part of both parent and erstwhile child—as if both parties were scoops of ice cream placed for a benedictory moment in the sun, and all the rumples, ridges, and rills smoothed to leave uniform balls of benevolence. To the contrary, the aged seemed to seize only more stiffly into who and what they had always been—their rumples got bumpier, their ridges peaked, their rills ran deeper—so that if you could compare them to ice cream, it was more to the sort so hard that you couldn't ram a spoon into the carton. Into his dotage ever more vainglorious, Dod was bafflingly unembarrassed by neighbors bringing pies, church congregants doing his grocery shopping, and volunteers from age-related charities replacing the rotten floorboards on his porch. He took the obeisance as his due. These many gestures would have constituted karmic goes-around-comes-around had the imperious codger ever done for others himself, but Daniel Dimmock had never in his life run chores for the elderly, much less baked anyone a pie.

More disconcertingly still, far from "softening" himself, far from gaining a sense of perspective on a father's minor failings, which he might soon recall with a backhanded tenderness, ever since intuiting during yesterday's phone call from Raleigh that this time his father wasn't planning an encore, Peter had flushed with waves of rage. It was as if in the next day or two he had to fit in all the pique he'd suppressed for decades, because once his father was dead there'd be nothing to do with it—the way you scurry about duty-free spending the last of your foreign coinage on chocolate. There wasn't any earthly point to fuming at a corpse.

Given that he had been through this dash to bid farewell several times, with its customary saying of last things, it would seem unlikely that there were any last things left to say. Nevertheless, Peter's head roiled with speeches, and they resembled nothing like, *Father, you've set such a fine example of a life well lived, and Esther, Luke, and I have always been grateful to enjoy such an accomplished, brilliant, distinguished, formidable . . . WHATEVER*, since the one thing that fathead didn't need was another compliment! Instead, Peter pictured railing at his father's bedside, *How come you think you're so* special? *You never bat-ted an eye at the hours and hours I spent—days, weeks even—arranging for your whole ground floor to be wheelchair-ramped in preparation for your return home with that hip, and getting the master bathroom ripped out, railed, and installed with a roll-in shower. I still have a life, or I did—I have kids who are young adults and need my counsel, but no! I have to fly back to RALEIGH.*

"Sir—you're up," nudged the woman behind him, not unkindly.

"Oh, sorry!" Peter placed a premium on competent air travel, and hurried to remove his tablet, per usual providing the iPad its own sep-arate, giant gray tray. He fished out his cell, change, and keys. He re-moved his overcoat, folding his sports jacket neatly beside it. Though its modest buckle shouldn't have set off the detector, he slid his belt through the loops, and nestled it by the coats in a tidy coil. From the same prudence, he unstrapped his slender watch. He tugged off his shoes, ruing the second-day socks. He pulled out his Ziploc, *no larger than one-quart size*, containing shampoo, deodorant, and toothpaste, *no more than three point four ounces or one hundred milliliters*, making sure to put the baggie, in accordance with the standard specifications, *on top* of his overcoat, DESPITE THE FACT THAT THE STUPID BAGGIE IS GOING INTO A GODDAMNED X-RAY.

Okay, yes, true—during this calm, methodic execution of his du-ties as a responsible flier, who completely understood that all these precautionary imperatives were contrived only for the safety of himself and his fellow passengers, he did feel a *teensy-weensy* twinge of irri-tation. The liquids protocol was inane. It had been roundly demon-strated that determined malefactors could concoct a successful science fair project with miniatures. Worse, the tiny bottles so consumed TSA agents, who took a malicious pleasure in confiscating costly moistur-izers of three point *five* ounces, that they forgot entirely to look for detonators wired to big wads of Semtex. That was why the agency finally lifted the ban on cigarette lighters in carry-on luggage. In test runs, its officers had found the lighters all right, veritably every one, but had left the guns.

Peter scanned the signage—no sharp objects, explosives, or fire-arms—to confirm he'd been fully *compliant*. It was a creepy word, beloved of authorities everywhere, who treasured its ambience of sim-pering eagerness to please, spineless groveling, wormlike subservience, and pants-wetting terror. *Compliance* admitted of no resistance; if you pictured the word as a thing, it was floppy and flaccid and on the floor.

Raising a hand to the folks behind him in apology that he hadn't initiated this striptease in more advance, Peter rushed his four plastic trays down the rollers, while opposite a languid TSA agent with bright green nails looked on sullenly, blah-blahing in a monotone about liq-uids and gels. Once the last tray got traction on the rubber belt, he gave his pockets a nervous extra pat for a nail clipper or stray quarter. An-other agent waved him wordlessly to the scanner—the guy's only job. Nice work if you could get it.

The curved clear plastic doors opened, à la *Star Trek* elevator—this whole clunky pod thing had that cheap, knocked-together look of a set for 1960s television—and he assumed the position, fitting his socks into the blobby footprints, lifting his arms in submission. He'd read in the *Times* a while back that these machines were rarely serviced, and the quantity of whatever carcinogenic rays they shot through you was fre-quently off the charts. For a short while thereafter he had insisted on being a "male opt-out," delighting in putting staff to the extra trouble of a pat down. But the thrill wore off. They'd snap on latex gloves as if he carried some disease, clearly put out by this asshole who couldn't get with the program, the while feigning all that respectfulness: "Now, I'm going to run only the *back* of my hand down your inseams." At some point, a bubbly TSA officer had assured him that all those old health concerns had been seen to, and now Advanced Imaging Technology was perfectly safe. He had no reason to believe her. Yet from laziness, as well as resignation, because in the end the tyrants of antiterrorism would always triumph, ever since he'd been *compliant*.

You know, I finally looked up the Dimmock Shunt online—Peter's bedside tirade had meanwhile resumed—*and it turns out that nobody uses it anymore! So you did your part for renal medicine back in the day—a day* over fifty years *ago—what of it? Esther learned* Chinese. *CEOs of massive American companies ask your daughter for her advice.* Esther *is important. Luke is on* TV. *For that matter, why was it always so important to you to be important? Me, I may not have changed history or pulled in big bucks, but at least I have a feel for other people, don't I? Since it's hardly a surprise that as an MD you never worked with flesh-and-blood patients, more "drooling imbeciles" you might actually have had to talk to. And my clients* like me, *believe it or not—and they get better, they learn to speak more clearly, they remember more words or get them out without sputtering, and afterwards they're* thankful—

"Over here, sir."

"What?"

The African American agent who issued him off to the side would not have looked nearly as fat if her pants weren't so tight. Their waist bit at an unflattering point, cutting under rather than containing her stomach. The uninflected flatness of her voice reminded Peter of his "subtle" acting in college. Had his mind not been clamorous with that saying of last things, he might have noticed: perhaps far enough into her shift that the time had started to drag, yet not so advanced into her workday as to be buoyed by the proximity of its conclusion, this youngish federal employee exuded the kind of boredom that is dangerous.

"Raise your arms, sir?"

Peter was stymied. He'd taken out his tablet, removed his coats and shoes and change and keys, put his dinky toiletries in that insipid *baggie*, surrendered in stocking feet in their unconvincing plastic pod, and now there was still more procedure, more insincere suspicion, more Mother May I. Fair enough, he duly thrust out his arms on either side, as if to do that minute arm-circle exercise that looked lame but made your shoulders ache like a bastard. Yet he also allowed himself to say aloud, along with the suggestion of an eye roll, albeit brief and certainly not overdone, "Oh, for pity's sake."

And that was a big mistake.

For two reasons, the first being obvious, since the cardinal rule of air travel was Keep Your Head Down. It was as if he'd barely survived a mass murder, and had been lying motionless amid the bodies. But rather than continue to play dead, in emitting *Oh, for pity's sake*, he had effectively jumped up and shouted, "Wait! Over here! You missed one!"

The second reason Peter knew the grumble would prove a grave misjudgment was neurological: it connected mind with mouth. At airport security, your sole protection from capricious persecution, arbitrary search and seizure, and indefinite detention without charge was the privacy of your head. An eternal infuriation for enforcers of every sort, a riot of apostasy, sedition, and mutinous insult—*your pants make you look fat*—was more than possible to entertain with disgraceful impunity *just so long* as these unacceptable sentiments were hermetically contained between ear, right, and ear, left. But to continue to provide a bouncy castle where a host of emotions lethal in the open air—disgust, contempt, derision—could imperviously leap, carouse, and interplay, this small, rounded safe house couldn't have any holes. Where the brain most commonly sprang a leak was around the upper and lower jaws.

With a warning glare after that *for pity's sake* impertinence, the TSA agent began tracing his spread legs and outstretched arms with a black plastic wand, which like all their other kit looked phony. It recalled those IED-divining gizmos some shyster had sold to the Iraqi army, in which its soldiers continued to place a superstitious faith at checkpoints even after the implement had been exposed as containing nothing but an unactivated credit card.

Alas, once mind was fatally connected with mouth, it was the dickens to close the valve. So the self-preservational part of Peter—which kept him from, say, hurling himself into traffic—tried frantically to summon his mental plumbers: *Hurry, this is an emergency, I need to shut the fuck up.* But until his cranial tradesmen answered the call, the back-sass percolating through his skull would dribble right into terminal five.

"But I already took out all the coins, the keys," Peter objected, his tone perhaps not overtly hostile but certainly a tad testy, when it should have been obliging, obsequious, sniveling even, and a far better line of attack would have run something like, *I'm so sorry, Officer, I seem to have made some grievous error that is all my fault, and I deeply regret putting you to any unnecessary extra trouble.*

"This scanner isn't a metal detector," she droned.

Which he knew, really, he supposed, he hadn't been focused, and getting that wrong was flustering, vexation being the very antithesis of what was required: perfect self-control. So when she ordered, "Empty your pockets, sir"—there was no *please*—he didn't say, *Oh, yes, certainly, sorry, whatever did I forget about? Why, you poor officers, you must get so tired of us scatterbrained passengers never getting the procedure right no matter how many times we go through this,* but:

"I did everything I was supposed to. If on top of the iPad and the shoes and the coats, the keys and the change and the belts, you're also supposed to completely and utterly empty all your pockets of *absolutely everything*—down to the fluff, and the threads, and the grit—the signs, or at least one of the officers out front, should have said so."

In concert with this *inadvisable* disquisition, Peter was indeed emptying his pockets; he was *complying.* But within reach, there was no table or surface of any sort on which to pile what little he could scrounge from his jeans: a crumple of dollar bills; a used tissue; a plastic unbreakable comb, bent by the curve of his buttock; in the watch pocket, perhaps having gone through the wash, an individually wrapped, long-forgotten cool-blue mint, soft and turning white; a to-do list ("take out trash"; "check in online"; "pick up and freeze small Junior's cheesecake for Dod, even if he won't live to eat it"); two tablets of Tylenol in a scrap of Saran Wrap in case of a headache now a virtual certainty. So he put the detritus on the floor. Since there really was nowhere else to put the stuff, the functionary might plausibly have forgiven his depository of choice, if only he had stooped to display these miserable wares in a suitably cringing spirit. While he certainly wasn't acting cowed, Peter would still have characterized himself as merely "placing" these offerings at the official's feet. Yet perhaps an observer who described him instead as "slamming" the wad of singles onto the linoleum would have been exaggerating only by an increment or two.

Her boredom moderated by a hint of relish, the plump overseer cried, "Supervisor!"

Just then, Peter made a connection between a last lump at the very bottom of his right front pocket and the scanner's output screen—on which a bland outline of a figure in a posture of surrender was accented by a single red spot on one thigh, like a child's representation of a boo-boo. His fingers closed around the source of this nonsense: a Chap-Stick. That was the boo-boo.

By the time the supervisor showed up—a swaggering thirtyish black guy in dreadlocks; oh, great, this encounter had every capacity to escalate into a race matter—Peter had *placed* the offending item amid the sad little pile of paper and plastic wrap on the floor, which looked so like trash that next he'd be accused of littering. He'd resumed his feet-spread stance and—because, after all, he had never been given permission to put them back down—thrust his arms back out, fingers outstretched, once again in seeming preparation for arm circles.

"You got a problem, mister?" the supervisor challenged, coming an intimidating inch or so too close. "You gonna *be* my problem?"

"No, sir," Peter said, jutting his chin but not in the man's direction. Avoiding the superior's gaze, he trained his own at a forty-five degree angle to the agent's face. Absurdly, he kept his arms extended. Bend-over-backward obedience could double as defiance. "I've done everything that was asked of me, sir."

"You gonna pick that stuff up off the floor?"

"Yes, *sir*. If you say so, *sir*. But I was ordered to take everything out of my pockets, *sir*." Peter had seen enough boot-camp movies to bark rigidly at attention like a green recruit.

"You in my *house*," the man purred, taking another half step into Peter's personal space. "Don't disrespect me in my *house*."

Peter couldn't help it; the mental plumbers had never shown up. "Begging your pardon, *sir*. With all due respect, *sir*. This is not your house. This is a public airport, *sir*."

So that was that. Allowed to scoop up his Kleenex, his to-do list, his ChapStick, his Tylenol, Peter was issued off to the little white room.

IN THE ISLAMIC State not long before, several women of Raqqa had been whipped for cladding themselves in abayas that were too tight and wearing Western makeup. But more than one immodest captive was given five extra lashes for "not being meek enough when detained."

Thus any agitation, or even the very fraudulent deference of which TSA agents themselves were masters, had now given way to a rueful, solitary repose.

Holding the specimen between thumb and middle finger, Peter Dimmock contemplated the source of his undoing. The ChapStick was the original kind, whose black-and-white wrapper had not changed appreciably in his lifetime. He never bought the brand's more innovative lip balms—not even tame variants like spearmint and strawberry, much less candy cane, or cake batter—because his father always used the original flavor, and he liked the smell. Peter associated that almost medical waxy plainness with his boyhood, when Dod was still "Father," and would lean down and smack his youngest on the cheek, leaving an invisible smear. He never wiped it off. It emanated a residual waft of unadorned masculinity, of a piece with his father's folded, freshly laundered cotton handkerchiefs, starched white shirt collars, and cool-blue-mint breath. Self-respecting men of Daniel Dimmock's generation would never be caught dead with cake batter lip balm.

Older and rechristened, Dod stopped kissing his sons, settling for a shoulder clap, or a handshake once they were grown. Thus Peter associated the smell of that original-flavor ChapStick with the unabashed adoration of a little boy, not yet compromised by the curse of mature clear-sightedness. If only because it was one of the sole props in his possession—they said they'd retrieve his tablet, coats, and carry-on, but no one seemed in any hurry—he ran the balm around his lips, which were dry. The smell was the same, and recalled his father in sharp relief, with a rush of affection this time, and then he knew he would never wish to launch into a harangue at the poor man's bedside about how the Dimmock Shunt was obsolete.

The officer who eventually grilled him about "making a scene" in airport security, "refusing to obey an officer's instructions" (flagrantly untrue), "flying into a rage" (TSA-speak for becoming mildly irked) and "endangering his fellow passengers" was visible for half an hour through the crack of the office door, exuding that time-killing idleness that in an earlier era would have expressed itself with a cigarette. Foolishly, Peter had committed the one unforgivable crime in the world of air travel—which wasn't, of course, holding a box cutter to a flight attendant's throat, but *having a bad attitude*—for which he had to be made an example, lest other fliers come to imagine that they were within their rights to get annoyed. Thus this wait was deliberate, its length carefully calculated to make him miss his plane.

Peter was raised in a family that taught him a great deal about power, especially about not having any—which should have been ideal training for flying from any airport in America in the twenty-first century. TSA agents were deputized with the kind of petty power that was especially horrifying because it wasn't really petty. They could ensure that you would be a no-show at a lecture you'd been engaged to give all year, damaging your professional reputation and having what would have been a lucrative honorarium withdrawn. They could make you sacrifice your hotel deposit or miss your own wedding. They could keep you from being present at the birth of your grandchildren. And they could most certainly guarantee that you would not see your father one last time before he died.

Negative Equity

THE LANDERS' PREDICAMENT came home to them when they decided to divorce and then nothing happened.

Graham must have been working himself up to the scene for weeks.
With sympathy born of habit and temperament alike, Rosalind felt
sorry for him; why, no wonder that for the last several evenings he'd
come home from the restaurant feeling ill. In the end, it was a relief for
them both. The decision to dissolve a marriage of nine years' standing
made for a warmer, sweeter evening than they'd conducted in months.

"I don't quite know how to say this," he'd begun, and even in this
declaration of inarticulacy Rosalind detected rehearsal. "I don't want
you to think there's someone else. There isn't."

"Who isn't someone else?" Honestly, she was trying to help.

They were sitting at the ample rough-hewn table made from a barn
door that so many dinner guests of yore had envied. Alongside, a
generous six-foot prep table divided the dining area from the kitchen
she'd always pined for, with cast iron dangling from the ceiling, slate
flooring, funky lines of mismatched spice jars, and retro tomato tins
brambling with spatulas and tenderizers. The triple-glazed skylights
that Graham had special ordered and the french doors onto their long,
lush garden would welcome fierce shafts of sunlight in the morning; at
well past midnight, the open-plan ground floor glowed quietly from an

array of inset down-lights on a dimmer switch. It was a beautiful house. Whatever the property websites claimed, this semidetached Georgian freehold was no less fetching than it had been a year before.

"It just shouldn't be possible!" Graham burst out opaquely. She sensed this presentation was already muddled, as if his mental Power-Point had frozen. "See, one of the waitresses—"

"Which one?" Way ahead of him, Rosalind sifted through the possibilities. In the "credit crunch"—a newsreader thumbnail that made the misery of millions sound like a chocolate bar—Graham's cozy city-center bistro Say La Vie had already let one waitress go. Of the remaining three, one was a cow, the other over sixty. How hard was it?

"It doesn't matter which one. We haven't done anything. We haven't had an affair."

He insisted that he didn't want to leave his wife *for* Chantelle, a willowy, athletic blond a decade his junior whom he persistently refused to name. But for even his eyes to stray, he said, his passion for Rosalind must have waned. Whether she believed him that there'd been no quickies in the pantry was of no importance. He wanted a divorce, and it really didn't matter if an ex-husband was a liar.

Rosalind would enjoy plenty of leisure to contemplate the nature of the worm in their marriage. To indulge Graham's dream of starting Say La Vie five years earlier, she'd been game for moving to Sheffield, closer to Graham's family, with an eye to having their own—though in current economic circumstances they'd put off a pregnancy yet another year. She got on better with his parents than with hers, and one could be a dental hygienist just about anywhere. Still, she missed the sense of possibility in London, and particular friends. Perhaps she'd been a little depressed. She didn't feel depressed, but depression appeared to concern less what you did feel than what you didn't.

Yet never mind the autopsy. They'd taken out a massive home equity loan when the restaurant's clientele first began to flag. It had seemed to make sense; the loan might see them through the downturn, and the house had appreciated a staggering fifty percent. But now that the property market had sagged as well, they owed more on the house than it was worth. If they sold now, they'd be saddled with debt that would snuffle at both their heels for years like a scabby stray. Graham may have been suffering from workplace lechery or worse, but for the time being, like it or not, they were stuck with each other.

For the proceeding fortnight, Rosalind and Graham experienced a curious flowering of their relationship. They'd both sensed something amiss, and getting it out in the open shed the toxic buildup of the unsaid. As housemates rather than spouses, too, they were much more courteous—remembering to say *please* could you pick up some milk, *thank you* for doing my laundry as well, or *sorry!* when they bumped into each other in the hall. Rosalind took unusually careful phone messages—printing neatly, ears ever pricked for a voice that sounded blond. As they fixed their separate breakfasts, Graham offered to boil an extra egg. She actually listened to him when he described that night's specials, even suggesting that the celeriac mash might benefit from a dash of horseradish. He actually listened to her when she described scraping the tartar off a patient's lower right molar the day before and having the tooth come out horrifyingly in her hand. Sticking to his story that he'd done nothing to be ashamed of, Graham insisted firmly that letting Rosalind stay in the master bedroom and moving his own things down the hall was driven by chivalry, not guilt. In all, the new politeness was shocking, since it emphasized the contrasting obliviousness and even rudeness into which the two had hitherto slipped. Rosalind knew she shouldn't allow herself to misinterpret the transformation, but the fresh descent of kindness and consideration couldn't help but get her hopes up a bit.

Meantime, while breathing through her mouth at the surgery to keep from recoiling from cases of chronic halitosis, naturally she pondered what had gone wrong. The difficulties with Say La Vie hadn't helped. After only one exhausting year, Graham had confessed ruefully that if you really loved to cook, the last thing you should ever do is open a restaurant. She'd admired his candor, though he was not a quitter.

Yet in addition the couple seemed to have lost, well—a sense of occasion. Initially, they'd both made a fuss over each other's birthdays, with piles of presents, many of them silly. Wedding anniversaries had sponsored a grand splurge, gloriously, at someone else's restaurant. On their second Valentine's Day together, Graham had lavished hours on a great heart-shaped onion tart, with tiny cutout pastry hearts scalloping its edge. Back in London they'd bought Christmas trees, one year decorating the fir with a culinary theme: whisks, egg slicers, and dangling wooden spoons. Stockings having been her favorite Yuletide ritual as a child, the woolen knee-highs they'd hung from the mantel in Kennington were as lumpy and bloated as the gout-ridden legs of a stout old man. Rosalind used to spend days finding droll trinkets for Graham's stocking: garish candies in the shape of pizzas, hotdogs, and fried eggs; gadgets like mussel holders and strawberry hullers that he'd never use, but utility hadn't been the point. Stockings were vessels for the small, the frivolous, and the tender.

What had happened? Boredom, practicality, and running dry of ideas. Birthdays had grown perfunctory. Rosalind might find him a package of Dalmatian-print boxers and not even bother to wrap it. Graham might find her something for the house—stainless-steel coasters to protect their beloved barn-door table—that was really for them both. Never mind a card, much less a tart, it was a miracle if either even remembered to say "Happy Valentine's Day!" on February fourteenth. As for Christmas, proximity to Graham's family had allowed them lazily to rely on her in-laws' festivities. They'd given a tree a miss since moving to Sheffield; the needles made such a mess. Why, this last Christmas they bought the obligatory bits and bobs for Graham's family, but made a pact to economize and skip buying presents for each other—the kind of pact you were meant secretly to break. Yet they'd kept their words! The problem wasn't the loss of any one holiday or marker; it was collective. In failing to celebrate a host of small occasions, Rosalind and Graham had neglected to celebrate the biggest of occasions: their lives together, abruptly so truncated and finite.

* * *

THE SECOND HONEYMOON came to an end on a Monday, when Say La Vie was closed. Graham was out late, without explanation. He didn't owe her explanations anymore, which didn't keep Rosalind from waiting up and fretting.

"Where have you been?" she snapped when he walked in at two a.m.

"Well, I *could* say," he said cautiously, "that's none of your business."

"*Could* say, or is that what you're saying? Because if it isn't, don't say it!" The corners of her eyes leaked mean, aggrieved tears.

"Ros. I realize it doesn't look like it, but we're separated. If I want to go out to dinner, I don't have to ask your permission."

"You don't even like going out to dinner! It's been 'demythologized,' you said! Restaurants are a waste of money, and a real treat nowadays is to eat in!"

"I've *also* said," he reminded her gently, "that the main thing you pay for isn't food but venue. It's like renting eight square feet of elsewhere for the night. Which, with our current arrangements, is exactly what I needed."

"It's that *Chantelle*, isn't it?"

He didn't deny it. She was inconsolable.

He shook his head. "This isn't working. I'd get my own flat, but I'm not sure I could manage the rent, keep Say open, and still meet our mortgage payments. But I might manage to let a room . . ."

Rosalind got herself together, for she suddenly realized that the only way to keep him—and part of what she realized is that she wanted to keep him—was to keep him in this house. "No, no, even a room would bust our budget. I guess the only thing I can't stand is secrecy. Being shut out. Obviously, you have every right . . . But since you *do* like nothing more than a night at home, next time . . . Well, why not bring her here?"

THUS THE FOLLOWING Monday, Rosalind found herself enmeshed in what was lightly christened *romantic comedy*, something of an oxymoron in her view; nothing about romance had ever struck her as funny. When Graham rocked up with this Chantelle creature, Rosalind had prepared the dating couple a candlelit dinner. Begging off joining them, she declared gaily, "Just think of me as your *waitress*"—flicking her not-especially-estranged husband a wicked glance. Becoming the other woman in her own home was rather stimulating, really, and Rosalind didn't, as she had feared, mope through the courses or fall into fits of weeping. Instead she was bright, witty, and hyperactive. Whisking around the prep island to lift dishes and condiments, she made a great show of graciousness in relation to Chantelle, asking where her family was from and where she'd gone to school.

"Of course, Say La Vie *must* be a 'day job,'" she gushed warmly. "Have you thought about what you really want to do?"

Chantelle had begun the evening understandably guarded, answering Rosalind's many merry questions formally and with few words. It was an odd situation, as they'd all agreed at the outset. Yet gradually the girl had relaxed, coming to find the circumstances a bit of a kick, and perhaps anticipating what a good story she'd have to share with girlfriends when they were binge-drinking at the weekend. She had that uninvested, dismissive nonchalance typical of her age. As a group, her Whatever Generation displayed a flip, arch airiness, as if apathy were a mark of sophistication. But Ros had seen plenty such girls come and go at the surgery, and soon enough they all developed adult-scale attachments. Life didn't let you get away with being blasé for long, if only because everybody cares about pain. And Rosalind had to concede that, with long, swaying straight hair like a palomino's mane and legs at which even another woman couldn't help but stare, the young lady was fetching.

"Have you considered becoming a dental hygienist?" Ros proposed. "Now, I know it seems a turn-off at first. But if you work for a private dentist, the pay's pretty good, and your day's over at five sharp. You're doing something important, and when you clean up some lad's smile, that came in coffee gray and tobacco stained? You've made him a lot more confident about himself in just half an hour, and it's surprisingly satisfying!"

Of course there was a subtext: You can train as a hygienist and then you can get married and buy a house and put your assets into a fledgling business, until your husband hires a waitress like you. Perhaps fortunately, Chantelle didn't extrapolate quite this far, and when she said she'd consider the career, she seemed to mean it.

"Well, even if Chantelle and I don't work out, at least you two will still be fast friends," Graham said after he returned from driving the girl home; at twenty-four, Chantelle still lived with her mum. "I felt like a right third wheel."

"Well, it's obviously, you know, awkward," Rosalind said, loading the dishwasher. "I was trying to set her at ease."

"Went a bit overboard," Graham reprimanded, though he was smiling.

"I wasn't attempting to co-opt her or anything."

"Oh, no? Always telling, what people say they're *not* doing. Though I have to say"—Graham balanced an oatmeal cluster on a slice of peach—"with just the amount of clove so it's strong but not dominating . . . Your crumble's top drawer."

IT WAS INEVITABLE, Rosalind supposed, that after the next Monday's dinner those two would decamp to the guest room and close the door. If only to safeguard her dignity, when a patient was flirtatious the following week she lured him home. She hadn't meant to start a contest, only to preserve her sense of herself as desirable and to restore a certain domestic balance. Let *Graham* find out what it was like to wake in his own house and have to make small talk with a total stranger who'd just shagged his spouse.

With Aiden, Graham was not himself given to Rosalind's approach—football badinage, invitations to play golf, offers of complimentary glasses of champagne at Say. To the contrary, he was gruff and visibly put out. So the gambit worked splendidly—if gambit is what it was. What a shame, then, that Aiden's halitosis had not cleared up after the cleaning, not even once he followed her advice to brush his tongue.

Yet with Christmas around the corner, it wouldn't do to be seen drooping through the holiday pathetically on her own. Thus she kept up the pretense of seeing Aiden, claiming that, since Graham had been so horrid to her swain over kippers, they preferred her boyfriend's flat. To explain her continued presence at breakfast, she paired an imaginary erotic tradition of preprandial passion with a truthful preference for waking in her own bed. Aping the jaunty liberation of a soon-to-be-divorcée discovering a whole new lease on life helped her in some measure to inhabit the role. Still, Graham's trysts were real.

All too real as well were her visits to property websites, which left Rosalind increasingly dejected. A pretend boyfriend was no consolation in the harsh blue glare of the computer: The market in Sheffield was recovering. The value of their comely Georgian freehold would be going steadily back up.

"SO WHAT ARE your plans for Christmas?" Rosalind attempted the airy delivery she'd learned from Chantelle.

"Oh, Chant and I will go to my parents', I figure," Graham said with an identical airiness. "Do the usual prezzies, soup-to-nuts palaver. What about you?"

"Well, my parents will be in Spain, so there's no point in my heading to Wimbledon." Being honest about this bit made it a tad easier to append more fanciful information. "Aiden's not on speaking terms with his family," she extemporized, curious what this tragic falling-out might possibly be over. Storytelling was so demanding! She'd no understanding of how novelists and other congenital liars managed. "So we thought we'd splash out on a big holiday meal at Kenwood Hall, just the two of us."

Since Graham could resort to the more seasonally apt comforts of home and hearth, she'd no idea why his expression grew so wistful.

* * *

ROSALIND'S PRIDE IN her budding narrative prowess wilted on the
realization that she was now obliged to make herself scarce on a day
she had no earthly thing to do. On Christmas Eve, her new powers of
invention failed her dismally, and to Graham she made up something
lame about "a party," with none of the details like where and whose
that would make it ring true. She doubted people ever threw parties
on Christmas Eve, and if Graham had been paying attention—if he
weren't himself so oddly distracted and perhaps even a shade forlorn—
he'd have smelled something fishy. He said "Chant" wanted to spend
Christmas Eve with her own family; he'd probably just stay in.

Thus at the door around eight p.m., Rosalind stalled in one of her
best frocks—in which to head to a pub by herself, and that was assuming she could find one open. Graham was settled contentedly in front
of a recording of *Ramsay's Kitchen Nightmares* on their set-top box,
sipping a glass of stout. It was cold out. She yearned to fling off her
coat, along with the pretense of this apocryphal "party," and join him
in one of his signature suppers, simple but stylish, a knack for which
had lured him so disastrously into conceiving Say La Vie. But when he
said, "Have fun then!" she was trapped by her own theater. She spent
the evening around a bunch of pawing drunks who, presumably like
poor Aiden, were also not on speaking terms with their families—for
good reason, as far as she could tell.

Christmas proper was even worse. She kept waiting for Graham
to leave that morning, while he seemed, oddly, to be waiting for her
to leave as well. In the end, they left the house together, waving with
forced smiles out on the pavement and then walking off in opposite directions. Not wanting to drink and drive, neither had bid for the car.
Rosalind was ostensibly meeting Aiden in the city center, and Graham
could walk to his parents'.

Rosalind trudged just long enough to confirm that the atmosphere
in the city was like one of those postholocaust films, after a plague
or a neutron bomb. Not a soul on the streets, and everything closed.

Tracing a route sure not to intersect with Graham's, she circled back. It was Christmas, it had started to rain, and she wanted to go home. Some Stinking Bishop in the fridge and a handful of savory biscuits in the breadbox could stand in for the fabulous bash at Kenwood Hall she'd be obliged to fabricate when Graham returned, like feeding the five thousand from a few loaves and fishes.

Yet when she rounded the corner onto their street, there was Graham not twenty feet from their gate, approaching the house from the opposite side.

"What are you doing back here?" she asked.

He sighed at his hands. "Truth is, I've never got up the courage to tell my parents we're splitting up. They like you. So I could hardly show up with Chant on my arm, eh? And coming alone would set off alarm bells."

Rosalind unlocked their front door, with its lovely curlicue pattern in the frosted panes, eager to get out of the rain.

"But what are you doing back here?" Graham asked behind her. "Have a fight with Aiden?"

He'd handed her an excuse. Plopping into a dining chair and drying her face with a tea towel, Rosalind declined it. "Oh, there is no Aiden."

"For a figment of your imagination, he sure had powerful bad breath."

"I mean there hasn't been an Aiden for weeks."

"Ah," he said. "So you won't mind my having borrowed your Kenwood Hall story. I told the family we'd decided to have Christmas just the two of us."

"Well, why don't we?" she proposed shyly. "I mean . . . I'm starving, aren't you?"

Of course, there was no turkey browning in the oven, no pan of roasties crusting in goose fat, but together they rustled up the very sort of ad hoc supper that Rosalind had envisioned the night before. He caramelized oodles of sticky garlic while she whisked up a toasted pumpkin-seed oil vinaigrette; he roasted walnuts for the salad while she shaved

Parmesan. They'd always made a good team—in the kitchen, at least. It may have lacked cranberry sauce and mistletoe, but this holiday had, however wanly, a sense of occasion. According to her Web research, this would be their last Christmas together. So they were celebrating the end of celebration. But maybe that beat not celebrating anything at all.

"To be honest, I don't mind taking a break from Chant," Graham confided, adding another slug of olive oil to the garlic. "She's a sweet kid, but . . . Lives on chips and ready-meals. Can't tell a good Amontillado from Red Bull. And the music! Oh, and you know she really *is* planning to train as a dental hygienist? She said to thank you, by the way."

"It's a good career," Rosalind said, grinding pepper into the dressing. "In this economy, it's important to be doing something *necessary*."

"Unlike restaurants."

"Say La Vie will recover, sweetheart," she said passionately, forgetting herself with the endearment.

Graham uncorked a red while the pasta water was still coming to a boil, and Rosalind popped off to what it still didn't feel natural to call "her" bedroom, returning to sheepishly slide an overstuffed woolen knee-high on the table. She'd originally planned the stocking's delivery for Boxing Day—always a bit of a downer. Fittingly this time, it was a day of overness, of disappointment, of closure.

"I know we shouldn't be buying each other presents, this of all years," she said. "But all those evenings I pretended to be with Aiden . . . Well, I had to occupy myself somehow."

Indeed, she had applied herself to his stocking with all the ingenuity and humor that had escaped her in years previous. One by one Graham pulled out the individually wrapped cherry pitter and pastry crimper, a chocolate-mud-pie-flavored lip moisturizer, a packet of fennel pollen, Grand Marnier truffles, a miniature of avocado oil, and a clockwork chicken—all mixed in with dark-chocolate Smarties, kumquats, and books of Post-it notes for marking recipes. Seeming abashed that he'd not got her anything in return, Graham finally worked himself down to the folded, rolled-up piece of paper in the toe, beribboned like a diploma—for it betokened a graduation of sorts.

Rosalind bowed her head. "The rest is just a goof. That's your real present."

Graham pulled the ribbon, unfolded a page of printout, and looked baffled.

"Upmystreet dot com," she explained. "See that graph of property prices in Sheffield?" She took a brave breath. "We can sell the house."

Graham cocked his head. "But don't you want candlelight with your Christmas dinner?"

"I suppose, but . . . ?"

Rolling the printout back into a cylinder, he strode to their cooker and poked the paper wand into the gas burner under the pasta pot. With the flaming page of A4, he lit the tapers on the table, then tossed the rising graph from upmystreet.com into the sink.

They sat down to dinner, and Graham raised his glass. "To negative equity!"

"To negative equity!" she returned with a boisterous clink, then tucked into a garlic pasta and rocket salad supper that, while hardly conventional, had all the makings of a long, joyous, and faithfully kept tradition.

Vermin

I DON'T KNOW if the moral of this story is that you should never buy a house. That's a pretty useless moral anyway, in a country where home ownership is enshrined as such a wholesome aspiration that mortgage interest is tax deductible. Who would listen? And I'm reluctant to reduce what happened between Michael and me to such humdrum advice. Yet other stories would seem to distill to the same cautionary chapter heading of a marital guide: Never Buy a House. Not long ago in Manhattan, some geez in the midst of a divorce was so incensed by the prospect of his ex getting her hands on their landmark Upper East Side town house that he blew it up.

I came across another local story, too—subtler, so you had to read between the lines. A rich banker married a younger woman shortly after his first wife died. These newlyweds also bought a flashy house in the city worth millions, and spent three years doing it up. But by the time the couple finally moved in, the marriage was on the rocks. He packed up after a few months. I read about the court case. The banker was appealing the decision that he had to keep paying fifty grand a month in mortgage payments since his former wife still lived there. Apparently in the divorce papers he'd charged she was "unreasonable." I laughed. It wasn't in the article, but I knew what had happened. They fell out over the house. He learned the kind of

woman he'd married only when she started obsessing over the wainscoting.

But that's not my story, exactly. We never had any wainscoting.

I'LL NEVER FORGET first walking into what I would shortly baptize
with affection "the Little Dump." Michael and I had been together for
just under a year, living in his studio in Greenpoint. With my paint
box having to compete with propagating guitars, amps, and recording
equipment, the apartment was cramped. So we were looking to pool
our resources and rent something more spacious.

Until that afternoon, the search had been depressing. Properties in
Brooklyn were proving way beyond our budget, and every place had
something wrong with it. Even if the apartment didn't keep the refrigerator in the living room and the bathtub in the kitchen, we picked up
right away that the previous residents had been unhappy there. It's
funny how you can tell; misery steeps into soft furnishings as indelibly
as tobacco. So exhilarated with one another, we spurned other people's
residue of gloom.

Yet the Little Dump was cheerful. In the sleepy family neighborhood of Windsor Terrace, it was located at the very end of a cul-de-sac
called Trevanion Close, a designation somehow both intimate and no-
ble. The street was unnaturally secluded for New York; when we met
the owner out front, neighborhood kids were sprawled in the middle of
the road drawing castles in colored chalk on the tarmac. The jabbering
owner hadn't let us in the front door for more than a minute before I
twirled in the big middle room and declared, "I think we could live
here." I hadn't even seen the upstairs.

Granted, this tumbledown two-bedroom was cheaply built and
flimsy. Wooden parquet maybe, but the floors were thin and creaked.
Nothing was plumb: the sill of the back window canted at a good fifteen
degree angle to the baseboard below; the bedroom doors upstairs were
hung askew. The result was a goofy, fun-house discombobulation that
made you slightly seasick. The fittings were trashy and surfaces fake;

patterned to look like granite, the kitchen counters were plastic. Over the years, the grungy brown carpet on the stairs must have absorbed gallons of cat pee.

And yet, the enclosed front porch was faced with a bank of sun-drenched windows. At the back, the windows of the kitchen and dining room were overgrown with an enormous grapevine, reaching beyond its square-framed trellis in the tiny yard and climbing the exterior brick. I admired the vine's ambition. In late September, its leaves were still broad and green, and I wondered if we might pick them for making Greek *dolmades*, or collect the next harvest of fruit and try our hand at homemade wine. (Okay, we never attempted either project. Grape leaves have to be brined, and if I wasn't up for that, I definitely wasn't up for wine. Still, the caprices were enticing at the time.) The foliage tinted the air green, and so canopied the panes that they wouldn't need curtains. In all, a happy house—or it was.

Besides, a junky, knocked-together quality was intrinsic to the property's charm. The house didn't take itself too seriously—it was a joke house—which meant that we wouldn't have to take it seriously, either. In those days, we cherished a drollness to our environs, a lightness and silliness and transience reflecting the fact that wherever we stood was mere backdrop. That's what it's like when you're first in love. You feel so hyper-real, so radiantly authentic, that no one and nothing else can compete—as if you and your beloved alone are three-dimensional, and the rest of the world is flat. That's why the frank fakery of this ramshackle dive on Trevanion Close was so appealing, like its farcical excuse for marble around the bathroom sink (more plastic). The two-story hovel had the atmosphere of a cardboard city in Hollywood, and that made us the stars of the show.

Even our negotiation of the lease with the landlord was bogus, a mere gesturing toward due process. I guess the place had been empty for weeks, and *Bob* was desperate for cash. (Once months had gone by and he still hadn't repaired the leak in the porch roof, we'd be pronouncing his name in eye-roll italics.) We'd been worried that this nervous, shifty-eyed owner would insist on a credit check, or recoil from our bohemian self-employment. But all he cared about was his deposit, until Michael finally asked in puzzlement, "Don't you at least want to know what we do for a living?" So *Bob* asked, but only because Michael had told him to. God, we couldn't believe we were in New York. I mean, we weren't squatters and we were responsible and we would, somehow, by scraping for every job, pay the rent on time, but *Bob* didn't know that. From someone who proved a pretty dubious character himself, the trust was baffling.

I remain certain that for close to two years Michael and I were supremely contented in that house, although it saddens me that what happened later inserts a dimming scrim between then and now. The present so shades the past that it's amazing we can remember anything at all, really—and maybe we can't.

The romances of strangers are somewhere between inaccessible and incomprehensible to other people, so you'll just have to take my word for it how vertiginously I was in love with Michael Espiner, and he with me. (Sadly, at this point I have to take my own word for it.) There was something about his hips, his excruciatingly narrow hips, and the way the thick black leather belt settled on them just so . . . He was a gigging musician then, and when I watched him strum in clubs I remember being jealous of his guitar. On breaks between sets, we'd cocoon on one of the ratty sofas that lined the funky, pass-the-hat dives he played, my head on his shoulder with, I now realize, the kind of dreamy, gooey look in my eyes that makes other people sick. I've a feeling we may have been the butt of a few jokes, but even if we'd known that, we wouldn't have been fazed. We were impervious. Which is just what makes folks who don't happen to be in love themselves especially nauseated by swooning couples: that you so obviously don't give a shit that you're making them sick.

Sure, the whole musician thing was a turn-on, but I wasn't enchanted solely by the mystique of Michael's smoky, freewheeling life. I loved his music. Not rock exactly but a bluesy, reflective, sorrowful style that I could best compare to Jeff Buckley. The lazy, lingering, lateral feel of his tunes also infused Michael's manner. Sitting, he'd prop his tailbone on the edge of a couch, stretch his long legs straight out as if daring someone to trip over them, and extend both arms along the back cushion with the fingers draped. He exuded a savorous lack of urgency that was relaxing, and that sank us into moment by moment as into a sequence of plush pillows. He was a man whose unusual inhabitation of the present tense made you wonder in what distant temporal dimension everyone else was living.

Michael also had an impetuous, fuck-it side. On one amble through the East Village, he pulled me into a chic retro shop and demanded the woman's hat in the window—a cocky red number with a partridge plume—without even asking the price. It was $140. He couldn't afford it, but he didn't blink. I still feel badly that the feather got bent in our final move.

Yet if Michael had a cool career, I liked to think that I did, too. Maybe I've attended to those news stories about mansions ruining people's lives because back then I was hired to work in many similar east side town houses in Manhattan. I painted indoor murals: a nature scene on a bathroom wall, a jungle theme for a kid's room. The duller but harder jobs entailed daubing plaster columns with the swirls of marble, streaking Sheetrock with the fine, variegated layers of wood grain, or pointillating a surface with the multiple grays, pearls, and blacks of a pebbled beach—making the bald artifice of our countertops back home seem fitting. The latter sort of work had a particular art to it. You had to stylize the execution just enough to indicate that you knew you weren't fooling anybody. Yet fakery done well enough, painstakingly and honestly enough, has a beauty all its own. By the time I met Michael I'd accumulated just enough clients by word of mouth that I could do my part in keeping *Bob* off our backs.

The point is, we were both freelancers, so we made our own schedules—though maybe it's time I clarified that despite the seat-of-the-pants finances we weren't kids anymore. Michael was thirty-five when we met, so I must have been thirty-three. Both old enough to have been through the romantic wringer; old enough to get worried. That it was never going to happen for us. That a cold roast chicken from the deli section of Key Food, noshed straight from the plastic tray while propped before yet another rerun of *Requiem for a Dream*, with no one to whom to marvel why this incredible film still seemed so culturally obscure, well, that's what life was going to be, period: getting chicken grease on the remote and talking aloud to yourself in front of the box. So on top of being in love, we were grateful to be in love. I do remember that much. I remember being grateful.

Looking back, I feel apologetic toward Ed and Sandy, who lived next door. We routinely ate dinner out on the enclosed front porch at midnight, even later if Michael had had a gig; we rarely got to bed before four a.m. We must have been noisy, laughing and chattering over a bottle of wine, cranking up the stereo when Jennifer Warnes' marvelous cover of Leonard Cohen got to "Famous Blue Raincoat," our favorite track.

That said, we didn't make nearly as big a racket as the bird. What we called "the Crazy Bird." Later a neighbor explained that the bird perched in the big pin oak across the street every night was a mockingbird, known for its ability to imitate the calls of other species, but I almost didn't want to know this. I liked our bird just being a little nuts. We developed a whole bio for this bird: how it was too socially inept to grasp that birds weren't supposed to sing their hearts out at three in the morning, and that's why it didn't have any friends. Since it couldn't settle on one song but broadcast the avian equivalent of the iTunes Party Shuffle, it was obviously schizophrenic. Having compared the Crazy Bird's sophisticated melodic lines to the riffs of Yusef Lateef, Michael vowed to record its after-hours concerts; he could see doing a whole CD inspired by those long minor-key medleys. Later I'd be sorry that he never got around to it.

One night, an untended car alarm was getting so irritating that I asked Michael whether we should report it to the police, until he walked outside and realized that the sound was coming from the upper branches of the opposite tree. It was the Crazy Bird, doing the whole sequence: *aaaaah-WOOO, aaaaah-WOOO, aaaaah-WOOO! YOW-ah-YOW-ah-YOW-ah! BEEEEEE-baaaah-BEEEEEE-baaaaah-BEEEEE-baaaaah* . . . More dysfunction: the mockingbird had mastered the mating call of a Toyota Corolla.

Yet the very finest entertainment during those raucous wee-smalls was the raccoons. Trevanion Close was blocked at the dead end with a brick retaining wall that ran right alongside our house. Out the porch windows we'd follow these stout, hunched creatures big as bulldogs as they lumbered across the top of that wall, obsidian eyes catching the light of the streetlamp, long, conical snouts snuffling the brick. Wearing concentric circles of black and white fur like oversize spectacles, they looked intelligent. (In due course, no amateur naturalist from across the street would need to assure us that raccoons are very smart, since we'd get altogether too up to speed on this North American "procyonid" through the internet.) Michael liked to peer out the front door and meet the animals' gaze square on. He believed that he could communicate with animals, really connect on their wavelength, and I indulged this little vanity since it was harmless. Anyway, everything about Michael beguiled me then, and I found the conceit endearing. Me, I got pretty good at imitating the creatures' throaty trill—*trrrrrr, trrrrr*—halfway between a growl and a purr.

Oh, I knew raccoons could be aggressive, and we were careful not to scare or tease them. I also knew they were notorious for getting into garbage cans and strewing trash all over the street. But maybe because they were so well fed by our next-door neighbor's exposed backyard compost pile, none of our nocturnal visitors ever pried the tops off our cans to scrounge, despite the fact that their paws have five long, prehensile fingers. Given what I read later, those animals could have assembled flat-pack furniture.

At some point during our first summer, one of the raccoons got *really* fat, and we made jokes about how it should become an inspirational "weight diversity" speaker until one night it—she, apparently—waddled down the wall having slimmed down quite a bit, five babies in tow. Real heartbreakers, too. The whole family took to foraging in our grapevine. Whenever I heard that telltale rustle on the trellis, I'd shush Michael and we'd both creep to the back window screen, not wanting to startle them away. Again, we were careful—a mother was bound to be defensive of her litter—so when Michael met the eyes of the mother through the screen he made sure to keep his gaze reassuring. Other nights the family would cavort at the end of the street, the kits scrabbling one at a time up the metal lamppost—we were astonished they could get any traction—then leaping to the wall: raccoon Olympic trials.

They also had a knack for disappearing. More than once we watched the mother lead all five kits across the top of that wall, until they'd pattered out of view alongside the house. So we'd skitter to the back window, expecting them to come out the other side and maybe jump down to forage on the trellis. But no raccoons. They simply vanished. It was a twenty-foot sheer drop to the parking lot on the other side of the wall, so it beat me where they went.

I'm sure there's an element here of you-had-to-be-there. A raccoon isn't an exotic creature for most Americans, but they were our raccoons, and they were exotic to us. Along with the Crazy Bird, a sudden rustle and trill in the grapevine, or another spotting of a lone male prowling down the retaining wall, contributed to a sensation that where we lived was special, that we were special. We inhabited a secret world at the end of a private little street where the night was alive. The raccoons were *wild*life. They encouraged us to believe that we were leading wild lives, too.

IT WOULD'VE BEEN early in our second summer on Trevanion Close that we got married—larkishly, in a quick civil ceremony in the Municipal Building in Lower Manhattan, acting with the impulsiveness with which most couples would go for ice cream. Meanwhile, we'd still bought hardly any furniture. We were surely the only couple on the block that kept a whole room without a stick in it: the dining room, a.k.a. "the ballroom," where Michael and I would dance to Counting Crows with a candle in the middle of the floor. I liked the place underfurnished—open, uncluttered, and preserving that just-moved-in feel that also reinforced the impression that any time we wanted we could just move out. We lived there lightly.

True, a number of things about the house were annoying, if you were going to be that way—to take the place seriously, that is, as the Little Dump naturally discouraged one from doing. Unanchored, the toilet rattled every time you sat down, and I was haunted by a vision of the bowl cracking off and sending a geyser of raw sewage pluming to the ceiling like an oil strike. The closets had those hideous louvered doors from the 1970s that were always slipping off their tracks. The kitchen linoleum was prehistoric and disastrously white, its protective surface degraded. By the time either of us got around to mopping, the floor would be practically black. But we grew accustomed to walking around the bucket on the porch, where the drips from the ceiling after a rainstorm syncopated Michael's latest recording, and none of these shortcomings bugged us much. I tried to keep the crumbs swept so we wouldn't attract roaches—some forms of wildlife were less than welcome—but otherwise, hell, Michael was a musician, and you know how blasé those guys are about domestic stuff. Me, I was raised in a slick, soulless suburban household in Scarsdale full of bagel slicers and electric bread makers that no one ever used; the toilets were unnervingly silent, and everything worked *too* well. So the kooky, jury-rigged nature of Trevanion Close was liberating.

Yet apparently this notion that we could just move out anytime was merely an idea of ourselves that we were attached to. See, one afternoon later that summer an impatient rap rattled our screen door. I recognized the bossy, busty woman who was subletting the house across from ours while the Carters were on an extended vacation in Crete. Though no older than I was, she had a matronly air. She'd attracted my attention before because she was forever barking admonitory or morally improving directions to her four-year-old daughter at a volume that carried to every house on the street—the showy parenthood less for the kid, I thought, than for the benefit of other adults. She seemed one of those modern mothers who are sanctimonious about having made the gallant sacrifice of reproduction, and always wanted credit for it.

"Ya think the owner of this house might want to sell?" she began in a piercing skirl, without introducing herself. "'Cause this dead end's real good for kids, you know? Like, with no traffic and everything?"

I kept the screen door closed between us. "I don't know," I said warily.

"Well, could you find out? My husband and I are looking to buy, and we've taken a real shine to this street." Meaning, they *had a right* to this street, and we didn't. Because it was *good for kids*. Maybe I'm touchy because Michael and I never had them, but really—parents these days think the world owes them a living and then some.

I made noncommittal noises and got rid of the bitch, but privately I began to panic. Ours was a rare New York enclave where people talked to one another. A neighbor must have shared that *Bob* was always hard up, and might part with the house for a price. Which was surely the case. That's when I realized that I loved this house, loved our late nights with the rustling grapevine and the raccoon Olympics and the Crazy Bird, and I wasn't about to let some blow in, ostentatiously Mommyish Mom buy these creaky parquet floors out from under me.

I'll cut to the chase. We bought the Little Dump. Although not, obviously, without making some changes. I confess that we got help from both our parents on the down payment. Still, no bank was going to give a mortgage to a self-employed mural painter and a blues guitarist who on a good night raked in forty bucks and a few free drinks. I hustled because I was good and motivated, and I don't think in the end it's turned out to be a bad career move to work at a commercial design firm—although while concocting a corporate logo or the cover of a computer probe catalog I sometimes miss painting Rousseau-like she-lions beside a six-year-old's bunk bed. Faux beach-pebble motifs didn't sit me in front of a screen all day, either, and I regret no longer coming home with streaks of cadmium yellow in my hair. Nevertheless, I get a kick when I spot a habanero sauce bottle whose label I designed, and a real job sure pays better. I grant that Michael's managing Slide, a little jazz club up in Fort Greene, didn't work out quite as well. While it had seemed a good fit on the face of it, when you're managing you're not playing, and the job was more about kegs than frets. But I'm convinced that our marriage would have weathered the transition to proper employment well enough if it weren't for the house.

The odd alarm bell should have rung before we closed the deal. Michael's demeanor had always been casual, stylishly so. He walked with a slow, syrupy saunter. He'd often insert a languorous pause between a question and his answer, just the length of a yawn, as if debating whether to bother to respond at all. Before we put in our fateful call to *Bob*, Michael had been impossible to rattle, convinced that over time most problems solved themselves. When I'd despaired during our rental search that we'd never find an affordable place that wasn't disgusting, he'd murmured that something was sure to come along that was perfect, and he'd been right. Yet while we were still haggling with our landlord over his outrageous asking price, Michael ruined an entire evening anguishing about how we'd never get homeowner's insurance for a house so clearly dilapidated, especially with ancient wiring that couldn't be up to code. At a midpoint in this mind-numbing hair-tear, I did a double take. Back when we first met at CBGB, I couldn't have imagined the words *homeowner's insurance* coming out of his mouth.

He'd never seemed especially concerned with housekeeping, either, strewing his dirty jeans around the bedroom. But even before we'd signed the contract, he suddenly became neurotically neat—jerking the bedspread for minutes until the piping aligned with the edge of the mattress and chiding me to hang my kimono on its nail.

Then when at the bank's insistence we had an engineer around to certify that the house wasn't about to collapse, we led the prissy, officious little man out the musty basement to the backyard. The engineer surveyed our grapevine, by then crawling deliciously to the second story and curling around our phone lines, and tsked. "Not desirable," he announced, making a rigid tick on his pad.

"The grapevine?" I said. "Why not?"

"Not desirable," he repeated like a robot. But here's the thing: I turned to roll my eyes at Michael, and instead of grinning along with me at this loser who was dissing our fantastic grapevine, my new husband was nodding along sternly, his forehead creased. From then on, too, I never stopped hearing about how the grapes attracted squirrels, and squirrels ruined our window screens. About how, when the fruit rotted, it drew insects. When I defended the vine as providing the kitchen and dining room—we'd already stopped calling it a *ballroom*—the luxuriant botanical tint of a greenhouse, he repeated with no detectable irony and in the same robotic drone, "It's not desirable."

I guess for some people who've always been free and easy, taking on responsibility makes them more solid and more grounded; that's what people say about becoming a parent. But there may be such a thing as becoming too responsible.

For my part, after the closing I was mostly excited about fixing a few of those annoyances I mentioned, neglecting to note the fact that before we bought the Little Dump I hadn't been that bothered by the kitchen floor. Which we replaced, and the bright red Forbo Marmoleum would have been fab, except that the moment it was installed Michael started Swiffering it, like, every day, and he'd lean down to scrape a little piece of squashed onion with his fingernail while I was trying to cook. I'd have been happy enough about replacing the sink unit in the bathroom, too, save that its apparently being called a *vanity* made buying one humiliating. Taking the term to heart, Michael sure enough swabbed the actually-not-plastic marble with Bon Ami every time he finished brushing his teeth, picking at any hardened drip of Colgate just as he did at the orts of onion on the Forbo downstairs. Meantime, I swear his walk was getting stiffer and faster, the strides shorter and a little edgy.

I was game for finally hanging a few prints, like posters from Michael's old gigs. Yet even after we fixed the leaky porch roof, Michael remained solely concerned with "structural issues." I'd sometimes come home and find him in the middle of the living room, worrying up at a pinprick brown mottle on the ceiling, and he gave the impression that he'd been craning his neck like that for quite some time. Saturdays he'd spend a good half hour stalking both floors, scowling into closets, searching out cracks. He wanted to get the points done on the front brick, a fissure filled in the stoop stairs, the fractured slab of concrete abutting our overgrown rat's nest of a backyard broken up and replaced. I had to observe that none of these dreary gray "improvements" would make living in the house the slightest bit more enjoyable. Michael explained with paternalistic patience that it was all very well to "prettify the place," but a house had to be *maintained*. I couldn't believe he used that word, *prettify*. He left me feeling girly and frivolous.

Well, all those therapists on the radio emphasize the importance of marital compromise. So when during our first summer as homeowners Michael grew concerned that the ten-inch gap between the Little Dump and the retaining wall collected rain (the enemy in my husband's life used to be trite riffs or computerized drum tracks; now it was *moisture*), I didn't say "Who gives a shit?" Instead, being a good wife—a word I still wasn't all that comfortable with—I agreed that, especially since the cavity was bricked up on both ends, it probably did collect a lot of rain. That side of our beloved front porch was clapboard, and for once Michael was right. The wood could rot and draw termites. So I acceded to bringing in a contractor to somehow seal off the gap. Nevertheless, this meant we'd probably squander hundreds if not thousands of dollars on what was surely the dullest square footage of the entire property.

Or so I thought.

"WHAT YOU THINK is *that*?" We'd invited a contractor for a price quote, and all three of us had clambered out the dining room window onto the trellis. As the contractor pointed his flashlight down into the dark recess between the brick wall and our house, Michael and I leaned forward to follow the beam. Something moved in the shadows, and I jumped. "Is cat?" He was Bangladeshi or something.

"I don't know, maybe." Gingerly, I peered back in.

"Look, is more than one!"

Just then the flashlight caught the whip of a furred tail, ringed in black and white.

When I registered that our delightful family of raccoons, the kits nearly grown old enough to have babies of their own, was actually nesting in that deep, narrow gap between our house and the retaining wall, even I experienced something of a change of heart. So they weren't nocturnal visitors. They were tenants.

I tend to blame Michael, but to be fair this territory thing is pretty primitive, and there's a huge emotional difference between hosting guests and invaders. These animals weren't quite living in the house itself, but close to it, and sizable shitting, peeing, rutting mammals bearing whole litters on the other side of our living room wall made me, too, a little queasy. Be that as it may, Michael did not experience merely "something" of a change of heart.

"They're *vermin*," he declared over his computer that very night, loading Web page after Web page. "That's how they're classified in New York, but the city refuses to take any responsibility for them. They *bite*. They get *rabies*. Their feces can carry *roundworm*."

"Oh, big deal," I said distractedly, trying to fit a bowl of pasta on the table where he was working.

"It *is* a big deal," he said in the officious daddy voice that apparently accompanies homeownership. "This last year, two kids got infected with roundworm, and in *Brooklyn*, too. From raccoons! Some little baby's brain damaged, and a teenager went partially blind!"

"So they're *not desirable*," I said, deadpan.

"Better believe it they're *not desirable*," he said, failing to pick up on my allusion. "And guess, just guess, what's their favorite food?"

I took a stab. "Human eyeballs."

"Grapes."

My stomach sank. That was it for the vine.

THAT VERY WEEKEND Michael went at the main trunk of the grapevine—six inches thick, big as a tree. With only a handsaw, the job took half an hour, and he got blisters. Once the cut was all the way through, the vine's many tributaries didn't even tremble, looking vibrant and perky and oblivious, still dangling picked-over clusters of tough-skinned green grapes as if nothing had changed. It was like watching a chicken run around a farmyard with its head chopped off. Soon the cut began to bleed sap, as the stump would continue to do for many weeks thereafter, like an undressed amputation.

We'd borrowed a lopper and extension ladder from next door—one of the last favors we'd ever be able to ask Ed and Sandy, since within the week Michael would permanently chill our relations with a set-to over their compost pile. ("You're *never* supposed to keep a heap of garbage like that without it being totally gated off," he later snarled at the poor eco-conscious couple—meek, agreeable people who tore the cellophane from envelopes for recycling and had remarkably never complained back when we'd caroused loudly so late at night. "I quote," he read from his printout, *"Don't put food of any kind in open compost piles; instead, use a securely covered compost structure or a commercially available raccoon-proof composter to prevent attracting raccoons and getting exposed to their droppings.* I mean, no wonder this street is overrun!") Michael ripped down branch after branch as the grapevine's tendrils clung desperately to the brick; it was for all the world like tearing screaming children from the arms of their mother. Grimly, I lopped the fallen climbers into smaller, uniform lengths and bound them with twine for collection. It was murder. I was in no doubt about that.

The project took all day, and when we arose the next morning I couldn't remember when I'd last gone to so much effort to make my life worse. The light blared from the back windows, loud and flat; before, the quality of the light had resembled the warm, companionable glow of a banker's lamp, and now it was more like a naked hundred-watt's glare from the ceiling. Suddenly the whole ambience of the Little Dump was transformed. I can't explain it except that the house felt more ordinary. More plain and stark. As the sun rose higher, too, the July heat really baked the place. I noticed only once we'd hacked it brutally to pieces how cool the vine had kept the lower floor.

Meanwhile, Michael was spending every night online, providing a running commentary akin to regular email advisories from the World Wildlife Fund. "Did you realize that these wily bastards are so strong, so cunning, and so agile that they can pick an avocado from a tree and hit a barking dog from twenty feet? They attack pets, you know."

"We don't have any pets," I'd say wearily.

"The Carters have those cats. And we're giving comfort to the enemy." Raccoons had apparently replaced *moisture*.

"That cemetery on the other side of the Prospect Expressway?" he might note a bit later. "We thought it was just us, but they're inundated! They've trapped over five hundred of the monsters in the last ten years, and this cemetery guy thinks the grounds must have thousands of coons. Eating the flowers. Digging up the lawn. In Brooklyn, it's an epidemic!"

"*Epidemic* is for diseases."

"Whatever. Infestation, then." He glowered.

I thought, this is the sort of nitpicking point scoring that I'd noticed other couples engage in—couples I'd pitied.

Of course, Michael was primarily fixated on the gap—I didn't know what else to call it, since this space between the house and the wall was such a strange, dumb segment of our property that it didn't really have a name. The contractor had proposed filling the space with concrete, but somehow we had to get the animals out first. I was afflicted by the image of screaming baby raccoons buried alive in wet cement, like a lesser Edgar Allan Poe story.

"There are outfits you can hire to trap them," Michael fumed. "But trapping costs a fortune, and these filthy freeloaders have memories like elephants. Take them miles away, and they come *back*. The real danger of eliminating their habitat is that they stay here but they try to get inside. You know they can turn doorknobs?"

"Not if they're locked."

"They love to make dens in attics, and chimney flues. We'd better check the roof." Sure enough, early the next evening I discovered the upstairs hatch open and Michael up on the roof. He was binding some cockamamie construction of chicken wire around the little aluminum chimney for our furnace.

I suppose this ranting over the computer didn't take more than a week, though it was a long week. In the end, we did engage the contractor to fill the raccoon den with rubble and cement, and also to figure out a way of scaring the creatures off first. Michael was convinced that when their home was threatened they'd attack, flying into our faces with bared claws. He was certain, too, that they'd take revenge. "Like *how*?" I'd say. I recognized my arch, humoring tone from other spouses' supermarket bickering, audible from the next aisle.

"They're very destructive," he'd say with a returning condescension. "You haven't been doing the research. You have no idea what they're capable of. They're not cute, cuddly little woodland creatures, Kate. They're diseased, they're violent, they stink, they shit everywhere, and they're vermin. *Officially*."

The night before the contractor was due, we were treated to another sighting of our tenants, trundling across the wall on the way back home. But instead of poking his head out the screen door to meet their glittering gaze in that special cross-species communion of yore, Michael rushed to close the front door, and locked it, though the screen door was already latched. Then he hurried to the back, slammed all the windows shut, and locked those, too. Without any cross-ventilation in July, it was sweltering. We ate dinner in silence, sweat pouring down our necks.

In the end it was pretty simple. The contractor, who seemed more amused than frightened by our predicament, pulled our garden hose onto the trellis and blasted the chasm. Two drenched adults and an adolescent scrabbled up the debris that served as their entrance and exit ramp, and skedaddled across the trellis to Ed and Sandy's—where presumably a three-course lunch awaited on the compost pile. After all Michael's hand-wringing, the low-tech pest control was an anticlimax.

That night, after the "habitat" had been smoothed and sealed gray, we heard a trilling mewl outside the kitchen window. It was a younger kit, not a baby but the human equivalent of a ten-year-old. Presumably the kit had been out and about during the afternoon's commotion, and had returned home to discover its relatives cleared off and its house smeared up solid—like a latchkey kid who comes back after school to find an eviction notice slapped on the door and the locks changed by the landlord. It didn't know where its mother was, and cried and cried on the denuded trellis—where it must have been hungry as well, since this once well-stocked outdoor pantry was abruptly bare of grapes. After a while I couldn't stand it, and as soon as the dishes were done I proposed that we turn in early.

Michael stayed paranoid about the raccoons taking "revenge" for the rest of the month. He swore that rinky-dink metal screens were no better protection from these ravaging creatures than spiderwebs. Dining on the front porch with all the windows shut during a heat wave was unbearable. The stifling, static air intensified the sensation that nothing was happening and that nothing would happen ever again. For the first time we felt that metaphorical hopelessness of living at a dead end.

Once our aggrieved raccoons had refrained from clawing through the roof or burrowing past his poorly secured chicken wire down the chimney, by August Michael relented. Slide was closed for staff vacations. On one of those weekend evenings now rare for a couple with full-time jobs, we once more stayed up late over a bottle of wine and opened the windows. By three a.m., I called his attention to an eerie quiet.

"The Crazy Bird," I pointed out. "It's gone."

Over the next few months I strained to detect the Party Shuffle in the pin oak, but the mockingbird had fled, and never again returned to its perch high in the branches across the street. Maybe mockingbirds and raccoons have a symbiosis, but *I* thought we were being punished.

I realize it took a while, and I don't want to be simplistic; there were other problems. Meantime, we did get the points done on the front brick facade. We replaced the shattered cement slab that held the drain in the backyard, even if the new slab cracked as well within the year. We duly replaced the furnace when Michael worried about its age, as we duly replaced the water heater once Michael would no longer leave for the weekend lest it flood the basement. We installed a new toilet, anchored, that didn't rattle. The house is now better waterproofed than when we bought it, although I doubt any of these "improvements" seriously increased the value of the Little Dump when we sold up. Oh, the break was *amicable*, as they say, and we agreed to split the proceeds and contents fifty-fifty—although we'd each so little capital once the equity was halved that we both had to go back to renting.

Marriage may be a covered dish, but it's as dark and unfathomable under the cover as from above. If you asked Michael what went wrong, I bet he couldn't tell you. As for me, I know this is only a story I tell myself. But I still believe it all came down to the raccoons. We murdered the grapevine and we drove off the "vermin" and we obviously convinced the Crazy Bird that life on Trevanion Close had got a bit too sane. We'd lost the wildness, you see. In fact, soon after we filled that gap between the house and the retaining wall, it began to seem that we hadn't so much driven the wildlife away as allowed the wildlife to escape. The wild life had up and left us.

The raccoons did come back from time to time, of course. According to the internet, groups of raccoons establish a regular latrine separate from where they live. I sometimes wonder how far our evicted tenants routinely traveled to the cement hulk of their former den to leave smelly black signatures of their disdain.

Paradise to Perdition

BARRY MENDELSSOHN'S STORY began where so many stories conclude.

Films about bad-assery divide into two classes. In the standard prototype, the *malefactors*—a ravishing word that Barry had come to embrace—go down in a hail of bullets, or they turn on one another, or the cops find the stash of cocaine. Barry had come across somewhere that the plots of all those 1940s black-and-white noirs were then legally required to illustrate that crime doesn't pay. What a joke. Look at Congress.

But in many a contemporary thriller, the audience is expected to side with the creeps. While as a matter of formal obligation it's touch and go, whatever the heist or con or double cross, our antihero gets away with it. Modern or no, any genre has conventions, and the traditional surprise-surprise signage of guess-who-slipped-the-net-after-all is a pan of our crafty protagonist with a drink in his hand (or her hand: equal opportunity depravity). Swanky glass, booze icy and preferably a bizarro color like electric blue, bamboo umbrella optional. Our lovable villain is *always* on a beach—either leaning over a weathered wooden rail at sunset or laid out in the sand sporting a mean tan, and we'd never have guessed that this guy who's never taken off his leather jacket in colder climes has such a hairy chest. We know he's far, far away from whatever went down, and he isn't coming back. The single shot of a sly smile over the lip of that glass is all we ever see of our ingenious little friend's future, since presumably we can fill in the rest. A life of ease, elegance, and all-you-can-eat sashimi extends infinitely to his horizon.

Apparently, Barry bought the conceit, down to the Curaçao and alluring condensation. Amazing how you could sell a vision of the next forty years with a cocktail.

To be sure, when he first landed in his new life of languishing, luxury, and abandon, it was pretty damned swell. After the half-pint plane touched down onto a dot in the Indian Ocean and taxied into an airport circa 1962, its handful of bleary passengers stumbled down onto the tarmac and shambled in the searing sun—funny how simply being spared a Jetway had become exotic—toward what resembled a cottage. With a peaked tin roof, its windows laced with wooden crosspieces, the tiny terminal was painted a soothing sea green. Barry's wife, Tiffany, would have squealed about how the facility was "simply adorable," and he was relieved to skip it. Along the walkway en route to baggage claim, outlandish blossoms burst through the latticed fencing; when you had enough money, no one would razz you for not knowing what all those jazzy foreign plants were called. The journey from plane to belt was as short for luggage as for passengers, and Barry's bulging leather gear smoothed to hand within sixty seconds.

He'd cleared immigration on the main island—hesitating over telling the pretty, smiling agent whether he had arrived in the archipelago for "business" or "pleasure"; taken with sufficient seriousness, wasn't pleasure itself a full-time job? So he rolled his chattel directly to the curb, sweat trickling his spine. At midday in this time zone, the air was syrupy, thick, and sticky, but the close atmosphere sure beat January in New Jersey, where takeoff had been delayed by snow. As a tribute to what really should have been a one-way ticket (which always raised eyebrows), he'd discarded his black down parka on a bench in the last airport's primitive waiting room. Some sucker heading in the wrong direction was welcome to it.

For a moment dismayed that his courtesy car was nowhere in sight, Barry remembered that he was traveling on a fake passport. His driver would be the one holding a sign printed RODRIGO PEREZ. Italian on his mother's side, Barry could pass for Latino in a pinch. Still, he decided impetuously that hereon he would go by "Rod." Forceful. Sexy.

In a freshly ironed canary-yellow uniform, the lean African driver flashed a smile, the first blazing ivories that Barry had seen in years that wouldn't have been the result of violent tooth whitening. "Meester Perez!" he exclaimed, extending his hand with the joy of meeting a long-lost uncle. "Welcome to our beautiful island! I do hope your journey was not so grueling."

Barry didn't care whether the young man's manner of spirited obsequiousness was sincere. Obsequiousness was a quality that you bought. Fraudulence merely made the fawning seem more expensive.

The driver wouldn't even let him hoist his own carry-on, and immediately handed his passenger a cold bottle of water. Bloated from business-class flights whose attendants were obsessed with hydration, Barry wasn't especially thirsty and didn't know what to do with the thing, which dripped in his hand; he wasn't one of those water people. Personally, he'd have preferred champagne, but there was plenty of time for that, and the three separate legs from Newark had involved such an unending river of alcohol that a breather was judicious. As for the water he didn't need (they might have made it Perrier), what mattered was the gesture. That bottle marked the beginning of a new life in which a host of flunkies ceaselessly wracked their brains over whatever Barry Mendelssohn—whatever *Rod* Perez—might possibly want.

Beginning this last link to his final destination, he'd been in transit for twenty-one hours—twenty-four, if you counted from shutting the front door of his undistinguished bungalow in Paterson for the very last time and ducking into his taxi. So he could have done without the tour monologue from the front seat. He was much too pooped to give a hoot about "takamaka trees," or the complexity of cooking fruit bats, or how locals cut cinnamon boughs to make their houses fragrant at Christmas. (What houses? Amid the crazed vegetation, whose profusion allowed only enticing glimpses of a beach wide and white as the driver's smile, the only structures he'd been able to discern thus far were big hotels.) Presumably he was within his rights as a priority guest to tell the driver to put a lid on it, but rudeness and imperiousness must have been prerogatives you had to grow into. Likewise Barry might have objected that the SUV was air-conditioned like an abattoir, but hitherto he'd led a modest life; bossing around underlings and acting oblivious to whatever the help might prefer would take practice. He missed his parka.

Turning a blind eye to its funereal connotations, as well as to the fact that the initials "ER" were powerfully associated with catastrophe, Barry had selected Eternal Rest because it was the most expensive resort in the region. Not a perfectly reliable measure of quality, but exorbitant didn't usually correlate with complete crap.

As they curved onto the grounds, Barry concluded with satisfaction that Eternal Rest was anything but crap. The landscaping was exuberant yet tidy; none of the palms had drooping fronds, and beds of colossal flowering bushes were cleared of dead underbrush. Connected by paved switchbacks, the vast residential units were set widely apart, their long gunmetal roofs settled into still more extravagant foliage for further privacy. At reception, the open-aired structure overlooked a sheer drop, below which lapped water whose inland strip was—get this—the exact color of Curaçao. Having done his homework online, he didn't need the plump, un-Britishly unctuous general manager to list out the facilities: pool, obviously, big, obviously; spa, fitness suite, business suite, game room; multiple bars, one beachside for sundowners; five restaurants, of varying ethnicities, including Japanese. In addition to hiking and snorkeling, diving and boat trips could be arranged. Participation in a weekly rota of management cocktails, hosted barbecues, discos, and karaoke nights was elective.

A businessman himself, Barry noted the fact that no lowly receptionist but the GM herself had greeted him with lemongrass tea. The resort might have charged over a thousand bucks per day, but hiring a large permanent staff to cover busy seasons and flying plenty of Western goodies into the island daily, establishments like this operated in the black only if they kept occupancy rates high. Even if they could afford to linger, rich folks were restless, and guests who prepaid their first six months would have been rare as hen's teeth. Had the administrators of Eternal Rest known that he'd embezzled a big enough bundle to put his feet up in this joint until he stroked out at ninety-two, who would have met him then? Oprah Winfrey?

That's right—*embezzled*. What of it? He was an *embezzler*, another pejorative that, like *malefactor*, he had embraced—or would learn to embrace—was working on embracing. Cinema's standout bad guys didn't hanky-twist their lives away whimpering, *Gee, am I doing something wrong?*

Barry and the GM, whose name he'd high-handedly forgotten, whirred off with his bags in one of the many electric buggies with which a small army of boundlessly cheerful staff ushered guests from place to place, lest they become perilously enmoistened by a five-minute walk. With one of the best views of the beach, his premier villa wasn't much smaller than his house in Paterson (to which Tiffany was now welcome). Packed with aromatic unguents, the bathroom was capacious as a two-car garage. The minibar was stocked not with sad little miniatures but full-size bottles (finally, his champagne). But the kitchen he planned to boycott. The living and dining rooms wouldn't see much use, either. He'd spend most of his time here watching CNN (well—or porn) on a mattress you could get lost on, or lounging on the sea-facing deck, which spanned forty feet across—where he would dawdle his left-hand fingers in the plunge pool, keeping the right hand firmly around that icy, iconic blue drink (well—or his dick).

When she'd finished showing him around, the stout head honcho stood in the foyer with her eyebrows arched, looking expectant. A beat too late, he realized he was supposed to effuse. "It's great," he said dutifully. When she clearly wanted more, he embellished, "I mean, *really* great."

He'd meant it was great, too. Yet as she left him to get settled, the tiniest worm in his mind niggled, *Is this all?* He suppressed an ugly apprehension that the worm could grow to a snake.

THEREAFTER ENSUED A blowout party for one. Barry began a typical day by ravaging the breakfast buffet, mounding his plate with *pain au chocolat* and gnarly, unearthly fruit labeled *mangosteens* and *rambutans*. He complemented made-to-order omelets with the locally smoked marlin-and-salmon combo. A bit of loitering over a latte would see him through to eleven a.m., when he'd hit the poolside bar, throwing down a beer or two before warming up to lychee martinis, cloudy concoctions with a blobby albino olive at the bottom to which he took quite a shine. The Japanese restaurant was next door, so he could glide to lunch with his buzz on; he'd never quite seen the point of raw fish, but he dug the prawn tempura. After dispatching the green tea ice cream with its fan-shaped cookie shard, Barry drifted the afternoon away on a fat canvas beanbag in the pool, occasionally signaling for a mojito.

By five, it was back to his villa to freshen up. While undressing for his shower, drying off with a blindingly white bath sheet that he left on the floor, and slathering top to toe in orange-blossom moisturizer, he kept CNN yammering in the background. Yet whatever was happening elsewhere seemed muffled and far away, as if the ructions were occurring on another planet. He'd gather that something had blown up, but couldn't have said whether the misfortune had occurred in Iran or Texas. By the second week, he started short-shrifting the news for Jennifer Aniston movies on the Romance Channel.

Dinner was a suitably elaborate affair, with delicate seed-coated breadsticks, heart of palm salad or mango-dotted ceviche (which didn't *seem* like raw fish), and imported Scottish rib eye or New Zealand lamb shanks—all washed down with zingy South African Sauvignon blancs and chewy Chilean Malbecs. A little unsteady, he'd be whizzed by buggy to his villa, where he could crack open the Hennessy and find out whether Jennifer got her guy. Unfortunately, he usually fell asleep before the couple got their act together, so that his experience of the Romance Channel was one of ceaseless heartbreak.

Rarely finishing a film before he passed out was, alas, only one of several flies in his orange-blossom ointment. Having long prided himself on his Mediterranean genes, Barry hadn't taken the equatorial sun into account, and at this latitude even his swarthy melanin-rich skin could singe. When by the end of the third week he'd started to peel, vanity demanded wearing his robe at the poolside bar. In the shower, rinsing off molting brown shreds made the ablution feel rather grubby.

Obviously he'd have to dial back the alcohol a bit *in the fullness of time*, an expression that imparted grandeur to his good intentions while not binding him to forthcoming virtue with any disagreeable specificity. The blur to his edges from rarely being completely sober lent the palms and the blooms and the coastline a vagueness that was probably wasteful. In all honesty, he missed the blissful entitlement of slogging through the office day on the forty-third floor in Midtown and enduring yet another bottlenecked commute across the bridge to Paterson, finally to take that first glorious chug of a new craft beer. He didn't think of himself as one of those work ethic saps who had to earn their happiness, but reward wasn't, well, as *rewarding* when all you were being compensated for was getting out of bed.

Some mornings, of course, getting out of bed ought to have earned him a medal. All those ill-gotten gains in an offshore account couldn't buy him out of a hangover.

Yet the biggest challenge was sewing indulgences end to end without any gaps, through which uninvited reflection was wont to seep. A lapsed Catholic, Barry recalled that the very word *indulgence* applied not only to a midafternoon Balinese massage, but also to the church's official grants of reprieve from stints in purgatory for one's sins—stays of execution, if you will. There'd been some sort of scandal way back when about indulgences of the theological sort being bought and sold. He had therefore purchased from Eternal Rest indulgences of both the secular and religious varieties, and panicked when they ran out.

Nevertheless, it was tough to eat, drink, and be merry every minute of the day. Unextended by chitchat, dining solo was too efficient, even when he padded the meal with soup and cappuccino. Cocktails in solitude, too, had a tendency to evaporate. Waiting for another bill to sign, drumming his fingers between refills, or idling his feet in a pool hot as the air, Barry would find himself muttering, "Assholes got what they deserved. Divaggio and Hobson'll make another billion in no time anyway. Get to keep the whole pile, too, with me out of the picture. *Ten percent.* Can you believe it? Love to see their faces first time they get a look at the books. Took me for a fool."

Only once the largely one-way conversation had dwindled did he realize that he *was* a fool—for not keeping his trap shut with one of the wives waiting for her husband at the bar on the beach. Her face was creased from too much sun, but he was a sucker for any woman who could still get away with a bikini in her forties. So he'd explained expansively about having founded a company that installed motion-activated lighting systems, "to spare the consumer the exhaustion of turning on a switch." That line had always earned him a chuckle before, and he should have pulled up short when she didn't crack a smile. "Gave us green credentials," he went on instead. "Having lights come on when you enter a room and fade off when you leave conserves electricity and cuts bills. Oh, MADCIS has done whole office buildings, coast to coast. Our systems can also power down computer and AV equipment that would otherwise keep purring away on standby. The savings add up."

"Mad kiss?" she asked hazily.

"Motion-Activated Domestic and Commercial Illumination Systems," he spelled out like an idiot. Did he *have* to name the company? What if the story made the papers? "Whole concept was my idea. The tech side's pretty simple. Motion activation has been around for decades."

Fortunately her husband showed up, or he'd no doubt have loose-lipped about how his partners, roommates from college he'd known for twenty years, had inserted some conniving fine print in the incorporation documents, the upshot of which was that the guy who came up with the whole concept—"The whole concept!" he'd come to grumble repeatedly to no one in particular—was due not an even-Steven third but a mere tenth of the profits. If she'd stuck around, too, he might even have blubbered about leaving his wife behind. "You can't believe the stress of the last few months. I mean," he might have shared, lifting his glass, "why do you think I'm on my third one of these? The secrecy was murder on my nerves. And there was a load of complicated finance to master. Tiffany didn't understand, and naturally I couldn't explain why I was so, you know, tense, hard to live with. But I couldn't tell her, see, unless I could be ironclad certain she'd come with. And I bet she wouldn't have. Has all these friends, you know, golf buddies. I was hoping till the last minute . . . But I couldn't take the chance. What if she ratted me out instead?"

No, he didn't blab to well-preserved bikini lady about Tiffany, but the encounter still shook him. He needed to shut up. He needed more to do.

From then on, Barry threw himself into Eternal Rest's organized diversions, which he had previously spurned as too summer camp. He took up snorkeling, though breathing through the tube with his head submerged induced an anxious drowning sensation that was embarrassing in two feet of water. He went on the boat trips, which made him vomit. He taught himself backgammon, though by then the muttering aloud had gotten sufficiently out of hand that soon no one would play with him. ("Right, sure, Divaggio and Hobson were the 'brains.' They were the 'tech savvy' ones," he'd sneer alone in the game room. "But the technology was Tinkertoy! Who came up with the whole concept?" Since no one was listening, he could non sequitur to, "And nobody *reads* contracts. I only did what everyone does: flipped through the incorporation documents looking for the signature lines." He often rounded on the more sorrowful incantation, "But I couldn't take the chance. What if she ratted me out instead?") He entered the Ping-Pong competition, but got so worked up declaring, "*Ten percent!* Can you believe it?" that he failed to keep the ball on the table. Besides, he couldn't kid himself. He wasn't really busy. He was *occupied*.

Extracurricular activities having never seriously interfered with the rigors of hedonism, the inevitable day came, too, when Barry was toweling down in preparation for another four-course dinner and caught an unguarded glimpse of himself in the dressing room's mirror. His face might have been drawn on a balloon that was then inflated to bursting point. His body always had a squareness about it, which Tiffany claimed to like; she said his strong right angles gave him a masculine bearishness, and as an object he appeared "impossible to knock over." But now his corners were *round*.

Nuts. He talked to himself incessantly. He was a drunk. And did this ever happen to those suave antiheroes who absconded with the loot in the movies? He was getting—he wasn't even *getting*. He was fat.

Thus was born Rod Perez, Reformed Character. (Alas, no one ever called him *Rod*. The resort imposed an atavistic respectfulness, and it was all *Meester Perez* this, *Meester Perez* that.) He foreswore the pastries, the *parathas*, the petits four. He renounced lunch. He trained waiters to bring him Perrier and cucumber sticks, or occasional bowls of consommé, no croutons. He hit the weights and stationary bicycle in the fitness suite, which was always deserted, and which he came to regard as his personal fiefdom. While the other guests dawdled on the sidelines with wine and sunblock, he swam laps. Resolved to walk everywhere, he was incessantly badgered by well-meaning buggy drivers insistent on giving him a lift, and saying no took so much energy—energy that no one on a cucumber diet could spare—that most of the time he gave in.

Turned leaf or no, the slimming was slight and slow. Moreover, becoming a fitness paragon made him even more of a pariah at a luxury resort in the Indian Ocean than talking to himself like a homeless person. Once when reclining poolside next to a fetching young woman in a lavender one-piece after ninety minutes of breaststroke—the only breast he'd stroked in this joint being his own—he began doing crunches in his lounge chair. Obviously, the lady was impressed. He'd seen her no-ticing him while he was still swimming, and now she was cutting eyes in his direction when she thought he wasn't looking. But after a couple of minutes, she put her book down. "Could you please take that some-where else?" she requested in an American accent. "Some of us are trying to *relax* here."

In the end, his corners still not restored, Barry was miserable, and he couldn't continue to sanction a life of unremitting denial in para-dise. Breakfast was a torture: sawing a single wedge of honeydew into translucent slices amid platters mounded with bacon, the while enticed by the aroma of toasting brioche and melted butter. This was the worst place in the world to go on a diet. With a clientele of honeymooning couples, families with hardworking parents on breaks they'd saved for years to afford, and Middle Eastern sheiks and Russian oligarchs whose cultures didn't run to exertion, Eternal Rest was also the worst place in the world for exercise freakery, which his fellow guests found not only strange or irrelevant but actively repellent. What was he pay-ing all this money for—to suffer?

Yet once he restored a civilized lunch and allowed himself a bread roll at dinner, Barry discovered the real slimming secret of the filthy rich: fastidiousness. Persnicketiness. The upturned nose. Interestingly, this was a form of abstemiousness with which the staff was clearly familiar, and clearly more comfortable. And he wasn't feigning the fussbudgetry, either. The glut of food and drink had seemed so fabulous at the begin-ning. But now he wondered if the chefs had changed, or the personnel who ordered provisions had been replaced by more stinting procurers. Nothing tasted nearly as good as it had when he arrived. So he sent back breadbaskets for being stale or overbaked. He complained that the jack-fish had been seasoned too heavily with cumin, and left three-quarters of his dauphinoise potatoes because he "wasn't keen on the nutmeg." He rejected countless bottles of wine for being too tannic, too thin, or too fruity, and abandoned ordering lychee martinis at the poolside bar; be-sides being a bit cloying, they'd developed a tinny aftertaste. He'd ceased to eat or drink to excess, but discipline didn't enter into it. Everything that grazed his palate was disappointing.

At length, however, what he grew truly starved for at Eternal Rest wasn't a coconut custard that lived up to expectations. It was resistance. No matter how many times he insulted the cooks and waiters to their faces about how the roasted vegetables were burned to a cinder, or how the prawn and garlic stir-fry was spiked with so much chili as to be roundly inedible, all that came back was *Yes, Meester Perez. So sorry, Meester Perez. We always grateful for suggestions to improve our service, Meester Perez.* Desperate to get a rise out of these amenable minions, Barry began lambasting dishes that had in fact been prepared impeccably. He accused the red snapper of being "a month old if it was a day." Though the waiter assured him that the fish was meant to have been caught that morning—which was surely the case—the bastard *still* apologized, explaining "there must have been some meestake in the keetchen." There was no mistake in the kitchen! Why couldn't he hurl back, "Look, you son of a bitch, you won't get fresher fish without diving into the sea and chomping down on that snapper while it's still swimming!" Or at the pool, when he tossed his towel back to the attendant snarling that it stank of mildew, he yearned for the guy to give it a sniff and say, "You crazy. Nothing wrong with thees towel. Something wrong with *you*." But no. *Many apologies, Meester Perez. New towel right away, please forgive delay of your sweem today.*

No matter how much abuse he chucked at these people, they absorbed the blows. It was like sparring with a punching bag filled with pudding. Now the drowning sensation wasn't from snorkeling in the shallows, but from being eternally submerged in a warm bath of hospitality. Every day was one long can-I-help-you-sir. He was choking on all this geniality, obligingness, and turning of cheek; he was suffocating under the plumped pillows of everlasting pampering. In what he had begun to think of as *real life*, Barry had been a combative man who relished trading good-natured insults with colleagues over a beer, and now he was flailing from a deficiency of friction, as if every surface in his surround had been sprayed with silicon and he couldn't get enough traction to walk across the floor. He yearned for quarrel, back talk, and contradiction. Sure, the customer was always right, but when you claimed two and two made five and you were right, there was no such thing as right. He had landed himself in a world of goo, where he was slathered with affirmation, flattery, and affable comments about the weather like the pink-smelling liniments of those never-ending spa treatments. It was a world in which he was never held accountable—where all that mattered was not what he thought or what he'd done but what he wanted.

What he wanted was to go home. Abruptly on an arbitrary Thursday afternoon, he showed up at reception with his packed bags, announcing that his flight to the main island left at five thirty. Within the hour, he was through the farcical airport security and seated in the waiting room. For once he was glad that this hop had no business class, hence no business class lounge, with its open bar, its free Wi-Fi, its buffet of miniature quiches, stuffed vine leaves, and ripe cheeses. He was glad of the hardness of this slatted bench, its lack of poofy cushions. He was glad to have to move over to accommodate shy local schoolgirls and pecan-colored professional travelers in dopey hats—to not be treated as if he were special. He was already looking forward to the invigoration of the prison yard, in which a man couldn't buy a place at the top of the pecking order, but had to struggle to establish himself in the hierarchy of other men; where if he so much as looked sideways at one of his fellow convicts he'd earn a sock in the jaw. In a cellblock, yes, but he still looked forward to folding his own clothes, matching his own socks, and changing his own sheets, *the whole concept*. He looked forward to celebrating the fact that this was the day of the week the penitentiary canteen served individual frozen pizzas, and that pizza, with a bland, congealed sauce of tomato soup concentrate, would taste more sumptuous than the Mediterranean focaccia with rosemary, anchovies, and kalamatas at Eternal Rest. Cinematically, this ending may have hewed to an old-fashioned plotline, but Barry had always liked those black-and-white noirs.

The flight was delayed by a tropical downpour, which crashed against the terminal's tin roof like an audience of several hundred breaking into applause. The dark beams crisscrossing overhead provided the snug, muggy room the atmosphere of a hunting lodge. Delicate wooden Xs over the upper windows stitched the building like an edging of crochet. He wished Tiffany were here. This airport really was adorable, and somebody should say so.

The Subletter

A NOVELLA

SARA MOSELEY KEPT track. She was not so pathologically tightfisted that she never picked up a dinner bill, but she would remember if she paid last time, and how much.

Sara didn't *want* to remember tabs. The information would simply blip into her head unbidden, like a software update. In her defense, she did exercise social restraint. If, at the electric arrival of the lacquer tray, her companion placed a single tenner on a £26 lunch bill and then began routing intently about her bag for pound coins—despite the fact that the month previous Sara had put the whole £57 for their dinner on her Visa, and Maeve had merely left the tip—she kept her mouth shut and grubbed for her wallet, if with a pressed white rim around the lips. Well brought up, she never blurted in public, "But I only ordered a salad!"

Fundamentally, Sara expected other people to hold up their end; in exchange, she would hold up hers. Was that so terrible? This rigid sense of justice ought logically to have corresponded to a right-wing outlook— down on handouts, keen on mandatory prison sentences—but Sara had liberal, Bennington-educated parents, and theoretically endorsed the spread-the-goodies tenets of European social democracy. Had Sara ever been personally subject to the Continent's horrendous upper-bracket tax rates, her politics might have lined up promptly with her more conservative inclinations in private life, an American sensibility that came down to covering your own ass.

Yet keeping track was not attractive, not even to Sara herself. Helplessly, she kept a lengthening mental ledger of trifling material grievances: Moira had never returned Sara's bone-handled umbrella after that downpour. Despite fulsome promises at the time, Patrick had yet to replace the blue-and-white china platter he'd cracked at a raucous dinner party years ago; Sara hadn't reminded him, but neither had she forgotten, and the friendship itself had suffered from a fine fissure ever since. After she'd splurged on a round-trip flight to Boston for his birthday, Brendan had returned the gesture on hers with a lone Terry's Chocolate Orange once their romance had gone off the boil. But she knew her list was shameful, and its extent and incriminating detail were well-kept secrets.

Sara yearned for a visitation of grace. She envied insouciant sorts who flapped cash about in restaurants from an excess of sheer joie de vivre, who arrived at the door bearing boxed Pavlovas without a thought of payback in kind, who sprang for champagne when an unassuming Italian white would have more than sufficed. She couldn't remember having met such people, but she was convinced they were out there, perhaps in droves; they simply didn't gravitate toward ledger keepers and lunch-bill talliers like Sara Moseley. The trouble wasn't that she was incapable of generosity, but that if she was generous then she remembered being generous, to-precisely-what-penny generous, and remembered generosity didn't seem truly generous, quite.

Sara had been raised in a nest of recycled aluminum foil, where Kennedy half dollars glinted with exaggerated wealth not only to the child but also to her mother. Were she to lobby for animal crackers at a grocery checkout, Mom would deduct the cost of the impulse purchase from her weekly allowance of thirty-five cents. Apparently the gene for small-mindedness was passed down maternally like the one for hair loss. If on some private campaign to become a Better Person Sara stifled the host of grudges she bore, issuing a blanket forgiveness of picayune, antediluvian debts, her resentments subsided only to rage more virulently than ever in a few days' time. Suddenly the whopping international phone bill that her sister ran up while quarreling with a boyfriend on a visit in 1991 would blister in Sara's mind like a recrudescence of shingles. Besides, why fight it? A long memory for slights had lent Sara Moseley an intuitive grasp of Northern Irish politics.

AFTER EARNING HER journalism degree from Tufts, Sara had taken six years to work her way up from proofreading annual reports on Patriot missiles for the Raytheon corporation to writing up street fairs for the *Brookline Newsletter*. Unable to divine a clear path from documenting the rise of "slouch socks" to covering the civil war in El Salvador for the *Boston Globe*, she sold off the contents of her entire household in the summer of 1986—a fit of disencumbrance of which nowadays, a clatter of salad spinners and silver-plated serving spoons later, she was in slack-jawed awe. With the proceeds of her dispossession, she backpacked around Western Europe in a flight of youthful exuberance that, however commonplace, fortified in then-adventurous Sara Moseley a determination never to live in the dumpy old United States again.

Sara hadn't moved to Belfast so much as run out there—run out of money, run out of wanderlust, run out of Europe. Waitressing with a master's degree seemed less ignoble abroad, so Sara began slabbing up fabulously pneumatic lemon meringue pie, taller than it was wide, at the Queens' Espresso on Botanic Avenue. That was shortly before the IRA bombed Enniskillen, in Northern Irish time; Ulsterfolk conventionally located personal cornerstones by their proximity to atrocities.

A virtual obligation of her new home, she soon fell in love with a voluble, abusive boozer with delusions of grandeur—or, as Sara soon learned to say, an *arsehole*. Said Arsehole was a working-class Protestant from the grimy, famously militant Shankill Road, where the failure rate at the Eleven Plus exam neared one hundred percent. (In recent years exclusive to Northern Ireland, the UK primary school test brutally separated brain surgeons from bank clerks before they were old enough to spell "social determinism.") But Arsehole had bootstrapped himself to Cambridge (the *real* Cambridge). After sowing a few oats as a drummer in a one-hit-wonder rock band in London, he benevolently returned to his grubby Shankill roots to woo his dole-dependent, Carlsberg-hoovering mates from the misguided gore of violent paramilitary loyalism. (Granted, the predominant loyalist modus operandi at the time—getting roaring drunk and arbitrarily shooting any old Catholic in the head—left something to be desired in the political panache department. While loyalists claimed to be securing Ulster's continued membership in the United Kingdom, these grisly acts of obeisance mysteriously failed to endear them to the motherland.) The real enemy, preached Sara's temperamental new boyfriend, wasn't the Taigs or the Provos but firebrand opportunists like Ian Paisley and even the soft-core Ulster Unionists, bent on deploying the cream of Protestant manhood to fight the IRA without bloodying the creases of their tidy bourgeois cuticles.

Having imagined previous to 1987 that *Paisley* was a pattern on ugly ties, *unionists* organized labor strikes, and *Provo* was the majority-Mormon hometown of the Osmonds, Sara plunged into a private crash course on the Troubles in her spare time—first to impress Arsehole, later to beat Arsehole at his own game. By the time she had digested an alphabet soup of paramilitary acronyms and could rattle off the casualty totals of pub bombings as she could once recite the Red Line's timetable at Porter Square, she cared for neither impressing nor beating Arsehole, since it turned out that Arsehole was, well—an arsehole. But by that point she had a quirky flat, a blender that ran on European current, and an embryonic journalistic expertise. She saw no reason to pull up stakes.

Eleven years later at forty-one, Sara the Anglo-Cajun American no longer asked herself why she was still living in Belfast—a question that, on detecting an accent that had never quite gone native, taxi drivers and pub patrons asked her repeatedly. Eschewing the real story as undignified for an independent career woman (it had too much to do with a man), she had distilled a string of answers more plausible than true, and selection was a matter of mood: (1) She was "fascinated by the politics"—while to the same degree that she was fascinated, she was bored. By 1998, mention of *decommissioning, parity of esteem, confidence-building measures,* or *cross-border bodies with executive powers* smote her with the impotent claustrophobia of dreams in which she could not scream. (2) "The people are so warm and good hearted"— another half truth; that famous Ulster friendliness candy-coated a contempt for Americans to which Sara fancied herself inured, although hate mail snidely addressed to "Little Miss American Pie" still smarted. (3) In Belfast, she'd "found her journalistic niche."

There was some accuracy buried in this last sop, though the niche was poorly paid and odd. Sara was a professional American. She wrote a Saturday column for the *Belfast Telegraph* called "Yankee Doodles," in which she was expected either to convey the American slant on the latest local calamity, or to comment on current affairs in the States. Diatribes against capital punishment, permissive US gun laws, or the illicit funding of the IRA by Irish Americans through NORAID had proved abidingly popular. She recorded spots on Radio Ulster explaining the origins of Thanksgiving, or why nearly one percent of her countrymen lived behind bars. When in blessing an ill-fated IRA cease-fire in November 1995 Bill Clinton touched down in Air Force One to work the entire province into an evangelistic rapture—thousands lined Royal Avenue that day, waving inflated red, white, and blue baseball bats in the rain—Sara hustled between TV panels, radio appearances, and guest op-eds in a lucrative Rent-a-Yank stint whose proceeds saw her through Christmas.

Ironically, it was a lukewarm allegiance to Uncle Sam that had facilitated her expatriation in the first place. In fact, across the globe the foofaraw of nationalism left Sara indifferent, and she was sometimes puzzled by having adopted, of all places, a statelet where the clamor of rival national loyalties dominated local discourse. So for Sara to earn her crust explaining American customs and American politics and American viewpoints was perfectly ridiculous. Visiting estranged friends in Boston for a month every summer provided about the same exposure to contemporary American culture as regular trips to the cinema on the Dublin Road. She devoured both the Protestant *Tele* and the Catholic *Irish News* six days out of seven, but often left the issues of her father's *Atlantic* gift subscription encased in cellophane. Sara Moseley's expertise on how Americans really felt about the Monica Lewinsky scandal derived from BBC vox pops, and as a professional American she was a fraud. But Sara needed the money.

The *Telegraph* paid £100 per week. With occasional book reviews (of novels by *American* authors) for the *Irish Independent* or panel appearances on Radio Ulster meant to put folks straight on why American secondary school students got itchy trigger fingers during algebra, Sara got by, but only just—to the tune of about £600 per month, or barely $1,000. Granted, Sara's £225 rent was modest even for Belfast, where by the mid-1990s flat rentals had soared perplexingly sky-high. Her budget had rarely to cover luxuries beyond a smart secondhand denim jacket from the Oxfam shop, a jar of Thai curry paste to throw on the same old steamed cabbage, and, of course, the occasional addition of another Michael Collins or William of Orange coffee mug to her burgeoning collection of Troubles ephemera. So in material terms her income was adequate. At once, it was not a grown-up income. Somehow a scraping by that was admirable in one's twenties seemed eccentric or even lazy in one's thirties, and Sara worried that a single woman this skint into her forties drifted inexorably to the social fringe. Maybe young, carefree bohemians aged into bog-standard poor people.

Or perhaps the problem wasn't simply money. Maybe the problem—and Sara was only beginning to realize that there was a problem—was Belfast, whose people were developmentally stalled at about the age of thirteen and had made her commensurately juvenile. She'd been happy in this town, but that was a past-perfect determination facilitated by the fact that she was happy no longer. And it wasn't really fair to blame

Belfast when the problem wasn't Belfast itself but the fact that Sara still lived there.

"I DON'T GET it," Lenore said, leaning back at a skeptical slant on her big blue couch. "You look good—your eyes only crinkle when you smile. And you say *please* and *thank you*? So how come you're still single?"

Dark, knurly haired, and busty, Lenore Feinstein was a former roommate from their grad school days with whom Sara kept up because the woman had tang. Yet as the three-year-old sleeping upstairs attested, Lenore had strong convictions about at what age one does what, which sometimes set them at odds. Sara was not following the Program.

Sara gazed through the wide picture window at the inviting wooden porch of Lenore's newly purchased Somerville clapboard. She resisted relaxing into the maternal bath of Boston's hot August air when she was headed right back to a chill, dimly lit drizzle in September. This Rorschach of sun through oak leaves put Sara on her guard. On average it rained in Northern Ireland over three hundred days a year, and she was used to it. She had to stay used to it.

"Oh, with locals in Belfast I always seem to hit a wall," Sara speculated. "I'm a foreigner, which they like at first—I have novelty value— but that's also in the end what they can't stick. I'm unable to 'share their *pain*.' Besides, all the bright sparks in that town clear off. The men who stay put are losers. If I really wanted to marry a Northern Irish boyo with spunk, I'd move back to Boston."

Sara's argot was a confused hash of colloquialisms from both sides of the Atlantic. Some remaining American friends found her Ulsterisms charming; others the lingo annoyed.

"So why *don't* you move back here? Sara, my *lassie*, you're not even Irish." Lenore the Ulsterisms annoyed.

Sara shrugged. Even a year ago, she might have put up a passionate defense of her adoptive town. Yet ever since this last April's signing of the Good Friday Agreement, relentlessly lauded as "historic," she'd been afflicted by the nutty impression that Belfast didn't need her anymore.

Though she'd done nothing but cheer the ostensible end of the Troubles from the sidelines in "Yankee Doodles," the agreement felt idiotically like her own job well done, meaning that she was now obliged to pad barefoot into the sunset like David Carradine at the end of *Kung Fu*.

"I don't feel quite at home in the States anymore." Like the lifting Gaelic lilt at the end of her sentences, the claim would read to Lenore as another pretension. "I fall between the stools. I'm not Northern Irish, and I don't try to be. But I'm not only American, so I'm not." An Ulster tic, the reflexive syntax was a joke, but Lenore looked put out; she didn't get it.

"What you are is stuck," Lenore announced, palms on knees. "Okay, Ireland used to be interesting—"

Sara winced. She hated when Americans called where she lived *Ireland*, as if the island were all one country.

"But now you say yourself that the politics are old hat," Lenore continued. "If coverage of that agreement thing in the *Globe* is anything to go by, the hatbox is wrapped up with a bow. Meanwhile you make no money. Your career is parked. No man, no kids. You're getting older, and sooner or later you're going to look it. Wake up. Go somewhere else. Belfast is over."

Sara glowered. She didn't like being lectured. Seeing each other only a few days a year, they couldn't commiserate over daily travails— the scheming of Lenore's colleagues in Lowell's psych department, last week's atrocious subediting of "Yankee Doodles"—but were obliged to discuss the Big Issues. The little issues were more fun.

Sara objected, "I know it's hard for you to appreciate—"

"I came to visit you in ninety-two, remember? You were so proud of that place, as if it were your private discovery or little ward, your *wee* friend who's a bit slow and needs a defender. Okay, that was sweet. But for me to humor you at this point wouldn't do you any favors. Sara? *Belfast is a dump.*"

Taken aback—surprisingly offended—Sara could only correct, "You mean, a *tip*."

Lenore plowed on. "The architecture is either sooty and morose, or tacky and plastic. The restaurants stink, and they're larcenous. As for the local 'cuisine'—fried potatoes, baked potatoes, mashed potatoes, or potatoes stuffed with potatoes garnished with a little potato, and seasoned with a *soupçon* of potato flavoring."

"*Spud* flavoring," Sara contributed forlornly.

"There's nothing to do in that frumpy burgh but watch American movies with assigned seating, or get shitfaced by noon. No wonder they blow the place up! You'd said up front that the one thing you couldn't bear to do again with a houseguest was to rent a car and drive up the Antrim coast, but what did we do? Out of *desperation*? Rent a car and drive up the Antrim coast! And the hairpin turns made you carsick. Then there's your friends. All they talked about for hours on end was whether the U-FDA was an illegal offshoot of the U-PLO, the U-NCAA, or the U-NAACP, or whether some poor schmuck got his knees shot off by the Provisional IRA, the Marginal IRA, the Not Ready for Prime Time IRA, the Mother's Own IRA, or the Really, Truly, Absolutely the Genuine Article IRA—"

Despite herself, Sara laughed.

"Okay, I confess there's some addictive *thing* going on with you and that jerkwater that's beyond me," Lenore admitted. "But I'm only quoting you back to yourself if I say that the romance is played out. You can get just as destructively hung up on a good-for-nothing town as on a no-account man, can't you? *I* think you're running away from your life, but if you get something out of this expat shtick, that's your business. So at least dust off the passport, goyfriend. What about Bangkok?"

The suggestion was not out of left field. Their mutual friend Karen Banks had been working for an NGO in Thailand and was leaving on a one-year project to study the empowerment of women in South Korea. On the off chance that someone had itchy feet, Karen had emailed all her friends that her Bangkok flat was available for sublet.

"What would I do in *Bangkok*?" Sara slumped in the armchair, chin jammed to her clavicle.

"You're a freelance journalist. The fall of the *butt*—or whatever their money's called—just triggered the economic collapse of Southeast Asia. Why not cover that story? There's more going on in Bangkok than Belfast. The deal is sealed in Ireland. The story is dead. Besides, you read that email. Karen's apartment house has a pool and a tennis court. With the *butt* depressed, it still costs less than that worm-eaten Victorian attic you rent now. And it would be *wa-a-a-rm* . . ." Lenore cooed.

"You mean hot," Sara said sullenly.

"That's the other thing. Your garret in Belfast is fucking freezing."

It was freezing. Her flat at the end of Notting Hill (a distant poor relation of London's fashionable district) had no central heating, just a single clanky gas fire installed in each drafty, cavernous room. The gas had a dodgy smell, moldy and suspicious, to which Sara became accustomed over the winter, but after this trip to the States the odor was bound to bother her for a while in September.

"You've always told me," Lenore said soberly, "that staying overseas turns your life into 'one long adventure.' Well, where's the adventure in Belfast? You've been there *eleven years*. Your adventures lately must run to, like, taking out the garbage."

"Rubbish," Sara furnished with a wobbly smile.

"That's enough for you? Swapping *garbage* for *rubbish*, that still gets you off?"

A trill from the foyer delivered Sara from this savage campaign that she abandon her only home. While Lenore answered the phone, Sara dismissed the Bangkok lark as physically impractical. Sara Moseley was clingy, hoarding, and cheap. She had no idea how she'd got up the antimaterial zeal to divest herself of everything she owned at twenty-nine, but she knew she didn't have it in her to shimmy through the tag-sale striptease a second time. On the other hand, she wasn't about to carton everything up and pay, what, hundreds, maybe thousands of quid to shift all her worldly goods to the other side of the world on a whim of Lenore's. What if it didn't work out? Another small fortune wasted on schlepping the chattel back again. Adventure was all very exhilarating so long as you were foisting it on someone else, and didn't literally have to pay the freight.

"I do have her number there, but this month she's in the States," Sara overheard. "In fact, this week she's staying with me. Would you like to speak to her?"

Lenore returned trailing the cord, and extended the receiver. "Friend of a friend," she whispered. "Don't know her."

"Hello?"

"*Sara.*" The name sounded insistent, almost accusatory. "I'm very pleased to have found you," a youngish female continued with disconcerting solemnity, as if playing grown-up. "I'm a friend of Evelyn Mc-Auley, whom you may not know. Evelyn said her friend Lenore Feinstein knew someone who lived in Bel-*fast*. This must be fate, reaching you with one local call. I'd been prepared for overseas day rates."

Sara would have thought the same thing, but wouldn't have said it aloud. "So how can I help you?"

"My name is Emer Branagh. I'm on my way to Bel-*fast* next week, to stay for at least nine months. Since Evelyn said you've been over there a little while—"

"Eleven years," Sara provided pointedly.

"I was hoping you might have a room to let. Or could suggest where else I might start looking."

Sara shuddered inwardly at the vision of this notional flatmate, whose aggressively ethnic name implied another root-grubbing *Irish American*. Worse, the affected brand that stressed the second syllable of Bel-*fast* as a badge of authenticity. (Try this for truly authentic hairsplitting: Locals in *Ba-al*-fahst gently stressed the second syllable only when the city was preceded by a directional modifier, like "West Bal-*fahst*.") The Yankee Bel-*fast*er was a one-upsman. The gasping emphasis induced anxiety in compatriots that in referring to *Bel*-fast they'd made unwitting asses of themselves for years.

"Have you tried the internet?" Sara asked coolly.

"I was thinking more along the lines of personal connections. You see, I'm an author. I'm hoping to write a memoir about my experiences there."

Good lord, not another *My Year in Bel-FAST.* Its dialogue would be riddled with apostrophes and quaint respellings like "Nor'n Iron," its profiles of the writer's overnight fast friends—all, by coincidence, Catholic—recounting for the umpteenth time the heroic struggle of the *second-class citizen* against the repressive occupation of *the six counties* by British *Crown forces.* Unfortunately for our budding memoirist, on the heels of the Good Friday Agreement ructions in the Old Sod were winding down, but that was part of being clueless: having no sense of timing.

Unkindly, she even resisted steering the girl toward the *Belfast Telegraph*'s classifieds. The *Tele* was *Sara's* newspaper, both her local daily and her employer. She felt protective, jealous—jealous of what was already hers, but it's funny how you can covet what you have.

Yet curiously, it was thinking about the *Telegraph* that occasioned a turn.

While on holiday, Sara filed "Yankee Doodles" from the States. The column was due Friday morning. It was Wednesday afternoon, and she'd yet to decide on a topic. A Monica Lewinsky reprise would backfire; Northerners refused to hear a word against Bill Clinton, because he came to visit. She'd lethargically considered this week's anniversary of the Hiroshima A-bomb, but that peg was out, too. *Tele* subscribers would rather be bored witless by their own Troubles than concern themselves with anyone else's. Sara had been writing "Yankee Doodles" for nearly nine years, and as of this day exactly, with no forewarning, she had nothing more to say.

"Now that you mention it," Sara supposed into the receiver, looking Lenore in the eye, "*my* flat may be available for sublet. I'm headed for Southeast Asia."

DIZZY FROM HER mental plunge, Sara still insisted on taking Lenore and her husband, Caleb, out for dinner that evening. Though her one-child, two-income hosts were awash in cash, Sara was determined to express official thanks for being put up the previous week. Lenore had visited Belfast only that once, so balancing the scales by hosting her friend in return was unlikely. (Lenore protested that being spared even one more night in Belfast was compensation enough.) When Lenore remarked that they could always whip up some pasta and finding a sitter was kind of a hassle, Sara chose not to get the hint. Her rules of reciprocity were militant. She would be *grateful* over Lenore's dead body.

For Sara was a stringently conscientious houseguest. Per custom, she'd shown up in Somerville with her own ground coffee, Melitta filters, pint of milk, and grease-spotted bag of cranberry scones. Rather than filch cold cuts, she skipped lunches, and for the odd nightcap didn't mooch from Lenore's crowded liquor cabinet, but scrounged through her carry-on for Drambuie miniatures squirreled away on British Airways. So scrupulously did she not impose—buying a whole bottle of shampoo for a few nights' stay—that she may have disconcerted her benefactors, who'd never have begrudged her the Herbal Essences in the shower stall. In truth, she was guarding against the very disproportionate resentment she'd herself feel toward a freeloader who used up her coffee beans, cadged her shampoo, and expected lunch.

To celebrate that afternoon's rash pronouncement, Sara opted for a Thai curry house. She reminded Lenore over lemongrass chicken that Karen's flat in Bangkok might already be taken, half hoping that it was. After she swallowed a whole green chili in one bite, Sara's forehead broke into a cold sweat. To what had she just committed herself? Had she the remotest qualifications to freelance about economic collapse? So over coffee, she regressed to more commodious subject matter: Emer Branagh.

"Most of these seeker types are so unsussed," Sara despaired, "that they're oblivious to being clichés. They're always convinced they're, like, *Mayflower* passengers in reverse, and no American has ever set foot on the shores of Antrim. I guess this makes them lucky, but they never notice that they're objects of derision. Locals are sniggering into their pints, and meanwhile these memoirists think they've found their true home away from home and everybody loves them." Sara had tried to leaven the diatribe with feigned sympathy, but the tirade came out acrid.

"Doesn't that make *you* a cliché?" Caleb asked.

"Of course," Sara concurred cheerfully. "Although contrary to convention, I'm a unionist, so I don't hero-worship convicted murderers. And at least I know I'm a cliché—"

"Sara, what's this girl to you?" Lenore broke in. "You've never even met her."

Sara pulled up short from asserting *You don't understand*—a regulation Northern refrain with foreigners, the better to shield a tawdry, quotidian bickering that, given opportunity, outsiders might understand all too horribly well.

"On the face of it, she's a known quantity," Sara said instead. "I've met stacks of Americans passing through that town: conflict junkies, reconciliation missionaries, human rights watchdogs, the odd genealogical quester whose, you know, third cousin five times removed hailed from Carrickfergus and who snaps a whole roll of prints when he finds 'McErlean' on a bakery sign. If they're not naive or loud, they're naive *and* loud, and the combination is desperate. Most visiting Americans have embarrassed me, or at least made me mad, since—when they know what one is—every single one, without exception, has turned out to be a nationalist. So I guess I'm prejudiced."

"How can you be prejudiced against *Americans*," Caleb exclaimed, consternated, "when you are one?"

"It's more than possible," Sara said, not backing down, "to be prejudiced against yourself. Still—Lenore's right. I don't know this *Emer* person, and I shouldn't make harsh assumptions based on the thousand credulous eejits who preceded her." For the rest of the evening Sara didn't mention Emer again, though she was surprised by how much restraint the omission demanded.

* * *

KAREN NOT ONLY emailed that her flat was still available, but also offered to give her old friend a thumbs-up with the features editor at the *Bangkok Post*, a well-regarded English-language broadsheet looking for new voices. As a financial backstop Sara could also edit publications for the UN, which always needed native English speakers to catch second-language gaffes and to cull enough bureaucratic twaddle to make text faintly comprehensible. The reports were soul-destroyingly dull, Karen warned, but the pay was super. Thanks to the Asian economic crisis, both Korean Air and Thai Air were offering scandalously cut-rate fares. Sara's whim took shape. It was doable.

Subsequently, other Boston running buddies of yore proved if anything too enthusiastic about this Bangkok caprice, betraying a widespread consensus that she'd been in a rut. Sara was abashed to discover to what extent she'd become the subject of her friends' conspiratorial despair. But frankly, they were dead on. She'd started out such a world beater, game for anything new or anywhere fresh, which is how she ended up in Belfast to begin with. Unbeknownst to herself, she'd become as much of a stick-in-the-mud in Northern Ireland as she might have had she never left Medford. Why, knowing nothing about Bangkok was good reason to go there. Had she lost faith in her capacity to learn? She didn't used to know a *loyalist* from a hole in the ground. What would stop her from mastering the causalities of Southeast Asian recession?

In binding herself to fragile intentions, Sara seized on logistics. Accordingly, Emer Branagh proved key. Sara could neither afford two rents nor shift kit and caboodle to Bangkok sight unseen. But subletting her Notting Hill flat had proved a tall order in the past. Sara inhabited the attic story of an older Scottish couple's creaky Victorian manor, and a tenant was obliged to ascend by the central staircase of the main house. Whenever she'd tried to sublet to students from Queens for her summer stint in the US, they'd recoiled from the incursion on another family's home. So she'd have to make nice with the bird in hand. Besides, if Sara didn't act on this kooky impulse right away, she knew she'd go back to Belfast, dawdle over "Yankee Doodles," churn daily on the stationary bicycle in the Windsor Lawn Tennis Club fitness suite, and mesmerized by her soporific routine would dismiss the whole Bangkok folly as temporary insanity. Clueless, maybe, but Emer was also a godsend.

Sara and Emer spoke perhaps three more times. Attempts to meet for coffee were scuppered by Emer's preparations for her flight to Bel-*fast* on the evening of August fourteenth. Sara's own ticket returned her to *Bel*-fast on September tenth. So she proposed to post Emer a duplicate key. Emer could move into the flat while Sara was still in Boston, locate a temporary room elsewhere for when Sara returned for perhaps three weeks to wrap up her affairs, then move back for the duration once Sara left for Thailand. The arrangement was cumbersome, but no doubt desirous of a place to lay her head on arrival in a strange city, Emer agreed.

In explaining the eccentricities of her abode, Sara took pains to ingratiate herself. Relating her waterless technique for cleaning the cast-iron skillet with heat and salt, she furnished a degree of detail that was deliberately comical. Tentatively identifying a few items that Emer might avoid using, she made light of her attachment to a gaudy Belgian beer glass lugged all over Europe. Yet through the smoke screen of self-ridicule Emer must surely have concluded she was a nut.

Sara was a nut. An honest catalog of the cherished items of which Emer should beware would include every bit of bric-a-brac in the flat. Sara was a passionate custodian of the lowliest appurtenance. All that she owned was implicitly cherished for the very fact that she owned it, helping define the vigorously defended boundary where the rest of the world stopped and Sara Moseley began. Arguably, it was the perfect impermeability of her own perimeter—that militant distinction between what was hers versus what was other people's—that explained most profoundly why at forty-one Sara Moseley remained childless and unmarried, and why she might be attracted to a foreign polity whose consuming obsession was *the Border*.

Emer as well seemed eager to please—neither wanted the other to get away—although wont to endear herself with oppressive sincerity. She attended to prolix explanations about the skillet with grave patience, and no amount of Sara's self-mockery could tempt her subletter into a shared chuckle. Dangling herself as a professional asset, Emer volunteered a host of do-gooder contacts in Southeast Asia whose causes "as a responsible independent journalist" Sara would have a moral obligation to promote. Over the phone, Sara would find herself jotting down the address of a pressure group that was campaigning to have the Khmer Rouge leadership brought to trial in Cambodia or the phone number of a little outfit that refurbished computers for underprivileged Thai schoolchildren. Once Emer rang off, Sara would look at the scribbles on her notepad, mutter *What's all this shite?*, tear off the pages, and throw them away.

Sara knew the type. Emer sounded exactly like the American volunteers for the Peace People on the Lisburn Road, who organized lemonade and biscuits for cross-community day camps. The unmitigated earnestness of these virtuous summer interns always dumbfounded local pub patrons at the nearby Four in Hand, who after repeatedly fruitless attempts to engage the visitors in slag-for-slag banter would contrive the same pitying dispensation for the Yanks as they might have for the simpleminded.

Emer emphasized that she had written a memoir before. Attaching herself to a small international school run for the children of diplomats, she'd lived for a year in Burma. The resultant first-person account was published by a Vermont press of which Sara had never heard, "with very good distribution," the girl stressed sternly.

Sara embellished. Young Emer's involvement with the region doubtless hailed from some stimulating undergraduate foreign policy course at, say, Sarah Lawrence. The professor would have been a seductively unstable Vietnam vet with whom the smitten Emer conducted a torturous affair. After graduation, the girl had beelined for the most fucked-up country left in Southeast Asia—*to impress Arsehole.* Arsehole wasn't impressed, since arseholes never are.

At least this much was not Sara's invention: the girl was clearly in the heady throes of Newbie Author Syndrome. That is, an unimpeded life of letters seemed to have opened before her. One after another, she would tame trouble spots to the page. Sure, thought Sara grimly, it was a pretty picture—as yet unsullied by word processor chain-smoking, dismissive squib reviews, flyspecked remainder copies, copacetic editors exiled to genre imprints, demands for massive rewrites meant to presage outright rejection of whole commissioned manuscripts, the odd close-call brush with mortality that makes our heroine gun-shy since sometimes trouble spots weren't merely theme parks but were actually dangerous, and joyless authorial alcoholism.

Cheerfully weaving the innocent's threadbare future, Sara formed a vivid picture of Emer Branagh, whose lifeless chestnut hair would be shoulder length and straight. Bangs. Thin if physically weak, she would disguise a passable figure with dowdy liberal clothes: loose corduroy slacks, plaid flannel button-downs, and lace-up umber Timberlands with corrugated soles. The girl was certainly short. However even-featured, her face would lack the hint of subterfuge that might have made it sexy. She was bound to sport big doggy brown eyes, and perpetually to wear the trusting, how-can-I-help expression of a pre-burnout social worker.

The plain-Jane mind's-eye portrait was satisfying, but Emer's Burmese escapade gave Sara a pang. A brutal regime conferred cachet, just as the Troubles had laced the bracken of a wet, underpopulated island with belladonna. On the heels of the agreement, the only peril Ulster reliably afforded was a dander to the shops without an umbrella. And while violence made any boondocks exotic, the same could not be said of a bland, business-section recession. Momentarily, Sara faltered, nervous that rather than flying to Thailand she should really be booking for Iraq.

AT 2:45 P.M. on Saturday, August fifteenth, 1998, a fertilizer car bomb exploded in the town center of Omagh, County Tyrone, killing twenty-eight people outright, and injuring over three hundred; a twenty-ninth victim would die in hospital by September. The bomb would be claimed two days later by "the Real IRA," the military wing of "the 32-County Sovereignty Committee"—both names that, owing to the scale of the casualties, countless television commentators would be forced to deliver on camera with a straight face. Though instigated after a formally brokered peace, the bombing of Omagh's town center was the single most lethal atrocity in the history of the modern Northern Irish conflict.

Troubles maven Sara Moseley learned of the tragedy a full thirty-one hours after the fact. She and Lenore had gone on a weekend camping trip to the Cape, and had pitched their tent out of the range of newspapers, televisions, and satellite signals since the previous Friday evening. Only when fiddling with the car radio as Lenore drove back to Boston late Sunday afternoon did Sara tune into: " . . . *including a young woman pregnant with twins. Northern Ireland's first minister David Trimble has denounced . . .*"

"Jesus, what's happened?" Sara exclaimed, cranking up a John Hume interview full blast. "I'm away for one bloody fortnight, and the place goes to shite!"

"Turn your back for a minute, and the natives revert to savages?" Lenore asked, owing to the volume of the radio obliged to shout. The news moved on to Clinton's impending testimony on Monica Lewinsky to the grand jury; Sara turned it down.

"It's just, you sounded so, well, colonial," Lenore said.

"It may seem as if bombs go off there all the time and what's one more, but that high a body count is a big deal."

"Are you worried that the casualties might include a friend of yours?"

"Oh, that's unlikely." Sara detested bystanders and hangers-on who milked atrocities for secondhand pathos. "Omagh's a ways from Belfast. Still, this bomb is bad news for the agreement. In the assembly, the UUP has a pro-agreement majority of only two seats. This one republican up-yours could push a few crucial UUP assemblymen into the

No camp. They don't trust Sinn Fein; the idea of going into government with pond scum already makes them gag. Also, whoever did this—and money down that it'll be disowned as a *mistake*—the Provisionals are sure to get the blame at first. On the other hand, that statement from Gerry Adams was gobsmacking. Did you hear that? He's 'totally horrified by this action,' and 'condemns it without equivocation'? I mean, knock me over with a feather!"

Lenore had failed to insert the grunts of someone at least pretending to listen. Sure, an associate professor of clinical psychology at Lowell had no reason to grasp how dumbfounding it was that the man the dogs in the street knew was the leader of the Provisional IRA had actually denounced a republican bombing, as journalists had ritually begged Adams to do for decades. But Sara was frustrated. She yearned for a convocation of chums in her drafty Belfast sitting room, where they could tease out Omagh's intricate political implications like patiently working snarls from windblown hair. The caucus would have been nostalgic. Ever since the signing of the agreement in April, Sara and her coconspirators (largely Catholic unionists—to republicans, Irish Uncle Toms; to Sara, unflinching freethinkers who refused to walk in lockstep with corner-boy fascists) had found themselves at a loss for material, and her dinner parties wound down before midnight. But after turns of the wheel this sharp, such evenings always ran boisterously into the small hours.

By contrast, here in Massachusetts she and Lenore spent the early evening searching three separate minimarts for Diet Peach Snapple iced tea. On the last leg to Somerville, silence fell between the two women, leaving Sara to her thoughts.

These were embarrassing thoughts. Abstractly, Sara was sorrowful. Yet mourning the death of strangers is a blunted, butter knife experience, bearing no resemblance to the slicing, machete-like bereavement of losing someone you know. Hence Sara was left to brood on more peripheral considerations, all obscenely selfish.

First, Sara felt left out. It wasn't fair. She sticks over a decade of weeklong downpours and winters when the sun sets midafternoon until the biggest cataclysm to hit Northern Ireland in thirty years goes down, and Sara is sunning on Cape Cod.

Second, she feared for her own sense of narrative resolution. Beginning with the death of eleven civilians around Enniskillen's cenotaph on Remembrance Day 1987, Sara had loyally turned the pages of Ulster's turgid multigenerational saga, of which the Good Friday Agreement had appeared to constitute a happily-ever-after last chapter. Because she'd been as addicted to the serial as any nineteenth-century Dickens fan, certainty that in the main the story was a wrap had made it vastly much easier for Sara to contemplate departure for Bangkok. But Omagh could very well mark the end of the Provisional IRA cease-fire. Were there to be an extended epilogue or, heaven forbid, a sequel, getting herself to quit Northern Ireland altogether could prove impossible.

Third, it was bad enough that nine days earlier the US embassy bombs in Nairobi and Dar es Salaam had gone off fractionally too late for Sara to repeg her *Belfast Telegraph* column for the following Saturday; thus at the same time other American journalists were finally taking terrorism seriously, Sara Moseley was filling out eight hundred words about the hokey faux Irish pubs off Harvard Square. But after Omagh's catastrophe, yesterday's "Yankee Doodles"—a bit of belletristic fluff on pretentious Americans who say "Bel-*fast*"—would have scanned to her aghast readership as beyond crass.

These matters aside, what throbbed uppermost in Sara Moseley's mind was the fact that yesterday was August fifteenth, on whose very morning Emer Branagh was to have assumed the Notting Hill flat. Sara accepted that her resentment was absurd, and she'd be hard-pressed to justify this impression of having been cheated. Hazily, her consternation was of a piece with that ruling compulsion to *keep track*. The bitterness was all bound up with her meticulous accounting of credits and debts, with her vigilant policing of the frontier between her personal province and the province of the world at large, and even with her fierce grip on bagatelle, for Sara clutched a skillet or a beer glass with the ferocity of a toddler with a stuffed bunny.

So it was childish. But now Emer Branagh could boast to all her little Irish American friends that she arrived in Belfast on the day of the worst bombing in the history of the Troubles, after paying for this claim to fame with a single morning of bleary unpacking. But if Omagh justly belonged to any foreign interloper it belonged to Sara, who had purchased wholesale anything faintly interesting in Northern Ireland with eleven draining years—for it is no mean effort to become exercised on a daily basis about other people's problems. Along with other misappropriations like the bone-handled parasol, Omagh had been stolen from her. Omagh got added to the List.

TAKING THE AIRBUS from Belfast International the morning of September tenth, Sara bobbed against the window. Sheep on passing hillsides jittered with the electric jolt characteristic of having missed a night's sleep. The sumptuous sunlight in which these storybook fields basked was duplicitous, a Tourist Board scam to lure her away from Bangkok. It rained here all day, every day, and *that* was why the pastureland gleamed such a seductive green. Priming herself for Asia, Sara encouraged her own weariness with the desolate residential architecture: stark white pebble-dashed boxes with dark-stained window frames. Still, as Belfast Lough curled on the horizon, the sight of Samson and Goliath, the two massive Harland and Wolff shipping cranes stapling the skyline, made her heart leap. However unaccountably, this was home.

To the indigenous she'd always be a foreigner, and that was an ineluctable fact, which Sara tried never to fight. But deferential guest-of-the-nation status couldn't dull an imperialistic glint in Sara's eye as the Airbus puttered down Royal Avenue and the wedding-cake dome of Belfast's pompous city hall hove into view. To all appearances, her possessions were few. She didn't own a microwave or washer. Her computer was a dinosaur, with an *E* that had started to stick. On the other hand, she did own all of Northern Ireland.

Which might have come as a surprise to the other people who lived there. Yet recognition that her personal deed to Ulster was ludicrous didn't compromise the sensation in the slightest. Ownership is as much state of mind as legal entitlement. For that matter, absence of birthright made Sara's title to the province possible. She wasn't vying for the North with locals, who seemed to possess their own country in a different dimension. In Sara's parallel universe, her only real competition for Ulster's sheep-strewn acreage was *other Americans.*

Mindful that this turf war was insensible and potentially all in her head, for her first several years here Sara made a concerted, compensatory effort to be, if not quite warm, at least cordial whenever she encountered her countrymen in Belfast. Yet other visiting Americans had repeatedly acted aloof in return, whereas the rare fellow expat full-timer had proved positively icy. Rearing back at the Crown Bar, compatriots would refer blithely to IRA contacts as if name-dropping rock stars. They booby-trapped their conversation with tests: Sara *had* seen, hadn't she, the latest Committee on the Administration of Justice report on the RUC? So a tacit rivalry between American political hobbyists in respect to territory that wasn't theirs to fight over was not purely the product of her private neurosis. Most nationals clung gratefully to one another abroad, but Americans in Northern Ireland seemed at once drawn to one another, and repelled.

Maybe deep down they made one another feel ashamed. Theater requires an audience, and this raunchy cabaret had run for three decades. Throw in the professional Peeping Toms—from CNN, *Le Monde*—and the statelet had staged a noteworthy portion of its seamy antics to titillate the overseas voyeur. Which made them all *enablers.*

So these days, Sara preferred simple avoidance to good manners. Take that rumpled late-thirties chap sitting at the front of the Airbus who'd boarded ahead of her, remarking to the driver in a strong Texas accent that the price of a return to Glengall Street had gone up. (Academic horn-rims, tweedy sports coat: Austin, Sara concluded. They had a conflict studies department. Open collar, nubby jumper, funky leather luggage: left-leaning, in the States. Translate: *nationalist*.) Of course she'd noticed him, while taking local passengers for granted as part of the scenery, like more sheep. Yet Sara had seated herself in the back, as far from the fellow as she could get. In truth, Sara was standoffish not so much because she was afraid that she might not like the man, but because she was afraid that she might not like herself.

For had she sat next to him, he'd have tossed off the name of the peace institute that sent him on this junket, perhaps proceeding to share his street smarts. *You wouldn't believe it, but Belfast is pretty safe. All the same, watch your back in republican estates like Twinbrook or Poleglass, where if the Provies aren't looking the joyriders will boost anything that moves* . . . Within ninety seconds he'd apprise his seatmate that he'd been here several times before. After all, that was the sole aim of his remark to the bus driver, who hardly needed to be apprised that the fare had increased.

Sara would mention how long she'd lived in Belfast herself not as a point of information but purely to gain social advantage. She'd reference *Chuckies* and *culchies* to show off her fluency in the regional idiom, and exaggerate the contamination of her vowels, pronouncing *house* as *hyse*. She would cluck-cluck over the Omagh bombing in order to insinuate her nuanced grasp of this autumn's delicate political state of play. The worse for this notional encounter, piercing American voices carry uncannily in small spaces. So throughout the genteel antagonism, every passenger on this bus would be eavesdropping. Sara had learned the hard way from an onslaught of anonymous hate mail forwarded by the *Tele*: no matter how erudite, subtle, and insightful about the North they might sound to themselves, the silent verdict of their audience would be devastating.

Thus Sara had refrained from speaking to the Texan at all, because the fact that this who-knows-whom, who-knows-what, who's-been-where-when-what-blew-up combat between foreign-born Troubles fanciers was unendurably gross never seemed to prevent Sara from throwing herself into the humiliating competition for all she was worth.

Geographically, Ulster was little larger than Connecticut, a state that provided for more than three million Americans with relative grace. Yet apparently Northern Ireland wasn't big enough to accommodate more than one.

The complex anthropology of the political parasite went some distance toward explaining why, as the Airbus drew nearer to the hideous Europa Hotel and thus a taxi ride away from a flat now installed with a compatriot's what-all, Sara bridled. She resolved to eradicate the least remnant of her tenant on arrival.

AS HER BLACK taxi wound to the top of the rise, arriving at a majestic if ramshackle manor at the road's end, Sara's proprietary sensation crested as well. Never mind that she merely let the top floor; this was *her house*. The fact that the deed was not filed in her name was a technicality, nay, an economy. It saved on taxes. The driver was suitably awed by the four-gabled grandeur of her residence. "Fair play to you, pet. Not many of these big old girls left in these parts, so there aren't."

However increasingly ambivalent about Belfast—eleven-year residence at a dead-end menaced with metaphor—Sara was always happy to return to the *hyse* itself. Her grounds scraggly with wildflower gardens, her wings attended by stately cedars like loyal footmen, the "old girl" had character. The posture of the house on the hill was drawn up, bosom high, like a turn-of-the-century dowager a few too many cream teas on. Though decrepit, she was vain into her dotage. Cosmetic restorations—the newer, lighter-hued slates patched ineffectually over a rotting roof, or the freshly applied magnolia paint already flaking from damp—blazed self-deceit, like foundation slathered over a once alluring face. While nowadays greatly reduced in circumstances, no. 19 retained the haughty reserve of old money, and from her elevated perch shot withering looks at the garish nouveaux riches monstrosities and dinky bourgeois bungalows that had replaced the august relatives of her own generation. The Miss Havisham of Notting Hill exuded a musty redolence of mortality and decay that sometimes frightened small children. She was indeed a house better let than owned, since the cantankerous old biddy hoovered money by the bin-full, which was why her guardians were forced to rent her top floor. Yet she sucked up the kind of cash that never made one's day-to-day any better, but merely ensured that life for her inhabitants deteriorated at a somewhat slower pace.

As a tenant, Sara ordinarily embraced this crumbling hulk with the devotion of a niece, a sentimental relation who didn't have to pay auntie's medical bills or clean up the messes of an incontinent. Today, however, a thread of foreboding tangled Sara's homecoming. Emer Branagh would have been nesting in no. 19's attic for four weeks. While the kid had promised to make herself scarce as of earlier this morning, Sara had encouraged her subletter to leave a few things behind if necessary, a companionable offer that she now regretted.

Forbiddingly, too, there was more than one way to take over. As a teenager Sara had mocked her mother's possessive exclamation, "You've tracked mud all over my clean floor!" *What's this "my floor,"* Sara had jeered to herself. *It's Dad who bought it.* At last after keeping her rented Notting Hill garret in impeccable order year after year, she understood. You could own something just by taking care of it. If you swept it, and mopped it, and waxed it, the linoleum was de facto *your floor.* Yet a host of wife beaters and IRA bombers had shrewdly detected a shady corollary. You could also own something through violation. If you abused it, and disfigured it, and ruined it for everybody else, it was yours, too.

As the driver hefted her bag up the porch steps, Sara reflected uneasily that she didn't have the constitution for subletting, which routinely entailed wear and tear. You needed to grasp that if few objects were perfectly fungible, most objects were loosely fungible. You had to register the fact that your territory on the most profound level could never be measured in square feet. You required a sense of proportion from which Sara had never suffered, and you had to be able to let little things go.

Sara counted out the exact metered fare. (A Belfast cabby didn't expect a tip, so an extra quid would have seemed gauchely *American*.) Inside, she bumped her heavy suitcase up the stairs; it was bulging from coffee beans, sports socks, and printer cartridges, all cheaper in the States. So big deal, Sara reasoned, she'd have to live with a stranger's sack of clothes (corduroy slacks, flannel shirts, stumpy shoes). She was mostly dreading those tiny, creepy markers of invasion: brown hairs in the drain, maybe the lingering whiff of a misfortune with fresh sardines.

Pushing the bag through the entry to her own lair on the upper floor with her bladder bursting, Sara hustled urgently to the loo. She noticed that the toilet roll was down to cardboard only when it was too late. The spare rolls that Sara always kept on hand in dread of this very calamity were evidenced only by more cardboard in the wastebasket. Irked at being so stranded in her own home, Sara searched her pockets, at last tearing open the airline overnight kit. Finally one of those flimsy gray bed socks served a purpose.

Washing her hands, Sara found only a sliver of soap, magenta, like the fat bar she'd left in August. On a hunch, she ducked into the bath next door. Sure enough, her shampoo and conditioner were down to a drizzle, and *someone* had opened her new bag of safety razors. So far, this homecoming was evincing a distinctly Three Bears texture.

Lugging her suitcase up the final flight of stairs, she naturally expected to confront her extensive poster montage of Goons with Guns on the landing's wall. The IRA and the loyalist Ulster Freedom Fighters were equally represented, as Sara's contempt for terrorists was nonsectarian. The montage was for grins. Eyes beady behind his ski mask, AK trained on an invisible foe, each fierce patriot of Ireland or Britannia looked like a little boy playing army whose overprotective mother feared for colds.

Of some twenty posters, only pinholes and Blu Tack remained. Well, if that wasn't a bit of nerve. Sure enough, those patronizing Brits were right: at least *some* Americans had "no sense of irony." Maybe a newcomer to this carnival whose sensibilities were still delicate wouldn't want to come home every day to losers with their heads in socks point-ing automatics at her forehead. But that array had taken years to ac-crue, and time to put up. Couldn't the girl have waited until Sara was in Bangkok?

Abandoning her luggage, Sara ventured warily into the adjoining study. She'd figured Emer for a save-the-whales type who'd bequeath her landlady a few bottles for recycling, but who would otherwise leave the flat shit-eatingly shipshape, a lone suitcase cowering in one corner, a jam jar of daffodils propping a welcome-home note . . .

The study was a wreck. The carpet was grotty, what little you could see of it. The floor was ankle deep in papers and splayed books from *Sara's* library. Crumby plates and scummy glasses punctuated every surface. Desk drawers coughed open, as if the place had been burgled.

Which it had been, rather. Half a ream of A4 was missing. An alien laptop was connected to *Sara's* inkjet, poised to deplete *Sara's* car-tridge. Printout underfoot was cheerful with *Sara's* parti-colored paper clips. Long faxes curled lavishly over the carpet like white chocolate on gateau, so no wonder the machine was out of paper. The scattered felt tips—capless—had once been stored in a "Reservoir Prods" mug, which was now—oh, no!—absent from the desktop. Sara whiffled in an adenoidal panic before discovering the rare evidence of Protestant wit—the mug's tough-guy silhouettes of Mr. Orangeman, Mr. Union, and Mr. Boyne pointing revolvers in dark glasses—decorously ob-scured with a hankie.

Numerous pages of the Black 'n' Red hardback notebook bought in July for the next volume of Sara's journal (£4.95!) were looped in a con-niving cursive. *This country is like a mirror,* a stray entry began, *from which gazes back at us our own reflection. Yet the mirror is warped, and what we see is distorted, a fun-house contortion of either what we wish to see, or what we fear . . .*

Oh, for fuck's sake, what horseshit.

She collected the books from the floor. Emer hadn't seized sensi-bly on hard-nosed references like W. D. Flackes's *Northern Ireland:*

A Political Directory or Malcolm Sutton's *An Index of Deaths from the Conflict in Ireland*. Instead, she'd been drawn to the *poetry* (Ulster's poets outnumbered its poetry readers by ten to one) and gentle volumes like Dervla Murphy's sweet but damp-eyed account of a Northern cycling trip, *A Place Apart*, or yet another Yanks-in-the-bog memoir, *O Come Ye Back to Ireland: Our First Year in County Clare* (a review copy—Sara had slammed it).

Enough. Time to case the rest of the flat, which, if she didn't miss her guess, was lacking that jam jar of daffodils. Funny. Emer had sounded so tidy over the phone.

In the kitchen, her precious Belgian beer glass, which Emer had promised to store safely out of harm's way, was pulpy with orange juice, and tilted by the sink against a mound of potato peelings. The sink itself was crammed with encrusted crockery. From among Sara's trove of Troubles coffee mugs, the rather prosaic one from the SDLP (good Catholics: no goons, no guns) poked from the sludge. Soaking at the very bottom, rimmed with rust, was the cast-iron skillet. Apparently those water-free heat-and-salt directions had been difficult to follow.

Shoes kissing the sticky lino, Sara surveyed her larder, whose inventory as of early August, from a lifetime of *keeping track*, she recalled to the bean. The comestibles had been pilfered wholesale. Five formerly unopened bags of pasta were reduced to stray shells. Apropos of the Three Bears, a family-size bag of muesli was down to a handful; Emer had literally been eating her porridge! The six missing tins of tomatoes must have contributed to the industrial-size vat of what looked like vomit in the fridge—a pinkish slop clotted with curdled bits that she theorized from a safe distance was tofu spaghetti sauce. Multiple unopened jars—green olives, dill pickles, gooseberry jam—were now stored in the refrigerator door, in anticipation of many complementary culinary delights to come. The subletter had splurged on her own liter of milk. But the only sign of Emer's having bought any nonperishables for herself was a single shaker of sea salt.

Eyes slit and jaw set, Sara picked the green olives, dill pickles, and gooseberry jam *out* of the refrigerator door, thank you very much, and slid the jars *back* into their cabinet.

Sara dragged her case down the long center room, where dozens of cassette tapes littered the bookcase, out of their cases. It's altogether feasible to disdain a stranger's taste in your own music. Emer had been playing Loreena McKennitt, Clannad, and Natalie Merchant—the wick, edgeless singers from Sara's morose period after breaking up with Arsehole. In the columns of unmolested tapes, the labels of *We Hate the IRA* and the two-bigotries-with-one-stone classic *The Pope's a Darkie* had been *turned to the wall.* "Sense of humor bypass," Sara announced aloud.

She stuck her head into the sitting room, hopeful that in the vaulting, underfurnished expanse, with its comely round-topped dormer window, sloped ceiling, and comforting pigeon warble overhead, she might locate her customary serenity.

Pigeons, certainly. Serenity, not quite. More books, everywhere— pulled from the shelves where they'd once been alphabetized by author. But Sara saw red only when she glanced at the far wall, where more precisely she saw nothing.

The dozens of photographs that documented her eleven years in Belfast had all been taken down, and were strewn carelessly on the guest bed: an *Irish News* clipping in which Sara's indistinct head at an IRA funeral was circled in highlighter; Sara and Arsehole; Sara at a meeting of the Belfast City Council; Sara aglow at her first loyalist bonfire; Sara's much younger face smiling alongside her debut "Yankee Doodles" column, yellowed in its frame. At a glance, none of the archive looked damaged, so she was a little at a loss to explain the flash of rage. This was subletting. Still, where would the harm be, keeping that collage in place?

But maybe the bedroom took the prize. Oh, by now she wasn't surprised to come upon what might have been the aftermath of the famous wire hanger scene in *Mommie Dearest*—although unnervingly the clothes flung onto every available surface featured not corduroy and flannel, but rayon and silk. The bedclothes snarled in a heap seemed par for the course; after sloshing through that wading pool of stationery in the study, Sara hadn't envisaged the sheets fresh, the spread smoothed, the pillows plumped. But she had not been prepared for completely rearranged furniture (pushed beside the window, the bed blocked the closet door—now, that made sense). And she had not been prepared for the shrine.

Or whatever it was. On the dresser, a peaked wooden cabinet was faced with two brass-knobbed doors. Ceramic incense holders bristled burnt joss sticks. Strings of fragrant cedar beads looped each knob of the mirror, while around its frame seasonally premature Christmas lights winked in a variety of merry colors. The Cranshaw melon looked like an offering of sorts, circled as it was by candles, which had drooled red wax on the bureau's veneer.

"Bloody hell," Sara mumbled. "Not only is she a slob, a cheapskate, and a sponger. She's a fruitcake."

The churchy aura of the assemblage made Sara superstitious, and she let it be. But she saw no reason to abide Emer's launderette decor, and beavered about the room whisking up kimonos, lacy underthings, and posh angora jumpers. Amid one armful, Sara identified her own denim jacket and hand-knit cardigan from Dublin (IR £119). Cheeky bitch! Retrieving the loaners, Sara heaped the rest unceremoniously into the interloper's open-mawed suitcase. How odd. When moving out for at least three weeks, why hadn't Emer seen fit to pack it and take some of this frippery with her? For that matter, Sara had yet to come across some scrap scrawled with Emer's new temporary address. She hoped the girl would ring, since she was planning to give the kid what for.

Collapsed onto the unmade bed—*in front of the closet*—the rightful owner of 19 Notting Hill grappled with an emerging dilemma. She still needed a subletter, and waiting until she found a more docile, respectful neat freak could terminally delay the trip to Bangkok. Retaining Emer but giving her a hard time about the state of the place would be dangerous; you don't want anyone staying in your home in your absence who bears you a grudge. The flat had been left in poor enough condition when Emer had, tangibly at least, nothing against her.

Furthermore, the office supplies, the grub, the toiletries and cleaning products—in their totality these moochings constituted a significant financial drain, and together they betokened a rank opportunism. The resourceful Emer Branagh had purchased nothing that she could scavenge from Sara's flat instead. Yet item by item, each presumption was trivial. What was Sara to do, chew Emer out for using her *paper clips*? Betray to another living soul a mentality so small change that it detected in a bedside box of coins a significantly lower proportion of 50P pieces?

As for the slovenliness: yes, the carpet was tatty, the lino sticky. There were the clothes, the tapes out of cases, the books in piles. But now that relief was already in sight in the bedroom, she had to admit that the mess was superficial.

As for the disassembled poster and photo montages—the erasure of Sara's twisted sense of humor and political tourism was well within Emer's rights. Excepting these few weeks, the girl had moved in for nine months or more, and quite reasonably wanted to make the flat her own. And hadn't she, just. The girl couldn't have arrived with many possessions, so their having been deployed to maximum effect suggested, as Lenore might say, colonial intent. The systematic effacement of Sara Moseley from her own home implied a decontamination, and the perfect absence of any homage to the primary tenant—like, when she's due home you at least do the dishes—was defiant.

Well, she would efface Emer Branagh right back. Weaving with exhaustion, Sara put a shoulder to the stead and began to shimmy the heavy double bed back where it belonged.

"Sara? I didn't mean to startle you."

Sara was startled, all right. While the intruder could only be Emer Branagh, the woman in the doorway didn't *look* like Emer Branagh.

In most cases, a fragile preconception is instantly banished by the overbearing materialization of the real McCoy, but Sara clung so to her fantasy subletter that she might have introduced the figment to the figure before her and asked them to shake hands. For one sustained moment Sara insisted stolidly to herself that plain, dowdily dressed, doggy-eyed telephone Emer was her real subletter, and this slippery, sidling item was an impostor.

The pretender sported hair not a shy brown, but jet black. If anything, she had a couple of inches on Sara, who herself measured a respectable five six. Indeed, the only thing about actual Emer that was short, stylishly so, was that hair, clipped designer-close, with pin curls lifting before pierced ears. Her build was less *thin* than *sleek*. While she wasn't dressed up, she was dressed chic—snug black jeans, low-heeled black boots buffed to a sultry luster, an oversize jumper of the sort imported from South America of late, a weave of bright yellow, red, and green against a black ground—vivid and intense without, somehow, looking loud. Eyeliner, and touches of tasteful jewelry that looked like presents. Presents from men. She had the kind of alabaster skin that might bring pallor back into fashion, treacherously sharp cheekbones, and guarded gray eyes—in all, a face that contained well more than the mere hint of subterfuge that made a woman sexy. A woman. That was the other surprise. This wasn't a girl.

"I—I'm sorry," Sara stuttered, nodding to the bed. For Sara, this impulse was typical, compulsively furnishing an apology to someone who owed *her* one, and obscurely of a piece with her other inane habit of fending off panhandlers in Boston with *No, thank you.* "I just thought—with the bed here, you can't get into the closet."

"I don't need to get into the closet," Emer said evenly.

That's because you keep all your clothes on the floor. Pity—all Sara's best lines were wasted because she hadn't the audacity to act on what were in all other respects the splendid natural instincts of a harridan.

"I may need to," Sara said, furious with herself for this persistent tone of beseechment. Why, in *her own* flat, when she was moving *her own* bed to where *she* preferred to sleep, did she feel as if she'd been caught at something naughty?

"I had this idea you were coming back a different day." Emer's own tone was one of quizzical bemusement.

Regarding the shambles, the rampant plunder, the fact that there *wasn't even any fucking loo roll*, the most minimal contrition was not forthcoming. As for having got the date wrong, the ploy was inspired. Prepared, Emer might have tidied the flat, but now we'll never know, will we? Meanwhile all this *crap* planted in every room like flags on Everest had an excuse, which may have been why a mild little smile now danced on a face that could otherwise appear rather hard to read.

"That's strange," Sara said. "Didn't you email me only three days ago to confirm my plans?" Having skirted as close as she dared to *you lying sack of shit*, she veered abruptly: "If I'm going to stay awake, I have to make some coffee."

Sara left the bed in the middle of the room, halfway between where it had been and where it was going, a limbo giving physical expression to an identically neither-here-nor-there uncertainty in the air as to who was in whose flat. As she burrowed into her luggage for a pound of french vanilla roast, Sara swallowed the impolitic lambaste she had entertained earlier, but the voice inside her head was not so easily quieted: *What are you doing here, woman? You're meant to have cleared off. Can't you see I'm knackered? That I just want to unpack, finish cleaning up your grot so this flat feels like mine again, and zone out with a glass of sherry in front of the Channel Four News? So could we please save this getting-to-know-you carry-on for another time?*

When Emer failed utterly to (a) leave, or even (b) fill the conversational void—really, the least she could do as the only person in the room sufficiently well rested to string together a grammatical sentence—Sara solicited with all the decency she could muster, "Is the flat working out for you?"

"It's quite acceptable." As Sara swept past, Emer pivoted so reluctantly from the doorway that Sara brushed the South American sweater. The woman seemed put out at having to shift her backside at all in—

In her own flat. Not quite sure of its dimensions, Sara was nagged by the impression of a developing situation here.

"Ach, I tried to warn you over the phone that the place was falling to bits," Sara prattled after Emer trailed her to the kitchen. "The plaster's crumbling, and splinters of frame come off in your hands if you're not gentle with the windows. You must have noticed that evil black fungus on the sitting room ceiling—it wipes off, but comes back. Damp . . . And the decor is desperate really," Sara blithered over the coffee grinder after Emer contributed nothing. "This floral wallpaper looks like a dog's breakfast, and the furniture is shite . . ."

At last Emer submitted soberly, "I don't care about any of that."

Springing to the defense of a flat Sara adored this was not. She would have to do the honors herself. "I guess I mustn't either, because the place suits me down to the ground. Quirky, offbeat. Quiet, a good place to write. I like the skewing of right angles with the slanted ceilings . . ."

They both seemed to notice at once that Sara was making only one cup of coffee. The mere two tablespoons of dark roast, the smaller-sized Melitta cone propped over a single *An Phoblacht* mug—in Sara's own book, this was the height of rudeness, the very sort of slight that, in Emer's place, she herself would have added to the List: *Wouldn't Even Offer Me a Cup of Coffee.*

Accepted: she was being horrid. And make no mistake. Under ordinary circumstances, Sara would spare anyone, a plumber, a cup of coffee. But just here and now, the last few shells of pasta seemed to rustle in their ravaged bags, restless for retribution. A muffled rattle exuded from the cabinet behind her, where the green olives, dill pickles, and gooseberry jam trembled like newly sprung kidnapping victims. And when Sara had scrounged through the breadbox for Melitta filters—there were three left, out of a nearly full box of forty—one of the subletter's sole contributions to the Notting Hill larder had crackled inimically against her hand: a cello bag labeled *Muesli Extender.*

Specifically, it was the *muesli extender* that ensured Sara would grind no more than two tablespoons of french vanilla roast this afternoon, for the premeditation its purchase implied had evaporated her very last modicum of hospitality. Forget a groggy mumble the Sunday after Omagh's town center exploded along the lines of, *Dear me, nothing to eat but that nice Sara Moseley's cereal. Maybe she wouldn't mind if I made myself free this one time—gosh, I'll try and remember to replace it when I'm out and about* . . . Oh, no. We see Emer Branagh stalking the aisles of Framar Health plotting how to make her landlady's unopened two-kilo bag of Marks & Spencer Luxury Almond and Apricot Muesli stretch to an extra fortnight. Having already been taken soup to nuts, Sara could not, absolutely could not bring herself to be taken for another coffee bean more.

Once Emer noticed that the welcome wagon was not being rolled out, rather than (a) leave, or (b) at least make a little headway on that mountain of smelly dishes, the subletter reached for Sara's tin of Twinings Earl Grey, in which a handful of tea bags had survived. Since the lithe young memoirist's punctuational punctiliousness appeared less powerful than her aversion to washing up, she gave the scummy SDLP mug in the sink a miss for the clean ULSTER SAY'S NO one, into which she ladled three teaspoons of Sara's demerara sugar with a feline smile. Helping herself to water from the electric kettle, she glided to the fridge, shook the Dale Farms carton at her ear, whitened her tea, and flipped the carton in the bin.

Sara took her coffee with milk. But the benefits of handing off a kitchen did not, apparently, work both ways. Coffee black, mood blacker, she launched to the sitting room to dispatch this impromptu klatch as expeditiously as possible.

IF EMER'S MANNER was dominated by a single quality, it was *indiscriminate gravity.* A contemplative lag seemed to precede anything the woman did or said. Hence only after two minutes' reflection did she decide on the weighty matter of taking her refreshment in the sitting room, too. Meanwhile, anxious to mark out the most rudimentary of territory, Sara had successfully staked claim to her usual cream-colored armchair, whose left-hand arm had gone a satisfying gray from propping a balanced representation of Protestant and Catholic newspapers.

Emer assumed the matching armchair opposite, knees together, ankles demurely crossed, one hand laid funereally on the other in her lap, back straight, head bowed—not so much in shyness as in reproof. Composed and reserved, she quaffed her Earl Grey with the solemn, sedate sips of a Japanese tea ceremony. Sara had the sick-making suspicion that this was not a woman who intended to go anywhere any time soon.

"Sorry to displace you like this." Taking a slurp, Sara winced; the coffee was bitter, and she had just apologized again. "But I should be buying that plane ticket to Bangkok within the week, which will give you a firm date by which you can have the flat back."

"Yes. That would be helpful."

Emer spoke oddly, but it was mostly what she didn't say that seemed bizarre. For instance, she did not say, *Really, it's no trouble*, or *I don't mind*, which you're supposed to claim even if you mind fantastically—especially then. Despite the palpable awkwardness, she'd still not yakked nervously to bridge a conversational chasm, a refusal to pull her weight altogether of a piece with a refusal to buy her own food. Nor had Emer delivered any of those costless compliments that one contrives in another person's home—admiration of some trinket, a passing ooh-ah over the expanse of the place for the price—whose sincerity is immaterial. Most strikingly, Emer hadn't expressed an iota of curiosity about the woman among whose possessions she'd been living for four weeks.

"I noticed—an arrangement, in the bedroom." Sara might as well have been giving meeting-a-stranger lessons: this is how you show interest in someone else's life. "The candles, incense, Christmas lights? I wondered, not to pry, but—"

"I'm a Buddhist."

"Ah, I see." She didn't. "Funny, I'd have thought, with your name—"

"My family is Irish Catholic."

Big surprise. "How long have you—?"

"Since Burma."

"That's unusual." *That's pretentious.* "I wouldn't think you'd find many fellow travelers around here."

Emer's stern, uninflected set-piece response finally connected this arch, snobbish woman with the sexless wooly do-gooder who'd spoken on the phone: "There are approximately one hundred Buddhists in Ireland. About forty of them live north of the border. It's a small but closely knit community. Many Buddhists here find respite in Zen from the demand to choose sides of the sectarian divide. We meet in each other's houses. If you were interested, I could find you some literature."

"Thanks, I'd like that," Sara lied, hastily rewriting Emer's memoir— *The Northern Irish Conflict: A Buddhist Perspective.* International bestseller.

Yet Sara felt soiled by the company of her own cattiness, even in her thoughts. The violent black coffee was giving her heartburn; to stay awake, she'd have to go buy some milk. It was possible that this woman was not the most annoying person she had ever met, but if so that happy discovery would have to wait for another day.

"So!" Sara said, getting down to business. "Where have you found to stay while I'm back?"

Emer didn't flinch. "I haven't."

Sara's anger since arriving home had been sustained at such a draining pitch that she did not grow angrier still; she went blank. "Sorry?"

"I haven't," Emer repeated dutifully. She had not understood that *Sorry?* meant not *I didn't hear you,* but *I'm going to give you a chance to say something else.*

"What went wrong? Did some opportunity fall through at the last minute?" Sara felt her face sting; it must be turning red.

"No," Emer said lightly. "I made inquiries. Hotels are out of the question. Even a B&B—I can't afford one." For once Emer's usually guileful, opaque expression shone with the translucence of truth. Read: cheap, messy, bonkers, and *broke.*

"What about youth hostels?"

"They limit length of stay. And I'm thirty-five, top price bracket. IYH is more expensive than you might think. More than here," Emer noted, "for example."

"But there are plenty of independent hostels, whose rules are more lax."

"Too lax," Emer purred. "I couldn't leave my computer at such places during the day."

"Did you ring those accommodations offices, at Queens, Jordanstown, and Stranmillis?" Sara charged hotly. "Did you check the Saturday *Telegraph*? Or outside the Common Room, where lecturers post lets for their holidays? The term doesn't begin at Queens until October, and I gave you very detailed directions for finding the notice board."

"Mm . . . I don't remember. In any case, nothing turned up."

That's when Sara realized that Emer had made no "inquiries" whatsoever.

"Where are you proposing to stay, then?" Sara asked. Aggressive stupidity can be a serviceable, even inspired tactic, but in this instance it amounted only to delay.

"This is a large flat"—Emer gestured toward the corner—"with a spare bed. And we can split the rent."

"I'm a little old," Sara growled, "for a flatmate."

"What are you, forty-four, forty-five?" Emer chided. "That's not so old."

Sara was a petite woman with excitable strawberry blond hair. A persistent pouty petulance gave her what she preferred to think was a child*like* aura, as opposed to child*ish*. Over a decade of ghastly Irish weather had protected a creamy, lightly freckled complexion. Thus even when trying for accuracy over flattery, strangers customarily underestimated Sara's age by six or seven years. Emer, who looked nowhere near thirty-five herself, would be habituated to the same mistake. Notwithstanding her wholesale incuriosity, the subtenant may have understood her landlady ominously well.

Sara tried the sympathy angle, though it was late for that. "I'm leaving a place that means a great deal to me, and heading to a part of the world where I've never been. I could use some solitude, some time for meditation, which a Buddhist should appreciate. If I'd wanted to share the flat, wouldn't I have proposed that you stay on to begin with?"

"That being the simplest solution, I thought it was strange that you didn't propose it." Emer punctuated the rebuke with a censorious frown. Though the younger of the two, she had a schoolmarmish side, and delivered this verdict as if administering a hard, disagreeable lesson that Sara was bound to see later was for her own good.

"This isn't what we planned before you moved in."

"What you planned was to put me to considerable inconvenience and expense," Emer said. "It was not practicable."

"But you agreed to it."

Tame for most folks in the face of impudence, but for Sara this was holding her own with amazing tenacity. Indeed, she may have been fascinated by conflicts like Northern Ireland's out of covetousness. Hell-raisers had something Sara wanted. She didn't think of herself as timid, and her stridency in print had put numerous noses out of joint. But that was on paper about politics, not face-to-face about gooseberry jam. Regarding matters of personal importance, Sara was all too often a doormat. Were she ever to have overcome her fear of duking it out, she might have diminished her coterie of friends, but would assuredly have secured the return of her bone-handled umbrella, the replacement of her blue-and-white platter, and most crucially a reduction of fatiguing resentments on the List, each of which extracted a fractional emotional debit per month, as if she were compelled to rent them storage space in her head.

Sara's expat-at-home-in-a-rough-town toughness was all surface. In truth, her feelings were readily hurt. Since most opponents struck her at the outset as less bruisable, battle presented itself as synonymous with defeat. Furthermore, while she was a very selfish person, Sara was uneasy about that fact, and consequently uncomfortable with the naked defense of her own interests for the sole reason that they were her interests. She thought it looked bad, which of course it did. But then, wily combatants embraced their own ugliness. To scrap well, you had to give up on getting your antagonists to like you, and get them to bend over instead. Pugilistically, a woman's classic Achilles's heel was her horror of appearing *unattractive*, since you couldn't come out swinging and seem like a nice person at the same time.

Emer didn't suffer from this complaint. She wasn't above endearing herself, but only to a purpose. In Boston, she had sucked up to Sara to get into Sara's flat. This insinuation accomplished, she dropped the charm. Her chin opposite jutted at the truculent what-are-you-going-to-do-about-it tilt with which a man would project physical threat.

For that matter, Emer's passive occupation of 19 Notting Hill amounted to physical intimidation of a kind. Her things were installed in the flat. She had a key to the downstairs door. What's more, she was quiet, or at least she had the presence to make a distinction between what she said and what she felt—a distinction that was oddly un-American, come to think of it—which had provided her ample opportunity to observe her talkative quarry. She would have already concluded that Sara Moseley was not the type to turf silk blouses out an upstairs window or to sling a grown woman over her shoulders and dump the trespasser like a sack of potatoes on the porch.

So the wrap-up was a formality. "What about bulletin boards in the Egg, the Bot, and the Elms?" Sara asked glumly. "Students are always letting an extra room."

Emer sighed with regret. "A room really wouldn't do. An artist needs space to dream, don't you think?" Over the phone in Boston, the assertion would have sounded naff, but in person, with that coy, pressed smile, it came across as mocking.

Standing with her cold black coffee and not looking Emer in the eye, Sara said, "Well, fait accompli, then." But she meant *coup d'état*. As she hustled feverishly from her flat like a refugee, Sara had never been more grateful to need milk.

* * *

WHEN SARA PUT the carton away, the green olives, dill pickles, and gooseberry jam were stored once again in the refrigerator door, the jars sweaty from temperature tug-of-war. Sara lifted the jars *out*, and slid them *back* in the cabinet.

She went to unpack, only to discover her case zipped up and propped outside the bedroom door, which was shut. A susurrating hum emitted from inside. Sara rapped a perfunctory warning, and walked in.

Emer's clothes were folded righteously into an open dresser drawer, its previous contents stuffed into a plastic bag alongside. The bed was back blocking the closet. The candles were lit and dribbling, while incense fugged the room with unconvincing gardenia. Mumbling hocus-pocus before her shrine, Emer was pretzeled into a lotus, hands palm-upward on her knees, thumbs and middle fingers pinched, eyes closed, face raised to bask in the sunshine of enlightenment.

For once Sara restrained herself from apologizing. "Emer, this is my bedroom," she said flatly.

More mumbo-jumbo.

"Emer, not to put too fine a point on it, get out." Eleven years in Ulster should be good for something; if the woman refused to budge, Sara could always blow her up.

Emer took a deep breath and opened her eyes with a flutter. "Excuse me, what did you say? Because it really would be best if we talked another time."

"No, it wouldn't." Were Emer to provide opportunity for much more invigorating practice like this, she might justifiably bill her landlady for assertiveness training.

"What seems to be the trouble now? My dear Sara, I thought you said you were tired!"

"That's why I want my bedroom back. Please."

"There's no cause to be snippy—"

"I did say *please*."

"We have a problem, then. This is my bedroom, too."

"Not anymore it isn't." At last Sara clocked why some people not only fought their corner, but sought corners to fight. This joust was exhilarating.

"Let's discuss this rationally before you get in a twitter," Emer admonished with a condescension that appeared habitual. "You're only here for a couple of weeks. Your things are already in a suitcase—"

"My *dirty* things are in a suitcase."

"Mine are put away in the dresser—"

"*My* dresser."

"And I've already set up my altar here—"

"Which you can move."

Emer clasped her hands and bowed her head. "There's only one bedroom in this flat. And you will also, I assume, work in the study?"

"In *my* study."

Emer shot Sara a reproachful look, as if there were a Buddhist edict against the deployment of possessive pronouns. "Then I should pay less than half the rent."

If this was victory, Sara didn't trust it. "Like how much less?" she asked warily.

"I'd be willing to pay fifteen pounds a week." The figure was prepared.

Sara paused to estimate that a full half share was closer to £28/week. For the next three weeks or so, what mattered was her privacy. "Fine, fifteen quid. Just make like a tree, okay? *Please?*" This time the imprecation was genuinely pleading.

Emer lifted a foot off each thigh and blew out the candles. Red wax spattered the looking glass. "Sara, you seem like someone who's done some interesting things in her life, and I'm sure you have a lot to offer. But I do wish you'd make a little more effort to be neighborly. This time will be more enjoyable if we try to get along, don't you think?"

Repressing the urge to slam it, Sara shut the door behind her subletter and plopped onto the bed, which she couldn't be bothered to shift again. It had seemed so narcotic at first, standing up for her rights. But she'd just been bamboozled into buying her own bedroom.

* * *

THE NEXT MORNING Sara lay abed until she could no longer hear banging and footsteps. Before making coffee, she padded trepidatiously about the flat, confirming that Emer was out. In the kitchen, the empty muesli bag garnished the rubbish, along with the empty carton of Sara's milk. Another dirty bowl, slopped with excess milk, crested the dishes in the sink.

Sara couldn't stand the mess, and did the dishes. Subsequently, she scavenged the flat for anything belonging to Emer Branagh, and deposited the lot on the sitting room's now-unmade spare bed. In gleeful acceptance of her own immaturity, Sara tacked her most bellicose paramilitary posters back on the landing's wall. She'd planned to ring some bucket shops in London to track down a cheap ticket to Bangkok, but by the time she remembered, the day had been swallowed by household restoration, and the bucket shops would be closed. It was Saturday; that meant an extra day's delay.

Emer returned around dinnertime flashing a perky *Father Knows Best* hello and no groceries. Putting the kettle on, she reached blithely for the SDLP mug, which had magically cleaned itself for all the mention the washing up appeared to merit. Idly dunking the last Earl Grey tea bag, she inquired by the by, "Don't you find that some of your guests are offended by those posters? Or maybe you don't have visitors much."

"I have any number of friends," Sara said, pouring herself a sherry. "But they can all take a joke."

Leaving the used tea bag to leak on the counter, Emer turned to face Sara for emphasis. "Thousands of innocents have died in this country. Many more thousands have been injured—maimed, crippled, blinded. Children have been orphaned, families often multiply bereaved. It dismays me how you could regard so much anguish as funny."

"That so?" Sara said. "Your loss." She scooped up her sherry and strode to the sitting room, where she applied herself to the *Tele*. For as long as she could engross herself in the opposite page, Sara held the paper with "Yankee Doodles"—filed minutes before her ride to Logan Airport—facing out, byline bold.

But Emer didn't drift in for another half an hour, at which time she assumed what was now her chair with a pair of chopsticks and a huge bowl of pasta. Sara recognized a potpourri of shells, rotelli, and elbows as the bag dregs in the cabinet. The sauce, oily and pale, smelled distinctly like Sara's last jar of marinated artichoke hearts.

"Would you like some?" offered Miss Hospitality 1998. "There's more in the pot."

"Yes, I bet there is," Sara said tightly. "But my appetite has gone off the boil."

"Must be jet lag."

"You like sherry with pasta? I wouldn't think they'd quite go."

"They do," Emer said. "You should try it."

Sara couldn't contain herself, and muttered over an *Irish News* op-ed urging contributions to the Omagh bombing fund, "In that case, I'd have to buy more pasta."

"Yes, I meant to mention," said Emer. "You're almost out."

EMER WAS GONE most of the following Sunday and Monday. While Sara was relieved, she was also jealous. Since the subletter was not forthcoming about what she got up to, Sara supposed that Emer's schedule was filled with the offbeat excursions Sara herself had contrived on arrival in Belfast, when the province was still otherworldly, even a little frightening—when keeping her conversational head above water in pubs was an athletic feat, and from context she'd strain to infer the meanings of *own goal*, *Stickie*, or *gob*. That was 1987–88—not an era about which she was strictly nostalgic. She'd often felt out of her depth, self-conscious about being "the wee Yank," famously easy pickings for hard-up Lotharios at last call. The rhythms of banter were rapid; while every self-appointed wag wasn't clever, they were all fast. Groping for words in the skirling back and forth, Sara was often slagged off within her hearing as "a dose" who wasn't even sure whose side she was on. Why, these days political uncertainty was the least of her problems—closed-mindedness and sanctimony more like it, just like her neighbors—and she gave pubs like Lavery's a miss most weekends for sherry and films on TV. Anything but sip glaze-eyed through one more poleaxed account of Bloody Sunday from a student who'd been four years old at the time.

For in one respect Sara had gone native. Locals didn't attend prolix lectures comparing Northern Ireland to South Africa at the Europa, and they'd eagerly pay the entry fee of three quid *not* to sit through a daylong conference on "Protestant identity." No one from outside cliquish West Belfast attended IRA funerals, black flags flapping on lampposts in the churn of low-flying army choppers. Solid citizens of the unionist community, of which Sara now counted as an honorary member, wouldn't be caught dead browsing the Republican Press Centre bookshop on the Falls Road (though it sold the best selection of Troubles coffee mugs in town). Rubbernecking blackened bombsites was frowned upon as ghoulish, and the middle class of both stripes universally regarded the Orange Order's marching season as the time to book for Majorca. So Sara no longer partook of Ulster's demented Disney World, either.

Was it middle-aged complacency that had turned her such a shut-in? Curled in her newsprint-smudged armchair that Monday night, having progressed only three pages into the section on Thailand in *Let's Go Southeast Asia*, Sara conceded that few of those diversions back in the day had been exactly *fun*. While at length republicans' hypocritical blend of thuggishness and faux-liberal indignation put her off *even* more than the drunken, flagrantly pathetic murderousness of their loyalist counterparts, fundamentally her factional predilections came down to competing aversions. By throwing in her lot with the stodgy, rectitudinous, law-and-order Prods, she might as well have joined forces with Sunday-go-to-meeting evangelicals in Iowa. Plenty of Protestant unionists were perfectly pleasant people, but they were also a big drag.

To be more candid still, Sara had never quite located the backslapping, more-the-merrier animation that was ostensibly so Irish, and definitive of Belfast's holy grail of "good crack." Perhaps the renowned boisterous-ness and loquacity that attracted American tourists to the island was a myth; sure Sara's sampling of pub life was duller and meaner than cliché would have it. Then again, Sara herself was a little tight of temperament, and didn't care for crowds. Maybe pub patrons were mean around Sara because they wanted her to go away. Maybe matey, Guinness-guzzling abandon was out there in buckets, but Sara couldn't raise the silver-tongued high spirits to jump in.

For all Sara knew, Emer Branagh had the goods. To date, the sublet-ter had proved cool, shut off, and po-faced, but one of the great frustra-tions of this mortal coil was that you could rarely know what someone else was like without you in the room. With no love lost between the two, Emer might have generated a dead mask of sobriety exclusively for Sara's benefit, thereby disguising a whole other frolicsome side of herself, some wild Irish rose that bloomed in the smoky fiddle-dee-dee pubs by the harbor.

For that matter, maybe this very night, while Sara stewed with this stupid guidebook feeling too torpid to get up and flip the Van Morrison cassette, Emer was down at the Rotterdam. A traditionally bunged, un-derlit bar that brought in live bands of tin whistles, Uilleann pipes, and bodhrans, the Rotterdam had proved too much a schlep from Notting Hill for burnt-out Iri-phobe Sara Moseley for donkey's years. But Emer was new here; a four-mile trip would still seem short. Maybe Emer had a finc fluty voice that lilted above the clink of glasses a cappella; maybe she knew all the words to "Galway Bay." Or maybe her very reticence, so un-American, would challenge the boyos to bid for biographical tit-bits with beer.

Sara could envision the subletter enthroned at one of the big front tables, surrounded by brimming pints with which half a dozen suitors have curried her enigmatic favors. In the swirl of fiddle music, at last a Mona Lisa smile creeps across the comely countenance aglow in lamp-light, as stout is hoisted high—"Slainte, mates! Here's to the luscious lass from Boston, Mass, God love her! Long may your woman dander the docks of Belfast City!" *This is Ireland.* Arms raised, patrons leap toe to knee. A dashing rogue, rugged, older than the rest, pulls the bonny American lady to her feet. Keeps to herself surely, but aye, she can turn a pretty jig. Look at those wee boots fly! Yet your man's eyes glint with a bitter business, about which our young visitor best be left in the dark. Ach, youse can never be sure who you're meetin' in our dark town, who in a crowd has shook hands with the devil hisself . . . *This is Belfast.*

Sara had to stop because she was going to hurl. She had clearly lifted the scene from a Carlsberg advert. Still, it wasn't incredible that while Sara was bored with this burgh Emer could be having a wonderful time, or that Sara was bored with Belfast not because Belfast was boring but because Sara was boring. And bollocks, she had forgotten, again, to ring those London bucket shops! Tomorrow, she would get that ticket out of here. But already the resolution had the hollow ring in her ears of those self-deceiving provincials in *The Three Sisters* who were still plaintively pining, "To Moscow!" in the last act.

SARA HATED GRAND schemers who were all talk, so the following morning she rang her editor at the *Tele.* When David Featherstone said squarely, "So you're leaving us, then?" her gut stabbed.

"For a few months," she hedged, though she'd promised Karen to sublet the Bangkok flat for a full year. Still, the notion of burning this of all bridges was more than Sara could bear. As she'd rehearsed a dozen times before picking up the phone, she threw herself a lifeline. "In fact, while I'm in Thailand—naturally traveling to lots of other interesting places like Vietnam, Laos, maybe even Burma—I wondered if you might like me to keep filing 'Yankee Doodles.' You know, the miracle of modern technology and all. And it might add a cosmopolitan touch—"

"Sara, Sara," Featherstone cut her off. "The *Tele*'s come a long way. We run the odd full-page comment from Adams now. We even carry stories from the South. But that's the south of Ireland, kid. Not south of Asia."

"David, you're always publishing interviews with some Northerner who's back from Tangiers—"

"Right you are, we'd interview a native son of Ballynafeigh who took a day-trip to Doncaster. But you're an American, just." He broke the news gently.

"Even though I've lived here for eleven years—?" Sara was trying not to whine.

"For the *Belfast* Telegraph, a Yank who lives in Timbuktu just isn't, ah—"

"In the picture," Sara finished heavily for him.

"Tell you what," Featherstone said, and for a moment his tone of concession raised Sara's hopes. "You must be at sixes and sevens, getting ready to head off. So let's stand you down as of this week. No need to get your knickers in a twist doing a dozen things at once—"

"Don't you at least want me to write a farewell column?" Her voice caught. "I wouldn't want my readers to think I just got, like, sick of them or something." Though wasn't that close to the truth?

"Only if you've time, so. I've another American girl—new arrival—might be interested in your slot. Fresh perspective—stranger in a strange land sort of thing, all wide eyed and what's-this. So don't think you're leaving me high and dry, just. That do us? Bon voyage, then. Send us a card, will you, Sara? That's a good girl. Ta."

Sara held the receiver out from her body like a dead fish. She couldn't move. She couldn't breathe. She couldn't blink. Finally she inhaled, and shuddered.

Who *else* would it be? That thieving bitch wanted to assume Sara's whole life, like those bioengineering thrillers in which an evil clone replaces the original twin, now buried in the garden. It all made sense now! In eating Sara's very food, Emer Branagh was *practicing being Sara Moseley*.

Given her state of shock, it was asking too much of herself to ring those bucket shops, and Sara made no more headway on her plans. Instead she worked up a hot, resentful sweat in the deserted Windsor

Lawn Tennis Club fitness suite, stamping furiously on the StairMaster. *What does Emer bloody Branagh know about Northern Irish politics?* Sara fumed half-aloud, having jacked the random-climbing program to level 12. *Could she detail off the top of her head the Byzantine decision-making rules of Stormont's new assembly? What do you want to bet that she thinks "D'Hondt mechanism" has something to do with digital TV? Besides, Featherstone, you'll never get any finished copy from that bleeding heart. She'll sag over her computer harrowed by the* anguish *of it all, and short out the keyboard by busting into tears!*

Later that afternoon, Sara made a stab at a farewell column for "Yankee Doodles." In the first version, she let fly all the scathing derogations of this conceited, inward-looking statelet that she had stifled as counterproductive these many years. She accused the Northern Irish of being misshapen as much by self-pity as by violence. Catholics and Protestants alike had been pandered to and fawned over, for with its plethora of initiatives, commissions, subventions, and peace funds the whole province was *spoilt*. She used words like *navel gazing, precious*, and *overblown*. She decried the thousands of novels, documentaries, miniseries, movies, and rock songs that had fetishistically elevated into an insoluble impasse of mythic proportions a down-and-dirty, small-minded brawl. Regarding the tiny extent to which she herself had helped inflate the North's vanity with her own attentions, she expressed profound remorse. It was a scandal that a dispute over the border between two virtually indistinguishable democracies in the EU had led to the slaughter of so much as a stray cat. Thousands had died here all right, but the ultimate tragedy was that each and every one had died for *nothing* over *nothing*.

Getting the diatribe out of her system was cleansing, but on review she could see that it backfired. The repudiation misleadingly implied that she'd had a terrible time here; that, perhaps having been wounded in some fashion, she was gunning for payback. Ulsterfolk didn't seem nasty; she did.

In the second draft of her swan song, Sara confessed that leaving

Belfast presented the biggest challenge of her adulthood. She said that especially in an intellectual sense she'd grown up here, and that the North had provided a richer, more nuanced political education than she might have received at Harvard's School of International Affairs. As for her take on the conflict after all this time, again she reached for the word *small-minded*, but qualified it with *seemingly*—going on to explain that she herself was a "remembering person," who had difficulty dismissing so much an unreturned umbrella. The grudge she might bear over an unreturned husband or sister staggered her imagination. Finally, she conceded that though she had always been mindful of her place, respectful of the fact that she wasn't born here, during her tenure Northerners had gone out of their way to make her feel welcome, down to including her in the exchange of ideas in this very newspaper. It was trite, of course, for Americans to extol the friendliness of the Irish, but Sara accepted the risk of cliché. She'd never encountered a people as a whole who had a warmer, lighter touch in the doings of daily life, and far more than the adrenal rush of bombs downtown or eleventh-hour intrigue at Stormont Castle she would miss good-natured banter with her neighbors when she idled down the road for soda bread.

By Tuesday evening, it was Sara who sagged over her keyboard, and it was Sara who burst into tears.

FOR THE REST of the week the two women negotiated one another's proximity with the wary caution of two paramilitary antagonists on mutual cease-fire. Nothing Emer ever said was precisely rude, but she continued to project a monolithic lack of interest in Sara's life. The indifference offered protection of a kind—when she went out, Sara needn't worry about rifled journals, steamed-open post, or browsed floppy files—but the very safety of these documents felt like an insult.

Frustrated, Sara began to fling herself before her subletter with a brash immodesty that with a man would have come across as slutty. If the phone rang while the two were reading—at each other—in the sitting room, Sara would conduct the conversation at full voice. "So now that the *Real* IRA has declared a cease-fire," she might posit caustically to a friend at Radio Ulster, who shared her indignation that the agreement provided for the wholesale release of paramilitary prisoners, "does that mean the lowlifes behind Omagh get off with a year and a half inside? . . . I'm serious! The Good Friday Agreement is potentially one big kill-one, get-one-free sale! Coin yourself a paramilitary outfit—make the name really moronic sounding, so they know you're legit. Mow down anybody who gets on your tits. Call a *cease-fire*, give yourself up, and bingo, you're out the door by May 2000!"

Every time she rang off, she'd feel sheepish. They'd both know she was showing off.

Yet clips of "Yankee Doodles" left pointedly in plain view never tempted the subletter even to peer at the lead. Flatteringly vitriolic hate mail was left untouched. The only belongings of Sara's that excited Emer's curiosity were her groceries.

Alas, Sara could not pretend to indifference in return. But with Emer so guarded, asking flat out whether she had indeed applied for Sara's "Yankee Doodles" slot seemed prohibitively degrading. While phone calls for Emer were few, she always took them in the study with the door closed. The one line from these calls that Sara had ever made out when she just *happened* to be passing by was, "I don't know how much more of this I can stand."

As far as Sara could discern, Emer had disliked her well before they met. A self-styled free spirit wouldn't have fancied picking up where another loudmouthed American left off. When Sara fomented over the papers (as she did even when no one was there), Emer looked as if she were playing deafening music in her head, lest this strident claptrap corrupt the clean white pages of her virgin memoir.

More personally, Emer was doubtless annoyed that Sara was presentable. Women were more at ease with one another when there was no contest in the looks department, and Sara adjudged the two as running at a dead heat. Sara may have been the elder, but good gene stock and dedication at the gym had kept her slight and compact. While her loose strawberry hair contrasted with Emer's jet-black crop, they both had the sharp, shifting features at which men and women alike looked twice. Presumably Emer might have taken a shine to her readily enough if only Sara were fat.

Emer was as fastidious about her appearance as she was slovenly about everything else. She hogged the bath like a teenager, and the sitting room cum boudoir was eternally scalloped with clothesline laden with handwashing. She was never to be caught slumping about the flat in stained gray sweats with a face covered in cold cream.

Sara was slovenly about her appearance, and fastidious about everything else. Yet by the end of their first week sharing the flat, Sara was rinsing musty blouses from the back of her closet and ironing in secret. After grossly mismanaging a pimple into a pulsing goiter, she spent ten minutes in the lav meticulously doctoring the mangle with concealer before she caught herself on: she wasn't going anywhere for the rest of the evening besides upstairs. Her relationship with the subletter seemed to be degenerating into a miasmic admixture of antipathy and a schoolgirl crush.

As for the Buddhist palaver, the religion seemed harmless enough, though if we are indeed ceaselessly reincarnated as we climb the ladder of enlightenment, Sara was bound to be returned relentlessly to earth until she got subletting right. (Perhaps she was already trapped in a hellish *Groundhog Day* loop whereby in her forty-first year an Emer Branagh cognate sponges gooseberry jam in ever-larger quantities as grudge-bearing Sara Moseley makes spiritual progress by the tiniest of increments.) At least Emer's flitting from hot spot to hot spot, shedding mercy and sagacity on the suffering of strangers, was pedantically consistent with the Buddhist concept of merit. Still: priggishly removing Sara's dribs of Stoli and Jameson to a far corner, Emer had reestablished her altar on the sitting room's ad hoc liquor cabinet, and whenever she passed the melon offerings and Christmas lights, she made a deep, pietistic bow—palms together, eyes closed. Sara refused to believe that Emer went through this folderol when no one else was home.

Sara continued to treat the sitting room as shared living space. At fifteen pounds per week, Emer wasn't letting more than a mattress. Emer hadn't got her nose in a sling about the matter, perhaps having calculated that, apropos of the kitchen, porous borders served her larger interests.

The source of Emer's income was mysterious. Evasive about whether her Ulster memoir was under contract, she was surely writing it on spec. Yet her clothes and jewelry were expensive. Rich family? Sugar daddy? For Emer's affected casualness about who-bought-what worked only one way. While Sara was obsessed with getting accounts to balance, Emer was equally obsessed with coming out ahead. In sum, Emer was a taker. Everywhere she went she would siphon off a little more than she gave back. The Emers of this world were levied on the whole species, like a tax. She pulled the pickpocketing off partly by being attractive, but also by being arty and passionate. She was dedicating her life to justice, empathy, and lamentation. The least the philistine ruck could do in return was to take up her logistical slack.

It was amazing, too, what you could get away with so long as you made a habit of it. Since repetition transformed the one-off impertinence to convention, Emer's tax on no. 19's larder was now routine. Surmounting her outrage, Sara began to indulge in the scientific fascination that drives clinical experiments on small animals. With crafted insouciance on their second weekend, she called as Emer started down the stairs, "You know, the mayo is down to scrapings. Could you pick up a jar on your way home? And I'm not usually brand conscious, but Hellmann's is worth the few extra P."

When Emer returned she'd forgotten, but Sara wouldn't let the matter drop. After two more reminders, Emer came home swinging a plastic bag for the very first time, in which nestled a single jar—the small size, but to give the woman credit, not the very smallest—of Hellmann's mayonnaise. Sara felt the same burst of triumph that must buoy pet owners when kitty finally poops in the litter box, until Emer mentioned in the spirit of afterthought, "Oh, that mayo was one pound sixty."

Sara's mouth dropped. "Sorry?"

"I'm glad to run an errand," Emer said with grave goodwill, survey-ing the shrinking stash of tins in the kitchen cabinet. "But this project is on a tight budget, and I will need to be reimbursed."

Sara stared. They called it *stones* in Boston, *chutzpah* in Israel, *co-jones* in Mexico, *cheek* in England, and *chancing your arm* in Ulster, but Sara decided that *motherfucking gall* would do nicely.

"I'm afraid I don't have any change," Sara stonewalled, resolved to fasten upon this ploy for the duration: politely request that Emer pick up groceries, never have cash at ready hand, feign the same maturity about piddly this-and-that with which the leech concealed her own un-remitting larceny, and forget all about it.

"No problem," Emer said at Sara's back. "I can just deduct the mayo from this week's rent. Oh, and would you like an olive?" She walked out, nibbling a pit. "Though I'm afraid they're not cold."

SARA TOLD HERSELF that it wasn't the olives themselves. It was the principle of the olives. Respect for another person's property, no mat-ter how paltry, emblemizes respect for its owner, and no one likes to be fleeced. Yet at bottom she knew better. It *was* the olives. It was the olives, at one pound ten.

In regard to a single quantity was Emer Branagh the soul of gener-osity. That would be edification. She was quite the authority on how to augment Sara's Thai curry paste with lime leaf and galangal, ingredi-ents unavailable in Belfast, without which a stir-fry was destitute. She delivered set piece anthropological lessons about her previous port of call—the Burmese prize celibacy; they don't have surnames—with the overpatience of a schoolteacher reviewing a unit before a test.

But one Burmese did have a surname: the opposition leader Daw Aung San Suu Kyi. Brave, virtuous, self-sacrificing, and pretty, the Nobel Prize–winning dissident was Emer Branagh's idol, whose name she couldn't mention enough times, showily rattling off the whole mouthful, which Sara could never remember. (Defiantly, Sara would refer to "Dawn Ann Sally Sukiyaki," "Susie Sun Myung Moon," or

"Molly Moo-goo-gai-pan," grimly satisfied that Emer took offense.) When speaking mournfully about Sukiyaki's difficulty meeting up with her critically ill English husband in Britain before he died, Emer might have been one of those Midlands tabloid readers still torn up about Dodi Fayed and Princess Di. Since American liberals took it for granted that any new acquaintance was *one of us*, Emer presumed that Sara, too, agonized over oppression in the martial state, and would not rest until its newly elected president Dawn Ann Sally Sukiyaki beamed from the cover of *People* magazine in a knockout new dress.

Though she'd no time for tyrants, Sara's working herself into righteous lather in her Belfast sitting room wasn't going to spring a single prisoner of conscience in the opposite hemisphere. (Her own diatribes against the IRA had never spared a single RUC reservist a sniper's bullet, either. But then, political consternation was like sex: arousing to partake in, embarrassing to watch.) A purely practical reluctance to get exercised to no effect must have read to Emer as callousness. When the subject of Burma arose after ten days or so, the subletter's eyes burned with contempt.

Up to a point, Sara *was* interested in Emer's expertise on Southeast Asia, whose tap water she would soon be avoiding herself. She might have welcomed reminders to keep your mouth closed in the shower and not to order salads in restaurants, if only she'd been allowed to pay for the advice with her own. But Sara couldn't even tell Emer the location of the nearest public library. Emer would cut her off flatly, "I'm already a member at the Linen Hall." Well, excuuuuuse *me*.

Moreover, Emer stymied any attempt to find common ground. When Sara once alluded to "Myanmar" (hoping to impress), Emer upbraided her that Burma's official name implied sympathy with its military government.

"Just like Northern Ireland," Sara said gamely. "Whatever you call the place, you give your politics away . . ."

Emer's eyes drifted to the book in her lap, *Grief in the Gorse* (or whatever).

Sara got the message and put a lid on it. Oh, she could have produced a handy little cheat sheet on which of a panoply of names for this blighted bog corresponded with which affiliations. Yet the adroitness with which Emer dodged using any of these terms suggested a surprising shrewdness. She'd obviously never cite the baldly Protestant *Ulster*, but she also never employed the gutless nationalist appellation, the *North* of *Ireland*, either. Why, she'd not once referenced the moderately impartial *Northern Ireland*. She was more wont to nod passingly at "here," wherever that was.

For what most frustrated Sara about the dratted woman was the elusiveness of exactly where on the finely gradated spectrum of Northern politics the subletter put herself. As best Sara could guess, Emer belonged to the finds-it-all-too-painful-to-bear set whose prissy nonalignment implied that to choose sides was to become *part of the problem*.

But hatred was not a spectator sport. To understand this squishy mire, you had to sample firsthand the fuel that powered the Troubles' perpetual-emotion machine, and that meant coming to detest, *detest and abhor*, at least one of its factions, without equivocation, to your very marrow. Accordingly, Sara Moseley hated IRA-supporting republicans, hated them with a factual simplicity that was almost elegant. While she'd nothing against Catholics per se (some of her best friends—well, they were!), she also plainly disliked Northern nationalists with an expansive, elective abandon that made it the more interesting prejudice.

For Sara, the Northern Irish nationalist had transcended political classification to character type. Although by local definition a *nationalist* aspired to a united Ireland achieved by peaceful means, Sara had met the Northern *nationalist*, in a temperamental sense, all over the world, and many samples of the species would mistake Michael Collins for a mixed drink. Indeed, the disposition increasingly dominated discourse on both sides of the Atlantic, and not via sheer numbers, but by hitting a distinctively shrill rhetorical register, like those high frequencies broadcast outside convenience stores that drive young people insane. The ilk was technically nonviolent, but squealing that people will do almost anything to get to stop amounted to terrorism of a kind.

A nationalist is a Moaning Minnie, a bellyacher. He's hard done by; he's been abused and deserves recompense. Yet no matter how many concessions you shovel him, they will never suffice, for all penance is paltry, any attempt at reparation an affront. Like a bunny in a briar patch, he glories in violation. He feels sorry for himself, of course, but this self-pity is competitive; it bristles around rival brands. And it is *triumphalist* self-pity. A nationalist uses his suffering as a cudgel to beat you over the head. He never does anything wrong himself. And he never shuts up.

While brandishing his minority status, the nationalist runs in packs. Drunk on Dutch courage from his mob, a nationalist is a bully. But he's never satisfied with merely getting his way; it has to be achieved at your expense. A nationalist is never happy unless he's making someone else miserable. That said, he's never happy. The happy nationalist is an oxymoron.

Accordingly, the worst thing you can do with a nationalist is to attempt to give him whatever he claims to want. He may love his children, his parents, his dog—nationalists are people, too—but the one thing that a nationalist loves above all else is his grievance. Any effort to fulfill a nationalist's ostensible agenda will read as malicious: you are trying to take his grievance away. A nationalist will bite the hand that feeds him.

Nationalists, in this metaphorical sense, were everywhere. As a temperamental class, they weren't necessarily predisposed toward devotion to kin and country, and a goodly proportion of the genus had never set foot in Northern Ireland. Nationalists were determined to ban fox hunting in Britain, and the average nationalist over a lifetime of dinner parties would lavish hundreds of times more indignation on vulpine anxiety than on genocide in Rwanda. Nationalists trampled seedlings of genetically modified crops. Nationalists campaigned for prayer in the schools; nationalists campaigned against prayer in the schools.

Nationalists insisted on special degree courses in Inuit Studies. Nationalists were book burners; nationalists decried book burning. Nationalists were into "power walking," and nationalists wrote letters to the editor to complain about cyclists who run traffic lights. Nationalists sponsored referendums to require that creationism be taught alongside evolution as an equally credible scientific theory. Nationalists had nut allergies; it was thanks to nationalists that you could no longer get a proper packet of peanuts on airplanes, but only chalky pretzels. Nationalists demanded untimed SATs for students with Attention Deficit Disorder. Nationalists wouldn't let you use the word *retarded*, even in reference to yourself. Nationalists murdered abortion doctors out of dedication to the sanctity of human life. Nationalists boycotted products developed through animal testing, and nationalists bombed cancer labs full of researchers and hamsters out of love for all creatures great and small. Nationalists were vegetarian, and nationalists would never rest until you were vegetarian, too.

Was Emer Branagh a nationalist? Spoiling for a showdown, Sara resolved to lure her subletter out into the open.

"CHECK THIS OUT," Sara commended in the sitting room, and read from the *Irish News* in her lap: "'A Belfast hospital has come under fire for flying a Union flag over its grounds.' Shockers. A Union Jack. Which so happens to be the flag of *this country*."

No reaction, save a slight shift in the facing armchair, perhaps the suggestion of a prim sigh.

"Now, Ranger fans are Protestant, Celtic fans Catholic, right?"

"Of course," Emer said tightly.

"'An irate caller to the *Irish News* also claimed a security guard directing traffic into the car park at the Ulster hospital in the mainly loyalist Dundonald area was wearing a Rangers hat.' Can you credit it?" Sara glanced up. Emer was looking twitchy. "'"It was a disgrace," said father-of-four from Portadown. "I felt intimidated going into the hospital grounds. You'd think that a hospital would be a safe haven from sectarianism."' And get this: Sinn Fein Councilman Alex Maskey has raised the issue of *football caps* on hospital *parking attendants* with the British *Secretary of State*, who has promised to *look into it*. Tell me this place is not *Romper Room*. Tell me, Emer, that it's *not funny*."

Slowly Emer lowered her book, and looked at Sara with pained parental disappointment. "You're being rather insensitive, don't you think?" The gentle castigation, *don't you think?* was Emer's favorite phrase, its coercive inclusivity calling Sara to her nobler self. "After living in Bel-*fast* for so many years, you must have learned the significance of symbolism in this place. I have to say, you surprise me, Sara." Emer's scolding way with her flatmate's Christian name made Sara want to snatch it away from her.

"After living in *Bel*-fast for so many years," Sara returned, "I have learned that these people get up in the morning to be offended. Now, they can fill my newspaper with nonsense, but they can't force me within the privacy of my own home to take their trumped-up grudges on board as anything but calculated nuisance. I hate to pull rank, but if you think this sorry father-of-four whinge-bag in Dundonald is doing anything but yank Mo Mowlam's chain you haven't been here long enough. It's all wink-and-nod, Emer. They know what they're doing. And dig deep enough under every brown-nosing British concession to rename their streets '*Oglaigh na hEireann* Avenue,' and paint '*Bruscar*' instead of 'Rubbish' on their wheely bins, and reroute yet another Orange march around their delicate cultural sensibilities, and you'll find a gun. The Brits are piss-in-their-pants terrified of these people, and Sinn Fein is making the limies dance. It is funny. But it ain't pretty."

"*These people*, as you call them, have suffered greatly," Emer said. "I worry that you forget that."

"Please," Sara implored, "don't lose any sleep over the state of my soul."

Emer closed the book in her lap slowly and placed her palm on the cover as if on a Bible in the dock. "Maybe *you* should lose sleep over your soul. *Sara*," Emer remonstrated, nodding at Sara's newspaper. "Is

Bel-*fast* anything to you but entertainment? Does it exist to you, as a city that people live and die in, or is it only an amusement park?"

"Right, sure, it's an amusement park," Sara returned, glaring, and the meniscus that had been bulging from the drip-drip of Emer's confounding condescension finally broke. "After eleven years here, my friends are still cardboard cutouts—toys, paper dolls—and I care nothing about their health and safety. So it's a matter of supreme indifference to me if the shops they shop in—and, incidentally, I shop in—sporadically explode. In fact, if anything terrible happened to the people I live among *every day*, I'd be happy! More *amusement*. The Good Friday Agreement, since it's shut down the fun fair for now, is the worst thing that's ever happened to me here, and I can't wait for the whole thing to fall apart so the fireworks can start back up—you know, body parts flying through the air, maybe an arm or a leg of someone I know but—being such an awful person—don't give a damn about. As for the politics I've written about *every week* for *nine years*, they're a mere ha-ha to me, and I cynically manufacture a straight face on paper to reap my big fat *hundred pound* fee on Saturdays. You, on the other hand, have been here an *entire six weeks*, and so of course you've already learned to weep when Belfast weeps. I just hope you're in *my flat* long enough for some of your large-hearted, sober-sided compassion to rub off on my mean—shallow—callow—*insensitive* character."

After a pacifistic moment of silence, Emer replied stonily, "I see no need to be unpleasant." Again with that remote, rising-above refusal to get her hands dirty, she went back to her book.

Burrowing masochistically into her *Irish News*, Sara blackly tallied the clues: sense-of-humor lobotomy, moral superiority, entitlement complex that extends to everything from my shampoo to my very home . . . *Nationalist!* Whatever her tortuous position on the Border, Emer Branagh had tipped her constitutional hand.

SARA HAD PLENTY to do. She had to write Karen and get the email address of the features editor at the *Bangkok Post*, then introduce herself to the guy and get the professional ball rolling. She should photocopy a batch of her best clips. For running her laptop and epilator, she should investigate Thai voltage and the configuration of Thai plugs, buying converters and adapters as necessary. She had to change the billing address on her credit cards. She ought to pick up mosquito repellent, since *Let's Go* said malaria was still a problem outside Bangkok. She needed to make an appointment for hepatitis and yellow fever inoculations, as well as for tetanus and polio boosters. She should check out travelers' health insurance. On the assumption that this expedition was not to be a complete damp squib, she should stop by Dunluce Health Centre and get a new diaphragm and fresh spermicide; piquantly, her lone tube of Ortho-Gynol was past its sell-by date. She had to find out if AOL serviced Thailand, and if not, how to get online with another provider. Nuts, and did she need a visa? She probably needed a visa! More expense, perhaps more delay. And what about these other "interesting countries" she planned to explore? Vietnam, Laos—the third world always demanded visas, since they're nice little earners. And how the hell did you get into Burma, through pleading, bribery, or prayer? The prospect of asking Emer was intolerable.

But Sara could concentrate only on the wrong end of her expedition. She agonized over how to avoid paying monthly dues at Windsor Lawn Tennis Club in her absence without canceling her membership; they had a waiting list, and it could be difficult to get back in. She debated whether to cut off the phone—maintaining the same account would leave her vulnerable to an unpaid bill on return—although what tormented her was not the meanness of making Emer pay to reconnect, but the potentially permanent sacrifice of a phone number to which she was sentimentally attached. She searched out a foolproof hiding place for her cast-iron skillet and systematically depleted what little food remained in the kitchen, since a few preventive measures might keep the List from growing like knotweed.

Compared with the daunting task of controlling one's mind, controlling one's mere behavior was child's play. Regarding the latter, Sara was if anything too proficient. Each morning Emer poured another bowl of muesli from Sara's new bag (Tesco Finest this time, the cheap kind with sultanas but no nuts). The only signals of Sara's simmering fury were a clipped tone of voice while she talked about something else and a shadowy poppling from the rhythmic clenching of jaw muscles. But Sara purchased the surface civility of their relations with pitched internal apoplexy.

If Sara was to continue to indulge her habit of talking to herself, she could at least have been rehearsing a few Thai expressions from her new phrasebook—like *mai pen rai* ("you're welcome, never mind"), *pen kan ehng* ("take it easy, make yourself at home"), *jai yen* (calm, or "cold spirit"), and *arai kadai* ("it doesn't matter")—whose implicit heedlessness might have proved therapeutic. Instead Sara stomped down Notting Hill muttering, *I slice up half my bunch of broccoli, using the stem, which I don't much like, to make it last another night, and the next day I find all the fleurettes hacked off this amputated STUMP!* So unabated had her bitterness become that it triggered the cerebral equivalent of acid reflux.

Sara tormented herself with visions of Emer Branagh flouncing around her flat in silks after nasty, Troubles-know-it-all Sara Moseley was gone for good, perhaps "accidentally" breaking a few of the vulgar coffee mugs that celebrated Goons with Guns. But even more insufferable than turning over to a nemesis her beloved tumbledown digs was the imminent handover of Northern Ireland itself.

Despite the agreement's afterglow, no sheaf of paper could sort out in a single stroke decades of partisan antipathy; the average Northern citizen carried a mental list of grievances every bit as lengthy and specific as Sara's own. Nevertheless, earlier that summer Ulster's political future had seemed largely to comprise tedious mop-up chores, the civic analogues of picking up beer cans and taking down risers at the end of an unruly rock concert. For the spectator, it had seemed time to go.

But Ulster's woes had never seemed more exquisitely intractable as they had in the last three weeks! In the wake of Omagh, both communities had talked big about overcoming their differences to end this madness, but the feel-good unanimity wouldn't last. The row over the decommissioning of paramilitary weaponry was heating up fast. Chris Patten's report on reform of the Royal Ulster Constabulary, due next summer, was certain to raise a ruckus if it so much as recommended a change of the force's name. And with the agreement under belt, this year Northern politicians were sure to snag the Nobel Peace Prize! Blair and Ahern, or maybe Hume and Trimble, but would they include Adams? Would Oslo be that out of touch, to award the man responsible for 1974's Bloody Friday a *peace* prize because *this* year he declined to mastermind twenty-six criminal explosions in one day? A travesty, but opportunity for a bang-up column in "Yankee Doodles" . . . Sara kicked herself. She'd resigned.

Meanwhile, Karen had mailed several back issues of the *Bangkok Post*. Thus Sara had the means at her disposal to concern herself with endemic corruption in the Thai construction industry, the extraordinary cost overruns of Bangkok's Sky Train mass-transit system and its controversially poor provisions for disabled travelers, and rejuvenated devotion to Buddhism amongst a Thai middle class disillusioned with capitalist materialism following the collapse of the baht. But Sara had only skimmed the *Post*'s front pages, rapidly abandoning these alien talking points for the familiar annoyance of the *Irish News*. She could hardly be expected to read about *Buddhism*, a topic that invariably drew her mind to decapitated broccoli.

To make matters worse, the North was experiencing one of those rare blushes of Indian summer, and the weather was maliciously beautiful. When she met with her BBC pals for a farewell dinner at Patrick's house, Sara lost all memory of the fractured blue-and-white platter in a gush of precognitive nostalgia. The *good crack* never ran dry, and she realized that after eleven years of practice she could keep pace with Northern banter as easily as holding her own in a round of "Row Your Boat." The booze was abundant and the spuds were *al dente* and she wove home blubbering.

* * *

IT WAS FOUR weeks into this sour marriage, and the two reluctant flatmates were faced off in their traditional sitting room armchairs. Sara peeked round the *Telegraph*'s "international" section (one article about a flood—the only stories the paper covered beyond the Irish Sea had to do with weather). As ever, Emer looked smashing, all decked out in creams: linen slacks, sisal flats, a loosely woven Chinese-collar vest over a sleeveless ivory blouse; fucking hell, she even matched the upholstery. Sara looked forward to winter. Gales would whistle through the rickety window frames and flap the drooping corners of mottled wallpaper panels. For sheer survival, Emer would have to smother those shapely bare arms in a plump, bunchy duvet leaking chicken feathers.

"*Sara*," Emer chided. "Have you bought your ticket to Bangkok yet? I would like that firm date."

Concerned by Sara's unresponsiveness, Karen had emailed that morning that she was readying for Seoul, and needed a solid commitment. Another friend would take her apartment if Sara wasn't interested after all. The email was stiff with the same sternness of Emer's reminder, and Sara felt that sheepishness of being called on in third grade when she hadn't done her homework.

"I have some temporary reservations, with a courtesy hold, but I haven't bought the ticket," Sara said evasively, engrossed in the paper. "The fare isn't great, and one agent said I might do better to wait . . ."

In truth, she had rung two bucket shops. One of the numbers was engaged. The other agent took down her particulars and promised to get back to her, then didn't. Sara had neglected to ring again. But to stand on semantics, she hadn't been lying. She did have reservations.

"Wait how long?"

"I don't remember exactly," Sara snapped. "There's some date soon when the airlines announce a whole new schedule of fares for off-season, okay?"

"I thought we had an understanding," Emer admonished.

"We also had an understanding that you'd stay somewhere else when I came home. We're talking a difference of hundreds of dollars to me, so maybe you could show the same flexibility I've shown you." Sara was aware that her stroppiness was all out of proportion to a perfectly reasonable question.

"But I've been under the impression that you don't like sharing the flat."

"Got that right," Sara mumbled.

"So I'm surprised you're not more anxious to be off."

This was the closest they'd come to acknowledging that they despised each other.

"I am and I'm not. I have a lot on my mind." Like olives, shampoo, pasta, and broccoli.

Emer went back to reading Paul Muldoon. More poetry. Incredibly for a memoirist in this of all places, Sara had never seen the woman read a newspaper—as if, by scorning the *Tele* and the *Irish News* for Michael Longley and Medbh McGuckian, she was drinking the conflict's surging groundwater, while Sara lapped at evaporating puddles. How Emer would take over a topical column like "Yankee Doodles" as such a purist was anyone's guess.

Emer looked back up with a crafty squint. "I meant to tell you, an acquaintance of yours says hello."

Sara felt instantly leery. It wasn't like Emer to volunteer information about what she did during the day, or whom she met. "Oh?"

Emer's delivery of the name was pregnant with the full knowledge that this character was well more than an *acquaintance.*

Arsehole!

"He's doing terribly well," Emer added with smarmy familiarity. "There's a fair packet of dosh on offer from the EU these days, to shore up the peace—"

"I *know,*" Sara said. *Packet* of *dosh* indeed! Sara had earned her own eclectic lexicon with eleven years' apprenticeship. A mere eight-week stay didn't grant Emer the right to lift the end of her sentences, to applaud *dead on!* or to call everything in sight from a midge to a Mourne mountain *wee*. For Sara's cadence and vernacular to have warped was only to be expected; for Emer already to be mimicking a faint Irish brogue was ridiculous.

"He's won a sizable grant to work with released loyalist prisoners and help them integrate back into the community. And I'm chuffed to report that he's stopped drinking." *Chuffed*? Perhaps Emer might further enlarge her vocabulary to encompass *prat*, *gobshite*, and *poser*.

Though Sara and Arsehole had formally parted on amicable terms, their relationship had been too sexual to round off into friendship. Residual attraction rapidly mutated into prickliness, and when they met—seldom, and only by happenstance—Arsehole always managed to slag off "Yankee Doodles," whose stewardship Sara had assumed consonant with their breakup. He would dismiss a recent column as "glib," or despair that she had no insight into the Protestants for whom she claimed to vouch, recommending kindly that she was really better off sticking to "the American carry-on." Sara would needle him about "showing a bit of scalp there," when in his rock band days he'd been so proud of his waist-length hair. The two didn't quite dislike each other, but they came close, because any appreciable temperance of their antagonism might have necessitated starting up the whole torturous entanglement all over again.

Sara could not imagine a worse fate. She harbored no more wistfulness about her infatuation with this histrionic megalomaniac than she would about a case of the flu. All the same . . .

The story of Arschole was a hefty chapter in her history, even if it was closed. He had crucially contributed to the greater legend of Sara in Ulsterland. As such, he lay on the near side of Sara's personal border. Though she had long before got past the humiliations he'd inflicted— the pub gatherings at which he'd shown off how badly he could treat his Yankee arm candy to his yobbish, tattooed friends, the gourmet dinners carbon-dating in the oven while he got poleaxed with some adoring French TV presenter in the Europa bar—she still begrudged him the right to walk and talk and live his life outside the perimeter of her own.

Arsehole was insulting and pompous and misogynistic and maybe even the Antichrist, but quite above and beyond all that, *Arsehole was hers*.

"He has quit drinking, or he told you that he's quit drinking?" Sara asked rigidly. "There's a difference."

"He's looking very healthy," Emer said.

"Watch your back," Sara warned. Though Emer recoiled from the smallest scrap of advice, the woman was really missing a trick here if she didn't take this one. "He's very manipulative."

"People change," Emer said breezily, turning a page with a polished fingernail. "I was given to understand you two haven't run into one another in donkey's years."

"Some people"—Sara leaned forward over her crackling newspaper— "*never change*." She collapsed back into the chair as if coining the simple maxim had sapped her.

Emer was reading again, but her expression was perceptibly victorious.

"Do you like him?" Sara asked limply.

"Sorry—like whom?"

"Do you *like* him?" Sara thrust out helplessly, unwilling to repeat the name.

"Oh. 'Like' him. I'm not sure I'd choose that word. He's a very interesting man. Complicated. Don't you think?"

Sara snorted. "That's one way of putting it."

Interesting, that was death, that was. Nice men whom you *liked*, they were safe as houses. But complexity would be a sticky trap for the likes of Emer, who would inevitably fall for Arsehole's mawkish self-pity disguised as sympathy for the downtrodden, and for the contradictions in his bio that covered for the ordinary fact that he didn't know who he was. As for Arsehole, he'd be all over Emer Branagh like a cheap suit. Not only did she look good, but she'd make him look good, which was always more the point.

Somehow this tipped the balance.

They would shag in Notting Hill's bed and get spunk stains on the Notting Hill sheets. Arsehole would lounge in this very armchair, from which he'd hitherto been banished. As the night's main event, they could uproariously take the Mickey out of aging, spinsterish, and spotty *Sara Moseley.*

Well, think again, cupcake, Sara steamed.

"Emer, I really owe it to you to tell you before anyone else." Sara blurted, "I'm not going."

"What do you mean, you're 'not going'—not going where?" Emer's shockingly everyday tone—offhand, and aggravated in a commonplace fashion, the way you get aggravated by a hole in your sock and not by the proliferation of nuclear weapons—revealed how coifed, how pin curled and teased and trimmed and blow dried had been every other sentiment to which she'd given voice since her arrival. Her accent was unadulteratedly American, and she sounded like a regular, defensibly peevish person whose plans had just been spannered.

Sara took a breath. She didn't feel rancorous anymore, or angry, and she even remembered that she no longer gave a fig about Arsehole, whom he nailed, or where. "I'm not going to Bangkok."

"Why *not?*"

Sara knew that she should concoct something—say, an irresistible journalistic opportunity that made her seem indispensable to Belfast's scintillating intellectual circles. But fabrication seemed too fatiguing, and she resorted to the truth out of laziness.

"I just can't. Can't bring myself. I'm too attached. To Belfast."

It hadn't been fair to accuse Emer of being "walled off." Sara had raised a barrier as well, as tall and razor wired as West Belfast's notorious Peace Line between Prods and Taigs. Tentatively, she clambered over her own menacing private fence.

"When I first came to this town, I didn't intend to move to Belfast. I just ended up here," Sara went on. "And for a long while I thought I was still on the road. In fact, maybe I've thought of myself as a bit of a vagabond until this very moment. And I thought of myself as young— don't we all? So Northern Ireland seemed like just one more way station of many. A lot like you: You want to go places, difficult places, strange places. And you're greedy, greedy in a good way, aware that there's not much time and there are so many countries.

"That's why I thought Bangkok made sense. I'd dawdled here long enough, and it was time to get a move on—to take on a whole new city, make a new set of friends, learn a whole new set of politics, and stay up late haggling with my lively adoptive coterie over, I don't know, structural adjustment? Kind of hard to picture.

"It was an appealing fantasy, and maybe you can pull it off. But I haven't. I'm not like that. I'm a nester. My family was always moving—my father was an academic, but he never got tenure—and I've always wanted a real home. I make fun of Irish Americans digging for their roots, or I give other Troubles groupies a hard time because they so obviously need to belong. But the truth is, I'm not any different. I like this place because I belong here—or I think I do, and if that's funny, I guess I'm a bit of a joke around town myself. I can handle that, though. I probably am funny.

"The thing is, I'm no Jack Kerouac. I'm not someone who's destined to go to a long string of exotic places. I've gone to one place. My life is dumpier than I realized. I can't head off to Bangkok, because I'm scared. I'm afraid I'll get disoriented. And lonely, and not give a damn about Thailand because caring is too much effort or I don't know how. I mean, hats off to you for living in Rangoon. I'm impressed. I bet that wasn't easy. And maybe you'll have a great time here, too. I hope you do. I have, in spots. I admit Belfast isn't fresh to me anymore, but then nowhere is after a while, so why not skip straight to the boredom and stay put? It's more efficient.

"Anyway, you will have to find another flat. I really, really apologize for pulling the rug out from under you like this. It's all my fault, and I haven't been playing games here. It's just taken me a few weeks to know my own mind. Maybe after you've found another place we could, I don't know"—it was well too late to propose long, giggly dinners with cocktails—"have a cup of coffee once in a while."

Emer may or may not have been grateful for the confidences, but suddenly being obliged to find another place to live had to have dominated her mind more than being passingly *chuffed* that some near stranger had spilled her guts, and she looked a little sullen. Sara would feel put out in Emer's place herself. They were hardly going to become fast friends simply because for three minutes Sara had stopped acting pissy.

"Well, I'll get on it tomorrow," Emer said with a sigh. "But for now, I'm beat, and I might like to turn in early. Would you mind?"

The unadorned selfishness, from Emer, was a relief, and Sara vacated the sitting room posthaste. While the subletter brushed her teeth downstairs, Sara composed a maundering, overly explanatory email to Karen Banks, declining the Bangkok apartment and encouraging Karen to give it to that friend who was next in line. As her modem hummed the message away to the electronic ether of Southeast Asia, Sara almost exclaimed aloud, "Come back!"—as if her alternative future were a lover, to whom harsh words had been spoken in the heat of the moment, and who had just driven out of range of her forlorn cry.

TO GIVE THE woman her due, when Emer did move, she moved fast. Two days later, she gave notice that she would be shifting from the flat in another two days hence. She spent most of this intervening period out, or on the phone with the study door closed, and the two women talked only in passing. Sara invited Emer to share a pasta supper before she moved out, but the subletter couldn't spare an evening and begged off. Sara was surprisingly disappointed; she yearned to provide her tenant a single bowlful of rotelli that she didn't begrudge. During this sudden denouement, Emer's small-scale impositions paled before one stark, ugly fact: Sara had been *unwelcoming*.

For years she had clung to a distinction between "having a problem with pettiness" and being an outright petty person. In the four days during which Sara was left to contemplate her sins—most of her unkindness had taken place in the confines of her own mind, but there might indeed be such a thing as *thought crime*—she worried that either there was no functional difference between being plagued by pettiness and being the very embodiment of pettiness, or that during Emer's tenancy she had made the leap.

Still, it was the second week of October, and Emer had yet to furnish even the meager fifteen pounds per week for September's rent that she had promised; Sara noted compulsively that for the first ten days of that month Emer was responsible for the full rent. That first third came neatly to seventy-five pounds, or a total of £120. Then there was rent for part of October, gas and electricity, the phone; when the subletter retired to the study for those protracted calls, Sara grew restive, glancing at clocks. She supposed she could square the phone bill once it arrived, but that involved a trust she didn't quite enjoy. After living with Emer Branagh for a solid month, she didn't really know the woman at all.

Obviously, the intelligent approach to these debts would have been to raise the matter point-blank, but Sara kept putting it off. The time never seemed right.

Hence as the two women lingered awkwardly on the landing by Emer's luggage as she waited for her cab, Sara had yet to prod the subletter to cough up some cash. In a strictly financial sense, she could afford to take the hit, but not, perhaps, in a spiritual one. She knew herself. She might demur from asking for the money, but *as usual* she would remember the debt, to the penny, for the rest of her life. Sara was haunted by her own disheartening aphorism: "Some people—*never change*."

"So," Sara began as Emer fussed with zips. "Maybe you should leave me your address, telephone? In case someone rings, I mean. Or you have post."

"I don't know what my address and number will be just yet. I'll send you a postcard."

"From across town?" Sara smiled. "Have I been that much of a shithead, that you can't stick ringing up?"

"I won't be across town," Emer said, with her usual sobriety. "I've been offered a post teaching English at an institute in Petersburg. A friend—never mind, it's convoluted. But the package is attractive. They're willing to fly me over, and cover any other travel expenses, as well as provide accommodation when I get there. So I'm taking the shuttle to Heathrow in three hours. Tonight, I'm on Aeroflot's red-eye to Moscow."

"Saint Petersburg!" Sara exclaimed in dismay. To cover the Pavlovian thought, *Now I'll never get my money*, she added inanely, "But what about 'Yankee Doodles'?"

"Excuse me?" Emer looked sincerely baffled. "What's 'Yankee Doodles'?"

Sara pinkened. "I mean, what about your memoir? *My Year in Northern Ireland*, all that?"

Emer checked her watch, and seemed, as ever, to be weighing something up. Maybe in the end she reckoned that after that gush of humility—not to mention humanity—from her erstwhile flatmate, Sara was owed a moment of ingenuousness in return.

"When you and I first spoke in Boston," she explained, "this project seemed to be falling into place so gracefully that I thought it was preordained. But since I got here, everything's been . . ." She left it. "Well, I decided I'd been misled. I don't think this is the right place for me. Burma was so lush, and despite the regime the people are full of life, always smiling. They have so little, their lives are so primitive, and with the junta they live under a continual cloud of fear. But they're still joyful, and amazingly unstinting. Here—if you must know, I find it depressing. Heavy. Gray. I hope you don't take this wrong, but I don't quite understand what you see in this town."

"And you think *Russia* will be any less heavy and gray?" Sara laughed. "God, you must really think Belfast is a horror show!"

"Oh, it's all right, I guess. Just a little *poky*. You can have it."

"Knowing what I do," Sara said, "I'm not sure I should thank you." The taxi tooted in the drive below.

"Russia might suit you at that," Sara added with a glint in her eye. "Plenty of suffering."

For once, Emer cracked a half smile. "There's only one kind of suffering I really can't abide," she admitted. "Mine."

Sara helped with the luggage, her stomach doughy. She hoped the sensation was regret about something larger than outstanding rent. She was just vowing with all the born-again resolution she could muster that this time she'd forgive and forget when Emer stopped on the landlords' ground floor.

"I'm sorry, I've been so distracted." The apology was Emer's first in their acquaintance. "I meant to leave you some money." She rustled into her carry-on, and hastily counted out a pile of twenties.

Sara accepted the wad with embarrassment, but did a double take when it proved so thick. "But Emer," she said, shuffling the notes. "This must be, what, close to four hundred quid! That's way too much."

Emer ignored the ten twenties that Sara proffered back, and shouldered her bags again. "Oh, I don't know, there's the rent, utilities. I made a couple of calls to Petersburg. And, you know, I used a few of your groceries and stuff. Keep the change."

Helping bundle the baggage into the Fone-a-Cab, Sara wished her subletter luck, and meant it.

Once the taxi had wended down the drive, Sara ambled back up to the flat, counting the notes again in astonishment: £460, all told. This was not the Emer Branagh of yore, who expected reimbursement for mayonnaise. Whether the woman had experienced a change of heart or merely a change of circumstances was impossible to say. Maybe the lavish overpayment was intended to shame Sara for having kept such exacting mental accounts, though how would Emer know? Or maybe it was Sara's reward for having been a tolerable flatmate for four whole days. In allowing that she was "impressed" by Emer's trip to Burma, she had said one thing nice; in confessing that she was too scared and stuck in her ways to go to Bangkok, she had said something modest; and she had *offered* Emer a bowl of pasta. If the wages of common decency had proved excessive, this fat roll of twenties delivered a downright Buddhist lesson about karma. That is, "keeping track" might assure just the compensation you were due, or somewhat shy. Generosity could boomerang back to you with dividends.

Standing at the middle room's tall front window, Sara gazed out at the hazy hump of Black Mountain on the horizon. The sky was low and dull. Ulster's brief Indian summer was abruptly at an end, and it had started to bucket. The weather could easily remain this unremittingly dim, wet, and dreary through to next May. Saint Petersburg! The city's architecture was supposed to be entrancing, and like Burma's the problems faced by post-Soviet Russia made Northern Ireland's seem small beer.

Sara tidied the flat, having anticipated this moment as one of triumphant reclamation. Yet her mood was unaccountably doleful. Once the dishes were done, the carpets hoovered, Emer's bedclothes tossed in the hamper, the flat still looked tatty. She couldn't help but keep noticing that the plaster was cracked, that the gas-fire flames had left dark smudges on the walls, and that the furry black mold on the sitting room ceiling, so recently wiped down, was growing back apace. The air was clammy with a biting chill, and when she lit the fire in the sitting room it smelled chemical and tainted, measurably more nauseating than the faint residue of gardenia incense it overcame. For once she looked at the garish floral wallpaper and didn't hate it with affection, but simply hated it.

A phone call to her editor was short but not sweet. Diffidently, she informed him that her "plans had changed," and she'd like to take her column back. *Ach, after we printed such a pretty farewell?* Featherstone chided. In short order, she was close to begging. *You've had a good run, pet. What's it been? Ten years?* Only nine, Sara corrected mournfully. *Maybe we both need a change, don't you figger?*

Plunked in her usual chair, Sara treated herself to a sherry a little early. Listlessly she rifled the *Telegraph.* For the life of her she couldn't imagine how *decommissioning* could have seemed scintillating for an instant. The truth was that she had stopped attending IRA funerals and Orange marches not because she was getting old, but because the Troubles were getting old. Like it or not, she had outgrown them.

There was still, of course, the good crack, the friendly banter with her neighbors when dandering out for wheaten bread and a chunk of Coleraine cheddar. But with Emer Branagh off to down *piroshki* and caviar with shots of frozen vodka, Sara felt swindled. Sure any old bog could seem priceless so long as some other patsy was willing to fight you for it.

About the Author

LIONEL SHRIVER's novels include *Big Brother*, the National Book Award finalist *So Much for That*, *The Post-Birthday World*, and the international bestseller *We Need to Talk about Kevin*. She has contributed to the *Guardian*, the *New York Times*, the *Wall Street Journal*, and many other publications. She lives in London and Brooklyn, New York.